PUSHING UP ROSES

REAPING COVETOUS VI

MJ MAY

Pushing Up Roses
Reaping Covetous VI
MJ May

Cover design by cheriefox.
Edited by Michelle Rascon of Rascon Revisions.
Proofread by Rogena Mitchell-Jones of RMJ Manuscript Service LLC.

❀ Created with Vellum

CONTENT WARNINGS:
Death and dying
Domestic abuse
Homophobia
Mental illness
Murder
Pet loss/euthanasia
Police violence
Self-harm
Suicide attempts

Mental illness is an important topic worldwide. In the United States, the national suicide hotline number is 1-800-273-8255. Never be afraid to ask for help, to reach out, and try for a better future. You are not alone.

This book also contains the importance of friendship, recognizing and accepting help when offered, protecting your family—related by blood or not—the furry ones that make our houses homes, prickly reapers, humor, learning to be tenacious when needed, and romantic intrigue.

Who you're born to and into what environment are beyond your control. I was fortunate to have a stable home with parents who loved me and wanted me. The tragedy of our world is that far too few can claim the same. Thank you, Mom and Dad, for being parents—for being there when I needed you as a child and for being there for me as an adult.

1

"I'm gonna kill that fucker." Dave's fingers repeatedly clenched while leaning heavily with his elbows on his knees. Dave's profile was tense, his jaw rock-hard and eyes narrowed to little more than slits. "I can't believe that asshole did this. I—" Some of the steam went out of Dave, but that did little to subdue his anger.

"Don't say that too loud. That lady from CPS could come out any minute, and we don't need her to think you're a violent guy." One hand rubbed circles over Dave's back as my eyes trailed to the door they'd taken Marshall through, a woman named Maggie from child protective services hot on their heels. Maggie wanted to interview Marshall first, then she said she'd be out with us.

"Christ, Leah." Dave sat up, scrubbing his hands over the top of his head. His bristly hair sounded rough below his heavy palms. "Why didn't I listen to those damn messages? Why didn't I just answer the phone? One time." Dave held up a single finger—not the middle one for once. "One time would have been all it would have taken. I would have ripped

Marshall out of that house so fast it would have made my asshole father's head spin."

I knew that feeling well. "Shoulda. Coulda. Woulda," I murmured. "Trust me, Dave. That kind of thinking never leads anywhere productive."

Snorting, Dave settled his hand on my leg, squeezing tight before releasing it. He clasped his hands together, eyes wandering toward the end of the hall and the doors where Marshall was being examined. "How much longer do you think it'll be?"

"I wish I knew. Aunt Joyce didn't mention anything about that."

I'd called Cecile on our way to the hospital. After quickly filling her in, Aunt Joyce got on the phone. It was weird, getting used to the new reality where my aunt didn't treat me with mistrust. She'd taken in the situation, asked pointed questions, and had given me the skinny on what to do and expect within less than three minutes. Aunt Joyce's immediate knowledge made me wonder just how often suspected child abuse cases came through the ER's doors. I didn't like the implications and managed to detour my brain before it could run down that twisted road of pain.

Dave turned his head just enough for me to see his haunted blue eyes. "Do you think I should have argued more? Should I have stayed with him?"

Marshall's doctor had asked him if he'd like Dave to stay. At fourteen, Marshall was still a minor, but he'd been allowed to make his own decision regarding Dave's presence. He'd chosen to go alone.

"No. I don't think that would have been a good idea. I don't mean this in a mean way, but you and Marshall aren't close. He's probably not comfortable with you there."

Dave's eyes widened, a wounded air sparking in those seas of blue.

"It probably wouldn't have mattered, even if you were close." I tried to console him. "Most likely, they're asking him a lot of uncomfortable questions right now. Chances are he wouldn't want you in there to hear anyway." I tried to remember what I'd been like at that age. It was only nine years ago, but it felt like a thousand. Sometimes I found it difficult to imagine I'd ever been that innocent—that naïve.

Soul-stealing warmth washed through my body fleetingly. Andy was nearby. Sitting in the Covetous Community ER waiting room, I wasn't sure if Andy was close because of me or if he was there on reaper business. That was the problem when you were kinda-sorta dating a reaper. Not that dating seemed like the right word. Calling Andy my boyfriend sounded all kinds of wrong.

"What's with the face?" Dave asked, his head turned toward me.

"Nothing important." I didn't want to get into the rabbit hole that my brain had just wandered down while thinking about my reaper.

Dave stared at me for a couple more heartbeats before giving a faint nod, letting it go. "What do you think's taking so long?" His mind strayed back to worry. I could hardly blame him.

"I don't know. I guess it'll take as long as it takes. Trust me, the police like documentation. You want them to do a thorough job. Evidence is a good thing, especially with where I think you're planning to go with this." I gave Dave the side-eye, my eyebrows raised in a question I'd hardly needed to ask.

"If you mean I'm planning to keep Marshall with me and never allow our fucked-up father access to him again, you're on the right track."

After my parents' murders, I'd lived with Aunt Joyce and Uncle Jack. I didn't have a lot of memories from around that time, something I was grateful for. What I did know was that CPS liked to keep kids with family. No one could get ahold of Marshall's mother, Cindy. As Marshall's adult sibling, Dave fit nicely into the family category. From what I understood, CPS would need to do an investigation—into Dave's dad, Marshall's case, and Dave himself. If he passed and Cindy wasn't *available*, he'd at least get temporary custody.

Andy's nearby warmth faded. I missed its presence, but I no longer ached with the need to run out and track him down. Things were different now. In a way, we were sort of living together. Or that's the way I thought of it. I had no idea where Andy had been staying, if anywhere. All I knew was that when he could, he was at Dave's old apartment in Ink No Evil with me. I didn't know if I'd ever be able to live in my previous apartment again. The lease would be up soon, and I couldn't imagine signing a new one. Dave and Chama told me I could stay as long as I wanted. It worked for now, but memories of Ashes clung to a lot of surfaces there too. Dr. Cross was right. I needed somewhere new, different, somewhere I didn't see Ashes curled up in every corner.

I didn't want to forget Ashes, not that I ever could, even if I wanted to. I just couldn't stand the constant reminders of what I'd lost. Every time I thought I saw her, caught a glimpse out of the corner of my eye, my heart would kick up only to crash in the pit of my belly as realization sank in that it was just a memory—a fleeting image that my overcrowded brain had randomly plucked out. It was like constantly picking at a scab, never allowing the wound below to heal.

Dave leaned back in his chair, a wooden structure with a vinyl seat cushion that had seen better days. Mine wasn't much better, but it was decently comfortable. Considering how long people usually had to hang out in the emergency waiting room, it was a good thing. I probably wouldn't want to sit on them for too long during the summer. The vinyl would stick to uncovered thighs. Since it was late October, I didn't have that problem with my khaki pants.

"None of this shit would have happened if my mom was still alive."

Dave's hushed words fell into my skull with the weight of a twenty-megaton bomb.

"My father wasn't great when she was alive, but he was better than this."

I swallowed hard, the burn of rising bile hitting my throat. Dave's mom died of pancreatic cancer when he was five years old. The spirit I'd seen clinging to the locked doorway in Dave's father's house reflected that scenario. I'd been pushing away thoughts of Dave's mother's spirit, concentrating on the catastrophe of the moment. Dave had no idea his mother's spirit hadn't passed on. I hadn't either until about two hours ago. I could have gone a hell of a lot longer without that knowledge plaguing my overloaded brain.

"She had a way with him," Dave went on, words soft with a childhood memory. "I don't know how she did it. Looking back on things, I don't even know why she married him." Dave heavily leaned his head on the wall behind him, then rolled it toward me. "I might not remember things right. I was just a kid then."

I stared into the singular eye I could see.

I'd never met Dave's mother, Charlotte. She'd died before Dave, Bobby, and I'd met. That didn't mean I didn't recognize the spiritual woman lingering on the second floor of Dave's childhood home. I had no idea why Charlotte hadn't moved on. I also had no idea how I would tell Dave she hadn't.

Now didn't seem like a good time. Not that there'd ever be a good time for that particular conversation. Licking my dry, cracked lips, I started, "Dave, there's some—"

"There she is." Dave jumped up. A few quick strides, and he loomed over the woman CPS had assigned to Marshall's case. Dave wasn't a huge guy, but he wasn't small either. Maggie Littleton was taller than me, but she was still a good half foot shorter than Dave.

"Slow down, Dave." I had to jog to keep up with him, but I grabbed Dave's shoulder and pulled him back. "Give the woman some space."

Dave barely spared me a glance. "How is he?" Dave didn't even try to conceal his worry. "Can I go see him now?"

Dave made a motion to step around Maggie. Deftly and with practiced ease, she stepped in front of him, blocking the way. "Marshall's doing okay. His doctor is finishing up, and he'll be out soon. In the meantime, I've got a few questions I'd like to ask. Maybe we could go sit down." Maggie gave a kind but tight smile. The type of smile I couldn't interpret.

Eyes longingly looking toward the door Maggie had just walked out of, Dave reluctantly answered, "Yeah, sure. We can do that."

We found our way back to the private little corner where Dave and I'd been hanging out for the last couple of hours. Sitting across from us, Maggie Littleton sat her bag beside her, pulling out a computer tablet and tapping the screen a few times. With one hand, Maggie grabbed her reddish-brown hair, twisting it at the base of her neck. Sliding a pair of reading glasses on, she settled them on her lightly freckled nose, her deep brown eyes peering over their frames when she looked at Dave.

"Now then," she gave Dave another one of those smiles I couldn't interpret, "it's my understanding that Marshall attempted to get a hold of you several times over the past couple of weeks, but you didn't respond. Tell me, Mr. Masters, why is that?"

Dave flinched when she called him *Mr. Masters*. Reaching

over, I clasped his wrist, squeezing tight, offering whatever support I could.

Sucking in a deep breath, Dave started, "It was my father's number. He and I don't exactly get along, and I didn't want to speak with him. I . . . I never even thought it might be Marshall, or Devlin, for that matter." Dave slumped forward. "Believe me, I will beat myself up for that one for a long time to come." Head shooting back up, Dave's lips twisted, his eyebrows deeply furrowed. "Marshall's fourteen. Didn't he have a cell phone?" Dave turned his attention to me. "Doesn't every teenager have a cell these days? I wouldn't have recognized the number, but I would have at least listened to a voicemail if it had been something different from my dad's number."

Maggie tapped a few things out on her tablet. Not bothering to raise her head, she said, "According to Marshall, Dean Masters confiscated his cell phone almost three weeks ago."

"Christ," Dave hissed. "That mother fu—"

"That's why Marshall had to use his home phone," I interrupted before Dave could say more.

"It appears so." Maggie made a few more notes before raising her head again. "What made today any different?"

I glanced at Dave. A quick nod gave me the permission I was looking for. Holding up my hand as if I were still in class and had the answer the teacher wanted, I said, "Uh, that would be because of me."

"Mm-hmm, and you would be . . ."

Well shit. I hadn't thought this through. At that moment, I'd never hated my name more. Not the name itself, but all the shit it carried with it. Opening my mouth, I started to answer when Dave beat me to it. "She's Leah McKnight, my best friend. You can think of her like my sister."

Maggie kept typing, her fingers stuttering to a halt. I

couldn't make out her facial features with her head down. She snapped her head up. Pulling down her reading glasses, Maggie stared at me. I could see the wheels turning, that glint in her brown eyes made all the brighter by the overhead fluorescent lighting. "McKnight?"

I gave a slow nod. "Correct." Thomas Birkingham's spirit chose that moment to show up on the emergency room floor. His screams and wails filtered through my consciousness, and I barely avoided the automatic flinch his antics typically instigated. After spending all that time in Bobby's room, begging my brother to wake up from his coma, you'd think that I would have gotten used to Thomas's ranting. The more I heard it, the more I thought getting used to that level of animosity would be impossible.

Maggie blinked, her blanched lips little more than a thin line. "Forgive me, Miss McKnight," she finally started, "but given your relationship with Mr. Masters, I'm afraid I need to ask a couple of questions."

Dave swung his arm around my shoulder, pulling me in close. Dread swamped me. Would my past influence this woman's decision? Maggie Littleton thought my brother was a murderer. She had no idea Justin Turlington's spirit had been the actual criminal. I didn't think my involvement in Liam's mother's death would go over well, either. I was a magnet for those with homicidal tendencies, and that was saying nothing of the self-inflicted damage I'd done. Self-consciously, I twisted my wrists, tugging at my jacket to ensure my scars and tattoos were covered.

Leaning farther into Dave, I finally answered, "Ask what you need to."

Maggie's eyes flickered between Dave and me. "I know these questions can seem invasive, but they are necessary. Right now, I am Marshall Masters's advocate, and he is my top priority."

"As it should be," Dave answered.

"Good. I'm glad we're in agreement. So, Mr. Masters, you cla—"

Dave held up a halting hand. "Sorry, but please, call me Dave."

"I can do that," Maggie swiftly agreed. "You said Leah McKnight is your friend, your *sister*." She stared pointedly at Dave's arm slung over my shoulder. "You are not involved more intimately?"

Dave and I shared a look that resulted in both of us rolling our eyes. "Why does everyone always think that?" he asked, eyebrows raised with the first glimpse of mirth I'd seen on his face. Squeezing me a little tighter, Dave answered, "That would be a hard no. That would be a little too close to incest for either of us."

I was afraid Dave had gotten a little too visual with his comment, but Maggie smirked, and an abbreviated chuckle escaped before she became serious again. "Message received. Miss McKnight—"

"You can call me Leah, although surprisingly, I don't have the hang-ups about my last name that Dave has."

"Leah," Maggie corrected. "I understand that your brother, Bobby, was recently killed. Is that correct?"

Bobby had died, protecting me, over two months ago. It was knowledge I carried with me like weighted baggage. That weight would have been lighter if Bobby's death had resulted in what it should have—eternal peace.

Guilt and Regret. The stuff reapers were made of—the stuff my brother had in spades when he died. Bobby wasn't drifting in a haze of blissful slumber. Bobby was a reaper, his district just north of Andy's. Too close and yet too far away.

Shaking thoughts of Bobby's fate from my mind, I answered, "Y-yes. That's correct. Dead and buried." *But not at peace,* my mind quietly supplied.

Maggie stared at me long and hard before she relaxed back into her chair. "Forgive my lack of empathy, but that's good to hear. I'm not intimately familiar with your previous situation, but Bobby was a constant threat to you and possibly those around you from what I've read." Looking back at Dave, Maggie nodded in the direction of the arm he had draped around me. "I would have had serious misgivings sending a fourteen-year-old boy to live with you, Dave, if Bobby McKnight were still alive and a possible threat, especially given your close relationship to Leah."

I blinked a couple of times before answering a quick, "That's fair."

"So, you said it was because of you that Dave finally listened to his messages."

"Dave's phone rang while we were in his Jeep together. It's not like him to ignore it. I, uh . . . pestered him about it, then grabbed his phone and took a look myself. I'd just finished listening to the messages when Jenny called me."

"Jenny?" Maggie glanced up.

"Detective Jennifer Riggins," I clarified. "From what I understand, Officer Michaels was on the scene, and once he figured out who Marshall was related to, he put the pieces together and knew enough that Dave and I are together a lot. He called Jenny, and she called me." I finished my explanation with a shrug.

"By that time, I'd started listening to Marshall's messages," Dave picked up the story thread. "Once I knew there was a problem, we headed straight to my father's house."

"I see." Thankfully, Maggie moved on from me. "Has anyone been able to reach Marshall's mother, Cindy?"

A low growl erupted from Dave. Removing his arm from me, Dave pulled out his phone, lighting it up and checking for any missed messages. With a frustrated shake of his head, he said, "No. I got Cindy's cell number from Marshall. I've sent her a couple of text messages. I've tried leaving voice-mails, but it says her box is full. The police have tried to contact her too."

Maggie pulled her reading glasses off before pinching the bridge of her nose. I wasn't sure of Maggie Littleton's age, but at that moment, she appeared older than I'd initially thought. I didn't envy her job. Marshall's situation wasn't great, but I figured it didn't rate in the horrific pile she'd mentally cataloged over the years.

"I'll try contacting her too." Settling her tablet off to the side, Maggie clasped her hands in her lap. "I asked Marshall if he was aware of any other contact information for her. He couldn't give me an address beyond saying she'd moved to Miami, Florida, with his older brother, Devlin. If I understand correctly, Devlin started college at a university in Miami, and his mother followed, leaving Marshall in the *care* of your father."

I squeezed Dave's hand—hard, warning him to keep his thoughts regarding his stepmother locked up tight.

Jaw clenched so firm it was a wonder he was able to speak, Dave answered, "That's my understanding, though I didn't know until tonight."

Cocking her head, Maggie gave Dave an assessing eye. "I'm sorry, Dave, but the whole situation is confusing to me. It's clear you care about Marshall. You're obviously very upset and angered by what happened today. And yet, Marshall tells me he hardly knows you, and I get the impression from what we've discussed that's a correct statement. You live what, ten, maybe fifteen minutes away? Why have you been so absent in his life?"

Dave's knee bounced, his whole body vibrating. "It wasn't by choice," he finally ground out. "I willingly left that house when I was sixteen. I moved in with an older buddy of mine."

"Chama," I filled in.

Dave nodded. "Yeah, he's my business partner now," Dave clarified for Maggie. "Those first few years, I tried to stay in contact with my brothers. I sent birthday and Christmas presents. Cards too. But my father and Cindy didn't want me in their kids' lives. They told me to butt out and not contact Marshall or Devlin again. I was young."

Dave was still young. Twenty-four and only a year older than me.

"And," Dave shot me an apologetic look, "there was other stuff going on in my life. At the time, I just kind of . . . let it go." Dave gave his folded hands a mournful look as my stomach dropped. "Don't." Dave twisted so he could look me directly in the eyes. "Don't do that. It wasn't your fault."

"But . . ." But it was my fault. "How can you say that? You were trying to take care of me after—"

"It's history, Leah. Maybe not as ancient as I'd like, but it's in the past, and even knowing what I do now, I wouldn't change a thing I did back then, not with you. You needed me then. Marshall needs me now. Thankfully, there's enough of me to go around." Dave's lips pulled back, giving a signature Dave grin. It was the smile that told me everything was going to be okay, the smile that pulled me through my darkest hours, the smile that had helped save my life.

"Hey." Marshall was barely audible beyond the pounding of my heart. Somehow, we'd all missed his entrance. We might have been slow on the uptake, but now he had all our attention.

Quickly getting to his feet, Dave's fingers slid under Marshall's chin, lifting his face and reacquainting himself with the damage. The tick in Dave's jaw grew steadier the longer he looked.

"It's not as bad as it looks." Marshall pulled his head away, tucking his chin. "I've had worse."

Dave took in a harsh breath. I knew him well enough to

know Dave was barely keeping his shit together. Dave wasn't a physically violent person—at least not to living flesh and bone. Recent events pushed his limits, and I didn't want to see where that imaginary line was drawn.

"It's bad enough." Dave finally answered.

Marshall's lip was split and puffy. His cheek looked the worst. A couple of hours ago, it had been a red, swollen mass. It was still swollen and red, but deep purples and angry greens had filtered in.

Jacket slung over one arm, Marshall shifted from foot to foot. "The doc says I need to take some Tylenol. Do you have that at your house, or do we need to stop somewhere first?"

"I've got Tylenol," Dave answered.

"And Oreos," I threw in. "There are always plenty of Oreos."

Marshall offered a half smile, lifting the uninjured side of his face. "Cool."

Maggie stood too, making me realize I was the only one sitting, so I stood as Maggie said, "I'll follow you home, if that's okay, Dave? I need to do a cursory walk-through of your home to make sure it meets Marshall's needs. There will be a complete inspection and report soon, depending on what Marshall's mother says when we contact her."

Marshall tensed. Given Dave's narrowed eyes, I didn't think he missed the reaction either. I wasn't sure about Maggie. I got the impression she didn't miss much and hoped she took note.

In the distance, Thomas Birkingham's rage-fueled words grew stronger in their cadence. He was coming back around, and I didn't care to be there when he did. One bout of his insanity was enough for the evening. "Since my car's still at your place, you're my ride too."

"Come on then, short stuff." Dave slung his arm around

me, hugging me tight as the four of us headed toward the exit. "Let's get this caravan on the road."

The night was chilly, and I leaned further into Dave, soaking up his warmth. Winter would be here soon, and it would get a lot colder. I hated thinking about it. Fall was nice. Winter, not so much. Maybe with Andy around this time, it wouldn't be so bad. Warmth flooded my cheeks, probably pinking their usually pallid color. I wasn't sure if Andy would be there when I got back to Dave's old apartment. I hoped he would, but I wouldn't be worried if he wasn't. Free choice—free will. It was management's sticking point, and I'd stuck it to them good. Lizzie said there'd be consequences. Every choice in life came laden with those. I wasn't worried.

Yet.

2

Before I put my car in park, I knew that Andy was waiting for me inside. This late at night, Ink No Evil's parking lot was empty. Once upon a time, it had been a car dealership in the tattoo shop's previous life. Huge pillars with lights crowning their tops littered the massive parking lot. Dave and Chama only kept a couple of them in working order, nearer the shop.

The fluorescent lights buzzed as I climbed out of my car, their brightness blocking out most of the stars above. Dragging my tired feet, I headed for the side door that led directly into the apartment and not the business. The neon monkeys above the main entrance were turned off, allowing a sliver of darkness upon entry.

"You're very late this evening. Are you okay? You were at the hospital—in the emergency room." Andy questioned while holding the door open for me.

His nearness added external warmth to the fire building within me. I'd gotten used to that warm glow and didn't want to contemplate what I'd do if it was taken away again.

I went up on tiptoes while Andy leaned down so I could

press my lips against his cheek. His body shuddered at the contact. I wasn't sure if it was because of the kiss or simply his increased ability to feel when I was nearby. I liked to think it had more to do with me as a person and not as Andy's final soul.

"I'm fine. Physically." I doubted I'd ever be fine emotionally or mentally. Most likely, I hadn't needed to clarify with Andy. "I was there with Dave."

"Dave's injured?" The door closed behind Andy, whisper soft. I heard the snick of the lock as he made sure I was as safe as possible inside. Justin Turlington's spirit had been reaped, but there were still enough living, breathing people out there and many were just as mentally out to lunch as Justin had been. My coworker, Ricky, came to mind. Ex-officer turned private eye Levi Dickerson was another guy riding the crazy train.

"No." I tossed my purse on a nearby table before stripping off my coat and throwing it on the back of a couch. "It was his half brother, Marshall." Falling into the couch cushions, I reached out a hand, only to come up empty. It was an automatic movement; my fingers reached for a swath of gray fur that was no longer there. Pain squeezed my chest. A pain Andy acutely felt too.

Sitting beside me, Andy let me come to him. I wasn't sure why, but it was almost always that way. Without hesitation, I snuggled in close, word vomiting all over Andy as I filled him in on what had happened with Dave's dad, Dean, and his brother, Marshall. Andy listened, grunting and offering one-word comments throughout. Fingers raking through my hair, Andy's fingernails scraped soothingly across my scalp as I spoke.

When I finished, he quietly sat for a few moments before asking, "And before? You were upset earlier today as well."

That was one problem with dating your own personal

reaper—one of the many problems. Andy felt my emotions. Sometimes I thought he probably understood what I felt better than I did. Given that it was a one-way street, I was often left floundering, trying to figure out what was going through my reaper's mind.

Tugging at the fabric of Andy's shirt, I thought back to today's earlier revelations. That new knowledge burned, churning up the acid in my stomach and making me queasy. Clearing my throat, I muttered, "Yeah, well, it looks like Cecile and I share a little more DNA with Justin Turlington than we'd like."

Andy's fingers stopped moving only to pick up their soothing motion again. "Your grandmother?"

"Barbara? Yeah, looks that way. Chrissie's witch friend came through and figured out the password and retrieved extra footage that Levi had tried to erase." The thought of what Levi had done grated, churning my acidic stomach with anger. "He's such an ass," I hissed. "What kind of person does that kind of shit?"

Andy was silent for a moment before answering, "A deeply disturbed one. A person I want you to very much stay away from."

"Trust me, I have no intention to seek him out." I was getting the creepy feeling that Chrissie and Dave were right, and Levi wanted more from me than I'd ever willingly give. Surprisingly, I was happier when Levi thought I was a murderer. At least then he'd been disgusted by me, not . . . whatever the hell this new infatuation was.

"How do you feel about that?"

I cranked my neck, twisting so I could stare into Andy's green eyes, little flecks of gold dancing around their edges. "How do I feel about Levi being a nutter?"

Andy's lips twisted into something close to a smile as if he were trying not to laugh and barely managed. "No. I think I know how you feel about the previous Officer Dickerson."

My neck was getting a crick. Laying my cheek on Andy's chest, I said, "I thought you knew how I felt about everything and everyone."

"Mostly. Sometimes it's too vague. But in this case, I was asking about your relation to Justin."

"Oh . . . that . . ." I blew out a sigh.

"Yes, *that.*"

I shrugged within Andy's embrace. "It's not like there's much I can do about it. I'm not going to lay here and suggest I'm happy about having him so directly in my family tree, but I'm a firm believer that we've all got more than a few rotten apples and diseased branches in our family histories. As far as I'm concerned, this infected branch has been excised and burnt to ash. Not much more I can do."

The thought of ashes drew my eyes up and to a nearby shelf. Secretly Dave and Cecile had gone to the funeral home and picked out a nicer box. Ashes was there, her remains in a pretty wooden box with carved flowers on the top. I'd seen her spirit go with Francis—knew she wasn't in that box. For reasons I couldn't explain, knowing her remains were here, with me, brought some level of comfort.

"Hmm, that's a surprisingly healthy point of view." Andy sounded pleasantly shocked.

"Yeah, I know. It amazes me too." My brain generally rocked toward the worst-case scenario and had trouble seeing even the most blazing bright spot. "This is something I really have zero control over." I hadn't had a lot of time to digest this latest revelation but thought that might have something to do with my easy acceptance. Sometimes, in life, there really wasn't anything you could do. That often sucked, but it took the pressure off.

"How did Cecile take it?" Andy's fingers still danced along my skull, lulling me and making my eyes heavy.

"She'll be okay. I think it hit her harder that Grandma Barbara's fate could have been hers if not for the charm Chrissie had made for her. Seeing our grandmother's mental state toward the end of her life affected Cecile more than learning about Justin." I shuddered. Cecile was so vibrant, so alive, and ready to see what the world had to offer. Imagining her nearly housebound for the rest of her life, at the mercy of whatever emotional trauma a lingering spirit might still cling to, was too terrible to consider.

"You think it was just Chrissie?" Andy sounded skeptical.

"She's the one that made the charm." She was the one who had agreed to try, to do something she'd sworn not to do again.

"That's true, but none of it would have happened without you."

A flush of embarrassed heat colored my cheeks. "I don't think I had much to do with it," I argued. "You were right. There's no way I could ever hope to reap all the lingering spirits in Covetous. It was a stupid theory. I—"

Andy shifted, pushing me up to look directly into his fierce eyes. It had been a while since I'd had that disappointed look thrown my way. "Stop that. You're not stupid, and what you wanted to do, what you begged me to help you do, wasn't stupid either. It scared the hell out of me at the time, knowing what your request would mean, knowing that I'd have to be close to you. That's on me, not you. Was what you wanted to do possible?" Andy shrugged. "Probably not, at least not entirely, but it would have been helpful, and at the time, it was the best you could offer. Besides, if it hadn't been for your desire to reap Eliza Morgan, you wouldn't have reconnected with Chrissie Hollybrook. You would never have had a chance to learn she's a witch and that making a charm to help your cousin was even possible. Do not sell yourself short, Leah. I won't let you."

I squirmed, uncomfortable with where this discussion had suddenly gone. I knew Andy was right. Sort of. I still didn't think I deserved a lot of the credit. It just wasn't in my nature. To be fair, I didn't think that had anything to do with my murdered parents. It was a part of me, just like Justin Turlington's DNA.

Having no idea what to say, I finally settled on a half-hearted, "Okay?" which came out more question than answer.

Andy huffed something I couldn't understand before flopping back on the couch again. "What am I going to do with you?" Andy muttered, eyes closed and near exasperation. Thankfully the brunt of his frustration seemed to be aimed at the ceiling.

I laid back across his chest. Andy's arm snaked around me, hugging me close. "For starters, you can stay until I fall asleep." A wide yawn pulled at my mouth, muffling my words. The adrenaline fueling my body faded. The day and night had been filled with uncomfortable discoveries. "It's been a shitty day."

"You're worried about Dave?" Andy's fingers danced along my arm, sending pleasant shivers racing across my skin.

"Dave and Marshall. You didn't see what Dave's dad, Dean, looked like." I hated what too much alcohol did to people. "And Marshall . . . he's still just a kid." Fourteen was a tough age. Abusive fathers with alcoholism didn't make it any easier. "And where the hell is his mom, Cindy? Why would she leave Marshall behind and move halfway across the country to be with his brother Devlin? It just doesn't make any sense."

"I don't know, Leah." Andy had answered that way a

billion times. I hadn't believed him at first. For the most part, I did now. As far as Dave and Marshall's situation went, there was no reason Andy should know anything. However . . .

"Dave's mom, Charlotte . . ." I sucked in a deep breath. My body wanted sleep, my brain, as usual, wouldn't let it happen. "When I was at Dave's old house, the one he grew up in, I saw her . . . Her spirit didn't pass on."

Andy's fingers stilled. "Charlotte Deana Masters?"

"I'm not sure about her middle name, but yeah, that sounds like her. Do you know anything?"

Andy's fingers picked their rhythm back up. "No. Only that you are correct. Charlotte Masters did not pass on. She refused to come to me. I was not aware that was Dave's mother."

Again, once upon a time, I would have doubted that statement. Now I didn't. "Yeah, that's what I was afraid of."

"And tonight was the first time you've seen her?" Andy's skepticism was more than fair.

"When we were kids, Dave was almost always over at our house. I can count on less than one hand the number of times Bobby and I went over there, and I'd never been upstairs before tonight. That's where I saw here, hovering in front of a locked door." My mind replayed Marshall's warning. "Marshall told me no one ever goes into that room. There was a lock on it." There was also a padlock outside Marshall's room, something I'd yet to mention to Dave. "She looked . . . bad. Charlotte died of pancreatic cancer, and it looked like a light breeze could blow her spiritual self over."

"Does Dave know?"

I gave as much of a head shake as possible, given my position across Andy's chest. "No. Tonight, at the hospital, there just wasn't the right . . . I just couldn't figure out how to say it. And Dave was already so upset about what was going on with Marshall—beating himself up about not answering his

phone or at least listening to his voicemails sooner . . . I just .
. ."

Andy was quiet, the ambient sounds of Dave's old apartment nearly imperceptible. "Do you plan to tell him?"

"What? Of co—"

"He's lived this long without the knowledge, Leah. Does
he have to know? Would his life be better for knowing?"

"I—" I wasn't sure. "No, I don't think it'll make his life
better." A lot of shit I knew hadn't improved my life. That
didn't mean I didn't need to know it. "I'm still going to tell
him. I think he has a right to know."

I had no illusions. This would gut Dave. But I also had no
doubt he'd want to know. I'd tried keeping things from Dave
in the past. It had never worked out well. That wasn't to say I
wasn't still keeping the mother of all secrets from Dave. It
wasn't just Dave but Cecile and Chrissie too. I was Andy's
final soul, something I'd yet to convince myself they needed
to know.

"Okay."

"*Okay*? That's all you've got to say?"

"No. It's late, and you have to be at work early tomorrow.
You should try to get some sleep. I'll stay as long as possible."

My mouth opened, unknown words itching to exit. I
swallowed them, snuggling deeper into Andy's warmth.
Mind drifting, my soft chuckle filtered into the pitch-black
room.

"Care to share?" Andy's soft voice whispered against my
skin, raising the hairs on the back of my neck.

"Just remembering the look on Marshall's face when we
got to Dave's house, and he got a good look at how
Halloween had vomited all over Dave's porch. And then he
went inside . . ." An even quieter chuckle bubbled up. "I don't
know if he was appalled or thrilled. Probably a mix of both.
The CPS lady seemed to take it in stride at least."

"Hmm, I need to stop by Dave's." Andy sounded genuinely interested.

"You really do. It's a sight to behold."

Sleep found me with a rare smile lifting my lips. Andy and I should have tried going to the bedroom, but we didn't. I was too comfortable, lying on Dave's old couch, its cushions more friend than foe. Andy would stay. He may or may not be there when I woke up. I'd experienced both over the last few days. When he was gone, I was sad but not devastated. Andy would be back to help hold the nightmares at bay, at least for a while—another fact I no longer doubted.

3

"Oh my god, Leah, did you hear?" Lenny trotted by my right side, both of us on our way to clock in for the morning. Apparently, he'd been standing at the door, waiting for me to arrive. It had been a few weeks since we'd played this game. I hadn't missed it.

"Hear what?" I played along, more chipper than usual. I chalked it up to the five hours of sleep I'd managed last night. I couldn't remember the last time I'd gotten so much time in the land of nod, and I hadn't woken up to a nightmare but to the feel of Andy's shirt beneath my cheek. There were no spirits Andy needed to reap, and as promised, he'd stayed.

"My mom's best friend's sister lives a couple of houses down from where Dave's dad lives. The police were there last night, and they arrested Dean." Lenny hopped up and down, keeping pace beside me as we wandered through Handy Helpers' aisles on our way to the break room.

Lenny's typical breakfast consisted of Doritos. As hyper as he generally was at o'dark thirty, I figured a soda of some kind was in that equation too. I wasn't a coffee drinker but couldn't imagine pairing Doritos with it. My stomach hissed revulsion and churned at the idea.

I quickly gave up trying to figure out the chain of gossip Lenny had just laid down. "I know," I answered while I pushed on the break room door. "Dave and I were there."

"You were?" Lenny grabbed his timecard, sliding it into the slot and stamping it quickly. "Is everything okay? Was Dave hurt?"

My heart warmed at Lenny's sincere concern. Lenny loved gossip, but he wasn't one of those malicious tale spinners. Sometimes I felt it wasn't so much *gossip* on his end as genuine caring. "Dave's fine." I didn't know how much Dave wanted me to say. He liked Lenny, but it was Dave's business, not mine. I settled on a generic summary. "Dave's taking care of his younger brother while things get straightened out." I'd shot Dave a text this morning asking how he was. It had been early, but either Dave had been up, or he'd taken his phone to bed with him. I'd followed up my text and asked if he'd heard from Marshall's mom yet. He'd sent back a firm "no" with an exploding head emoji.

"Oh, that's good." Lenny leaned back on his locker, a small smile of relief pulled at the edges of his lips. "I texted Chrissie last night to see if she knew anything. She didn't and was concerned. I'll message her today and let her know Dave's okay."

It was probably a good idea to give Chrissie a heads-up that Dave had company of the uninformed type too. Lenny seemed to unknowingly have that well in hand.

Pulling out my Handy Helpers vest, I slid my dark purple armor on. Given the cooler weather and my long sleeves, I didn't need to wear my leather wrist straps anymore, and the vest slid seamlessly over my white, cotton sleeves. "That sounds like a good idea. I'm sure Chrissie would appreciate it."

"Congratulations, Lenny," Ricky's liquid voice slid like slime over my skin. "It sounds like your relationship with Chrissie is still going well."

Lenny and I turned, staring at Ricky's disturbingly bright smile.

"She's quite the catch. Especially . . . well, we can't all be blessed with . . ." Ricky waved a hand up and down, indicating the breadth of Lenny's body. "Chrissie must be a very solid person and able to look past what's on the outside."

Ricky closed his locker, whisper soft.

I slammed mine.

"See you out on the floor. I hope you have a good day." Ricky finished with another blazing smile, his teeth too white, like he'd been overusing the whitening gel.

"What an ass." I probably would have said it even if we hadn't been alone. It was just Lenny and me in the break room.

"No argument here," Lenny agreed. "I really don't like it when we work with him."

"Me neither."

Lenny worked with Ricky more than I did, but neither of us was scheduled with him too often. Berta oversaw scheduling. I kept meaning to get her a thank-you card for her efforts.

"You know he's full of shit, right?" I hated how, once upon a time, I'd kind of thought like Ricky. Chrissie was beautiful. Lenny . . . wasn't, at least not on the outside. But Chrissie had dated *beautiful* before, and she'd gotten a great kid out of it. What she'd also gotten was a lesson that looks were far from everything. Chrissie found other things about Lenny attractive. They were the qualities that wouldn't fade with age, that wouldn't wither into dust or change on a whim.

"Yeah." Lenny didn't sound convinced, and I hated Ricky a bit more for planting the seeds of self-doubt in Lenny's head. Not that the seeds hadn't already been there. Most likely, Ricky had just thrown some fertilizer and water on them.

"Come on." I grabbed Lenny's arm, pulling him out of the break room and onto the floor. "Time to get to work."

<hr>

It was late morning, and things at work were going smoothly so far. Gary was tucked away in his office, Daryl was on as manager, and I'd mostly succeeded in avoiding Ricky Levitson. I'd gotten true, honest-to-god sleep the night before, and Andy had kissed me before shooing me out the door this morning. Despite what had happened with Dave and Marshall last night, I felt . . . good. It was such a foreign emotion it took me until mid-morning to name it.

It was a shame that I'd barely had time to enjoy my epiphany when Levi Dickerson showed up. "You're a difficult woman to track down, Leah."

My back stiffened, the hairs on my arms standing at attention, irritatingly brushing against the long sleeves of my shirt. I was in the process of inventorying storage containers toward the rear of the store. I didn't bother turning. I didn't want Levi to think he was important enough to hold my attention.

Tapping a couple of numbers into the scanner, I said, "It's a small town, Levi. Somehow, I doubt I'm that difficult to find." I didn't want to encourage Levi, but his statement didn't make much sense.

"You haven't been back to your apartment." Levi's cold, matter-of-fact words shivered over my skin.

"Stalking again, are you?" It wouldn't be the first time.

Levi grunted, the sound almost a growl. "You say that like I have a choice. I've tried calling. I've left messages and—"

"And I haven't answered. Get a clue, Levi. You were an officer, and now you're supposed to be a PI. I don't think it takes training in either of those fields to figure out I don't want to see, speak, or in any way have anything to do with you." In other words, *fuck off.*

I caught Levi's murky reflection in the dark plastic of one of the containers on the shelf in front of me. It was difficult to make out, but the thin line of his lips, pinched eyebrows, and hard set of his jaw screamed unhappiness. "We still have a lot to talk about, Leah. Ignoring me won't make me go away."

Levi's words drew a bitter laugh from deep within, finally making me turn and face him. "Believe me, I know that all too well."

Briefly, Levi appeared contrite. For whatever reason, Levi wanted to rewrite our history. There was only one problem with that—I didn't. Levi was an ass. He'd made my life hell and was still making my life hell, only in a different way. There was no soft-squishy feeling when it came to the man standing before me. The only emotions running through my mind and body were bad ones. I didn't have a drop of compassion for Levi Dickerson. As far as I was concerned, helping to save his life should have bought me a Get Out of Jail Free card. All that action seemed to have gained me was a deeper level of interest.

Swallowing down whatever moment of regret he might have experienced, Levi soldiered on. "I might be willing to give you the password to the flash drive if—"

"I've already watched it." I waved a dismissive hand in front of my face before turning to scan the storage tubs again.

Levi's teeth clacked together. "How?" Anger fueled that lowly spoken word. Cold, brittle anger.

My heart sped. I didn't like Levi at my back. He'd healed a

little too well from his injuries for my comfort. The last time I'd seen him, Levi needed a cane. He didn't have one in hand now. That didn't mean Levi Dickerson wasn't without weapons, and I wasn't speaking about guns or knives. Levi's hands were large and strong. The bruise he'd leveled on my arm was gone, but its memory was alive and well.

Forcing down my growing fear, I tried for nonchalance. "It doesn't matter. All you need to know is that I watched the video—all of it, even the part you tried to delete. I don't give a shit about what else you think you have. I also don't give a shit about whatever else you're curious about. If you don't leave me alone, I'll see about getting a restraining order." I didn't think that would do much to deter someone like Levi, but it might embarrass him into leaving me the hell alone.

"Why won't you—"

"Leah? I'm sorry to intrude, but I could use your help with something."

I'd never been so thankful to hear Melody's voice before. Turning, I plastered on the most grateful smile I could. "You're not intruding, Melody. I believe I've sufficiently answered this customer's questions. Right, Mr. Dickerson?"

Mouth twisting into something sour, Levi's gaze bore into me before turning on Melody. With a stiff nod, he turned and headed down the aisle. Melody and I remained silent until he passed from view. The slight hitch in his gait was the only indication Levi Dickerson had taken a bullet to his leg and shoulder just a few short months ago.

"You okay?" Melody asked, her eyes still focused on the corner Levi had disappeared behind. "I really didn't mean to interrupt or eavesdrop. I wanted to talk to you. I was trying to patiently wait until you were done, but the more I heard . . . I didn't like how he spoke, and you didn't look comfortable."

"I'm glad you butted in." Relief flowed through my body, but it was tempered with the knowledge that Melody was alone. Since Rose was hospitalized last August, I hadn't seen Isaac in Handy Helpers. Now at home, in hospice, I didn't expect to see Isaac outside Rose's presence again.

"Okay." Melody blew out a heavy breath. "I'm glad." Finally focusing her attention on me, I noted the dark circles beneath her eyes. Melody's wrinkled skin had a sallow, thin quality I didn't like. Her glasses weren't as thick as Rose's, allowing tired eyes to show through. "I'm sorry. I know you're at work, and this probably isn't the best time, but I wanted to let you know that Mom's condition isn't great. She's . . . she's not doing well." Melody finished on a harsh swallow. "I doubt it will be much longer. I think she'd like to see you again before she passes. Mom is very fond of you, and you've been a big help to her these past few years."

Grief dug its cold claws deep into my soul again. You'd think I'd have better armor against the pain of loss by now. I didn't. If anything, my armor was more patchwork quilt than impenetrable steel. "I . . . I'd like that. I love Rose." I wanted to tell Melody that I loved Isaac too, but she wouldn't understand. Melody had never met her father, even though he'd been there from the moment of her birth and witnessed her grow and mature into the wonderful woman she'd become. Isaac was a devoted father. Melody would never know how devoted.

"She loves you too." Melody's face softened, easing and relaxing her lips. "Is it okay if I call or text you?"

"Of course. Give me a time, and I'll be there." Gary would more than understand if I needed some time off to visit Rose. Thinking of Gary, I asked, "Is it okay if I let Gary know?"

Melody gave another one of those soft, understanding smiles. "Mom would like that. She enjoyed coming into the store, and Gary always treated her right." With a kind chuckle, Melody added, "Mom's convinced that he told the staff to let you know when she walked through the doors. You always knew when she was here and came to help her."

But it wasn't Gary. It was Isaac. He'd found me, and where there was one, there was the other. And it would be that way when Rose passed. Soon Rose would know. She'd understand how much she'd been loved, that Isaac had been there every step of the way. My grief was selfish. Rose and Isaac would soon be free. But all humans were selfish—even past death.

4

Lizzie nodded in my direction as I walked out of Handy Helpers' doors. She rarely offered those too-wide smiles anymore, at least not since we'd come to an *understanding* about Andy. I also didn't think she was happy about my absence from my apartment. Oddly, moving out wasn't about her, although having Lizzie living on the first floor in Ellen Dykstra's old apartment didn't give me warm and fuzzy feelings.

I just couldn't do it. Memories of Ashes danced in every corner and swam across the window seat she'd called home.

I was halfway to my car when my phone rang. Seeing Dave's name light up across the screen wasn't a surprise. I'd barely gotten out a brief hello before he started in.

"Do you know what that woman said to me?"

"And what *woman* would that be?" I asked while sliding my key into the door of my car. I figured I had a pretty good idea but wanted to be sure who Dave was getting ready to verbally skewer.

"Cindy," Dave spat the name like it was diseased. "You

know, when Dad married her, I actually tried to give her a chance."

"And how long did that last?"

"Two days. That's when she started painting the house."

Dave's mom had loved the original woodwork in the old, craftsman-style house. Cindy didn't. She'd said it was too dark and painted all of it white. I didn't think Dave and Cindy would have ever had much of a chance, but if there had been one, she'd blown it with a single paintbrush stroke. Not that Cindy really cared that much either way.

Tossing my purse into the passenger seat, I dropped into the driver's side, pulling my jacket around me a little tighter. The cloudy sky kept the temperatures chilly. Halloween was right around the corner, and if the weather kept this up, the trick-or-treaters would need coats over their costumes.

"I take it you finally got a hold of her?"

"Oh yeah. Cindy finally got around to calling me two hours ago. I was her second call after the police. She sounded put out that she had to talk to me at all and couldn't figure out what 'all the fuss was about.' Can you believe that shit? Her fourteen-year-old son's lip is split, his cheek is swollen like an egg, and she can't figure out what the *fuss* is about?"

I took a deep breath. Anger rolled through me, but it was a dim flame compared to how pissed Dave sounded. "Is she coming back?" That was the million-dollar question. Cindy was Marshall's mother. The CPS representative had told Dave that they wanted Marshall back with Cindy if Cindy was a stable parent. Dave had been on the fence. He just wanted Marshall healthy and safe. If Cindy could manage that and she wanted Marshall with her, then he'd see it done. I couldn't imagine a mom not wanting her kid, especially given that Marshall wasn't a bad one as far as I knew. Evidently, Cindy felt differently.

"Only because she fucking has to," Dave seethed. "She's pissed because CPS threatened her with abandonment, but it's pretty damn clear she doesn't want to care for Marshall." Dave let loose a frustrated sigh.

I hated that he was going through this. "What did Marshall say?"

Dave typically didn't sugarcoat things, but I also couldn't imagine him blatantly telling Marshall that his mom didn't want him. Although, he probably had a clue from some of the things Marshall had said and some of the looks I'd caught when Cindy's name was mentioned.

"I haven't talked to him about it yet. He's been holed up in his room all afternoon."

Marshall's room had been my room when I'd stayed with Dave after Justin Turlington used Bobby's body to shove my nosy downstairs neighbor over the third-floor railing, cracking her skull and killing her.

"Besides," Dave went on, "I want a chance to speak with Maggie Littleton again to see what my options are. If Cindy really doesn't want him, I can look after Marshall. I might not know a hell of a lot about raising kids, but he'll be safe here, and at least I give a damn."

"He'll be more than safe with you, Dave." My best friend had a nurturing streak a mile wide. Marshall might not know it yet, but he was in good hands. "Are you going to make that offer to Cindy?"

"I'm not sure yet. I'll get with Maggie, talk to her and see if that might be a possibility. I'll ask Marshall what he wants first. If he wants to stay with me, I'll do everything I can to make sure that happens. Evidently, fourteen is the age in Indiana where kids have the right to say who they want to live with, but that usually means one parent or the other. I'm just Marshall's half brother."

I didn't think Dave was *just* anything and said so. "We'll

figure this out. Remember, impossible situations are our specialty, and this one isn't nearly as impossible as some of the shit we've run up against recently. Besides, Cecile's a member now, too, and we can solve any case between the three of us." I laid it on a bit thick, but Dave's laughter told me it was worth the effort.

"Hey, I hate to spring this on you last minute, but I've got some things at work to clear out and rearrange. Chama and Tonn Tonn covered for me today, but I need to talk the Marshall situation over with them. Any chance you could come over for a couple of hours and hang out? I know Marshall's old enough to stay home alone, but . . ."

"No problem. I just got off work, and my schedule's free." Turning the key in the ignition, I left the car in park but started to turn up the heat.

"Okay," Dave blew out a relieved breath, "that's good. I wasn't sure, you know, with Andy, what . . . uh . . . yeah, let's just settle on I'm just not sure and leave it at that." I hardly ever heard Dave embarrassed.

"It's okay. Most of the time, I'm not sure either." What I was, was content. It had been a long time since I'd been able to say that. "I'll see if I can coax Marshall out of his room, or at least I can ask him if he'd like to meet Lenny. I think they might have a few things in common."

Dave barked out a laugh. "No shit. I asked if he needed any help setting up his gaming system. Thank god he said no. I didn't have the first clue. That stuff's never been my cup of tea."

It wasn't mine either, but I'd absorbed enough from Lenny over the past couple of months that I might be able to hold a conversation with Marshall. Then again, when Lenny talked about his gaming prowess, I mostly sat there, nodding my head here and there. Most likely, I didn't know jack shit.

"I'm getting ready to leave Handy Helpers' parking lot. See you in ten."

"M'kay. Drive safe."

Dave ended the call, and I tossed my phone in the passenger seat. I should have probably talked with Lenny before I offered up his services. Pulling out of the parking lot, I saw Lenny headed for his car, and all I did was wave. I couldn't imagine Lenny as anything but over the moon about getting a new gaming friend. With that in mind, I headed for Dave's house.

<hr>

Dave wasn't kidding when he'd said Marshall was holed up in his room. I'd been there for over an hour, and beyond his, "Okay," when Dave shouted through the door that he was leaving but that I was around, I hadn't heard peep one out of him. It was time to change that.

Pushing off Dave's couch, I headed for the stairs. Eliza Morgan's spirit might have been long gone, but I still made a large arc around the spot she'd called home for over seven years. Memory was a strange thing, and I often caught myself doing a double-take of the area, thinking I detected a hint of her spirit out of the corner of my eye. It was just a trick of my mind, but I looked all the same.

Dave had refurbished the wooden staircase, polishing it into something near pristine. Dave's house was just another thing he took care of. Used to be that I was the front and center *thing* on that list. My spot was in jeopardy, and I couldn't be more relieved. As far as I was concerned, it was a prestigious list. I just didn't want to be at the top anymore. Other people needed his attention more than I did, and dear god, wasn't that a relief.

Marshall's room was on the opposite side of the main

suite. Turning left when I got to the top of the stairs, I headed for a door that, just a few months ago, I'd sort of called home. It was probably more accurate to say it was where my clothes had called home. Giving a quick, double knock, I said, "Marshall, it's Leah. Can I come in?" I heard the distant sounds of gunfire in the background. I shivered, remembering my own up close and personal experiences with firearms. This was just a game, an imitation of someone's idea of excitement.

The background noise lowered until I heard shuffling and shifting. The creak of old floorboards sounded as Marshall made his way to the door. Dave's home didn't have locks on any of the inner doors. I still wasn't sure why Dave's dad's house was different. It was one of many questions peppering a dimly lit list cowering in the corner of my brain. I hoped Marshall could shine a flashlight on a few of them.

The twist of antique workings invaded the quiet of the hall. The door to Marshall's room cracked open, revealing a whiskey-colored eye as it peeked through. Marshall didn't say anything, simply blinked a couple of times while keeping the door barely open.

Shifting uncomfortably, I gave a ridiculous wave. "Hey, Marshall. Have you got a couple of minutes?" I didn't think he had anything but time. It was still polite to ask.

"Why?" Marshall didn't sound belligerent, simply curious.

I shrugged. "I'm bored?" It came out more as a question than a statement. "Also, I had a couple of questions for you. You don't have to answer if they make you uncomfortable. I thought you might have some questions for me too, about Dave." Marshall and Dave weren't close. They barely knew each other. Dave was the one Marshall had tried to reach out to despite that. I had to think that counted for something.

Marshall's hesitant glare flicked off to the side before landing back on me, curiosity shimmering deep within. I caught a hint of a nod before the door opened farther. Scooting back, Marshall headed toward his gaming console. It looked like he was probably saving his progress. Satisfied, he plopped down on the bed.

Following, I flinched at the lavender-colored bedspread. Dave had purchased it with me in mind, not his younger brother. "Sorry about the bedspread," I offered while sitting on a rolling desk chair. "For a while, this was my room. I think Dave bought that," I pointed at the comforter, "thinking that if I liked the color, maybe I'd sleep in the bed."

Marshall glanced down at the fabric before asking, "Did it work?"

"Not really." My gaze caught on the window seat Dave had installed for Ashes, then my heart pinched before I looked away.

Marshall must have caught my line of sight. "Dave said your cat died recently." There was no sting in those words, simply a factual statement.

"She did," I swallowed hard. "She had kidney failure."

"That sucks." I figured that was about as much empathy as a fourteen-year-old was capable of. Besides, it summed up the situation better than fancy words ever could.

A thought suddenly struck me. "Do you have any pets? Do we need to go over to the house to take care of anyone or bring them here? Dave won't mind." I didn't need to ask him to know that.

Marshall shook his head, wincing when the action pulled at his lip. The redness was gone from Marshall's face, deep purples and ugly blues taking their place on his cheek. The swelling in his lip was diminished, but the cut was still there, still painful. "Mom never wanted the fur and Dad . . . I wouldn't trust him with anything like that." There was a lot of baggage in that statement. It was a sad truth that humans were allowed to have kids when they couldn't be trusted to care for a pet.

"Okay. I just wanted to make sure." The silence became awkward. My gaze tracked around the room, amazed that it looked more lived in than when I stayed there for a few weeks. I looked back on the gaming console and I decided now was a good time to bring up Lenny. "I've got a friend at work who is really into gaming. I'm not gonna sit here and tell you I have a clue what he's talking about most of the time, but if you want, I think he'd love to come over and play, or maybe do something online." I'd heard Lenny talk about that before, that he had friends online that he played with and against.

"That sounds cool." Marshall's fingers twisted a piece of the lavender comforter, not offering up much more on the subject. Still not meeting my eyes, he asked, "So, Dave said he had to go to work for a while."

I nodded. "Yeah, his partners covered for him earlier today, but there's some stuff he needs to take care of."

Marshall cleared his throat, eyes still downcast. "Dad said he does tattooing. Is that true?"

"It is," I answered proudly. "He co-owns a studio with his friend, Chama. It's called Ink No Evil."

Marshall glanced up, his eyes wide, and a wry smile twisted his lips. "Cool name."

I chuckled. "Dave and Chama certainly think so. They still argue with each other as to whose idea it was. If you ask Dave, he'll tell you it was his. To this day, I don't know who to believe."

Marshall was back to staring intently at his fingers. "Chama, that's who Dave left to live with. Right?"

"Yeah. They were friends already, and when Dave left your house, he moved in with Chama."

Marshall didn't say anything. He simply stared at his twisting fingers.

I decided to dig a little deeper. "Were you upset when he left?"

Marshall shrugged. "Not really. At least the house got quieter. For a while."

Little warning bells started ringing in my head. Dave and his dad had fought—a lot. It wasn't a surprise to learn things had quieted down after he walked out. In a way, maybe somewhere in Dave's subconscious, one of the reasons he'd left was to spare his younger brothers the animosity that was only growing stronger. The bigger reason was that he was afraid if he stayed any longer, he'd end up in jail for assault. Dave and his dad really didn't get along. Evidently, it had helped, but not as much as Dave had hoped.

"Just for a while?" I prompted.

Blowing out a deep breath, Marshall scrubbed his hand over the top of his head. He had a lot more hair than Dave, and the action left strands of wheat blond hair sticking up all over the place. "Maybe a year or two. But Dad's . . ." Marshall shrugged, the action too adult for someone his age. "Dad's dad and Mom's mom. There was a lot of yelling. And then, there wasn't." Marshall stared at the wall, his face grim. "I think Mom just kind of got fed up and decided it wasn't worth the effort." Marshall's eyes narrowed as he looked toward me. "I think Mom and Devlin both gave up, or at least they changed tactics. They had a plan to get out."

I swallowed hard at the implications. "Devlin graduated and moved away to college."

"And Mom followed." Marshall's thin lips looked grim.

"And you?"

Marshall looked away again, voice small. "I guess I wasn't worth it either."

I sucked in a harsh, painful breath. "Marshall, I—"

"This house," Marshall interrupted, "it's got a good vibe to it. It's not nearly as heavy as Dad's place." Marshall didn't call it *home*. I wondered if he felt like me, like he didn't really have a place that had earned that name.

I thought back to the locked doors and Charlotte's spirit. I could openly ask about one of those things. Maybe that would hint at the other. Clearing my throat, I asked, "Why isn't anyone supposed to go into the bedroom at the end of the hall?"

Marshall's body stiffened, his fingers twitching within the fabric of the lavender comforter. "We just don't," he answered, unhelpful.

I pressed a little harder. "It was locked from the outside. I think it's a little more than that."

Lips parting, Marshall appeared to struggle, twisting his body this way and that as he fidgeted. "It's stupid, and you wouldn't believe me."

"You'd be surprised what I'd believe. Dave too."

My response earned me a quick side-eyed glance. With a huffed, "Whatever," Marshall caved. "Weird sh—stuff happens in that room. Mom tried cleaning it out and changing it into a yoga studio . . . It didn't go well. Devlin told me it was Dave's mom's room. Kind of like a craft room or something like that. I don't know how Devlin knew, but he said she spent a lot of time in there . . . you know, before she died." Marshall swallowed hard, proclaiming Charlotte's death. "Eventually, Dad just closed it up and threw a lock on it. I don't even know where the key is. I never *wanted* to know."

Marshall was a teenager. That meant curiosity was almost always hardwired into their DNA. The fact he had no inclination to even try to sneak into a locked room was telling. "And your room?" I questioned. "Why do you have a lock on it?"

Suddenly standing, Marshall paced toward his gaming console, tapping it with the toe of his shoe. "That one's easy. Dad."

My blood ran cold, imagining all kinds of horrid scenarios. "Your dad?"

"Yeah." Marshall's hands fisted at his sides. "I came home one day, and he'd trashed my stuff. He denied it later, but come on," Marshall whined, "who else would have come into our house and just kicked the shit out of the stuff in my room? Nothing was stolen, just destroyed. I bought the padlock the next day. My stuff's been safe since."

"Shit," whispered out of my mouth, filling the room. "Well, one thing I can guarantee is that you'll never need that here."

Twisting, Marshall glared at me, his eyes far from sure. "You telling me Dave doesn't drink?"

I'd have to talk to Dave about this later, about Marshall's worries. Dave had never spoken well of his dad, but I didn't remember him calling Dean an alcoholic or stating he was violent when he did drink.

Standing, I took a couple of steps toward Marshall. "No, I'm not going to say that, but he doesn't drink a lot, and I've only seen him do it socially." Breathing in deeply, I told Marshall my suspicions about Dave's lack of inebriation. "I don't think he could afford to take the risk of being drunk when I was . . . I wasn't good . . . For a long time, your brother had to be on constantly. He couldn't risk being compromised, not with me and my screwed-up brain." I tapped my temple for emphasis.

Marshall stared at me like he saw me for the first time, or maybe finally believed for the first time. Seconds ticked by, turning into a minute, maybe longer, before Marshall asked, "Did your brother really murder your parents?"

I flinched, ready to defend Bobby, to shake my head no. It

wasn't Bobby but Justin's soul riding his body, forcing my brother's fingers to squeeze that trigger. Instead, I answered, "Yeah, he did."

"That sucks," Marshall said, his evident answer for anything tragic.

"Yeah. Yeah, it does."

5

The next day I was in the middle of a double shift, sorting wood in the Wasteland—my long-sleeved cotton shirt and purple Handy Helpers vest did little to block the cold wind—when heat stole through my soul, warming me from the inside out.

Andy.

With a smile, I turned toward my reaper. That smile faded quickly. "Andy? What's wrong?" I'd seen Andy's stoic face more times than I could count. That uninterpretable blank look that revealed next to nothing. More recently, I'd seen his lips twisted in amusement, smoldering desire, and soft want. What I'd rarely seen was a look of sad despondence.

Andy walked closer, enveloping me within the warmth of his arms. Breathing deeply, I clutched him tight, pulling his lean body into mine. "Andy, what—"

"Have you checked your phone messages recently?"

"No. Not for a few hours. I've been working." A fine shiver ran up my spine as fear constricted my chest. Andy was a reaper, any knowledge he had that I didn't couldn't be good. "What happened? Are Dave and Cecile all right? Chrissie?"

"They're fine," Andy assured, his fingers dragging through my growing hair, fiddling with a tangle at the end. "It's Rose."

My breath caught. "Rose? Is she . . . did she pass?"

"Not yet." Andy pulled away, not holding me at arm's length, but far enough he could look me in the eyes. "But I've started to feel the call of her spirit. I don't think it will be much longer, and I'll bet Melody has called you."

I started walking toward the doors leading back into Handy Helpers. Andy didn't follow. Out here, we were alone. Inside was a different story. Andy didn't like the reaper whammy he had on the living, at least not when he didn't need to use it. I appreciated that he didn't want to fuck with everyone's minds. It was another way he and Elijah were different. Elijah got a kick out of it. Andy was just annoyed.

"I'll see you there." Andy's words haunted me as my feet pounded along Handy Helpers cement floor. Lenny saw me scurrying and shouted something I couldn't hear, the cacophony of noise rushing through my brain blocking out everything else.

Shoving into the break room, I made a beeline for my locker. While digging through my purse, I vaguely caught the squeak of the break room door open and close. Lenny's too-close face popped up on the other side of my locker as I finally discovered my phone. It took me three tries to punch in my phone's code with shaking fingers.

"What's wrong?" Lenny asked, sounding scared. "You look really upset."

Lenny's voice drowned into the background as I listened to Melody's voicemail. Andy was right. Rose wasn't expected to live much longer. For a few precious seconds, I couldn't breathe. Hunched over, I heard Dave's voice, echoing through my head, telling me when to inhale and exhale.

Slowly, my vision cleared, the blackness receding. At some point during my meltdown, Lenny left and returned with Gary.

"Leah? Talk to me. What's going on?"

Blinking through unshed tears, I fought back the panic of impending loss. Still shaking, I set my phone back inside my locker, gaining enough strength to look at my boss. "It's Rose." I swallowed thickly. "Melody called. Rose doesn't have much time. I . . . I know I'm supposed to work a double today, but—"

"Go." Gary's eyes dropped with his own grief. "Go and say goodbye for all of us. Don't worry about this place. We'll be fine." Gary's usual ruddy color paled, draining away with sadness.

"I'll clock you out," Lenny offered, already on his way to the cards.

I thought I said thanks, but I wasn't sure. I'd already shoved my hands through the sleeves of my coat and was headed for the door and parking lot. Running to my blue Toyota, the cold, fall wind whipped at the tangled ends of my hair, making it hard to see. Or maybe that was the tears in my eyes.

"**T**hank you for coming."

Melody looked exhausted, worn thin, and frail with impending loss. She'd been taking care of Rose for the past few weeks, and it showed. I'd cared for Ashes, giving her fluids and medications, cleaning up her vomit, and coaxing her to eat. Caring for the diseased and dying ate away at your soul, taking little bites here and there, eventually making a meal of it.

"Mom's still coherent, but she comes and goes. We don't

think . . ." Melody's voice caught, choking. With a final head shake, she headed deeper into the house.

Melody's husband, Charles, sat on the end of the couch Dave typically claimed when we came over. He offered me a tight nod as I walked by. Following Melody, we quickly made our way to the back bedroom, where Rose had barely left in the past couple of weeks.

The room smelled of disinfectant and medications, weirdly taking on the ambiance of a hospital room. Walking through the doorway, I barely held in my gasp of disbelief. Rose had never been an imposing figure—her personality was large, her body not so much. But she'd never looked this frail, this pale imitation of the woman I'd come to know and love.

Isaac was at the head of the bed, spiritual fingers running through Rose's haphazard blue-white hair. He couldn't feel Rose's skin or the brush of her hair against his spiritual flesh. Maybe that's not what mattered. Perhaps it was the movement itself that offered comfort. Barely looking up at me, Isaac gave me a warm, welcoming smile that was full of relief. "Hello, Leah. Thank you for coming."

I started to tell Isaac that no thanks were needed but remembered at the last second that Melody wouldn't have a clue what I was talking about. Offering Isaac my own version of an appreciative smile, I moved closer to Rose, taking her skeletal fingers within my own. "How long does she have?"

"No one's sure," Melody answered, "but her breathing is slower, and she hasn't eaten anything in . . . I can't really remember the last time."

I nodded. "Can I sit with her for a while?"

"Of course. Take your time. My children and grandchildren have already said their goodbyes. It's just you, me, and Charlie at this point." Melody's fingers squeezed my shoulder. "I'll be in the living room. Call if you need me or if she starts to pass."

"I will."

Melody's soft footfalls carried her down the hall, leaving me alone with Rose and Isaac.

"I can't believe this is really happening." It was a stupid statement. Rose was in her mid-nineties. No one lived forever, and she'd lived longer than most.

"Rose has lived a good and long life."

My brain traveled back to what Andy had said, that Isaac's continued spiritual presence might have made Rose's life less, not more. I couldn't believe that. I wouldn't believe that. Maybe Andy was right. Even if he were, I couldn't think badly of Isaac for his decision to stay. I'd never seen love run that deep or true. Ignoring those doubts, I answered, "She has."

Isaac lifted his head, a sad, wistful smile tilting his lips. "She loves you very much, Leah. You've brought us both joy. Rose isn't in any condition to tell you that herself, but it's the truth, and she'd want you to know just how important you are to her."

I didn't think I'd done anything spectacular. "I'm not sure why, but I'm grateful. Besides, Rose has done far more for me than I have for her." My own flesh and blood grandmother had tried to murder me when I was little more than two years old. Rose might not have been directly related to me, but she was my chosen family, just like Dave.

"Hmm, still underselling yourself," Isaac gently scolded. "My Rose would definitely set you to rights if she could."

I laughed softly, thinking about the harsh words Rose would level at me. Rose had always been honest. Sometimes she'd been tough, but it always came from a place of caring. Rose wanted me to be stronger.

"She'd hate all this fussing," Isaac interrupted our silence.

"People have been coming and going, not seeing her at her best. Rose wouldn't like the attention."

"No, I imagine not. But she's well-loved, and they want to say goodbye, just like me."

"True." Isaac remained silent, both of us staying by Rose's side.

After a time, Melody came back in and pulled up a chair on the other side of Rose's bed, clasping her other hand. Minutes ticked by in oddly pleasant conversation. In some ways, I thought my presence was just as soothing for Rose's daughter as it was for Isaac.

Time slipped through our fingers, and eventually, Rose's breathing slowed to something incompatible with life. Her heart monitor stuttered, and those beeping complexes became increasingly sparse as Rose faded from the world.

A choking sob broke through Melody's calm demeanor, drawing her husband, Charles, into the room. Rubbing his wife's shoulders while she shuddered and cried, neither saw Andy enter the room. As always, I felt his approach before I ever laid eyes on him. Our gaze connected across the room, Andy's a reflection of the deep, aching well of sorrow I felt.

"He's come for us, sweetheart," Isaac's whispered voice floated through the room, calling to Rose's spirit.

Once again, my breath caught as Rose's spirit rose from her chest, a misty shade of blush pink. The haze swirled before coalescing into something more solid, something so much younger than the woman I'd come to cherish. A hiccuped sob caught in my throat, somewhere between grief and joy. Rose looked like that beauty in the photo she kept on a side table in the living room—the one that had been taken right before Isaac shipped out for the last time. She'd likely been pregnant when that photo was taken, though I don't know if she'd known at the time. Regardless, the spiritual woman floating before me embodied the Rose that Isaac remembered, the one he'd fallen in love with over seventy years ago.

"Rose," Isaac sounded awestruck.

"Isaac? Is that you? Is that really you?" Rose's voice was lighter than I'd ever heard before, something from her younger, more naïve days.

"It's me, sweetheart." There was so much emotion floating through Isaac's words. The air was thick with it, drowning away my sorrow. "I've been waiting for you for so long."

"Isaac!" Rose's spirit launched itself toward Isaac, twisting and melding into colorful shades of soft pinks and brilliant hues of golden yellow.

"Isaac," Andy's reaper voice cut through their reunion, drawing not only Isaac and Rose's attention but Melody's and Charles's too. I heard both of their shocked intakes of breath. Glancing over, they shared the same wonderstruck expressions almost all the living experienced when they beheld a reaper. I wasn't sure what either of them saw when they looked at Andy. In a few minutes, they'd forget he was ever there, and it wouldn't matter.

"Are you ready to go now?" Andy asked, a pleasing note hidden within his unnatural reaper voice. "It's been a long time coming, don't you think?"

Isaac's image was vaguely discernible from his melding with Rose's spirit, his words distant and barely audible. "I wouldn't change a thing."

"I know," Andy answered, "but it's time to rest now."

Isaac, or maybe Rose, said something, but it was no longer discernible. With tears leaking, I watched for as long as I could until both their spirits glowed so brightly they burned my eyes. Toward the end, I couldn't make out who was who, and I knew, deep down inside, that's the way it was always meant to be. I hadn't tried to speak with Rose when she'd left her body. Her eyes had been for one soul and one soul only—the one she'd longed for and never known was so close by.

Andy's warmth faded from my core, leaving me cool and alone with Melody and Charles, Rose's lifeless body lying on the bed between us. It was little more than a husk of the woman I'd loved like a grandmother. Easing my fingers from Rose's cold ones, I made my way around the bed to Melody. "I'm so sorry," I managed, wishing she'd been able to see what I'd just seen. Maybe then the loss wouldn't hurt so much.

Melody's glazed eyes stared up at me, clearing as memories of Andy fled. "Thank you, Leah. I'm glad you were here in the end."

I was, too, for more reasons than Melody would ever know.

"At least she's with Isaac now," Charles said, shocking me until I realized that was something the living said when a loved one passed, something to soothe their own sorrow and ease their hearts. I didn't know how true it was for others, but in the case of Rose, Charles was absolutely right.

"She is," I agreed.

Melody took my hands in hers, squeezing tight. "I hope so." Standing, she wiped the tears from her eyes, releasing my hands and leaning over Rose's body. Kissing her mother's forehead, Melody whispered something I couldn't hear, something Rose could no longer hear either. It didn't matter. Whatever those words were, they were more comfort for the living than the dead.

Straightening, Melody gave Rose's forearm another squeeze. Charles was up too, on his phone, alerting the rest of the family about Rose's passing. Turning to me, Melody's eyes shimmered beneath the lenses of her glasses. Taking my hand in hers again, she said, "There's something we need to talk about, something Mom wanted you to have."

6

"Holy shit, Rose left you her house?" Dave sat forward, elbows on Cecile's kitchen table. Cecile, Aunt Joyce, and Uncle Jack were there too. Uncle Jack and Aunt Joyce were preparing dinner, but all activity stopped when I released my little bombshell.

Uncle Jack recovered first. "You mean," he cleared his throat, "she wants . . . wanted," Uncle Jack corrected, "you to live in the house, like rent it from Melody?"

I shook my head. "No, as in she left the deed of the house to me. As in, as soon as it's all official, I own a house."

"Holy shit," Dave repeated, flopping back in his chair, eyes wide and dazed. "I knew she liked you but . . ."

"But to leave me her house." I nodded in agreement. "I hardly knew what to say when Melody told me." My fingers slid down the cool surface of my Mountain Dew can, leaving trails in the condensation.

"What did you say?" Uncle Jack sat next to a silent Cecile, her eyes nearly as wide as Dave's.

"I didn't say anything, not for a few minutes." I stared at

nothing while I remembered that totally bizarre conversation. "Charles must have thought I didn't believe Melody, or maybe didn't hear correctly, because he told me the same thing, reassured me that's what Rose wanted and that he and Melody agreed."

"Wow." Cecile's hushed voice finally filtered into the room. "Did you have any clue?"

"None." That was maybe the easiest question I'd ever answered. "I told Melody I'd have to think about it."

Dave's head shot up. "What's to think about? You love that house." There was genuine confusion there.

"I do," I agreed, "but I think it should go to Rose's family, not—"

"You are her family," Cecile interrupted, reaching for my hand and squeezing my fingers tight. "How many times have you told me that Dave's as good as a brother to you? He's your family, just as much as we are." Cecile's eyes rounded the room, taking in my aunt and uncle. "Just like Gary and Judy are family. Lenny, Chrissie, and Lilly too. Blood is just a part of what makes a family, and you know it. Family is as much a matter of choice as genetics." Cecile and I shared a meaningful look, both of us silently agreeing on who we wanted to discount as a family member.

"Cecile's right." Aunt Joyce stood next to Uncle Jack, a wooden spoon gripped within one hand, her other rested on his shoulder. According to Cecile, they were doing better, the arguing dimming to something near nonexistent. My chest tightened, and my heart warmed when Uncle Jack covered his wife's hand with his own.

Laying the dripping spoon on the counter, Aunt Joyce continued, "Rose was no shrinking violet and age didn't dim her mind. She knew what she wanted, and obviously what Rose wanted was you in that house—permanently. You were good to her, Leah, and she was good to you. For what it's worth, my advice is to gratefully accept Rose's gift. It would make her happy, thinking of you in that house, taking care of it with the same loving care she did." With a final pat to Uncle Jack's shoulder, Aunt Joyce picked the spoon back up and headed toward the kitchen.

"Yeah," Dave motioned toward the kitchen, "what she said."

I squirmed, shifting in the wooden kitchen chair. If Rose's spirit had stuck around, I could talk this out with her. It was a selfish thought. Selfish or not, it crossed my mind more than once.

"You said Melody and Charles were on board with the idea, right?" Cecile asked, and I nodded. "Then I don't see the problem. It would be good for you in so many ways."

Cecile wasn't wrong. I'd been thinking of looking for a new apartment. I'd never dreamed of looking for a house. "It's really big for one person."

"I'm sorry." Dave leaned across the table, eyebrows raised and a mischievous smirk on his face. "I wasn't aware Rose had a roommate. Cecile, did you know Rose had some mysterious other person living on the property?"

"Ass." I threw a napkin at Dave. The lightweight paper fell short. "She raised Melody in that house."

"Yeah, like over fifty years ago," Dave helpfully answered.

I blew out a frustrated breath. "I don't even use the one bedroom I've got, let alone three."

"Now you're just fishing for excuses. I've been in Rose's house. It's got a living room, couch, and TV. We both know that's all you need, for now. I've still got high hopes you'll find your way back to a bed." Dave waggled his eyebrows suggestively. Uncle Jack's lips contorted in confusion. Aunt Joyce and Uncle Jack didn't have a clue about Andy, and for now, I wanted to keep it that way.

I shot Dave a warning look, one that only deepened his smirk.

Thankfully, Cecile broke in before Uncle Jack could ask anything. "You could always get a roommate, someone to help out with the utilities and that kind of thing."

"A roommate?" I stared, unblinking at Cecile. "Who in their right mind would want to live with me?" At Cecile's startled and somewhat hurt look, I amended, "Present company excluded."

"Well . . ." Cecile looked to Dave as if he might have the answer.

Dave surprised the hell out of me when he answered, "Chrissie."

"Chrissie Hollybrook?" I asked while Aunt Joyce simultaneously asked, "The witch?"

Dave's eyes bounced from me to somewhere behind me in the kitchen. "Yes . . . to both."

My mouth opened, ready to spew all kinds of reasons why that made absolutely no sense, why it wouldn't work. But it closed just as quickly as those reasons fizzled out and died the moment they touched my lips. "You really think she might be interested?"

Dave shrugged. "No idea. She loves plants, and from what you've told me, she's turned her apartment into an indoor jungle. She'd love the garden at Rose's house. She'd probably still put plants all over inside, so I guess there's that, plus she's got a six-year-old daughter you'd have to deal with . . . I suppose those are things to consider, but it might be worth an ask. Besides, I like the idea of you having a roommate, at least a roommate like Chrissie."

Uncle Jack nodded like a loon.

"I take it you agree?" I asked my uncle.

"Let's just say I don't disagree," he answered.

Since truly accepting lingering spirits as fact, Uncle Jack

and Aunt Joyce had come around to believing in Chrissie too. Despite what Aunt Joyce had said earlier, I didn't think she disliked Chrissie. Given that Chrissie created the charm dangling around Cecile's neck, allowing my cousin a semblance of normal life, my aunt was ready to adopt Chrissie into the family fold.

"Jack, you wanna help me with this?" Aunt Joyce asked, dinner finally ready.

Uncle Jack hopped up, putting a hand on my shoulder when I tried to follow. Potato soup, French bread, and salad were on the table within a few minutes.

"God, this is so good." Dave barely took time to blow on his soup before shoving the steaming brew into his mouth.

"Glad you like it." Aunt Joyce sounded genuine. "Next time, you should bring Marshall over."

Spoon halfway to his mouth, Dave grunted. "He was supposed to come today, but Cindy finally showed up."

I stiffened, meal forgotten. "Did she . . ."

Dave caught my meaning. "No. Not yet. She's got an interview with Maggie from CPS tomorrow. From what I understand, they consider my dad unfit to get Marshall back. They want to keep him with his mom." Dave shook his head before stuffing his soup into his mouth, swallowing hard. "Personally, I don't think either is fit to keep him."

Cecile gripped Dave's arm, rubbing up and down in what I figured was a soothing motion.

"Why did his mom leave in the first place?" Aunt Joyce asked, her meal temporarily forgotten too.

"Who knows. I sure as hell don't, and Cindy dodges the question every time I ask her."

"Dodges the question?" Uncle Jack gazed from Aunt Joyce to Dave. "What does that mean?"

"Just what I said. When I ask her why she left her four-teen-year-old son alone with a man who evidently has a drinking problem and anger issues, instead of taking Marshall with her, she answers that Devlin left for college, as if that explains everything. When I try to dig deeper, make her explain, she moves on to something else. I can't figure her out. It's like she only has one son, and Marshall is . . . I don't know, an afterthought?" Dave shrugged. "Maybe Maggie can get more out of her."

"I can't believe that CPS would be happy with that answer," Uncle Jack offered before digging back into his soup.

"Yeah, but they're big on keeping kids with their mom or dad." Dave sounded halfway defeated.

He wouldn't give up that easily. I also suspected that this was one of those areas littered with red tape.

"You're family." Uncle Jack pointed his spoon at Dave. "That gives you an edge. Marshall's fourteen, and that'll help, too, unless he wants to go with his mom. In that case, she'll most likely get custody of him." With a shrug, my uncle added, "I'm sorry, Dave, childcare and custody aren't my field of expertise, but if it comes to that and you need a good lawyer, I'll point you in the right direction." My uncle's field of law ran more toward the mundane.

"Thanks, Jack. I appreciate it." Blowing out an exasperated breath, Dave looked to the ceiling. "I've got no idea what Marshall wants. He's zipped up tight, and I'm unsure how to reach him. Leah talked to him a couple of days ago, and that helped some, but . . ." Dave looked lost. That insecurity drove a knife into my heart. Dave was one of the most confident people I knew; it hurt to see him flounder.

"We'll get it figured out," Uncle Jack assured. Aunt Joyce nodded in agreement. "We always do." Pointing a chunk of bread dripping with butter in my direction, Uncle Jack said, "Leah's going to move into Rose's house, you're going to do what's best for Marshall, and Cecile's going to start veterinary technician training next year. We've got it covered."

Uncle Jack sounded sure enough for all of us. It was a promising outlook on the future.

I didn't trust it for a minute.

7

It was pouring rain the day they lowered Rose's casket into the ground. I hadn't seen so many people at someone's services since my mom and dad died, and I barely remembered that day well enough to compare it. Melody and Charles were there, along with their children and grandchildren. A lot of life had been born from Rose and Isaac's love—many generations to carry on their legacy.

Uncle Jack, Aunt Joyce, Cecile, Dave, and I were there, and a large congregation from Handy Helpers. Gary and Judy huddled under a broad umbrella. Daryl and his wife curled under another. Berta and Dennis under yet another. That left Lizzie as the odd manager out, and I figured she was the *person* holding down the Handy Helpers' fort. Lenny wasn't around either. He would have been, but he'd been kind enough to swap shifts with me so I could have the morning off.

Harry Nichols was there, standing beside someone that looked younger and perhaps related. I wondered if it was his nephew—the one that owned the lake cabin. I smiled when I thought of how irritated Isaac would have been to see Harry there.

Most of the people surrounding Rose's casket were expected. Ricky and Levi weren't.

I didn't think Rose had had much interaction with Ricky, and the little time I'd witnessed her with Levi didn't make me think he'd show up or that he even knew her that well, which made me wonder if he was there to stalk me instead of to pay his respects to Rose and her family.

Shelly clung to Ricky's arm like a limpet. A bulky raincoat encased her ever-dwindling frame. Ricky acted like he couldn't care less that she was there, and on more than one occasion, he tilted his umbrella a little too far over, exposing Shelly to the frigid rain. I wanted to go over and pull her away, shelter her under my own umbrella. I didn't. Instead, I stood there, fuming silently.

"You okay?" Dave leaned down, his breath fogged by the chilly air. "You're all tense."

I nodded in Ricky's direction. "Ricky's being his normal dickish self."

"Ricky's here?" Dave stood a little taller, craning his neck around the sea of umbrellas. "Did he know Rose well? He doesn't seem like the type she would have had much tolerance for."

I scoffed. "Not that I know of. He's been such a suck-up lately. Most likely, he's here to prove some type of asinine point that only makes sense to him. But that's not why I'm upset. He keeps moving his umbrella, allowing the rain to pour down on Shelly."

Dave growled something low in his throat. "What a dick."

"That's what I just said."

"And I'm agreeing with you."

We quieted as Rose's services got started. I didn't want to, but my eyes kept flicking over to Ricky, inadvertently catching Levi as well. The more I saw, the stranger things seemed. I'd thought Levi was probably here to harass me. A couple of times our eyes connected, the look on Levi's face was completely indecipherable. But for once, I wasn't the focus of Levi's sole attention. Instead, that honor belonged to Ricky and Shelly.

Rose's services didn't last long, and soon her casket was lowered into the ground. My chest ached with the pain of losing Rose and Isaac. I'd miss them. I'd miss when Isaac sought me out when Rose came into Handy Helpers. I'd miss being able to tell my secrets to him, and I'd miss Rose's advice and strength. In their own ways, they'd been there for me when I'd needed them. I could only hope that need had passed or would be filled by another.

Precious warmth seeped deep into my soul, filtering out and settling into my bones. Andy was nearby. He wouldn't come into the fray because his natural reaper aura would be too disruptive to the gathered people. I wanted to feel his arms around me, but this was part of the price I was willing to pay. I doubted this kind of separation was part of the consequences Lizzie harped about.

Dave, Cecile, and I made our way toward Melody and Charles to offer our final respects. "Damn, I hope this weather clears up by tomorrow. Otherwise, the trick-or-treaters are going to be wet and cold." Dave was looking forward to Halloween this year. He'd enjoyed tricking out his house, but what he was really anxious about was the kids dressed up ringing his doorbell.

"Is Marshall as excited as you?" I asked as we moved a little closer to Melody, the rain just beginning to let up.

"Probably not, but I think he's looking forward to it some."

Cecile ducked her head around Dave's large frame. "I'm glad Marshall stayed in the Jeep. It's so cold and wet, and his face is still bruised enough that people would probably stare and ask questions."

"Yeah," I agreed, "good call there."

We finally got to Melody and Charles. After quick introductions to the children and grandchildren I'd yet to meet, Melody leaned in a gave me a heavy hug. "There are some things we want to get out of the house. I'll let you know when you can move in."

"There's no hurry. I—"

"It's your home now, Leah. It's what Mom wanted. I'll get you the keys soon. We'll get the paperwork finalized, and then it will be all yours." Melody pulled away, her icy fingers stretched across my cheeks as they cradled my face. "Mom was so proud of you, Leah. She talked about you all the time, almost always with a smile on her face or a tug of worry at her heart. She wanted you to be happy. Mom would love to know she was a part of bringing a little more of that into your life."

I was glad for the rain. Its drops covered the tear that escaped my eye. Choking, I managed a half-ass, "Th-thank you," before Dave pushed me forward, shuffling us off and giving my aunt and uncle their chance to speak with Melody and Charles.

The rain trickled to little more than a drizzle, allowing us to lower our umbrellas. "I'm gonna head back to the Jeep to check on Marshall." Dave thumbed in the direction we were parked. "You coming with me?" He looked at Cecile and me.

Cecile nodded while I waved them off.

"I'll be there in a few minutes. Don't leave without me."

Dave and Cecile shared a look. I could see Dave winding up to argue, but I silenced him with a single word. "Andy."

Dave's mouth snapped shut while his eyes immediately scanned the area. "Where?"

I waved a hand in Andy's general direction. "Over there."

Looking half-exasperated and half-dubious, Dave swung his arm over Cecile's shoulder, pulling her in close. "You know, I think it's freaky how you can do that."

I didn't bother to explain. Dave and Cecile didn't know just how well I could feel Andy. They knew I could tell he was around when they couldn't, but they didn't know the particulars, and I wanted to keep it that way. With a raised eyebrow, I said, "I've done freakier shit."

Chuckling, Dave said, "Don't take too long," before heading for the Jeep. Cecile threw a wave and a wink over her shoulder as she was tugged along.

I watched them take a few steps away before turning. I traced a trail that led off to the side, near a small stand of three trees, toward Andy.

Appearing from behind a solid tree trunk, Andy's arms found me, wrapping me in his warmth. He didn't seem to mind how soaked he got, holding me. "What can I do?" he asked, voice soft against my ear.

A shiver ran down my spine that had nothing to do with the cold or rain. "You're already doing it," I answered, snuggling in deeper, sighing into Andy's shirt. "You'd blend in better if you wore a jacket." Andy didn't feel the cold or heat like the living, at least not when he wasn't around me.

"I blend in well enough."

That was true. "Aren't you cold now with me?"

Andy was silent for a beat before he answered, "Not nearly cold enough to move away."

Heat filled my cheeks, and I buried my face in Andy's chest. "It was a beautiful service, despite the rain." My words were muffled, but Andy still heard them.

"Rose was a special woman. I'm not surprised there was a large turnout."

"Isaac would have liked to see all the people here. Well, except for maybe Harry Nichols."

Andy's soft, agreeing chuckle eased down my spine like a warm blanket. "True. He—"

"I don't see what the problem is. As you can see, she's just fine. Aren't you, honey?"

Within my reaper's arms, I stiffened. Head tilted up, chin on Andy's chest, I stared into his concerned eyes. Eyebrows raised, Andy gave a questioning look when I pressed my lips together in a shushing motion. Without another word, Andy pulled us deeper into the trees. Three tree trunks hid us from view.

"I'd like to hear it from Shelly."

I stiffened further when I recognized Levi's voice.

"Well, I suppose that's fine. After all, she's right here. Shelly, tell the man you're fine, so he can report back to your brother that you're alive and well."

Shelly's soft tones were barely audible over the rustling wind and dripping leaves. Large raindrops fell on my head, dampening my hair and matting it to my head. "I'm okay. Really. P-please tell Brandon not to w-worry."

"There, see? Everything's fine. I don't know why Brandon thinks he needs a private investigator to look into my personal—"

"You know," Levi sounded almost bored, "it would be a hell of a lot more convincing if I couldn't see the bruises around Shelly's throat. Another fall? And if so, what the hell did you fall into to leave finger marks on your flesh?"

Shelly's gasped surprise was louder than her words had been.

Tucked away like we were, I couldn't see what was going on, but whatever it was sounded uncomfortable.

Ricky laughed, low, deep, and creepy with barely veiled threats. "Come on, Shelly, let's go home and get you out of this weather. And you," Ricky's voice lowered a couple of octaves, "please tell Brandon that Shelly is my concern, one that's becoming increasingly burdensome the more he inter-feres. Relationships are difficult even under the best circum-stances. They become near impossible when others constantly interfere. Isn't that right, sweetie?"

I wanted to vomit. The sappy sweetness flowing out of Ricky's mouth stank with toxic additives.

"Ricky, don't say—"

"Let's go, Shelly. I won't offer again. If you don't want to leave with me, then you'll have to find your own ride home."

The area silenced to nothing but the dripping overhead leaves, the sturdy oaks still hanging on to last summer's foliage. The breeze picked up, shuddering through the dead, hanging leaves, the sound restlessly haunting. Through nature's musings, I heard Levi let loose a heavy sigh before he walked away.

Andy peeked around the side of one of the trees, checking to make sure things were clear and we were truly alone. Ducking back into our little alcove, he nodded once. "They're gone." Lips pinched into little more than a thin line, Andy's fingers ghosted over my face, pushing my wet hair away and tucking it behind an ear. "I've seen him before. Both of them."

I nodded before laying my cheek on Andy's chest. "Ricky and Levi. The woman was Shelly, Ricky's unfortunate fiancée." I shuddered despite Andy's warmth. "She's in trou-ble, and it sounds like Shelly has family that still gives a damn about her and is worried." I didn't know exactly why they'd hired Levi. Maybe it was to try to dig up dirt on Ricky. Maybe it was because Shelly hadn't contacted them for a while. I wished they'd hired someone else. I'd hoped some-thing shinier, something more interesting, would come along and grab Levi's attention away from me. I just wished it still didn't hit so close to home.

"You need to stay away from them, Leah."

I barked out a crazed laugh. "Yeah? You tell them that. I

work with Ricky, and Levi . . ." I let loose a heavy sigh. "I have no idea what's going on with Levi. What I can tell you is that I've told him to go to hell. Repeatedly."

"Hmm." Andy's fingers stroked through my dampened hair. "One of them is definitely for Elijah. The other . . . time will tell. His spirit is murky."

"Which one's which?"

"They were too close together for me to tell. All I know is that one of their spirits will never be mine to reap."

I thought I had an idea and didn't think it was the guy who'd once sported a badge, terrorizing my life for the past six years.

8

I worked Halloween morning into the late afternoon. It was the first year since I'd started working at Handy Helpers that I'd asked for Halloween night off. Dave was throwing a party of sorts, nothing wild, consisting of Cecile, Marshall, and me. Chrissie and Lilly were supposed to stop by at some point. Lenny had the night off, too, and he'd been hinting for the past couple of days that their costumes were "epic" and something he was excited to show off. I didn't have a clue what they were going as.

Ricky was off work all day, and after what I'd heard the day before at Rose's services, I was glad I didn't have to look at him. Those grating smiles and sugary sweet words were becoming increasingly intolerable. I still wasn't sure if it was all part of some master scheme Ricky had concocted—the *drive Leah McKnight even crazier than she already was* plan. It seemed like a lot of work to go through just to mess with me.

Cecile was at Dave's when I arrived. The rain had ended the night before, and October 31 was sunny, clear, and cool, but not frigid.

"Hey, Leah. How was work?" Cecile asked while holding

the door open. I'd stopped by the grocery to restock our supply of Oreos.

"Not too bad. Where's Dave?" I asked while looking around the cluttered mess of the Halloween explosion. Dave had creepy Halloween sounds floating around the house from some internet radio station.

"He ducked out to get some more candy," Cecile answered as she disappeared into the kitchen. "I don't know why. I told him we already have enough, but he's paranoid about running out."

I looked at the mountain of Halloween candy piled on top of Dave's table and raised an eyebrow. "Just how many kids does he think live in Covetous?"

Cecile stifled a giggle. "More than you or me. It'll probably keep until next year, or else he can take it to work. I'm sure Tonn Tonn, Chama, and Hampton will help him eat it."

"Are they coming over tonight too?" I asked while hefting my bags filled with Oreos onto the counter.

"No. Tonn Tonn's having his own 'grown-up party.'" Cecile shook her head, her blond hair floating around. The tiny plastic spiders she'd artfully placed throughout threatened to make a break for it. Besides the spiders, Cecile's face was painted white, temporary tattoos of stitches here and there across her cheeks, forehead, and chin. She had on some Halloween scrubs—cats with witches' hats sitting in jack-o'-lanterns. I was still in my typical Handy Helpers gear of a white, long-sleeved shirt and khaki pants. I absently rolled the sole of my shoe across the floor, noting that the fresh packaging tape I'd strapped across was still in good order.

"Ah, I see." I wasn't sure what a *grown-up* Halloween party consisted of, but I figured I was good where I was.

"Is, uh . . . Is Andy coming over?" Cecile asked, her blue eyes peeking out from under her lashes.

Nodding in the general direction of upstairs, I said, "Not

with Marshall here." I kept my voice low, just in case he was somewhere nearby. "Neither of us want him to experience the reaper whammy."

Last I'd heard, CPS was still in discussions with Marshall's mom. I wasn't sure what was going on, but they seemed content to let him stay with Dave. At least for now. If anything, I hoped this would help Dave's cause. Dean Masters had been released but was pending charges of child abuse. He was currently in forced outpatient rehab and living at home.

"That makes sense. If Marshall stays, maybe we can see if Chrissie can make him a charm too." At my raised eyebrows, Cecile said, "We don't have to tell him what it's for."

I wasn't sure a fourteen-year-old boy would be too stoked about wearing a spelled crystal, but I didn't argue. I had something bigger I wanted to talk to Cecile about, something I wanted her opinion on before I told Dave. First, I needed to double-check on Marshall's whereabouts. "Is Marshall upstairs, in his bedroom?"

"Yup, door shut and all." Cecile began sorting the candy on the table, blowing out a disbelieving breath. "I can't believe he thinks we need more."

Ignoring the sugar mountain, I blurted, "I saw Dave's mom's spirit."

Cecile's fingers stopped moving. Her body froze as she leaned over the chocolate loot. "You . . . you mean, when she passed, years ago?" There was a note of disbelieving hope tucked into her wavering words.

"No." I sat down heavily. "Like in, just the other day when I went up to Marshall's room to see if he needed any help with his stuff."

Swallowing heavily, Cecile sat down too. If she'd known we'd be having this conversation, Cecile wouldn't have bothered with the white makeup because she wouldn't have needed it to achieve the look she was going for. "Just . . . j-just a few days ago?" When I nodded, she whispered, "Oh my god. Dave didn't say a word to me about it."

Twirling an escaped piece of candy across the table, I mumbled, "That's because he doesn't know."

"What?"

I inhaled deeply. "I said that's because he doesn't know. Not yet."

"You didn't tell him?" Cecile sounded incredulous.

"What was I supposed to say?" I defended myself. "Hey, Dave, I saw your mom's spirit upstairs while I was helping your beat-up brother grab his stuff. Shame she didn't pass on like she should have years ago when she died from cancer."

Cecile recoiled, chewing on her bottom lip.

"Sorry, I didn't mean to sound so snippy. It's just that I've been struggling with this. I don't have a clue how to tell him. Dave's got so much going on with Marshall right now, and it's not like all this just happened. Charlotte's been dead for over fifteen years. Her spirit's not going anywhere right now, so there's no time crunch."

Cecile blew out a frustrated breath before she gave a reluctant nod. "I see your point. It's just—"

"Dave needs to know," I finished.

"Yeah. It's probably going to hurt him, though." Head down, Cecile tapped dark purple, fake nails across Dave's wooden tabletop. "He doesn't talk about her much, and when he does, it's near worship status. He was so young when she died. Sometimes I wonder if his memories are accurate. I don't think anyone's as perfect as Dave believes his mother was." Cecile's tapping fingers increased, their sound a quick beat. "And if she lingered . . . if she didn't move on . . . there has to be a reason, and those reasons aren't always . . ."

"Yeah, I know." Leaning into my chair, the weight of this latest bit of knowledge compressed me.

Cecile's tapping momentarily stopped, her baby blues staring softly with concern. "Why do you think she stayed? Did you get any clues? Did she say anything?"

"No idea. She didn't say anything when I saw her, and frankly, I was too stunned to try to talk with her. All I can say is she was standing in front of a locked door at the end of the upstairs hall. She disappeared back through the door before I walked down the stairs." Flipping another piece of candy, I sucked in a deep breath. "I asked Marshall about the locked door the other day when Dave asked me to come over and hang out while he went into Ink No Evil."

"What did he say?"

"Only that 'weird stuff' went on in that room. That Cindy had tried to turn it into a yoga studio and something didn't go well with that plan. Dave's dad is the one who locked the door, and Marshall had no interest in trying to break in." I raised my eyebrows, letting Cecile see just how incredulous I found that.

"Yeah, I agree. Curiosity would have been too much for me too. Did he sound scared?"

I shrugged. "Not exactly, but he did sound like locking that door might have been one of the few things he agreed with his dad about."

"Damn." Cecile suddenly looked as exhausted as I felt. "I understand why you haven't said anything to Dave yet, but we need to. Soon. The longer this gets put off, the harder it will be and the more upset he'll be that we kept it from him."

Fidgeting with a loose piece of candy wrapping, I stared down at that shimmering foil as if it held all the answers. Unsurprisingly, it didn't. "You know . . . Andy questioned whether I should tell Dave at all. Not in any kind of malicious way," I hurried to explain. "Just, you know, that he'd gone this long without knowing, so . . ."

"So you figured what? That you could go in, find out why

she stayed, get her reaped, and Dave would be none the wiser?" Cecile sounded dubious.

"Maybe?" I answered without much confidence. "I told Andy no. Not that it's not tempting, but I think Dave has a right to know, even if Charlotte's reason for staying turns out to be something . . . not great," I weakly finished.

Cecile's hand found mine, but those long fake nails made it impossible for her to squeeze as tightly as usual. "We'll tell him tonight, after the trick-or-treaters leave and Marshall's back up in his room."

I blew out a relieved breath. It might have been selfish, but I didn't want to do this alone. "Thanks, Cecile."

She gave me a comforting smile before she turned her attention back to the candy. "Now, let's get this sorted before Dave gets back with more."

<hr>

Dave had far more trick-or-treaters than I thought he would, but still not enough to get through half the candy he'd purchased. As a general rule, I wasn't a kid person, but I did like to see them dressed up. Early evening we saw the younger ones, their parents in tow, openly gawking at the Halloween explosion that was Dave's house. Darkness brought out the tweens and teens, and they weren't nearly as much fun. Lots of them were barely dressed up and were mostly out to either cause mischief or just get a lot of free junk food. Bobby, Dave, and I'd done that too. I'd stopped caring about Halloween and all its tricks and treats after my parents' murders.

Lenny, Chrissie, and Lilly showed up mid-evening. Marshall had known their costumes straight away. Not surprisingly, they were the main characters of a video game. Chrissie was supposed to be a sorcerous, Lilly was a woodland fairy, and Lenny was dressed as an elf of some kind. Chrissie pulled me aside at one point to inform me her outfit had a lot more clothes than the character Lenny had shown her a picture of. She pulled the image up on her phone, and I choked on an Oreo. The temperature wasn't too bad outside for late October, but Chrissie would have been damn cold if those little scraps of fabric had been the sum total of her outfit.

After a quick introduction, Marshall and Lenny hit it off, and we left them to their corner to discuss . . . I'm not sure what, but there were a lot of hand and arm gesticulations involved, at least on Lenny's part. There were also smiles—on both Lenny's and Marshall's faces. Dave smiled too, something soft and full of relief. Before they left, Marshall asked Dave if Lenny could come back sometime, and he readily agreed.

While Lenny and Marshall were talking, Chrissie told me she'd like to come over and see Rose's house—my soon-to-be house—when I got the keys. I'd broached the subject with her a couple of days ago, and surprisingly, she said she might be interested. I was two parts excited, one part anxious about the idea of living with someone. Someone that wasn't Andy.

By nine forty-five, Dave turned off his porch light. Marshall had snuck back up to his room about an hour prior, bored with the trickle of trick-or-treaters that wandered up every now and again. Andy rang the doorbell around nine-thirty and was currently sitting on Dave's couch, exhausting the supply of Oreos I'd just purchased.

"That was a good night." Dave flopped down on one of his couches. Cecile plopped down next to him. Cecile's hair had seen better days, and most of her spiders had come loose, finding new homes among all the other Halloween debris littering Dave's house. "We had plenty of candy, but by the looks of things, Andy will take care of most of that."

I glanced over, and sure enough, Andy had moved on from Oreos to SweeTARTS. Instead of verbally sparing with Dave, Andy gave me hopeful eyes. "Can we take some of this back to your place?"

Dave answered for me. "Sure. There's plenty. You guys take some, and I'll bring the rest into work." Scratching the stubble on his face, Dave shot a look toward the top of the stairs. "I'll ask Marshall if he wants anything too."

Now that it was just the four of us, Cecile shot me a nervous, expectant look. Not ready to delve into things yet, I stalled. "Heard anything from Cindy or CPS?"

Dave grunted while he threw an arm over the back of the couch, easily encompassing Cecile in the move and tugging her a little closer. Cecile melted into his side. "She's back in Florida."

"Huh?" I blinked, my eyes flicking between Dave, Cecile, and Andy. "What the hell?"

"Tell me about it." Dave blew out an exasperated breath. "Long story short, Cindy's fine with Marshall staying with me. When asked what he wanted to do, Marshall told Maggie that he'd rather stay here, with me, and keep in the same school system. I think if Cindy gave half a damn, CPS wouldn't have been as okay with it as they were. It's pretty clear at this point that Cindy doesn't care about her son. I passed the criminal background check, so—"

"Bet you're glad you didn't haul off and punch Levi in the face like you wanted to a time or two," I cut in. "That would have put a pretty glaring blemish on your record."

"No doubt," Dave agreed. "Still might have been worth it," he muttered before shaking his head like a wet dog. "Anyway, I guess the little shenanigans I got up to when I was still a minor didn't count for much, not that what Chama and I got up to ever resulted in an arrest." Dave's mischievous smile and far-off eyes spoke of things I probably didn't want to know.

"So," Cecile filled in, "Marshall's here for the duration? Cindy won't take him. What about Dean? What if he sobers up and petitions the court to get his son back?"

Dave sat up, removing his arm from around Cecile's shoulders and placing his elbows on his knees while he leaned forward. "I'm not sure, and that's what I don't like. I want to see about making it permanent. I don't want this to be something Cindy changes her mind about on a whim. And I sure as hell don't want my father getting his hands on Marshall again." Twisting his head so he could look at Cecile better, Dave said, "I'm gonna talk to your dad. He said he could point me in the direction of a good family lawyer, and I'm gonna take him up on his offer."

"That could get expensive." Not having a plethora of it, money was never far from my mind.

"Totally worth it," Dave answered quickly.

"I agree with Dave." Andy had been quietly sating his sugar high, and we all looked at him when he chimed in.

"I'm sorry," Dave cupped his ear, leaning closer to Andy, "but did you just say you agree with me?"

For a surprising minute, it looked like Andy might throw a piece of candy at Dave. He changed his mind, popping it into his mouth instead. "I did. Peace of mind is a precious thing. Almost no cost is too high."

Dave's lips parted as he raised his eyebrows. I thought he might say something, but he simply nodded and leaned back into the couch cushions.

Back to Oreos, Andy's crunching echoed loudly in the empty space. Dave had long ago changed the music to something soft and light, no longer spooky. Sitting in the relative quiet, Dave with his arm back around Cecile, Andy's warmth radiating from where our thighs touched, it would have been easy to fall into a content state—possibly the most content I'd been. But *content* and I weren't on much more friendly terms than *hope* and I were.

Without looking, I felt Cecile's eyes bore into me. Head tilted down, I stared at where Andy's clothed thigh touched mine. Not long ago, he'd been afraid to touch me, afraid of hurting me the way other reapers' touch hurt. It was no small thing that Andy no longer hesitated to reach out. Needing his comfort, I reached over, lacing my fingers through the hand not constantly shoveling sweets into his mouth.

"This is nice," Dave interrupted my internal panic attack. "All of us sitting here, just—"

"I saw your mom," I blurted, unable to keep it in anymore. My heart raced, palms sweaty. Andy didn't seem to mind. He just squeezed my fingers tighter.

Quiet permeated the room until Dave finally said, "You . . . what?" Dave sounded more quizzical than upset. Obviously, he didn't understand. Not yet.

Clearing my throat, I tried again. "I'm sorry I just word vomited that out." Swallowing, my saliva burned my throat. "The other day, when I went to help Marshall get his things, I'm pretty sure . . . No," I shook my head, "I'm positive, I saw your mom's spirit." Raising my head, I realized I'd been staring at Andy and mine's joined hands. "Standing in front of a door at the end of the second fl—"

"Bullshit," Dave's cold, angry voice sliced through the room. Dave had never spoken to me like that, never cut through my soul so succinctly.

"Dave," Cecile's tender tones attempted calm. "You need to listen to Leah. She—"

"I don't need to listen to jack shit." Dave jumped up, pulling away from all of us as he started to pace. "Why in the hell would you say something like that?" Dave violently shook, rolling his shoulders as his pace widened. "Christ, Leah. That's so fucking cruel."

I'd expected a lot of responses. I'd never imagined this. I had no idea what to do with this version of Dave—this anger-fueled person, that rage directed at me. Hunching in on myself, Andy gave my fingers a harder squeeze.

"Dave." Andy's voice was calm and level. Given the charms Cecile and Dave wore, his reaper voice would no longer work on them. I had the feeling that if it had, he would use it right now. "This is not Leah's fault."

Rounding on Andy, Dave got right up in his face. "No, it's fucking not. It's yours." Dave jabbed a finger into Andy's chest, yanking his hand back when he felt the burning sting of cold frostbite. Pulling back, Dave loomed over my reaper, face red with anger. Dave's eyes narrowed to little more than slits. "If you'd just do your damn job, then none of this shit would happen." Shaking out his hand, Dave looked incredulous. "How can you stand to fucking touch him?"

Dave was deflecting, throwing up verbal roadblocks, trying to protect his mind from the news he didn't want to contemplate, let alone hear. Before any of us could say anything, Dave stomped away, repeatedly running the palm of his hand over his short strands of blond hair. "That can't be true. There was no reason Mom would have stayed." Dave shook his head so violently I thought he might give himself another concussion.

Cecile shot me a sympathetic look before going to Dave. I had to give my cousin points for bravery. I didn't think Dave would physically hurt her, but his words were pointy daggers, and, in many ways, they were far more damaging than a slap ever could be.

"Dave." Cecile approached Dave like she would a skittish, fear-aggressive animal. Cecile didn't say anything else. She just laid her hands on Dave's lower back, rubbing slow, deliberate circles. Turned away from us, I couldn't see Dave's face, but I heard the harsh hiccuped noise that might have been close to a sob. Shoulders drooping, Dave curled in on himself, breathing harshly.

Quietly sitting beside me, Andy popped another piece of candy into his mouth.

I wasn't sure how long Dave stood there, wrapping his head around what I'd said, not that he'd let me say much. Waiting for the worst of the storm to pass, Dave finally turned, eyes red-rimmed and face pale. Inhaling deeply one last time, he let Cecile wrap her arms around his waist. I was relieved when he draped an arm over her shoulders.

"Wh-what—" Dave cleared his throat. "What exactly did you see?"

I licked my dry, cracked lips, willing words to them. "I'm sorry, Dave. I—"

Dave held up a halting hand. "Just tell me what you saw."

"Okay." Shifting, I scooted toward the edge of the couch, never once losing contact with Andy as I relayed what happened the night we'd gone over to fetch Marshall. Dave's normally tanned skin was pale when I was finished, red splotches popping up here and there. Deciding to get it all out there, I told Dave about my conversation with Marshall, about why the door was locked and what he knew about it. By the time I was done, Dave was back on the couch, limbs shaky. Cecile sat so close she might as well have been on his lap.

Finished relaying everything I knew, I remained silent, giving Dave time to take it all in. Head in his hands, Dave bent forward, hiding his face and eyes. I needed to see those deep blue eyes. I needed to know he was going to be all right. Dave's response made me second-guess telling him. Maybe Andy had been right. Maybe I shouldn't have said anything at all.

"Dave." Cecile finally broke the silence. "I know this is hard, but do you remember anything that might help? Your mom seems to be . . . well, her spirit seems to have an interest in that room in particular." Looking at me, Cecile asked, "You never saw Charlotte before now, right?"

"No, but Bobby and I didn't go over to Dave's much as children, and I'd never been upstairs until I helped Marshall get his stuff."

"She's right," Dave agreed. "I hated being at home and was over at Bobby and Leah's house more than my own. I didn't have people over. As far as the room you're talking about . . ." Dave stared at his clasped hands. "I'm not sure. I know the one you're talking about, and Mom was in there a lot. I think Marshall's right that it was her craft room. After she passed, I couldn't . . . I didn't want to go in there. It was too hard."

Given that I hadn't stepped foot in my childhood home after my parents' deaths, I more than understood. "Admittedly, my experience is limited, but from what little I do have, I think the reason your mom didn't pass on has to be in that room somewhere, especially if she's actively trying to keep everyone else out."

"You think that's it?" Dave finally looked at me, the usual blue of his eyes dimmed within his bloodshot sclera's. "You think she's actively trying to keep everyone out?"

"I—" I looked at Andy, but he only shrugged. Frustrated, I answered, "I'm not sure. Maybe it's not intentional. Maybe it's just sort of an effect of her being there in general. Until I provoked her, Eliza didn't actively do anything here that we know of, but people who are more sensitive to things like that didn't want to be in the house. I don't know if the rest of your family has more of a spiritual radar than you've got or if it's something else. Marshall didn't specify when Cindy wanted to turn the room into a yoga studio, but he sounded like it was more than just bad vibes. I guess we could always ask Cindy."

Dave let loose a barking laugh. "Yeah, good luck with that."

I couldn't argue and didn't.

My best friend looked so damn defeated. I couldn't let him stay like that. "It's probably not as bad as it seems. Spirits hang around for all kinds of reasons. Maybe your mom's isn't all that bad. Maybe it's something that was important to her, but not tragic."

Head still bent, Dave's downcast eyes peeked up at me. "Even if it's not something that bad to you and me, it was obviously important enough to her. Right, Andy?"

"In my experience, yes," Andy answered matter-of-factly.

"Do you remember anything? About her?" Dave clarified. "Were you the one that was sent to reap my mom?"

Setting down his candy, Andy gave Dave his full attention. "I was. I didn't realize it was your mother until Leah asked me about her. I can't tell you why she didn't come to me, only that she started to but stopped and turned. After that—"

"She couldn't see you anymore," Dave filled in, tone flat.

"Correct."

"Shit."

Leaving Andy's side, the contact warmth left me, but the internal fire of Andy's presence remained. Sliding down on my knees, I wrapped my fingers around Dave's clenched fists. "Hey," I crooked my neck, awkwardly angling my head to look up into Dave's bent face. "This is what I do. Or at least it's what I'm trying to do. I've got this. I will figure out what's keeping her here and get it fixed. And now I've got Cecile to help too. We'll give Charlotte the peace she deserves. I won't stop trying until we've figured it out. Okay?"

Dave's fingers slowly unclenched, turning and squeezing down on mine to the point of pain. "God, Leah. I'm so sorry. I shouldn't have said those—"

"Water under the bridge. Besides, I'm sure I've said a lot shittier things to you over the past six years. We both know I was a train wreck for a long time, and I lashed out at everyone and everything. Lots of times, you had a front-row seat to my verbal abuse."

"That doesn't make it any better or any righter," Dave argued.

"No," I stood, running my hand over Dave's stubbly hair the way he did mine, "but what it does make you is human. It's what friends are for."

Dave grunted. "To take verbal abuse?"

"No, to forgive verbal abuse."

9

Five days after Halloween, I got a call from Melody. The papers for the house were ready to be signed. All I needed to do was put ink to paper, and I'd be the proud new owner of Rose's house. I could live there until I was ninety and I'd still call it that.

Uncle Jack agreed to go with me, just in case I had any questions. In the end, it was a fairly simple affair. Melody said she'd removed Rose's personal belongings but left some furniture behind. Considering I didn't have much, I was okay with that. Keys in hand, I left the lawyer's office and headed for what would be my new home. I'd called Chrissie the night before, and she'd agreed to come over and take a look while Lilly was at school. Chrissie's schedule was more flexible now that summer was over and Lilly was back in classes.

Uncle Jack had asked if I wanted company, going through the house. Surprisingly, I didn't. I wanted to spend some time there by myself. Parking in the drive, I got out of my car. The air was cool with dark, heavy clouds lying low in the sky. A cold north breeze pulled at the ends of my hair, chilling my nose. Pulling my jacket tighter, I took a quick glance around the front yard. The roses lining the front of Rose's house were dormant now, cut back and waiting for spring.

Hurrying up to the door, I slotted the key in place and opened it. It was weird, just walking in without knocking first, without Rose standing in the doorway, colorfully painted toenails gripping the doorframe as she welcomed me inside.

The old, wooden floorboards creaked, sounding mournful as I stepped inside, shutting the door against the cold. Melody had been by earlier and turned up the heat. I'd need to call the utility companies and change the bills to my name. It was one of the many things I had written on a slip of paper in my purse.

The hospital ambiance wasn't as prominent as it had been. The scent of cleaning agents pushed out the stench of disinfectants. My footsteps sounded loud in the silence of the house. The rooms Rose had once lovingly called home looked sparse, even with some remaining furniture. Memories of Rose and Isaac lingered in the living room and Rose's main bedroom. Lying in the middle of the mattress, Melody had left the picture of Rose and Isaac, the one that had been taken before Isaac had shipped out, the one that had sat on a table in the living room. There was a note on it that simply read, "It's yours if you'd like it. Mom would have wanted it to stay in the house. Love, Melody."

Tears stung my eyes as I stared down at the image. Rose's passing and both their reapings left an ache in my chest. It was a hole of loneliness I didn't have a clue how to fill.

The ringing doorbell pulled me from my melancholy, at least temporarily. Leaving the picture where it was, I headed for the front door, relieved when I found Chrissie on the other side. I'd wondered if asking her to move in with me had been a good idea. The emptiness of the house put that fear to rest.

Chrissie's neck craned this way and that when I opened the door. At the sound, her head flipped back, her long, blond ponytail whipped around her shoulder. Dressed in a thick, pale blue winter coat, Chrissie's cheeks and nose were red with the cold November wind.

I didn't get a greeting out before Chrissie offered, "The front yard looks great."

Smiling, I waved Chrissie in. "You ain't seen nothin' yet. If you like the front, you'll love the back."

Chrissie grinned as her eyes scanned the living room. "She really left you her house?"

I nodded while heading toward the back door. "As batshit crazy as it sounds, yes. Why don't we head outside and take a look around the backyard and gardens while you've still got your coat on." Besides, I figured that was the part of the house that Chrissie was most interested in.

"Sounds like a plan."

The tour didn't take long. Like the front landscaping, the back was just as dormant. Some people wouldn't have been able to see through that, to what it could be. Chrissie wasn't most people. She was a nature witch, and this was her element.

"The energy back here is fantastic." Chrissie moved around. She'd taken off her gloves, hands stretched out. Not for the first time, I was thankful for the privacy fence that surrounded the backyard. "The plants are really happy. They feel loved."

I didn't have a clue how Chrissie knew that just like she didn't have a clue how I could see lingering spirits. Not that I understood that either. I didn't have to understand to believe her. "Rose really liked gardening. I weeded a lot for her the past few years when she couldn't do it herself."

Chrissie half turned, her face in profile as she said, "I can tell. The plants are happy you're here."

"I—" I had absolutely no idea what to say to that.

"It's okay. You don't have to say anything. Let's go back inside so I can check out the rooms and see how things would work."

I appreciated Chrissie's no-nonsense, take-charge attitude. As a single mother, she probably had to be like that. Going back in, we took off our coats while I showed Chrissie around. The house was a three-bedroom, two-bath. There was an en suite in the main bedroom. Chrissie walked through the rooms, taking everything in, asking questions here and there, and nodding at this and that.

With a final tour of the kitchen, we found ourselves back in the living room. Flopping down on the couch, Chrissie's eyes wandered the room. "You really don't mind us moving in?" Her raised eyebrows looked skeptical. "I know you like Lilly, and she likes you, but you've never lived with a six-year-old. It's not always easy."

"You're right, but I think I can manage. It's a big place." It wasn't really, not by most home standards. Or maybe more to the point, it was average for a home in the area. Coming from a one-bedroom apartment, the place felt huge to me. Huge and empty.

"Not gonna lie. This is tempting." Chrissie tapped her fingers along her jean-clad legs. "It won't just be Lilly and me, though. I like Lenny, and he'll probably be over a lot too." Chrissie shifted uneasily. "I know he can sometimes be . . . a lot. Lenny's not everybody's idea of a good time."

I'd already thought about that. "I don't mind. I've gotten used to Lenny, and when he starts talking about stuff I don't get, I just kind of tune him out. Not trying to be mean or anything."

Chrissie chuckled. "No, I get it."

"Besides, if we're comparing significant others, then I don't think Lenny has anything on Andy." Twisting so I could see Chrissie's expression better, I asked, "How about you? Do you think you can live with a reaper coming and going whenever he wants?" I'd gone toe to toe with management, and I wasn't giving Andy up for anything, including Chrissie moving in.

Blowing out a deep breath, Chrissie's eyebrows pinched, her lips twisting in distaste. For a minute, I thought the whole thing was over before it really had a chance to get started.

"Grams would shit kittens if she knew. Thank god she's gone, or I'd never hear the end of it. I'm not sure I could have made a charm strong enough to keep her at bay." Giving another chuckle, Chrissie smiled. "I'm not gonna sit here and tell you I'm thrilled, but I think it's something I could get used to. I'm going to have to work up a better charm so looking at him doesn't give me a headache all the time. Lilly will need one too."

"Will that be okay? Having Lilly around a reaper?" I don't know why I thought it would be different for children, but I didn't want to do anything that would screw up Lilly's life.

"She'll be fine. Lilly's a smart kid, and I've been a lot more open with her about . . . what we are since finding out the reason Gram's passed away. It's Lilly's heritage, and I'm not going to deny it anymore. I'll always give her a choice, and when she's old enough, if she doesn't want to be a practicing witch, so be it. I won't pressure her, but there've been enough . . . incidents that I think she's got a lot of potential. It would be irresponsible not to train her properly." Chrissie gave me a significant look. "I mean it when I say there have been incidents. Things might get a little iffy around here at times, especially while Lilly's trying to learn control. If things get too bad, I might have to look into homeschooling." Chrissie's eyes shifted to her tapping fingers. "I have to admit, that's something that's been stressing me more and more. If that becomes necessary, and I need to stay home with her more, I'm not sure how to make ends meet. I'd definitely need to give up my extension college classes."

"Not gonna happen." Determination hooked its claws in good and deep. Rose was a single mom. She raised Melody without any help, and if anyone would understand and wanted to help out another mom and daughter, it would have been her. "The house is mine, mortgage-free. I'll have to pay property taxes, insurance, that kind of stuff. I figured if we could split utilities, I'd call it good. If worse comes to worst and you need to homeschool Lilly, we'll figure it out so that you don't have to give up on classes too."

"I—" It was Chrissie's turn to be speechless. "That's far too generous. I couldn't ask—"

"You didn't ask, I offered. If you feel bad about it, consider it payment for services rendered. There's not enough money, thanks, or free rent in the world to repay you for what you've given Cecile." I meant those words with every fiber of my being.

Chrissie just shook her head. "You helped reap Grams. If it wasn't for you, then I never would have known why she passed so quickly. Grams would have been stuck in this world. She never would have found peace. As far as I'm concerned, we're more than even."

I shrugged, looking around the barren house. I'd always feel Rose and Isaac here, see their smiling faces, feel their love, but those emotions had already faded. Just like Rose's spiritless body, the house was an empty shell of what it had once been. It was time to fill it back up.

"Then let's consider this a fresh start, a clean slate for both of us."

Breathing in deeply, Chrissie's lips pulled tight before

relaxing into a wide smile. "You've got a deal." She reached out, grasping my hand and giving it a healthy squeeze. "When do we move in?"

10

"Hey, Lenny, did you hear the news?" Generally, I hated this game. My oddly good humor this morning peeked through when I decided to turn the question tables on Lenny. The wide, beaming smile lighting up his face should have been answer enough.

"Chrissie called me last night." Lenny practically vibrated. If he'd still had that little rat tail cinched together at the base of his skull, it would have twitched like a fiend. "That is fantastic. All three of you will be under the same roof. That house will be oozing with good vibes." Lenny gave a firm nod as his own physical confirmation. "I think it'll be great for everyone. Chrissie loves plants, and now she'll get her own garden."

You didn't have to know that Chrissie Hollybrook was a nature witch to understand she loved the leafy green stuff. One step into her apartment was tip-off enough. It was a pretty fair bet that not every plant lover was a witch. Still, I wished Chrissie would let Lenny in on her secret. Trust was a funny thing. I wouldn't trust Lenny to restock the light bulbs, but I'd trust him with Chrissie's secret. Mine too, if it came down to it.

"Are you helping her move in?" I asked as we made our way into the break room to clock in. Lenny and I were both on for the morning and early afternoon shifts. I'd checked the schedule earlier and knew Ricky would overlap us some this afternoon. My stomach already felt queasy with the idea of seeing him again.

Since Rose's services, I'd had a few brief interactions with Ricky. He never showed any hint that he'd been aware of me during his odd dust-up with Levi. Andy and I'd stayed hidden well enough. I hadn't seen Shelly since then. Levi either. I was relieved about one, but not the other. Shelly's welfare was never far from my mind, and every time I thought of her, bile rose in my throat. I hated thinking of what her life was like but didn't know what else to do about it. At least her brother was concerned too.

"If you don't mind," Lenny thankfully broke through my pointless worrying. "I, uh . . . are you okay with me coming over? I don't want to overstay my welcome or anything like that. I know that I can sometimes be—"

"You're always welcome. Anytime, Lenny." I pulled us both to a stop, placing my fingers on Lenny's arm for emphasis. "Never doubt that, okay?"

Lenny's head tilted down and to the right, eyes downcast and a red flush creeping up his neck. "Thanks, Leah." Eyes tilting my direction, Lenny worried his bottom lip with his teeth. "But I need you to promise me that you'll tell me if I ever get to be too much."

I hated that Lenny felt the need to tack that on. "Will that make you feel better?"

Lenny nodded so quick and hard I was afraid his head might pop off, rolling down aisle three, crashing into the spray paint cans like a bowling ball. "It will."

"Okay," I blew out. "Then, for what it's worth, I'll let you know if you're ever bugging the shit out of me and if I wanna throw your ass out the door. Deal?"

Visibly relaxing, Lenny chuckled, low and honest. "Deal." Picking up where we left off, we made our way to the break room. "If that's the case, then I'll be happy to help Chrissie and Lilly move in. You too if you need anything."

"Between Dave, Cecile, and the group at Ink No Evil, my end is covered. Aunt Joyce and Uncle Jack might even lend a hand, depending on my aunt's work schedule. Besides, I don't have much."

Andy wanted to help too. It had been one of those moments where our situation hit home. Andy took the blow much harder than me. As far as I was concerned, I had more than enough help. But Andy wanted to be there. He still hadn't told me when he'd died, but our time together made me think he'd lived in an era where men were a bit more chivalrous with their ladies, especially ones they were kind of, sort of dating. I think not being able to help stabbed at his guy-cred.

"That's cool," Lenny offered while stamping his timecard.

It *was* cool. More than cool. There was a very dark time in my life, where I'd thought I was alone. Thinking about all the people ready and willing to help me do something as mundane and tiresome as moving was the reality check I constantly needed. Even Berta and Gary had offered to help. Offering up her children's services, Berta was confident that if I needed help cleaning, they'd get it done in no time. As for Gary, he'd offered free paint and deep discounts on whatever else I might need in the store.

"Aunt Joyce, Cecile, and I are going over tomorrow to start cleaning and painting. Chrissie wanted to be there too, but she has to work, and Lilly will be in school. After we get that done, then I'll move in. Chrissie's lease is up in December, but she said she'll probably move in sooner than that." As timing went, it couldn't get much better. Chrissie had been ready to sign for another year.

Closing my locker, I slid my arms through my Handy Helpers vest. Lenny and I headed for the door when it swung open as Ricky pushed his way inside. For the briefest of moments, I saw the real Ricky peek through. Jaw tight, lips thinned, and eyebrows pulled low, Ricky looked pissed about something. Forcefully pushing the door open, he nearly plowed right into Lenny. The snarl forming on Ricky's lips was so familiar it almost wiped away the months of simpering kindness we'd all been subjected to. And then, just like a light switch being flipped, Ricky's demeanor changed. Although tighter than usual, his lips pulled back into a forced but wide, beaming smile. His bright white teeth gleamed in the overhead florescent lights.

"Good morning!" Ricky's overly loud voice made me flinch. "Sorry about that, Lenny. I was a little too exuberant." Ricky's laugh grated along my spine, peeling off little pieces of flesh as it went.

Throwing me a disbelieving look, Lenny quickly shuffled to the side and gave Ricky a wide berth. "No worries," Lenny offered.

"Very kind of you." The words eased out of Ricky's mouth, but they had barbs hooked to their sides.

Lenny gave me a "what the fuck?" expression. His wide, questioning eyes begged for answers I didn't have.

Giving Lenny a small, silent head shake, I blurted, "I didn't think you were scheduled to work this morning." I didn't try to keep the disappointment out of my voice.

"Oh, I wasn't supposed to." Ricky's nonchalant words didn't match his tone. "Lizzie called early this morning and asked if I could come in. Seems like we've got a couple of employees who called in sick. Lizzie's not sure if it's just a cold or maybe the flu." Chuckling low, Ricky opened his locker and hung his coat up inside. Smoothing down his pristine, white shirt, Ricky pulled his deep, purple Handy Helpers vest out. Unlike mine, his had been hung up and was wrinkle-free. "The two of you need to take special care. We wouldn't want anything happening to Handy Helpers' best employees." For once, Ricky's smile appeared all too genuine.

Cold swept through my body. The usual warning bells Ricky's presence typically set off sounded just slightly louder.

"See you two out there. Let's have a good day." Ricky slid past Lenny and me, passing through the door a lot more gently than he'd entered.

"Leah?" Lenny's voice shook with his unasked question.

"Yeah, I know. Me too." Lenny and I left the break room, our moods soured, the joy of earlier squashed. It struck me again how unfair it was that one person could make that big of an impact. Life shouldn't be that way. Then again, life shouldn't be a lot of ways.

As it turned out, Aunt Joyce, Cecile, and I had a lot of wallpaper to strip before we could start to paint. Part of me felt guilty as another strip came off. Rose had obviously liked the pattern. It felt like I was losing another piece of her in some ways.

"I understand." Aunt Joyce popped up at my shoulder. Dressed in an old set of charcoal gray scrubs that had shots of lavender paint splashed here and there, Aunt Joyce had a scarf wrapped around her head, protecting her hair. Cecile and I'd quickly found out my aunt was the smart one. Experience was an excellent teacher.

Holding the strip of light blue wallpaper, soft yellow roses climbing vertically up its surface, I asked, "You do?"

"Mm-hmm. But as hard as it is to remember this, it isn't Rose's home anymore. It's your house now, one we're forging into a home. Rose wanted you here, and she was wise enough to know you wouldn't keep everything like it was. This place is meant to be a home, Leah. Not a museum. One day, when you eventually move out, someone else will come in and change what you did. And that's the way it should be. Your home should reflect you, not the dead." Aunt Joyce raised an eyebrow, giving me a meaningful look. "Now, get back to peeling."

My lips curled into a grateful smile. "On it."

"Good. I'll start on the other wall." Cecile was in the hall bathroom. It had been one of the few non-wallpapered rooms, and she'd gotten busy painting it a soft, warm gray. Chrissie had picked out the colors for that room and two bedrooms. We planned on re-wallpapering one of the walls in Lilly's room—a light pink paper with cats sporting unicorn horns—caticorns. I figured we'd take that down again in a few years, but it was cute as hell for now.

Aunt Joyce and I heard the music playing in the living room while Cecile hummed along, sometimes singing a line or two. We'd chuckle at my cousin's tone-deaf voice. I don't think either of us considered telling her to stop singing.

A couple of minutes slipped by like that, and it was normality at its most blissful. Hearing Aunt Joyce clear her throat warned me it was about to change, or maybe twist the meaning of normal. "So . . . I wanted to talk to you . . . about Thomas."

"Birkingham?" I asked while pulling at another stubborn piece of paper, ripping it before it got too satisfyingly long. "Shit."

"Here, you need to spray more of this water-detergent mix on it and let it soak a little longer. Patience, Leah." Aunt

Joyce started spraying my area, soaking it a lot more than I'd done. Again, the voice of experience.

"Patience and I aren't always good friends," I muttered while standing back, watching her spray.

"Me either," Aunt Joyce agreed, our conversation easy. Something deep down struck me. This is how it should have always been between the two of us. "There, now let's give it a little time."

We stood back before sitting on a couple of overturned buckets. We'd covered the hardwood floors with plastic, and it crinkled as we shifted our feet. "So, Thomas . . . What did you want to talk about?"

Aunt Joyce was in profile, her blond hair covered by the scarf she'd wrapped around it. Thin lines spread out from her pinched eyes. Her jaw clenched and unclenched for a few seconds before she started. "I don't like the thought of him wandering the halls where I work. Yes, I know how incredibly stupid that sounds. He's been there the whole time I've been working, and it's never bothered me before."

"You never knew about him before."

"Correct." Aunt Joyce nodded for emphasis. "And now that I do, I can't un-know about him."

I ducked my head. "I'm sorry. I—"

"I told you before, we're done with apologies, Leah. I needed to know. Well, maybe not about Thomas in particular, but about lingering spirits in general. I told you before Halloween that I didn't like the thought of him there. You said he's too angry to get much coherent from him."

It wasn't a question, but I still answered like it was. "Yeah, and I wondered if Cecile might be able to help." I was afraid that's where this discussion was headed. Aunt Joyce had seemed open to the idea and the time. But times changed.

"Hmm, yes." Aunt Joyce bent her head, looking at her

paint-splattered shoes. "While that might be true, I figure more information about Thomas couldn't hurt. Right?"

My head whipped around so fast that I thought I pulled something for a second. "What did you find out?"

Aunt Joyce squirmed, her overturned bucket tipping a little precariously. Picking at some of the wallpaper goo on her fingers, she asked, "Did you know there used to be a hospital wing named after him?"

Forget tipping my bucket—I damn near fell off it. "What? Are you sure?"

Aunt Joyce dipped her head. "I thought the name sounded familiar." She glanced in my direction. "You know after I got over the whole 'oh my god, ghosts are real' thing." Aunt Joyce twirled her finger in the air. "When I calmed down, I couldn't get the name out of my head, and I couldn't figure out why. I did some snooping around the hospital and found out why. The Birkingham family name is still on some older plaques crediting hospital donors. The hospital area that was specifically named for him was torn down during one of the remodels." Her eyes tilted toward the ceiling as if my aunt were thinking. "I'm not sure which one. Over the years, the hospital has been added on to, remodeled, and some areas were completely torn down." She shook her head. "New technology is always coming out, and there's competition between hospitals. Anyway, the Birminghams must have been well off to get a whole wing of the hospital dedicated to them."

"Wow." I stared at the torn wallpaper goading me across the room. "Dave did an internet search of Thomas, and we knew he came from a wealthy family, but . . . I can't imagine how much money it would take to get a hospital wing dedicated to you."

Aunt Joyce grunted. "More than any of us will ever see. That's for sure. You know, nowadays, with someone that wealthy, they'd be all over the internet. That long ago, not so much," she finished with a shrug.

We both silently sat while I pondered that latest bit of information. Finally, Aunt Joyce asked, "Do you think that has something to do with why he's still there, roaming around the hospital?"

I mulled that over. "I'm not sure. Did you find any mention of a woman named Beth? That's the name he keeps screaming about, claiming she was murdered."

"I didn't see that name on any of the plaques, but I wasn't specifically looking for it either. Do you know a last name?"

Unfortunately, I didn't and said as much. "I have no idea. All he says is Beth."

"Hmm." Aunt Joyce propped her elbows on her knees, leaning forward. "There's a chance one of the doctors I work with might know something. It might be a long shot, but Dr. Meyer has worked in the ER for fifty years. He's a good doctor and is due to retire in the next couple of months." Aunt Joyce straightened, her back cracking with the effort. "From what I understand, Dr. Meyer did his internship and residency at Covetous. That kind of thing doesn't happen very often anymore. They like doctors to get experience at different places. I'm sure Covetous Community wasn't called that back in the day. Hospitals change ownership, and they almost always change their names when they do, but the point is that Dr. Meyer has been in Covetous, working at its main hospital, for over fifty years."

I blinked, my eyes dry and crusty. "I know he's old and might have been alive at the same time Thomas was, but why do you think Dr. Meyer, in particular, would know anything?"

Aunt Joyce shrugged, her fingers twisting as she continued picking off the glue. "I'm not sure. But you said Thomas roams the hospital, claiming someone named Beth was murdered—and from what you've been able to gather, he blames someone at the hospital for that. Dr. Meyer might not know anything. Maybe what happened to Beth occurred before Dr. Meyer was employed by the hospital. I still think it might be worth a shot. Even if Dr. Meyer can just tell us who Beth was."

I didn't realize my jaw had dropped until it snapped shut. "That's . . ." I licked my dry, cracked lips. "That's a really good idea. Or at least it's somewhere to start. And you're right. Having more information before we confront Thomas again would be smart. Even if Cecile can calm him." I stared at the soaking wallpaper. It had probably been long enough, but I was still too stunned to stand. "How do I get to talk to him?" I didn't want to pay for a trip to the ER just to get information.

"His retirement party." Aunt Joyce sounded sad.

"He's leaving soon?"

Aunt Joyce gave a reluctant nod. "Dr. Meyer's a good man and a good doctor, despite his age. He's worked ER for decades and knows what he's doing. He's a calm presence, and I'm going to miss him."

"You respect him."

"Very much. Some stereotypes you hear about doctors are true and well earned. Dr. Meyer has never fit into that temperamental mold."

I started to apologize but figured I'd get scolded again. Instead, I said, "Thank you."

Aunt Joyce looked startled for a moment before her face softened into a smile. "You're welcome. They've started reducing his caseload in preparation for his retirement. Parties like this are normally spread through the floor the retiree works on and lasts for a few hours. I'll let you know when and you can *conveniently* stop by to pick something up for Cecile. If he does know something, he might not be comfortable talking in front of you. We'll have to see how it plays out."

Again, all I could say was, "Thank you."

"While I appreciate that, it's kind of self-serving. You'd be doing me a favor by getting Thomas's spirit to move on. As I said, I don't cherish the idea of him wandering our halls. You might be unique in being able to speak and see spirits, and Cecile might be the only one that Thomas's spirit truly injures, but I have to think there are others out there that can at least feel, on some level, when he's around. That kind of anger can't be good for those patients and the staff working at the hospital."

"N-No," I stuttered. "Probably not."

"Plus," Aunt Joyce slapped her thighs, standing with a soft grunt, "It's just plain creepy, thinking about him wandering around." Holding out a hand, Aunt Joyce helped me stand. "Better get back to work. This paper isn't going to strip itself."

"If only," I groaned. "I'm starting to think we should have rented one of those steam thingies."

"Naw, this will do." Aunt Joyce ran her scraper under the paper to prove her point, peeling it back easily. "See. No problem. We'll have this done in no time."

We didn't get it done that quickly, but it still went faster than I thought it would. Soon Aunt Joyce and I were singing along with Cecile, each of us vying for the coveted prize of worst vocalist in history.

11

————

I moved into Rose's old house on a Friday. Andy was still in a mood about not being able to help. He did pack a few of my clothes, carrying the bags and boxes out to my car for me the night before, when no one else was around. He'd held me tighter last night, whispering nonsense into my ear. Andy had a way of doing that—talking about past events without much context. It didn't bother me that I didn't know what exactly he spoke about most of the time. I just liked to hear his voice. Sometimes I wondered if he told the stories more for his benefit than mine. Either way, it didn't much matter.

As it turned out, Chama, Tonn Tonn, and Hampton couldn't help much. Ink No Evil was busy, which was a good thing. Uncle Jack took the day off from work and helped with some of the bigger things. He and Dave carried out the larger furniture from my old apartment. Tyson had come home from work and lent a hand here and there. He was sad to see me officially go, but given that I hadn't stayed in my apartment for the last month, he understood and was happy I'd found a new place.

Aunt Joyce had to work, but she'd more than done enough already as far as I was concerned.

Thankfully, Lizzie was working as manager of Handy Helpers and wasn't around when we emptied my apartment. I'd had to go up one last time to look around and make sure nothing had been missed. I'd choked on a sob when I looked over to Ashes's window, only to see that Dave had disassembled her window seat. It made sense. I didn't own the place, and we needed to leave the apartment in as much of the same condition as we could. It still hurt. I'd turned away from that naked window as quickly as I could. The rest of my recon hadn't taken long. At that point, I figured if anything was left, the next tenant could toss it.

By late afternoon, everything that could be moved in had been. Cecile had to go to work in the afternoon. Her dad dropped her off, and Dave planned to pick her up later. Rose's couch was better than mine, and I liked it more, so we'd kept it. The floral chair Dave had long ago claimed as his own somehow made a new home in Rose's old living room. It looked happier here than it ever had in my apartment.

Letting his weight fall into the aged cushions of the old, floral masterpiece, he leaned to the side, rocking back and forth, before settling in. I didn't know how or why, but Dave and the old chair just fit together for some odd reason.

Dave let his neck roll across the back of the chair while his eyes gazed at the sedentary ceiling fan. "You'll want to see about air conditioning come summer," Dave said absently.

Exhausted and flopped out on the couch, I agreed. "Rose never liked it much." And she'd never installed it. Dave had taken a look at the heating unit and said the ductwork was in place; I just needed a new setup. It was a good idea to start saving now.

Yawning, I asked, "What time's the pizza guy supposed to

be here?" That was probably sexist. Women could deliver pizza too.

Dave checked his watch. "Should be in the next ten minutes or so."

"Okay," was about all I could muster. I didn't have much to move, but it still wore me out.

Silence settled into the bones of Rose's house, filling it up and making the late afternoon peaceful. Or at least I was peaceful. Dave's fingers tapped along the chair, his tired body still restless. Knowing Dave had a lot on his mental plate these days, I asked, "How's Marshall doing?"

"Better." Short, clipped, and to the point. It wasn't a typical Dave answer, especially where his brother was concerned.

"Is school going okay?"

Marshall had gone back to school as soon as the bruising on his face healed. Dave's house was in the same school district as Marshall's dad's house, so at least there wasn't much change there.

Dave gave an awkward nod. "Yeah. I got a text from Lenny about an hour ago saying he'd picked Marshall up, and they planned to spend a few hours together playing video games." Dave grunted. "Christ, that sounds weird. Six months ago, if you'd told me I'd be getting text messages from Leonard Filliman, I'd have said you were batshit crazy."

"We both know I'm still batshit crazy," I said, lightening the mood.

"True enough," Dave huffed out but didn't say more. It was weird. I was the one typically stuck in their head, not Dave. I didn't like it.

"You okay?" It was as open-ended a question as I could come up with.

For a few seconds, I didn't think Dave would answer. Finally, his head rocked back and forth. "No. Not really. I can't get what you said about Mom out of my head." Twisting his neck, Dave's deep blue eyes found mine. "I'm afraid, Leah. More afraid than I've been in a long time."

Sitting up, I scooted toward the edge of the couch, settling my elbows on my knees as I leaned forward. "What are you afraid of?"

Dave blew out another breath. "She stayed. Why the fuck would she do that? What's so important—so wrong—that she didn't go to Andy when she had the chance?" Finally lifting his head off the back of the chair, Dave leaned forward too. "It can't be good." When I started to open my mouth, Dave shut me down with a single, narrowed look. "You know it can't. A big part of me doesn't want to know. I feel like a selfish little kid, hiding under my covers, hoping my mom will make the monsters go away. But this time, I think Mom needs me to do that for her."

I inhaled sharply, hoping Dave would understand my next words. "Not you, Dave. She needs me and maybe Cecile to do that. If you want, I can go in, talk to her, and see what I can find out. That doesn't mean I need to tell you what she says." I let that sink in for a few seconds before I asked, "Do you understand what I'm telling you? What I'm offering? It's up to you whether I ever breathe a word of what your mom says."

Dave's harsh swallow echoed throughout the room. "I hear you and . . . thank you, but . . . I don't think I could live like that."

I couldn't either. The truth was a tricky thing. Often, it was the not knowing that chipped away at your soul, taking little pieces a chunk at a time. Knowing the truth was more like ripping off the Band-Aid, exposing all your wounds at once. Experience taught me which one healed faster.

"Okay. We're agreed then? I'll tell you what she says?"

Dave gave a solemn nod.

"And Cecile?"

Dave's eyes flashed toward me.

"I'd like to take her with me. I only got a glimpse that one time, but your mom wasn't . . . she didn't seem angry or violent. Sadder than anything. It's time we test out what Isaac thought."

"You mean about this thing going both ways? That Cecile's emotions can affect lingering spirits the same way they affect her?"

I was glad Dave remembered.

"Yes. Aunt Joyce asked me to try to reap Thomas Birking-ham's spirit." I looked down at my feet. "He's pissed, and I can't get anything from him in his current state. If I've got a prayer at this thing working, then I need to get him to calm down. The only way I can see to do that is if Cecile can work some kind of emotional mojo on him. Aunt Joyce called it 'spiritual Valium,' and I think that's a fantastic way to think of it."

Dave nearly choked on his spit when I filled him in on Aunt Joyce's moniker. "Holy shit." Dave rubbed the palms of his hands over his stubbled cheeks. "If this works, then I'm getting Cecile a t-shirt that says that."

"I'll chip in." I sent a grin Dave's way, happy when he returned it. Sobering, I asked, "So, what's the plan to get back into the house? From what I understand, your dad's still living there. I can't imagine he'll be okay with us traipsing in, springing the lock on that door, and chatting Charlotte's spirit up."

"No, I can't imagine that would go too smoothly." Dave placed his thumb and forefinger on the bridge of his nose. "Marshall's still got things there, in his room. We've talked about going over and picking the rest of it up, but he's been reluctant, and I understand why. I haven't pushed. I think it's time I offered to go over myself. Leave Marshall out of the whole collecting business. I'll just take some boxes and shove everything I can physically carry into them because as far as I'm concerned, Marshall's never spending another night in that house again."

If determination alone could keep Marshall with Dave, then he didn't have anything to worry about. Unfortunately, we both knew better. "Have you met with the lawyer yet?"

Head bent, Dave's eyes peeked up at me through lowered lashes. "Yesterday. He said our best bet, or maybe the easiest route, would be if Cindy signed papers granting me permanent custody of Marshall. I can't imagine Dad would ever sign something like that, but Cindy might, and since she's got legal custody of Marshall right now, that's who we really need. To lock things up nice and tight, Dad's signature would be great too. Given Dad's history and Marshall's age, the lawyer didn't think my father's claims would amount to much."

"Do you think Cindy would do that?" I couldn't imagine a mother willingly signing over custody of a child she'd raised.

Dave grunted, his mouth twisting with disgust. "I think it's got a better chance than it should."

I let that ugly thought sink in for a few minutes before I returned to the issue of getting into Dean Masters's house. "So, we go in, clean out Marshall's room and sneak into the locked bedroom at the end of the hall. You can pack while Cecile and I communicate with your mom."

"Theoretically, that should work. Chances are Dad will leave us to it. If he's being a bigger ass than usual, I've got a few choice words to share, and that'll keep him busy and out of your hair."

I didn't like the satisfied smile pulling at Dave's lips. I could only imagine how that conversation would go, and leaving Dean with only a black eye and busted nose sounded generous. "Hopefully, he leaves us to it."

Dave shrugged as if it didn't matter either way. "You think it'll only take the one time?" he asked tentatively.

"I don't know. If not, then maybe we should 'accidentally' leave something of Marshall's behind, something we don't think he really needs but can be used as an excuse."

"Okay. That could work." Dave leaned back in his chair, checking his watch. I wasn't sure how much time had passed but figured the pizza should be here soon. My grumbling stomach hoped so too. "You, uh . . . It should be Andy, right? Coming for Mom's spirit. It won't be Bobby, will it?"

Dave and I hardly ever spoke of Bobby. In a way, my brother had become the silent elephant in the room again. Speaking his name brought a flood of nasty emotions, something Dave and I shared. There was nothing either of us could do for Bobby, nothing that would give my brother the peace we both thought he deserved, an opinion Bobby didn't share.

"I think it will be Andy," I answered.

"Can you ask him, just to make sure?"

Tugging on my sweatshirt, I started twisting the fabric, bunching it up into a wrinkled mess. "I can ask, but I'm pretty sure I can tell you what his answer will be." This was Andy's 'district,' but at the end of the day, reapers hear a spirit's call, and they go. Technically, Oleana's spirit should have been Andy's to reap. It had been the day she'd died. Later, when her spirit was finally ready to move on, Bobby had gotten the call, not Andy. Management was being pissy and disruptive at the time, a problem that was hopefully resolved. But management was tricky, and reapers were little more than pawns. Neither Andy nor Bobby had much control in the matter.

Dave stared at me until the doorbell rang. Pushing out of the chair, he headed for the door, paid the pizza delivery guy (and it *was* a guy), and carried that heavenly smell into the living room, setting the box down on the coffee table. "I'll grab some plates and drinks." Dave returned with paper plates, a roll of paper towels, and a couple of cans of Mountain Dew.

We ate in relative silence, lost to our own versions of mental limbo. Sometimes life was like that. I'd thought that "getting better" meant getting out of my own head. And, to a degree, that was true. But even the most mentally stable humans spent time wandering down never-ending mental highways, those roads often littered with potholes, cracked pavement, and washed-out sections of asphalt. Maybe that was just part of being human.

———

"When are you planning on trying to reap Charlotte?" Andy flipped through channels on the TV, not focusing on anything long enough to pick. I figured he was just messing with the remote to give his hands something to do.

Scooting closer, I leaned into Andy's body. His arm wrapped around my shoulders. The action was near automatic. Dropping the remote, the muted TV stopped on some sports channel—something neither Andy nor I cared about. Popping a piece of hard candy into his mouth, Andy silently sat, staring as a football player got tackled.

"I'm not sure. Dave needs to talk to Marshall first to make sure he's okay with us going over and getting his stuff without him."

"Hmm." Andy continued sucking on his candy, another piece already loaded in his waiting fingers. Soothing silence surrounded us while Andy's eyes tracked around the room. "It looks nice. Did moving in go okay?"

"No hiccups," I answered lazily, the stress of the day

settling in and making me sleepy. It was amazing how much better I slept with Andy around. His presence didn't always keep the nightmares at bay, but it was better by far.

"I wish I could have been here."

I'd lost count of how many times I'd heard Andy utter some version of that line.

"It's fine. I had more than enough he—"

A soft knock interrupted my reassurances.

Andy's body stiffened. "Are you expecting someone?"

I wasn't. "No, and everyone I know would text first. Maybe it's a neighbor or something." I would have sounded more confident if the knocking had come from the front door instead of the back.

Sliding off the couch, I left Andy's warmth and headed for the back door. Andy followed a few steps behind. Most likely, he'd try to stay out of sight as long as there wasn't a threat. I had no idea what he'd do if the person on the other side of the door meant to do harm.

There wasn't a peephole in the back door, and the closest window didn't allow me to see who might be standing on the stoop. I was just gearing up to ask who it was when a face popped up outside that window.

"Holy shit!" I jumped back, landing in Andy's arms.

"Good evening, Leah," Francis's muffled voice echoed through the window, his bushy beard wiggling with his words and bright smile. "I thought I'd be polite this time and knock. Isn't that the preferred method for humans?" Francis's eyebrows rose so high and innocent I almost believed him. The mischievous glint in his aqua eyes kind of gave him away.

With my heart hammering, I pulled out of Andy's arms, craning my neck so I could ask why he thought Francis was brightening my door. Andy didn't have any more of a clue than I did, and he just shook his head in response to my silently questioning eyes.

"May I come in?" Francis was more curious than pleading.

Now that my heart had calmed from the shock of his sudden appearance outside the window, it started to hurt in a different way. The last time I'd seen Francis was when Ashes died. Seeing him again, here where I was trying to make a new beginning, drove a spike of fresh pain deep into my chest.

Reaching for the handle, I unlocked the door and opened it just wide enough to allow Francis to come inside.

Despite the cold November evening, Francis was dressed almost the same as the last time I'd seen him. Pants with frayed edges kissed his dirt-streaked, bare feet. He had dirty blond hair that appeared to be hacked off here and there rather than properly groomed. Francis's beard wasn't in much better condition. Oddly enough, he was wearing a bulky jacket, something that looked out of place on his otherwise summery wardrobe.

Walking into my warmer house, Francis didn't try to remove his jacket. Eyes scanned the room, and he stared at every nook and cranny with more interest than Andy had shown. "This is a far sight better than that apartment you were staying in."

I shouldn't have been offended, and yet, I was. That apartment had been my first stab at freedom—freedom from my past actions and dependency on Uncle Jack and Aunt Joyce. It wasn't the Hilton, but it was what I'd been able to afford, and I'd always kept it clean.

"And Andrew, it's good to see you here." Francis gave a lewd grin. "You must have worked things out with management. I don't imagine they're too happy about the situation." Francis was overly pleased with management's displeasure.

From what little I understood, it was an ancient argument between them.

"Francis." Andy's cool tone blanketed the room. "It's odd to see you out and consorting with humans."

Francis grunted some type of agreement. "True enough. Although not as odd as seeing a reaper shacking up with his final soul." Francis chuckled, rocking back and forth on his bare feet while Andy and I stood there.

I couldn't speak for my reaper, but I didn't have a clue what to say beyond, "Why are you here?" I'd let Ashes go, encouraged her to move on, just like Francis had asked me to do. I had no idea what business he'd have with me.

The mirth lighting up Francis's face vanished so swiftly I thought its presence might have been a figment of my imagination. Eyes narrowed, thin strips of aqua shimmered between blond lashes. Lips pulled so thin his mouth nearly disappeared within his beard, Francis looked pissed. The air was thick with his anger. Taking a step back, I once more melded into Andy's chest.

Taking a deep breath, Francis's body relaxed, and his eyes slipped closed before they opened a little wider. "Sorry about that." I wasn't sure if Francis was truly sorry or just offering placating words. "I was just remembering the circumstances for why I'm here."

I shot a worried glance at Andy, afraid I'd done something. I wasn't sure exactly what Francis was. Dave and Cecile had seen his true form the day Ashes passed away. They both agreed that Francis looked like some type of fairy woodland creature. Since Francis was still firmly in the land of the living, I couldn't see his true form the way I did the dead. Regardless, I did know that Francis was old—ancient—and someone you didn't want to piss off.

Catching my anxious look, Francis gave me the assurance I needed. "It has nothing to do with you or Andy, so no worries. In fact," Francis's emotions took another one-eighty, turning him back into a jovial drifter, "the reason I'm here is because you aren't so bad, for a human."

Before I could ask anything else, Francis unzipped his jacket and shoved his hand deep inside. He pulled out a sleeping ball of dirty white fluff. "There was a fire. She is the only one that survived, and she's too . . ."

Francis's voice droned on, but I tuned him out. My eyes zeroed in on the sleeping kitten he held. Heart stuttering, it caught before starting up again, beating harshly against my ribs. Francis might have still been talking when I closed the distance and reached in to scoop the fluffy piece of living fur out of his palm.

She was small, maybe seven or eight weeks at most. She didn't feel that thin. Her mother had done well by her. What she was, was dirty. Ash- and soot-covered. Despite that, I still saw her white fluff and knew that's the color she should be.

". . . needs a home." The static plugging my ears cleared, popping with sudden clarity.

My head snapped up. "You're giving her to me?" I asked, incredulous.

I'd been thinking of getting a new cat, of going to one of the local shelters or trolling the internet for something. But every time I thought about it, I'd get this heart-sick feeling, like I was somehow betraying Ashes's memory. This might be different. This was like a gift. One I couldn't refuse.

Francis scoffed. "Animals are not to be *given*, despite what humans believe. What I am doing is offering her a place to stay, to rest and grow. Should she choose to remain with you, then that is her choice. Cats can be very particular, but I believe the two of you will suit."

I scratched her head, and rumbled purring filtered through the room. I didn't realize I was crying until the first tear dropped onto her fur. I couldn't take my eyes off her and could only offer a muffled, "Thank you."

Francis was silent for a beat before quietly answering, "You are welcome, Leah. Treat her with the same love and respect you did Ashes, and I'm sure she'll happily remain with you for years to come."

I didn't hear the back door open and close or the click of its lock. Andy's slender fingers lifted my chin. As always, I leaned into his warmth, my damp eyes staring into his quietly tender ones. "She'll need food and a litter box."

It was a good thing one of us was being practical. "Yeah, I, uh . . . I threw out Ashes old litter box. I'm not sure what Dave did with her food and water dishes." I doubted he threw them out. Most likely they were in a box at his house, stored away.

"Do you want me to hold her while you call?"

Truth be told, I didn't want to let her out of my arms, but it was time to do the job Francis had entrusted me with. Gently handing her over, the kitten looked even smaller in Andy's larger hands. Grabbing my phone, I called Dave and explained the situation as quickly as possible. Cecile was there with him, having gone to Dave's house after he picked her up from work. She squealed in the background right before she grabbed the phone from Dave and started firing questions at me. In the end, they decided to run to the grocery for me, pick up some supplies, and head back this way.

Grateful for the help, I ended the call and turned to see Andy's head cocked to the side, his eyes slightly glazed. I knew that look. Someone was about to die. It was time for Andy to be the reaper he was.

"Go." I reached in and peeled my new charge from Andy's cupped hand. "Dave and Cecile should be here soon.

Marshall might be over too, so you'd need to hide anyway. I'll be fine."

The grim lines on Andy's face told me he'd rather stay, but that wasn't an option. Walking toward the door, Andy turned and asked, "Have you thought of a name?"

I'd only had her for a few precious minutes. Looking at her soot-covered fur, I remembered Francis had said something about a fire and that this kitten had been the only survivor. Without needing to give it much thought, I answered, "Phoenix."

12

"Lilly can't stop talking about having a cat," Chrissie said, shifting the potted plant in her arms so I could see her face. "She's over the moon."

"I probably should have asked you if that was okay before I told Francis I'd take her."

Chrissie had decided to start moving some of her things into the house, a little each day with the final big push one week to the day since I'd moved in. Lilly would be at school and out of the way for most of it. Lenny was with her now, entertaining Lilly while Chrissie and I started moving some of her plants in. We would go back for another load and bring Lilly and Lenny with us that round.

"No worries." Chrissie set the plant on the kitchen countertop. "I've been thinking about getting Lilly a pet for a while, but our apartment complex wouldn't allow them. We would have had to move. This works out perfect." Chrissie's eyes scanned the room. "Where is the little fluffball?"

"I locked her in my bedroom. I didn't want her to get underfoot."

"Good plan." Chrissie and I headed back out to our cars.

We'd loaded each one up. Since we both had smaller vehicles, there wasn't much to unload, and soon, we were on our last trip. Chrissie's phone rang as she was setting down a box. Digging her phone out of her pocket, Chrissie's face lit up as she answered, "Hey, Lenny. Are you guys doing okay?"

Chrissie's smile faded, her skin paling at an alarming rate before a flush of red sped into her cheeks. "Say that again." Eyes narrowed, Chrissie's hand clenched her phone. A low, pale green shimmered from between her lashes. "I'm leaving now." Chrissie ran toward the door. I had no idea what was happening, but something had spooked Chrissie.

I followed.

As soon as Chrissie dropped the phone from her ear, I asked, "Is Lilly okay? Did something happen?"

Yanking her car door open, Chrissie was halfway inside before she answered, "Lilly's going to be just fine."

"But is she—"

"Mark's there." Chrissie slammed the door, started the engine, and peeled out of the drive.

Running up to the house. I locked the door and followed. The only Mark I knew was Lilly's sperm donor. From everything I'd heard, Mark had bolted out of Chrissie's and Lilly's lives shortly after Lilly was born. I had no idea what he was doing at Chrissie's apartment now but couldn't imagine it would be anything good.

"Fuckity-fuck-fuck," I murmured while hitting the gas, speeding through the neighborhood. I didn't know what Rose's neighbors thought of me moving in, but driving like an idiot through the neighborhood probably didn't get me a lot of brownie points.

Despite my wild driving, Chrissie beat me to her apartment. I could already hear the yelling when I got out of my car.

"Leonard Filliman? That's who you're shacking up with now?"

Running up the stairs, I couldn't see the owner of that voice but wanted to slap his face anyway. The sarcasm and contempt were thick and judgmental.

"Lenny's ten times the man you'll ever be, Mark," Chrissie spat so cold and low it sent shivers racing up and down my spine. "He doesn't run away when things get iffy."

"*Iffy?*"

I rounded the stairwell in time to see Mark throw his arms up, high and wide, as if he couldn't believe what was happening.

"Unbelievable. That's what you'd call what you are? Iffy?"

Chrissie reeled back as if she'd been physically slapped. "What I am or am not has nothing to do with this. What the hell are you doing here now, Mark? You told me five years ago that you were leaving, and I wouldn't ever have to see your face again. Looks like you're backing out on your word again."

Standing at the end of the hall, I wasn't sure what to do. Maybe I shouldn't have followed. Maybe this was private. I hadn't given it a second thought when I'd hopped in my car. Now I was giving it a second, third, and maybe fiftieth thought.

"Charming," Mark sneered, pulling at the sleeves of his coat. "I can't believe I ever thought you were worthy of my attention."

"Ditto. Again, why the hell are you here?"

Mark's face became an unreadable mask as he stiffened. "Why do you think? I came for my daughter."

While I stumbled back, Chrissie's fists clenched, her knuckles white. Chrissie's arms were covered by her long-sleeved jacket, but I didn't need to see them to read the tension.

Barely audible, so quiet I had to strain to hear her, Chrissie said, "Over my dead body."

Mark smirked, actually honest-to-god smirked. "Let's hope it doesn't come to that."

"What the hell." I lost my battle with silence. Mark's words froze my core. I'd seen enough death in my life, and making threats like that was no joking matter.

My words brought Mark's attention to me. Fully turning, I had an opportunity to get a good look at him. Chrissie and Mark had been high school sweethearts and were around four years older than me. I had vague memories of them from when I was in high school, but I wouldn't have been able to pick Mark out of a lineup. Staring at him now, I marveled at just how charming the two of them looked together. Mark was an all-American boy. Taller and beefier than Dave. Mark's hair looked like he highlighted it to bring out its blondness. I wasn't sure if his golden hue came naturally or from visiting the tanning salon a few times a week. Regardless, it looked good on him, and his white teeth gleamed when his lips pulled back.

Instead of a smile, I got a grimace. "Is this her?" He threw out a hand in my direction. "Fergus told me you had a new . . . *friend.*" It sounded like I was little more than shit on Mark's shoe.

While I thought, *Fergus?* Chrissie asked, "You've been talking with my dad?"

Mark snorted. "He called me, filled me in on what you did to your mother."

Chrissie took a step forward. "I didn't do anything to my

mom. Grams did." Shoving her thumb into her chest, Chrissie said, "I fixed things. I saved my—"

"She never would have needed saving if you weren't . . ." Mark waved a hand in Chrissie's general direction, "what you are, what you're trying to turn my daughter into."

Chrissie drew in a sharp, pain-filled breath. "I'm not turning her into anything. Lilly is my daughter. She's a descendant of Grams. It's who she is."

Standing out in the hall, anyone could hear what was being said. Right now, it just sounded like a couple of ordinary humans who'd had a child and strongly disagreed on how that child should be raised. In a way, they would be right. The witchy factor threw a lot of colorful shades into that story.

Mark shook his head. "It's not who she has to be, and that's why I'm here, to stop you from corrupting our daughter the way Oleana corrupted you."

"Funny how you didn't give a damn about that five years ago," Chrissie spat.

"Things change, Chrissie. People change."

Chrissie laughed, sharp and biting. "Not that much, Mark. Now, tell me what the hell this is really about."

Some of the bravado slipped from Mark's face, pale insecurity moving in. Licking his lips, Mark glanced from me to Chrissie. "There's nothing else. I just want my—"

"Bullshit." Chrissie inched forward, her movements threatening despite Mark being taller and outweighing her. Green fire danced in her eyes. You didn't threaten a mother with the removal of her child, and you especially didn't threaten one with Chrissie's abilities. I had to wonder at Mark's intelligence. Unlike Lenny, Mark knew what Chrissie was and most likely had an inkling of what she could do. I couldn't understand why he was being so reckless—so antagonistic. He could have come at this a lot of other ways, he could have—

"Don't threaten me, Chrissie," Mark whispered. "You're not the only one with friends on their side, and I assure you, the ones I've made are a hell of a lot more powerful than anything you've got to throw at me."

I sucked in a harsh breath while Chrissie came to a dead halt. "What?"

"You heard me." Mark tugged on his jacket again, moving away from the door at his back and toward me and the stairwell. "You opened up my eyes to a few things, Chrissie." Gaze darting back toward the closed apartment door, Lenny and Lilly safely tucked behind its steel frame, Mark's eyes tracked back to Chrissie. "She's my daughter, and I have just as much right to her as you do. And it turns out, some people in this world think I should exert those parental rights."

"Some people?" Chrissie turned, her eyes losing some of their green fire. "Are you sure that's what they are? *People?*"

Mark's foot caught on the cement landing, throwing his body forward and into the railing. Unlike when Ellen Dykstra hit the railing at my apartment, this one held. Regaining his balance, Mark's flushed face stared Chrissie down. "I'll be back, and when I am, I expect to see Lilly. You can't keep her from me. It's time she got to know her real father, not that loser you've taken up with."

Throwing me a final, disgusted look, Mark stomped down the stairs, taking his blond highlights with him.

Chrissie and I stood there. Her breathing was harsh in the quiet of the stairwell. Cold sweat dripped down my back, my body suddenly too hot. The zipper on my coat sounded loud as I yanked it down.

Having no idea where to start, I said, "Chrissie, I—"

"They can't have her."

My head snapped back. I'd heard that correctly. *They*, not he. "Who's they?"

Chrissie didn't answer. Frantically, she ran her hands over the top of her head, tugging at her ponytail. "This can't be happening. It just can't be," Chrissie murmured, her words tumbling over themselves in a rush to be free.

Closing the distance, I grabbed Chrissie's arms, pulling them down and holding her wrists in my clenched fists. "Who are they, Chrissie? Who wants Lilly?"

Shaking her head violently, Chrissie answered, "I don't know. Not for sure."

"What do you mean you don't kn—"

"Just what I said," Chrissie yelled in my face. "I don't fucking know! It could be any number of groups. I told you before, Lilly's got promise. She's . . . Fuck, she'll probably be more powerful than Grams was, more powerful than me. Having a witch like that under your control, under your thumb and doing what you want, not what they want, would tempt a lot of groups of *people*." Pulling out of my grasp, Chrissie leaned heavily on the wall next to her apartment door. Head tilted back, she let loose a heavy sigh. "Mark's an idiot. He has no idea who he's crawled into bed with. I don't know what they've offered him, but once he's got Lilly, they won't need him anymore. He'll be useless baggage."

"You mean they'll . . ."

Chrissie shrugged. "They may not have to kill him. I suppose it depends on the group involved and how much of a thorn in their side Mark is. If he knows the score and just wants to get Lilly away from me and dump her with them, they might let him go. If he really wants to keep her, then . . ." Chrissie spread her arms out. "Then he's probably a dead man walking."

"Shit."

Head down, Chrissie's chin lay on her chest, her face

cupped within her palms. "I have to figure this out. I have to think. I have to . . ."

Pulling Chrissie away from the wall, I hugged her tight. Chrissie had to bend down to get the full effect as short as I was. "What you have to do right now, right this very second, is get your shit together so that when you walk into that apartment, Lilly doesn't have a clue there's something wrong. After that, we speed up the timetable of you moving in with me."

Chrissie's breath sighed into my neck. "You don't mean that, Leah. Trust me, you don't want Lilly and me to move in with you now. This shit storm wasn't part of our deal, and I'm not going to put you in the middle of this."

"I've been in a few shit storms in the past, and so far, I've made it to the other side. You and Lilly are moving in, and that's final. Mark has something or someone on his side, well, you've got people too, and I don't think Mark has a clue what those people are made of. You're right. He's an idiot—all the way around."

Chrissie chuckled, the sound muffled against my shoulder. "Unless he's in league with the dead, I don't think you and your reaper are going to be much help."

"I've got more than the dead on my side." Oddly enough, I felt very confident in that statement. "And so do you. You've got a whole book of friends tucked away in a junk drawer in your kitchen. One of them already saved me from having to deal with Levi Dickerson more than I already had. I got a glimpse of those pages, and they're full."

Pulling away, Chrissie rubbed her finger under her nose. The sound of clogged snot filled the hall when she sniffed. "Grams' friends, not mine."

"I've got a feeling those friendships automatically transferred to you upon her death."

Chrissie's eyebrows pulled down in thought, her eyes

drying. "Maybe. Chances are slim, but it's also possible one of those names in that book is behind this."

Well, shit. I hadn't thought of that. "Okay," I said slowly, "then we go through the names in that book with a fine-toothed comb. We talk it out together and decide who might be the safest ones to contact first. We'll figure this out, Chrissie. I'm not a hundred percent sure how yet, but we'll get there."

Pink splotches covered Chrissie's face, her eyes red-rimmed from pain and anger. Staring up at her, Chrissie didn't look as defeated as before. She didn't look happy either. If I had to name the emotion, I'd call it resolved. With a final, firm nod, Chrissie redid her ponytail, smoothing her hair and getting herself as much back to rights as possible.

"You ready?" I asked after Chrissie had taken several deep breaths.

"No, but I've made them wait long enough. Lenny's good at bullshitting but not so great at lying. He's probably running out of things to keep Lilly occupied. Thankfully, Lenny knew enough not to let Mark inside. As far as I know, Lilly doesn't have a clue her sperm donor was out here at all."

Grabbing Chrissie's keys out of her hand, I unlocked the door and threw over my shoulder, "Then let's keep it that way."

Opening the door, I was greeted by Lilly's body slamming into mine, her arms wrapped around me and her beaming face staring up into mine. Innocence was a precious, fleeting commodity, and I planned on doing everything I could to keep Lilly's intact as long as possible.

13

Chrissie asked Doug for an extra day off, and with some help, she moved into Rose's old house the following day. All of us kept our eyes peeled for any signs of Mark. He never showed. Chrissie was edgy but tried to downplay it for Lilly's sake. I think Lilly knew something was up, but a quick introduction to Phoenix, and she was too preoccupied to pay much attention to anything else. Thankfully, Phoenix didn't seem to mind the attention.

As soon as Lilly went to bed, Chrissie got to work doing . . . other things. She walked the perimeter of the property, arms outstretched and palms down. I saw her mouth moving when she came into the pools of outside lights. Most of the time, she disappeared into November's cold, dark evening. When she finally came inside, Chrissie looked scary pale, and her fingers were ice cold. She collapsed into Dave's floral throne, hands shaky.

"Here." I shoved a glass of OJ into her hands, along with a candy bar. "Get some sugar into you."

"Thanks." Chrissie's shaking grew more obvious when she brought the glass of juice to her lips. Sitting on the couch,

I let her get fluids and food into her before I asked, "Do I want to know what you did out there?"

Quaking subsiding, Chrissie slid deeper into the chair. It didn't protest as much about her weight as it did with Dave's. "Nothing bad, at least not for you or anyone else that doesn't have ill will when they cross the property line."

"Define *ill will*." My brain didn't always play nice, especially against me, and history was a heavy reminder that I'd willingly tried to harm myself.

Chrissie's head tilted to the side, her eyes tracking toward me as a fingernail tapped along the nearly empty glass dangling from her fingers. "Mostly, it will alert me if someone has bad intentions toward you, me, or Lilly. Consider it a bonus that my casting will also tip me off if your brain decides to play stupid games with your health—mental or physical."

I swallowed hard, unsure what to think of that. "Chrissie, I—"

"It'll be fine, Leah. I'd never do anything to hurt you."

"I know," I assured. "I didn't mean to imply that."

Chrissie sat up, tilting the chair slightly. "I know, and no offense taken. Really, what I just did is pretty paltry. I'll want to beef up the alert system more, but first, I need to look into a few things. What I did tonight will just act as an early warning system. It won't keep anybody out, but it will let me know if someone we don't want around steps foot on the property."

My eyebrows shot up. "That sounds useful."

"Not nearly useful enough," Chrissie grunted. "But it's better than nothing. Since I'm a nature witch, winter isn't the best time of year for what I can do. Mark probably doesn't know that, but I'll bet whoever he's hooked up with does."

Chrissie jolted when we heard the front door open. I had my own early warning system where Andy was concerned and had felt the warmth of his presence before he'd walked through the door. "It's just Andy," I said when Chrissie started to get up.

"Shit," she cursed while settling back into her chair. "I need to add that to the warning system."

"Yes," Andy waltzed into the room, easing around the couch and sitting close to me. "That's a fine piece of crafting. Oleana would be proud." Head turned toward me, Andy's bright green eyes caught in the low lighting. His nearness made my heart rate tick up. "Good evening, Leah."

My stomach did that cliff dive I was getting used to, swooping low and making me lightheaded. "Hey, Andy." I scooted closer, wanting to feel his warmth from without as well as within. "Busy day?"

"Average." Andy's breath tickled my ear, sending a shiver through my body.

"This charm still needs a little more tweaking, but it's better than before." Chrissie's comment interrupted the cocoon of peace I'd wrapped around myself. "The edges of Andy's image are still fuzzy, kind of like they want to morph into something else, but it's holding steadier than before. At least looking at you isn't giving me a migraine."

"That sounds like progress."

Cheek resting on Andy's shoulder, I turned enough to look at Chrissie. This was the first time she'd been around Andy and me as a . . . whatever we were. I'd been afraid I'd find judgment on Chrissie's face. But that's not what was there. To my relief, there really wasn't much of anything. Chrissie looked relaxed, her head cocked to the side in what appeared to be clinical interest. If I had to guess, I'd say she was trying to figure out how to make her charm work even better.

"I suppose. It still needs improvement." She fingered one

of the charms hanging around her neck for a second before she asked Andy, "Could you really feel my casting?"

"Most definitely, though I was uncertain what your casting was searching for when I passed through it."

Chrissie's lips twisted. "Ill will. Which, I assume since I wasn't alerted to your presence, you have none toward anyone that lives here."

"None whatsoever," Andy answered breezily.

"Good to know." Chrissie let loose a wide, cracking yawn. "God, I'm fucking exhausted."

Since I wasn't a witch, I had no idea just how much casting took out of one. Given the few times I'd seen Chrissie do some major mojo, it looked like it really wiped her out. Add in the fact that we'd done a rush move, and most likely, she didn't have a hell of a lot left. "Go on to bed. Get some sleep."

Chrissie shot Andy and me a look. "You hitting the hay soon too?"

I shrugged against Andy's side. "Most likely I'm already there." I still didn't sleep in an actual bed very often. The couch was more home to me than my bed. "We'll see how the night goes."

Chrissie shot me a sympathetic look, one that was absent pity, thankfully. "Okay. Have a good night."

I watched Chrissie stand, ready to jump up and catch her if she started to waver. She was steadier than I'd feared she'd be and successfully walked down the hall and to her new bedroom. I heard the click of her bedroom door shut right before Andy said, "Chrissie laid down an impressive perimeter. Is there a reason I should be aware of?"

Thoughts of Mark tensed my shoulders. Andy's warmth relaxed them. Andy had been MIA yesterday, and this was the first I'd seen him since witnessing Chrissie's ex.

Shifting Phoenix around to settle in my lap instead of the

cushion beside me, I answered, "You could say that," and dove into what had transpired the day before.

Andy quietly listened. Every once in a while he'd ask a question or two for clarification. When I was done, he lifted me, settling my body within his own. Phoenix let loose a mew of irritation but quickly settled within the warmth of my lap.

"You attract danger like pollen attracts bees. It's a worrisome trait, Leah." Andy buried his lips in my neck, kissing against my skin, sending lightning-quick sparks of fire racing through my skin.

I leaned into him, savoring the feel of his skin against mine. "This isn't . . ." My breath caught as Andy's lips traveled to the shell of my ear. "Th-this time, it's not . . ." I tried again, not getting any farther than before.

"Oh, I'm well aware," Andy breathed against my dampened skin, sending even more shivers rippling down my spine. "Regardless, you're in the thick of it again. I'm not pleased." Andy pulled back, and his fingers twisted my head so he could look me directly in the eyes. "Be careful, Leah. Don't make me hear the call of your soul."

Those beautiful green eyes were marred with shimmering pain. The scar running through Andy's eyebrow pinched to near nonexistence.

I didn't know what to say, how to make Andy feel more at ease. "I can't abandon Chrissie or Lilly."

The barest hint of a smile lifted the corners of Andy's lips. "I know, and I'd never ask you to. All I ask is that you value your own life as much as theirs. You're willing to sacrifice for everyone but yourself."

"I—" My mouth closed, unsure what to say. Arguing the point would have been a blatant lie. I wasn't unfamiliar with lying, but I was trying to do it less.

"I know." Andy's fingers carded through my dirty hair, the

wear and tear of moving having taken its toll on my cleanliness. Andy didn't seem to mind. "Just be careful. That's all I ask. Okay?"

Offering a weak, "I'll try," was the best I could do, but it was still better than what I'd been able to offer a few short months ago. Trying was progress. Trying was a promise I planned to keep. Unfortunately, trying didn't always equal success.

14

I would have liked more time to get settled into my new home before Dr. Meyer's retirement party came around, but my timetable didn't figure into that. I'd also hoped to go over to Dave's dad's house to try to speak with Charlotte first. But there were a lot of logistics to work out with that one, including figuring out a time Dave, Cecile, and I were all off work and could do it. Dave wanted it to be when Marshall was at school. He still wasn't comfortable with Marshall hanging out on his own, at least not for long stretches of time. Dave had adjusted his work schedule to fit more with Marshall's school hours and so he could be home in the evenings with his half brother.

I wasn't surprised Dave had changed his life to mold to Marshall's. I would have been far more surprised if he hadn't.

A different pair of ladies were at the help desk guarding the emergency room. The last time, both had looked older, like they'd been retired for at least ten years and had shown up so they'd have something to do. One woman sitting behind the desk fit into that mold. The other was probably in her mid-forties to fifties. Or maybe she was younger and had just had some shitty-ass luck in life.

"Can I help you?" the younger one asked. Her words sounded right, but her tone screamed that I should turn around and jump off the nearest bridge.

"I'm here to see Joyce Miller. She's a nurse in—"

"I'm well aware of who Joyce Miller is," she snapped back at me. Her fingernails were too short to make the typical tapping noise I was used to when someone typed away at their keyboard. "Is she expecting you?"

"Yes?" It came out more of a question than I'd planned. "Yes," I said more forcefully. "She's expecting me. She's my aunt." I wasn't sure why I threw in the last bit, except this woman looked like I was something stuck to the bottom of her shoe.

Waving me to the side, she said, "Wait there so I can see to the people behind you."

I shot a look over my shoulder. Unlike the last time I was here, the ER didn't seem too busy, and only one person was queued up behind me. I took a step to the side.

"Let Joyce Miller know her niece is here to see her." I got a look at my *helper's* name tag when she lifted the phone to her ear. Deanna didn't sound any kinder to whoever she'd called than she did to me. Evidently done with me now, Deanna ordered a clipped, "Next person," to the unfortunate soul coughing behind me.

Thankfully, it didn't take Aunt Joyce long to pop up. Opening the same private door Tyson had led me through a few weeks ago, Aunt Joyce stuck her head out and waved me in. Dressed in navy scrubs, her blond hair pulled back into a messy bun, Aunt Joyce had plastic security cards and passes dangling from a chain hooked to a pocket on her scrub top.

"I've got Cecile's bag in my locker." Aunt Joyce leaned

over, conspiratorially whispering into my ear. "They'll just think you're here to get that." It sounded like a good enough plan since I'd come before to get something of Cecile's. Aunt Joyce thought this would be the best time to talk with Dr. Meyer, to see if he knew anything about Thomas Birkingham. I wasn't sure, but it was worth a go. If we pissed off Dr. Meyer for some reason, he was retiring anyway and wouldn't cause much grief for Aunt Joyce.

The hallway we walked down was a lot more jovial than the last time I'd seen it. Nurses, doctors, and assistants were still scurrying around, but their movements didn't seem as harried, and the sounds weren't as overwhelming. It still stunk like a typical hospital, not that I'd expected that to change.

I caught sight of Tyson out of the corner of my eye. He was in a room helping a nurse with a patient. Our eyes connected, and he gave me a head bob of greeting along with a quick smile. Given that he was busy, I didn't do more than wave back.

Turning the corner, the nurses' station came into view—decorated with balloons, a happy retirement sign, and a couple of rather pathetic-looking streamers, the area looked somewhat festive. A half-eaten sheet cake was propped up on a nearby table, along with tiny plates that refused to hold much more than a minuscule slice of cake. Even tinier plastic cups were stacked next to the cake, just enough for a shot or two of the red punch in a nearby pitcher. A few nurses and probably assistants huddled around the table. A woman in a white coat looked like she was probably a doctor. The man of the hour stood at the head of the card table, an almost empty glass of punch in one hand, his other tucked into his white coat pocket.

Age hadn't taken a toll on Dr. Meyer's hair. He still had a

thick crop of silvery-white hair, the edges neatly trimmed and swept away from his cracked, leathery face. Dr. Meyer looked like he liked to spend a lot of time outdoors. Time in the sun had taken its measure. Sparkling brown eyes shone beneath round-framed glasses.

"Joyce!" Dr. Meyer's voice was tender and full of respectful fondness when he said my aunt's name. "I haven't seen much of you today."

Aunt Joyce rounded the corner of the table. More than a few staff lingering around walked away when Dr. Meyer pulled my aunt into a one-armed hug. "Sorry, Dr. Meyer, I've been busy with patients."

"After today, no more of this Dr. Meyer stuff. You call me Ed."

Aunt Joyce pulled away, tutting softly. "No can do. You'll always be Dr. Meyer to me."

Dr. Meyer huffed but didn't bother arguing. "Have you gotten one of these minuscule pieces of cake yet? They're small but mighty."

I softly chuckled. Dr. Meyer was my kind of guy and thought the pieces were kind of dinky too.

"Not yet, but I'm on break, so I'll try one." Grabbing a couple of plates, Aunt Joyce slid a piece of cake on each one before she grabbed the punch and poured us each a glass. As she was pouring, she said, "Dr. Meyer, I don't think you've had a chance to meet my niece, Leah."

Dr. Meyer turned his megawatt smile on me. "Nice to meet you, young lady." He shot out a hand, and I shook it. "You've got a great aunt here. Best nurse I've ever worked with. Joyce knows her stuff and has kept me on track for the past decade or so."

Aunt Joyce flushed pink, shuffling her feet back and forth with unease. Deciding to make her more uncomfortable, I answered, "I know. I'm lucky."

My aunt's head shot up, eyes wide and searching. I maintained eye contact, making sure Aunt Joyce knew I was serious. Slowly, her eyes softened into something grateful. Shoving a piece of cake into her mouth, Aunt Joyce chewed quickly before swallowing. Emptying her glass of punch, she cleared her throat before launching into our cover. "Leah came to pick up something for Cecile."

Dr. Meyer's smile was softer this time. "I'm so glad she's doing better, Joyce."

My aunt thanked Dr. Meyer. I saw why she liked this doctor so much and why she'd be sad when he was gone. Working the ER hadn't dimmed Dr. Meyer's personality, and he treated my aunt with respect and care. I figured that held true less often than anyone would like.

I'd zoned out for a bit, but my ears perked back up when Aunt Joyce said, "I wanted to pick your brain while you're still around."

Dr. Meyer chuckled. "There are a lot younger minds than mine to go picking at, Joyce."

"True, but for this question, I think I need a mind that's got a bit more miles on it." Aunt Joyce kept her voice light, a teasing touch dancing around the edge.

Dr. Meyer ate it up. "What a polite way of saying I'm old. So, what can this aged brain offer that a younger one can't?"

"Information." Aunt Joyce's eyes briefly shot my direction to see if I was paying attention. "I saw a name on one of the plaques—one of the older ones acknowledging donors. For some reason, the name rang a bell." Aunt Joyce licked her lips. "Thomas Birkingham."

Dr. Meyer's reaction was instant. His body suddenly stiff, all his joviality slipped away as his lips tightened. "Now, there's a name I haven't heard in a long time."

My heart kicked up a couple of rhythms. Given his reaction, it was clear that Dr. Meyer knew something. The uncomfortable look he shot my way also made me think he wasn't about to dish what he knew with me this close.

"Hey, Leah." Tyson popped up on the other side of the table, eyeing the cake warily. "Who do they think they're feeding?" he asked, blessedly oblivious to the momentary tension spike.

Tyson's appearance broke the ice, and Dr. Meyer softly laughed. "Old farts like me, I guess." Dr. Meyer drank the rest of his punch before he asked, "Do you know Leah?"

Nodding while swallowing a piece of cake, Tyson answered, "She used to live in the same apartment complex, just down the hall. But she ditched me recently." Tyson threw me a wink I appreciated.

I also saw an opportunity. Waving Tyson over to my side of the table, I turned my back on Dr. Meyer and Aunt Joyce, hoping the illusion of privacy would get Dr. Meyer talking. It worked.

Not long after I'd turned my attention to Tyson, Dr. Meyer spilled what he knew. But it was a lot harder than I thought it would be, trying to listen in on two different conversations. For my already crowded brain, it was impossible. Leaning toward Tyson, I crooked my finger and indicated I wanted him to do the same. When he was close enough, I whispered, "I hate to do this, but I need to hear what's going on behind me. Only, I don't want them to know I'm listening in."

Tyson's eyebrows shot toward his hairline, his dark brown eyes wide. For half a second, I thought I'd overstepped, but a mischievous grin lit up Tyson's face, making him look more like a seven-year-old boy than a young man living on his own.

"Oh . . ." Tyson's eyes flicked behind me before settling back on mine. "This won't come back to bite me in the ass, will it?" Tyson turned serious. "Because Joyce is just starting to act human again, and I—"

"She's in on it too," I hastened to alleviate Tyson's concerns. "Aunt Joyce is good."

"In that case, what do you need me to do?"

"Just keep talking to me. I'll nod now and again, but I won't be paying attention to you."

Tyson shoved another piece of cake into his mouth, swallowing the entire thing whole. "Easy," he answered on a harsh gulp. "It'll be just like talking to my last girlfriend," he added with a wink.

Good to his word, Tyson started talking, and I tuned out. I'd missed some of their conversation, but then Dr. Meyer said, "Beth." He whispered the word, but it wasn't with fondness. "There's a second name I haven't heard for a long time, at least not in association with Thomas."

With my back to them, I couldn't see Dr. Meyer's expressions and only heard his tone. There was a break in the conversation when a nurse came up to grab some refreshments, congratulating Dr. Meyer on his retirement and telling him how much he'd be missed. In this case, I didn't think those were meaningless platitudes.

When the nurse left, Aunt Joyce offered, "If it's not something you want to talk about, that's okay. I was just curious. You know how my mind wanders, always picking at things."

Dr. Meyer gave a wane smile. "I do. That's one of the reasons you and I always got along so well. And, in that spirit, I'll tell you what I know, but keep in mind, it was a long time ago, and a lot of the backstory I'm going to share was given to me secondhand. When all that happened, I was young and inexperienced. The doctors working at the time didn't give two hoots about a young, fresh-faced doctor like me. Still, I was on duty the night it happened."

My ears perked. It sounded like Dr. Meyer knew a hell of a lot more than I'd hoped. I was maybe even more surprised that he was willing to share what he knew. As if reading my thoughts, Dr. Meyer said, "I hardly think anyone will care that I share this with you. It happened, what, over fifty years ago. Considering I was just an intern, it'd be nearer to sixty. God, time flies. It slips away, and you're old before you realize it."

Aunt Joyce started to say something, probably to protest that Dr. Meyer wasn't old even though he clearly was.

"It's okay, Joyce. We're dealing with truth here, and the truth is, I am old. Thankfully I've still got all my marbles." I couldn't see it, but I imagined him tapping the side of his head. "Or at least most of them," he chuckled. "Now, you asked about Mr. Birkingham. Did you know that at one time, one of the wings of the hospital had his name on it?"

"I did but wasn't sure how long ago that was," Aunt Joyce answered.

"A while. That part of the hospital has been rebuilt twice since then, a different name going up each time. That's the way money works, I suppose. Anyway, Thomas Birkingham was a wealthy man, came from a wealthy family, from what I understood. Don't ask me how they got their money because I honestly have no idea. But that money is probably one of the things that got Elizabeth into trouble."

"Elizabeth? Is that Beth?" Aunt Joyce asked.

"He often called her Beth. Or at least that's what he was screaming the night he hauled her in here, more than half dead already." Dr. Meyer paused. "Wish I had something a little stronger than punch to add to this cup." Heaving a sigh, one of those little cups went flying by my peripheral vision, landing in a nearby trashcan. "Then again, given the details of the story, maybe not."

Tyson grinned, his arms waving around like he was in the

middle of a really important story. Maybe he was. I hadn't been paying a bit of attention. I took that moment to smile and nod. I even managed a little laugh. All around us, staff speed-walked back and forth, the sound of machines not as distant as I would have liked.

Behind me, Dr. Meyer started up the tale again. "The short of the story, as far as I know it, is that Elizabeth was what we called a 'wild child' back then. She did what she wanted, when she wanted, and her granddaddy's money smoothed over any feathers she might have ruffled along the way. That's not so unusual, and not much harm was done until Elizabeth came of age and got her driver's license. Even that would have been okay if she hadn't had a penchant for downing a glass or five of alcohol before climbing behind the wheel."

"That couldn't have gone over well," Aunt Joyce broke in.

"You wouldn't think so, but like I said, money cures, or at least slaps, a Band-Aid on a lot of crimes. Elizabeth was nineteen when she caused her first major accident. Thankfully, the mother and the two sons in the other vehicle survived. No charges were filed, and the fact that Elizabeth had been drunk seemed to slide under the radar. Her second accident, the man in the other car wasn't so fortunate."

"She killed someone?" Aunt Joyce asked with awe.

I gasped softly, and for a hot second, Tyson's story faltered. Like a pro, he picked up again quickly. So far, this story wasn't going anywhere I thought it would. I'd imagined Beth to be some innocent victim, but this . . .

"She did," Dr. Meyer answered. "And not just anyone, but one of our emergency room doctor's children, Dr. Ben Davidson's only son, Adam." Breathing in deeply, Dr. Meyer sounded lost to memory. "I was there that day, when they brought Adam in. Looking back on it, knowing what I do now, there was nothing that could have been done—not then anyway. Maybe with the advancements since then, but not at the time. Adam's neck was broken. Even if he had survived, he would have been paralyzed. Again, given medicine at that time, it wouldn't have been a good life, whatever remained of it. Regardless, Adam didn't survive his wounds. He died that night. Ben wasn't allowed to work on Adam, but he refused to leave the room. Ben watched his son die, right there in front of him."

Aunt Joyce made a small noise, something that sounded like painful understanding. "Was Elizabeth injured too?"

Dr. Meyer barked out a laugh, far from humorous. "Barely a scratch on her. We see it all the time. The one all liquored up gets off a lot easier than the innocent person they hit."

"She was arrested this time, though, right?" Aunt Joyce asked.

"You would have thought so, but mysteriously, all evidence that Elizabeth Birkingham had been three sheets to the wind up and blew away, disappearing just like that." Dr. Meyer snapped his fingers. "Ben was devastated."

"Understandable." Aunt Joyce sounded pissed. I bet she imagined Cecile lying on that table, dying, instead of Adam Davidson.

"Yeah, but karma . . . she can be an interesting creature to anger, and when she comes back around for you . . . watch out." Some satisfaction slipped into Dr. Meyer's melancholy.

"What happened?" Aunt Joyce asked. I got the impression we were starting to get to the meat of what I needed to know.

"Like I said, karma happened. That is, if you believe in that kind of thing. Not three months later, Elizabeth got herself good and drunk and hopped behind the wheel of her brand-new car. This time, Thomas followed, chasing after his granddaughter. And this time, it wasn't another car she hit, but an unyielding tree. Thomas witnessed the whole thing. Keep in mind, we didn't have cell phones back then, and from what I understand, the accident happened out in the country somewhere. Thomas pulled Elizabeth from that wreck, laid her in the back seat of his car, and drove her here."

"Was she still alive?" Aunt Joyce asked, her voice a little breathy.

"She was. I was on that night as a first-year resident." Dr. Meyer sounded grim. "So was Ben."

"Well, shit," I whispered, momentarily afraid Dr. Meyer and Aunt Joyce had heard me. Thankfully, I'd spoken quietly enough that only Tyson's eyebrows rose.

"Ben was the senior ER doctor on staff that night. I was stitching people up and setting broken arms and legs while he handled the really tough stuff. Long story short, Elizabeth didn't make it."

Aunt Joyce was silent for a beat before she too asked, "Do you think . . ." She hesitated.

"Do I think Ben didn't do all he could to save her?" Dr. Meyer answered Aunt Joyce's unasked question. "I have no idea. No one did. The nurses working with him didn't contradict what he said, but it was a fog that lingered over Ben's head." Dr. Meyer sounded distant again, his voice clouded and sorrow-filled. "Some say that's why Ben did it, why he ended his own life a few months later."

My head snapped back as if physically slapped. My arms crossed, hiding already covered scars and tattoos. I wanted to bury my head in the sand somewhere. Hunched in on myself, I missed Tyson's move. His hands on my shoulders pulled me from my inner self-loathing. Staring into his concerned brown eyes, I offered a weak smile. Tyson's quirked brow told me that he didn't buy it. I gave his fingers a squeeze of reassurance I didn't feel.

When she finally spoke again, Aunt Joyce's voice was whisper soft, "Dr. Davidson killed himself?"

"He did." There was a lot of regret and anger in those two words. "It was a damn shame. Ben was a good doctor. He helped a lot of people, and the world was a worse place without him. Rumors can be nasty things."

No one was more aware of that fact than me.

"The rumor at the time was that Ben didn't do everything he could to save Elizabeth, that he let her die. I don't know if that's true or not. What little I knew of Dr. Davidson, I don't think it was. Personally, I think it was the grief over the loss of his son. Regardless, Elizabeth's actions not only cost her life but the life of a promising young man and, eventually, his father. It was a waste of life all around."

Silence surrounded us, the sounds of a busy hospital background noise. A couple more staff members dressed in scrubs swung by, grabbing a piece or two of cake, looking dubiously at the small portions and the even smaller glasses of punch. Dr. Meyer murmured words of gratitude. If pressed, I couldn't have recalled what he said.

"And what of Mr. Birkingham?" Aunt Joyce finally asked when they were alone again.

"Thomas? I'm not entirely sure. At the time of Dr. Davidson's death, Thomas was gearing up for a lawsuit against Ben and the hospital. Talk of that fizzled out after Ben's death. It was yet another rumor, that the fear of a lawsuit was why Ben put that gun to his temple and pulled the trigger." Dr. Meyer's tone sounded dubious.

"But you don't buy that either?" my aunt asked.

"I suppose it could have been, but doctors get sued. It's become part of the job. I have a hard time thinking that was the tipping point."

The tipping point. What had been Ben Davidson's tipping point? I knew what mine had been, the first time at least. I'd stared into that mirror in my aunt and uncle's spare bathroom and found my mother staring back. Only it wasn't my mom, it was an illusion, one that I found inescapable. It was worse seeing her reflected in me. I'd reached for those sheers, chopped off my hair, and then hacked into my wrists. If Cecile hadn't found me, bleeding out on the floor . . .

Aunt Joyce's question interrupted the swirling thoughts and guilt threatening to pull me back under. "Did Thomas pass on after the loss of his granddaughter?"

Dr. Meyer was quiet, and I got the feeling he was thinking. "I don't remember exactly when, but if memory serves, it wasn't too long after we lost Ben. I think he died at home, but I might be wrong. I didn't pay a lot of attention to the goings-on of Thomas Birkingham. By that time, I was into my first year of residency, and being the doctor with the least seniority is exhausting work." Dr. Meyer's voice lightened, as if his residency was a much fonder memory than Dr. Ben Davidson's death.

Clearing her throat, Aunt Joyce said, "That's some very sad history. It's not . . . I suppose it's not what I was expecting when I asked you about Thomas. I'm sorry. I didn't mean to drag up so many bad memories. Today's supposed to be a day of celebration, not . . ."

Aunt Joyce's voice faded off, mixing with the background noise. I thought I knew how she felt. Naively, I'd thought whoever Beth had been was someone innocent, someone who had died due to negligence or malpractice. And maybe one of those two things was true, but one thing certainly wasn't—Elizabeth "Beth" Birkingham was no innocent bystander.

"It's all right, Joyce. You didn't know. And yes, it is very sad history," Dr. Meyer agreed. "I haven't thought of Ben in . . . Oh, I can't really remember the last time, but he was a good man. You don't always find that combination—being a good person and a good doctor. Push comes to shove, when you're ill, you'll take a good doctor over a good human being any day of the week. It's nice when you don't have to choose and get both. Dr. Ben Davidson was the whole package."

"Kind of like you," Aunt Joyce said fondly.

Dr. Meyer stuttered. "Well . . . I suppose that's nice to hear. I'll let my wife know you think so the next time I'm in the doghouse. Thank you, Joyce."

"I'm happy to say it anytime." Aunt Joyce cleared her throat before raising her voice a little higher. "Leah, I'm sorry to interrupt. I know you haven't seen Tyson for a while, and it's probably good catching up, but we probably need to get Cecile's things so you can get them to her. Besides, we might be slower today, but I think I've loafed over here enough. If I don't get back to work soon, they'll hunt me down."

"We wouldn't want that." I turned in time to see Dr. Meyer give my aunt a one-arm hug. Then he said, "If something happens to me and I find myself lying on the bed instead of hovering over it, you better be here to take care of me." Given Dr. Meyer's age, the request held far more weight than most.

"If I'm not working, I'll tell them to call me in, just so I can be there to harass you into feeling better."

Dr. Meyer chuckled, his smile wide, deepening the wrinkles on his face. "I'll hold you to that."

"I better get back to it too," Tyson said, reaching around me and snagging a couple more pieces of cake. With a wink, he added, "See ya later, Leah. It was good catching up with you. It's always interesting." Tyson gave an odd type of salute, one of the tiny pieces of cake almost flying off the plate. If I still lived at my old apartment, no doubt Tyson would pound on my door tonight wanting an explanation. It was yet another reason to be glad I didn't live in Maple Valley Apartments anymore.

Aunt Joyce and I headed for the break room with a couple of final goodbyes. Opening her locker, Aunt Joyce lifted out the same floral duffel she'd handed me weeks ago. I had no idea what was in it, probably just some random stuff Cecile had thrown in earlier to make it look realistic.

"Murderers! You killed her. You killed my Beth."

I cringed, slamming my eyes shut as if that would close off Thomas's rants.

"He's here, isn't he?" Aunt Joyce's gaze darted around the room, looking a little wild. Just like Dave, she could no more see or hear Thomas than almost every other human on the planet. That didn't stop her from trying.

"Close, but not in this room." I blew out a deep breath. "I'm normally better at covering when I see or hear them, but Thomas is . . ."

"Loud?"

"Very."

"Hmm . . ." Aunt Joyce cocked her head to the side, hands on her hips. "What do you make of Dr. Meyer's story?"

Hugging Cecile's bag to my chest, I hung my head. "I'm not sure. It's not what I expected."

"Me either. Although, I'm not exactly sure what I did expect." Aunt Joyce's fingers lightly skimmed my coat, pulling at the edges and drawing my face up from the floor. "Are you okay? That couldn't have been easy for you to hear, and I'm sure it hit closer to home than you would have liked. I know it did for me."

Twisting the fabric of Cecile's bag in my fingers, I wasn't sure what to say. Finally, I settled on, "That could have been me. Well, not the whole doctor part and all, just—"

"You can be anything you want, Leah. But yes, that could have been you. Different circumstances, same outcome." Shifting closer, Aunt Joyce cupped my chin in her hands. Tiny puffs of air left my lips as Aunt Joyce's face swam in front of my tear-filled eyes. "I am so very thankful it wasn't you. I know I haven't always been as supportive as I should have been, as understanding . . . but one thing I was always grateful for was your survival. Never ever doubt that, Leah. No matter what went on in our past, I never wanted you gone, not like that. I hated seeing you in that much pain, unable to reach you no matter how hard we tried."

I managed a smile, tiny as it might have been. "I know," I softly answered. "I've always known that, Aunt Joyce."

"Good." Pulling me into a tight embrace, Cecile's bag trapped between us, I let Aunt Joyce hug me. It was the kind of hug I'd always wanted from her. It was the kind of hug I missed, the kind my mom would have given me. Maybe it wasn't as good as Mom's would have been, but it was a close second.

Pulling away, Aunt Joyce's eyes were a little shiny too. "You better get going if you're going to get to work on time." Rubbing a finger under one of her eyes, Aunt Joyce turned away from me. We were doing better, but it was still awkward, seeing each other not at our emotional best.

"Ah . . . the irony in that. All those times I got there super early, working for free, and today I might be late."

Aunt Joyce gave a strained chuckle. "Tell Gary it was my fault for keeping you."

"Sure thing," I easily lied. I'd never tell Gary that.

Saying a quick goodbye, I headed to the hall and toward the exit. Thomas must have moved on quickly because I didn't hear or see him anywhere. I did see Tyson again, shoving a piece of cake into his mouth. He'd been smart and stacked a couple more on his plate. We gave each other head nods, and I threw in an extra wave as I darted into the main lobby, ignoring a woman with a horrid-sounding cough waiting in line, the tall figure of a man's spirit hovering nearby. The spirit was blabbering nonsense while his hands kept slapping onto his head, pulling at his spiritual hair. I had no idea what had happened, why this man's spirit seemed stuck in that horrid existence. At that moment, I didn't want to know. Between Thomas Birkingham and Dave's mom, my spiritual plate was currently full.

15

Lenny and I didn't share a shift at work today. Chrissie was at work while Lilly was in school. From what I understood, Lenny was going to go over to the house so he could be there when Lilly got off the bus. It was a new routine for her, and there was also the worry about Mark. Chrissie said she hoped to be home by that time too, but Lenny was back up just in case. Chrissie had also notified the school that Mark was in the picture again and under no circumstances was he allowed to pick up Lilly or contact her in any way.

While restocking Christmas lights, I thought over a conversation Chrissie and I'd had earlier in the morning. Unfortunately, Chrissie had never sought sole custody of Lilly. It wasn't legal. Mark had up and left, and she'd thought he was gone for good. Out of all the concerns she'd had for Lilly, she'd missed the very human threat Lilly's biological father posed. Chrissie was doing a bang-up job beating herself up about it now. Dave had put her in contact with the lawyer he was using to help him get custody of Marshall.

"Christmas time again. Back in my day, this wasn't a thing at all."

My body hunched inward, muscles tightening. I hadn't had the misfortune of hearing Elijah's condescending voice in weeks. I hadn't missed it. Turning ever so slightly, I quickly scanned the aisle, noting we were alone. "Elijah. To what do I owe the displeasure of your visit?" I continued restocking the shelves. I didn't like having Elijah at my back but couldn't bring myself to give him the attention he so desperately desired.

From his low humming, I could tell Elijah wasn't standing still. Meandering back and forth, he finally came up beside me, picking up a package of LED multicolored lights and turning it over in his hands. "I can't say that I see the appeal, but the living spend money and time on all kinds of things that I don't understand."

Thanksgiving was still a couple weeks away. We'd had Christmas decorations out before Halloween was over. I'd never decorated much. I'd been rethinking that since I lived in an actual house now. Plus, there was Lilly to think about. Then again, I wasn't even sure if Chrissie and Lilly celebrated Christmas. I put that thought in the very back of my mind, further crowding an ever-growing to-do list.

"Always so much on your mind, Leah." Elijah scooted closer, annoyed I was ignoring him.

I took a couple of steps farther away and tried not to let it bother me when Elijah smirked triumphantly.

Annoyed, I asked again, "Is there something you actually need or are you just bored?"

Elijah shrugged. He wasn't wearing a coat, despite the forty-degree weather outside. I hadn't expected him to. With his long-sleeved, dark gray shirt and dark blue, almost black jeans on, Elijah's pale skin and white-blond hair shone brightly. His blue eyes glimmered behind his blond lashes.

Those eyes should have been beautiful, and I suppose, in their own devious way, they were. "I suppose a bit of both," Elijah dramatically sighed. "It is painfully boring, now that Justin and Hannah are gone."

Hannah had been Liam's murderous mother. She'd hoped to add me to that list. Isaac's quick thinking and Bobby's sacrifice had saved my life. I wasn't the least bit sorry she was gone. I was even less sorry Justin had been reaped. "Forgive me if I don't join in on your little pity party." Rolling my eyes, I got back to work.

"That's okay." Elijah leaned against the wall of lights. "There's a bright spot on the horizon." Leaning farther in than I was comfortable with, Elijah whispered, "I can feel it."

Panic shot through my soul, flashing down my spine and pulling me up taught. Spinning around, I took two steps back and stupidly asked, "What are you talking about?"

Elijah's smile was instantaneous and wide enough to show his pearly whites. "Oh, wouldn't you like to know?" Stuffing his hands into his pockets, Elijah danced back, grinning from ear to ear.

"Eli, what are you doing here?"

Even when I'd first met her, I hadn't liked Lizzie's voice. I still didn't, but for maybe the first time in my life, I was relieved to hear it. Lizzie Johnson wasn't just my management, but Elijah's too. If there was anyone that could kill his buzz, it was her.

"Lizzie." Elijah's smile fell, his lips pulled into a thin, pale line. "We've had this discussion before—only my friends call me Eli."

Lizzie's smile was brittle in its cruelty. "Then you must not hear it often, Eli."

I stood there, a couple boxes of colored lights in my hand. My eyes tracked back and forth, waiting to see who the winner of this outcome would be. I thought I had a pretty good idea, but so far Elijah was holding his own and not backing down.

A grin slowly stealing across his face, Elijah relaxed. "I find it curious that management backed down so quickly where Andrew and Leah are concerned." Elijah shook his head as my pulse skyrocketed. I didn't like Andy's name thrown into their little catfight. "Word is you've gone soft."

Lizzie stilled. Lizzie looked perfectly human to me without a reaper touching me or one of Chrissie's charms hanging around my neck. Elijah's chalky skin, blank face, and tense muscles spoke to something very different. It took a lot to frighten a reaper. Being dead probably made you a little more immune to threats. But whatever he saw on Lizzie's face brought Elijah's fear to the surface.

"Andrew's situation is . . . unique," Lizzie's soft, barely audible words grew in intensity. "And Miss McKnight made her intentions very clear. You are more foolish than I thought to believe there will not be consequences in the long-run—consequences that Leah and Andrew have accepted."

We might have accepted them, but neither Andy nor myself had a clue what they were.

"Now, I believe I know why you're truly here. You are drawn to him just as I am. Be patient, Eli. He will be yours, eventually."

For lack of a better word, Elijah pouted. "I don't like waiting."

"Neither do I." Lizzie shot me a look that sent chills through my core. "But sometimes, that is all we can do. His end will come, and you'll be there, waiting. You won't be the only one to enjoy his screams when you drag him away."

Elijah brightened as I sickened. I wasn't sure who they were talking about. It was probably a customer who'd come in or maybe an employee. Whoever it was, they were destined to be one of Elijah's souls, and no matter what they'd done to deserve their fate, that didn't make hearing about it any more palatable.

Blowing out a deep sigh, Elijah gave me a final grin. "I suppose I best be moving on. Have fun keeping house with Andrew." Elijah laughed, something cold and eerie. "Somehow, I imagine you are getting the shaft in that relationship." Elijah's grin spread into a full smile, his eyes alight with joy. "Then again, maybe not." With that parting, nasty comment, Elijah started humming as he sauntered away.

"Fool," Lizzie softly called after him before she turned her attention on me. "Eli's always so eager. Never any patience with that one." There was an irritatingly fond note in Lizzie's voice, as if she didn't find Elijah nearly as nausea-inducing as me. With an odd wave, Lizzie headed off, a faint, "Better get back to work," echoing over her shoulder.

I stood there, blankly staring at where Lizzie had turned down another aisle, disappearing from view.

"Leah, are you all right?"

I jumped, dropping one of the light boxes in my hands. Ricky stood not two feet away. Irrational as it was, I was annoyed he'd been able to sneak up on me. I'd been so zoned out, no sneaking would have been required.

"I'm fine," I hastened to answer, leaning over and picking up the dropped box.

I must have risen faster than Ricky expected me to because I caught the sneer on his face before he covered it with an overly wide, fake smile. "That's so good to hear. I worry about you. You've had so many difficulties in life, so much trauma. I hate to think of something else happening to you—something worse."

Swallowing hard, my throat ached. "I—" I had no idea what to say.

"Have a good evening, Leah. It's almost closing time, and

this time of year, it will be very dark when you head out to your car. Be careful. You never know who might be lurking about."

The light boxes almost made another unceremonious fall to the floor. Mouth hanging open, I watched Ricky walk away, a jaunty swagger to his gait, fingers tugging at his vest and mercilessly smoothing it down.

Had I just been threatened? Like so many times in life, it wasn't what Ricky said, but how he said it.

Not for the first time, I really wished Isaac would pop up so I could tell him what just happened. I missed my spiritual friend. The sharp reminder of that pain doubled the unease churning in my gut. As usual, it wasn't the dearly departed fucking up my life, but the living.

Clocking out that night, I went to my locker, unease building the acidity in my stomach. I'd started keeping antacids in my purse. I downed one the minute I had that little pill in hand. Checking my phone, I saw I had a missed text from Dave. He and Cecile were free tomorrow morning, and he wanted to know if I was up to going over to his dad's house to see if Cecile and I could figure out what was keeping Charlotte there.

As far as I knew, I was free and had the day off tomorrow. Lilly and Marshall would both be in school, which freed Dave and me in other ways. Typing a quick response that I was on board, I also added a quick note that I was getting ready to leave work and would call Dave when I got home to hammer out the details.

I knew the real reason I wanted to wait until I got home. Dave would be expecting my call, and if he didn't get it, he'd send out the proverbial hounds. Ricky's warning-slash-threat earlier had rattled me. I almost asked another employee if they'd walk out to my car with me but didn't want to give Ricky the satisfaction of knowing just how much he'd gotten to me. Was I being a stupid idiot? Probably. Pride was an idiotic vice, and being a living, breathing human, I still had my stupid share.

Old fears quickened my pace as I set out for my car, pulling my coat tighter against the mid-November winds. As cold as it was, no one would think less of me for hurrying to my car. Shoving the key in the door, I opened it as quick as I could, dropping down into the driver's seat and throwing my purse on the passenger one. Lightning fast, I locked my door before I shoved the key in the ignition. My old Toyota started right up, easing some of my fear. That fear reignited when I pulled out of Handy Helpers' parking lot. The lights of my car landed on a big-ass truck, a big-ass jerk standing beside the driver's side door, a cruel grin on his face as he waved goodbye.

Ricky Levitson was a devious asshole. The question was, just how devious and violent was he?

16

D ave, Cecile, and I arrived at Dean Masters's house a little after nine the next morning. Even more leaves were piled up around the house, blowing here and there. Given how neat and clean the surrounding houses looked, I'd bet Dean's neighbors weren't very fond of him either. The porch looked better, or at least the empty beer bottles were gone.

"You ready?" I asked while Cecile clung to Dave's hand.

"I think maybe we should have called first." Cecile worried her bottom lip. It was the same argument she'd brought up on the way over.

Dave shot her down again. "No. This way, he doesn't have time to build up a lot of steam."

I thought Dave was being a little too optimistic. From what I understood, Dean had lost his job. His wife had left him. His oldest son was now at college in Florida. And his youngest son had been taken away from him. Dean had been forced into rehab—never the best situation, and he'd always hated Dave, at least from Dave's perspective. Given Dean's free time, I figured all he had to do was sit and stew. Regardless of a warning call, Dean Masters was most likely in a good steam about something or other. Chances were good we were all about to get verbally burned. I just hoped we could keep it to words and not physical violence. Personally, I hoped Dean wasn't home. Dave had Marshall's key, and we planned to go in and do what needed to be done no matter what.

Sucking in a deep breath, Dave's chest puffed out as he took two final strides to the door, knocking with pounding efficiency. We waited about thirty seconds, and when no one came, Dave knocked again, louder this time. I was just getting my hopes up that maybe Dean was gone when something heavy skittered across the floor on the other side, followed by a string of curse words.

The door flew open, and my breath caught. Cecile's loud intake of air indicated I wasn't the only one shocked by Dean Masters's appearance. Wearing stained, threadbare sweats and an equally dirty sweatshirt, Dean looked as wrecked as his home. With dirty, thinning blond hair sticking out at all angles and at least a five-day scruff littering his cheeks, Dean smelled just about as bad as he looked. But one smell was absent—alcohol. It appeared as if Dean really was trying to sober up. At least he got a few points for that.

He lost those points when he sneered at Dave. "What in the hell do you want? I don't have any more kids for you to take."

Pushing forward, Dave forced his father back into the house. Cecile and I followed. I closed the door behind us.

"God, you stink." It wasn't the best opening Dave could have gone for. It was, unfortunately, very accurate.

Dean bristled. "Who gives a fuck what I smell like. Not like I was expecting company. Now, what the hell do you want, and why did you bring them with you?" Dean spat *them* like Cecile and I were diseased.

Cecile beat me to laying a calming hand on Dave's arm. Her fingers squeezed down tight, warning him to play nice, at least for a little while. Keeping my hands stuffed into the pockets of my heavy jacket, I stared toward the staircase. Charlotte wasn't there. I hadn't really expected her to be, but still, I looked.

Taking another attempt at a calming breath, Dave ratcheted down the anger. "We came to get the rest of Marshall's things. He's staying with me for the foreseeable future."

Dean let loose a harsh laugh, followed by a heavy coughing fit. "You?" he finally managed through stuttering coughs. "Cindy didn't want him either? Figures. No one wants the little fairy." Dean moved farther into the room, letting his body drop into a nearby chair that had definitely seen better days. The cushions were so stained I couldn't tell what the original color had been.

Cecile and I shared a look behind Dave's back. She'd caught the word too. So had Dave. "*Fairy?* What in the hell's that supposed to mean?"

"Dave," I started to caution. Dave held his hand up, silencing me while we waited for Dean to answer.

"What? He didn't tell you?" Dean snorted something unpleasant before he reached for his pack of cigarettes. Dean lit one up and blew out a heavy dose of smoke.

Cecile and I dropped back.

Dave moved forward.

An orange glow lit up the end of Dean's smoke as he sucked in, blowing out another breath. "Not a huge shocker. He probably didn't want to get kicked out of your place too." Leaning back, Dean used his feet to start rocking, making the loud creak of protesting springs sing through the room.

"Why would I kick Marshall out of my house?" Dave sounded far more reasonable than he should. I knew that cool voice, and it was far more dangerous than when Dave yelled.

Dean rolled his eyes. "He's gay, a homosexual, likes dick. However you want to say it. That's what Marshall is." There was so much spite in Dean's words that I took a step back. Cecile held her ground, but her hands were fisted by her sides. A flush of red crept up her neck and cheeks.

"Cecile, Leah . . . why don't the two of you head up to Marshall's room and start collecting the stuff on his list. My *father* and I need to have a little chat." Dave's tone was still cool, low, and painfully calm. Warning bells slammed through my head.

"Dave, I don't think we—"

"It's okay, Leah," Dave assured me. "I promise, all Dad and I are going to do is have a talk. I won't touch him. I wouldn't want to get contaminated with whatever's festering on his skin right now. We'll be fine."

I wasn't sure I was placated. Cecile went up on her tiptoes and kissed Dave on the cheek. "We'll be right upstairs. Holler if you need us." With that said, Cecile grabbed my wrist, dragging me toward the stairs. Both of us carted the bags and duffels we'd brought with us.

We were halfway up the stairs when Cecile let loose a sharp gasp while her hand clutched the charm around her neck. Before I could ask, Cecile offered, "She's here. I can feel Dave's mom. Or at least I assume it's Charlotte."

It was my turn to pull Cecile along. "Good. Let's see what we can find out and do it as quickly as possible. I don't trust Dave down there alone with his dad." Dave's intentions might not have been to haul off and hit his father, but intentions were only that. Dave wouldn't care one whit about Marshall's sexuality. What he would care about was the toxic filth exiting Dean's mouth—and the fact Marshall had most likely been exposed to that same filth.

Coming up to the second-floor landing, my eyes were immediately drawn to the end of the hall and the locked door. Charlotte wasn't there. She was probably behind it. We'd need to get in somehow. Marshall had given me the key to the padlock protecting his room, but he didn't have the key to the room Charlotte had claimed.

"Marshall's stuff first?" Cecile asked, throwing up a questioning eyebrow.

I nodded in agreement. "Yeah. We'll pack up as much as we can fit into these bags, then see what we can do about Charlotte." Take care of the living first. It was a mantra I'd been telling myself for the past few weeks. One day I might even believe it.

I slid the key into the padlock protecting Marshall's door. I'd half expected it to be open already, what with the way Dean was acting. Maybe he didn't want to go into Marshall's room anymore. Maybe Dean was afraid he'd catch "the gay."

Inside, Marshall's room looked like what I'd kind of expected. The kid might be emotionally damaged, but he was a neat freak. I'd noticed that the few times I'd been around him and in the room he'd claimed at Dave's house. There were a few tossed things here and there from his earlier hasty exit, but not much.

"I'll take the closet, you take the dresser," Cecile directed, and I hurried to comply. Beyond extra clothes, Marshall had asked for some of his knickknacks, along with some pictures of friends he had spread here and there. He'd already snagged the important electronics during his impromptu escape. He'd left behind some older video games, and I planned to throw those in too as long as there was room. Given how sparse Marshall's closet looked, I figured there'd be plenty of space.

I noted a couple of pictures of his brother and mom. Oddly enough, Marshall hadn't mentioned grabbing those. I tucked them inside a bag anyway. Maybe later, when things calmed down, he'd want them.

"How are you doing?" I threw over my shoulder, glancing in Cecile's direction.

"Almost done. There's not as much here as I thought there might be." Cecile was on her knees, tossing shoes into another bag. There'd be a fair amount to lug downstairs, but we could handle it.

"Don't forget to leave room for the bolt cutters." We'd tossed those into one of the bigger duffels, along with a brand-new padlock. With any luck, Dave's dad wouldn't notice the swap. That luck would run out if he tried to open it with the key he had. I wasn't sure how often Dean went into Charlotte's old room. The way Marshall talked, no one had been in there in years.

"I think I'll have room," Cecile assured me.

I wasn't keeping exact track of time but figured we'd been at it less than five minutes when Cecile and I both eyed the room, checking for anything we might have missed. Cecile even got down on her hands and knees again and checked under the bed.

"It's as neat under here as the rest of the place," she said, her blond halo of hair popping up on the other side of the bed.

In silent agreement, we left all the bags on Marshall's bed. I snagged the bolt cutters while Cecile grabbed the fresh padlock.

"You ready to do this?" I asked, the bolt cutters resting on my shoulder.

"Let's go." Cecile headed for the open doorway.

Out in the upper floor hall, we both paused, listening for voices below. I caught Dave's low rumble, his voice too quiet to hear. Cecile and I shared a worried look.

"No screaming." Cecile chewed her bottom lip. "I'm not

sure if that's good or bad."

"Bad," I quickly answered before speed walking to the door at the end of the hall.

Charlotte was still a no-show, at least on this side. "Is she still in there?" I asked Cecile as I raised the bolt cutters to the lock. There was always a chance Charlotte didn't stick to the upper floor.

"She's there." Cecile fingered one of her charms again. "If I'm reading her right, she's really worried. Or maybe upset?" She shook her head in obvious frustration. "Sorry, but those two emotions are really difficult to tell apart."

"Don't apologize. It's more than we had before."

Squeezing down on the bolt cutters didn't get me very far. I didn't have a lot of upper body strength, and for whatever reason, the padlock had been placed high on the door-frame, making me reach above my head.

Seeing my obvious struggle, Cecile jumped in, each of us pushed down on a side and managed to cut through the lock.

"Shit, that was harder than I thought it'd be." I silently lamented the fact Dave was stuck downstairs and not up here with us. He would have had the lock busted open in no time.

Pocketing the broken lock, Cecile reached for the door handle, ready to twist. With a heavy inhale, she squared her shoulders and turned the knob.

Neither of us was sure what we'd find on the other side of the door. Marshall had said the room had once been Charlotte's and that his mom had tried to turn it into a yoga studio. If that were true, it looked like Cindy had given up on the idea pretty quickly because precious little appeared to have been touched.

"It's like a memorial tomb," Cecile whispered.

I gave an absent nod. Overall, the room was small—most likely the smallest bedroom in the house. A long table took up most of one wall, sheaves of different colored and patterned paper stacked up along the edges. The middle of the table held a cutting board and several different-sized, full plastic containers. A tall stool stood in front of the table. There were a couple of larger dresser-like pieces of furniture with shelves along the walls filled with binders.

A fine layer of dust covered everything. Charlotte's spirit stood in front of the single window lighting the room. Its pale pink curtains were just as dust-covered as everything else.

"Wow," Cecile muttered. The old wooden floor creaked as she walked toward the worktable. "This is impressive." Reaching for one of the books, Cecile's breath caught the same moment my heart sped up.

"Yeah, I'd back away if I were you." I shifted closer to Cecile. "Whatever you're doing definitely got Charlotte's attention."

"I can tell." Lowering her arm, Cecile moved closer to me. "I got a spike of fear and what I think was anger. Again, those two emotions can be difficult to tell apart."

Charlotte's spirit didn't look any healthier than the last time I'd seen it. A pink-and-white floral scarf covered her bald head, chemo having taken its bitter toll, stripping Charlotte of the vibrant beauty she'd once held. Rail thin and pasty pale, Charlotte's spirit was a wispy hint of the woman who'd given Dave life.

The one thing that hadn't faded was the deep blue of her eyes, the same color that shone through Dave's. And right now, those oceanic eyes looked focused and pissed. Or, at the very least, guarded.

My eyes tracked toward the wall of colorful binders.

Stretching my arm past Cecile, I made a similar motion while keeping an eye on Charlotte's spirit. Her eyes narrowed, tensing while tracking my movements. Easing my hand back, Charlotte's spirit relaxed but still appeared vigilant.

"Yeah, that seems to be a hot zone." The million-dollar question was why. "I think it's time we ask Charlotte."

Cecile made a humming noise I took as agreement. Sucking in a deep breath, I said, "Charlotte Masters, I'm—"

"Get out!" Charlotte's blue eyes snapped in my direction, her anger clear.

"Whoa." Cecile clung tighter to her charm. "She's really scared."

"Scared?" I stared at Charlotte. "That wouldn't be the emotion I'd go for. She looks and sounds pissed."

"Oh, she's that too, but underlying it is fear. I know I said they can be hard to tell apart, but I'm not wrong." Cecile sounded confident, and I didn't have any reason to doubt her.

"Charlotte," I tried again, "I'm not here to—"

"I said get out!" Her spirit came toward me. Some of the loose papers on the desk shuffled and lifted off the table. "There's nothing here!"

Yeah, I didn't believe that for a second, but Charlotte was too upset and didn't seem inclined to listen to anything I had to say. We weren't getting anywhere, and time was short. "Cecile, I think it's your turn."

Charlotte's riled-up spirit hovered three feet in front of us. The fringe on the spiritual blanket she had draped over her shoulders blew on a spiritually induced breeze.

"Umm . . . are you sure? I mean, I don't know if—"

"And we'll never know unless you try. In the words of your mom, we need a little spiritual Prozac here."

Cecile wheezed in a breath, a less than confident, "Okay," dropping from her lips.

Keeping my eyes on Charlotte, I wasn't sure what to do beyond stand there and watch. Neither Cecile nor I had any idea if she could really influence lingering spirits' emotions the way Isaac thought she could. It made sense, though, and we needed to test it out. I couldn't think of a better time or place. Still, I planned to keep a wary eye on Charlotte. I didn't think she was as violent as Thomas Birkingham's spirit, but it was obvious Charlotte could move things, and she was damn protective of something in this room. If things got too dicey, I planned to haul Cecile's ass out of that room as fast as possible.

But the more I watched Charlotte, the less likely it seemed I'd need to throw Cecile over my shoulder. By slow degrees, Charlotte's spirit calmed, her eyes widening and thin lips plumping. Slightly dazed-looking, Charlotte blinked her wide eyes as the papers on her old workbench settled, fluttering to a stop.

"Cecile?" A small quiver ran through me.

"I . . . yeah, I think I might have this."

I didn't think there was any *might* about it. "I'm not sure what kind of Zen emotions you're exuding, but keep it up."

Cecile's face flushed, and for a hot second, she looked flustered. Gathering her resolve, she said, "I think you can try again."

Later, when we were away from Charlotte, I'd ask Cecile about the blushed fidgeting. Right now, we had a mission. Counting on Cecile to keep doing . . . whatever it was she was doing, I tried again. "Charlotte, I'm Dave's friend, Leah."

Charlotte's head whipped toward me, her blue eyes wide. "Dave? You know my David?"

I'd never heard anyone call Dave by his full name. Charlotte had passed before Bobby and I'd met Dave. Maybe she'd called him by his full name.

Pocketing that tidbit for later, I answered, "I do."

"She likes talking about Dave." Cecile sounded relieved. "Love. Pure and bright. Longing too."

That was far easier to work with than rage. "You raised a wonderful man," I honestly told Charlotte. Only my words saddened her.

Eyes downcast and shoulders hunched, Charlotte clung to the spiritual blanket she had wrapped around her arms. "He's just a boy, not a man. I left him too soon." She looked off and down to the side. "I tried to hold on, but . . ."

I still didn't have a lot of experience with lingering spirits. I'd spent most of my life ignoring them, silently walking by and making no attempt at engagement. My recent forays into conversations with them led me to believe that the passage of time wasn't something a lot of the lingering dead had a good hold on. Charlotte wasn't an exception.

"Charlotte, you passed years ago. Dave's twenty-three." Soon to be twenty-four come January. "He's all grown up and doing really well."

Charlotte's eyes sparkled. "Twenty-three?" Her eyes drifted toward the window. "So much time . . ."

By my count, eighteen years. I had no idea what it was like to think of all the time you'd missed with your child. "He misses you too." Maybe I shouldn't have said it, but I wanted Charlotte to know that she may have left Dave when he was young, but those five years they had together weren't forgotten and had made a huge impact.

Charlotte's smile was wistful. "He was a beautiful boy—so full of energy." A soft, warm laugh lit up the room, and I wished Cecile could hear it. From the smile lifting the edges of her lips, I thought Cecile might be getting the better part of the deal for once.

"He's still got a lot of energy, and he's still beautiful—inside and out," I truthfully answered.

Charlotte's gaze became scrutinizing as she stared me up and down. "Are you his girlfriend?"

"No." It was my turn to laugh. Cecile stared at me, eyebrows raised. "She just asked me if I was Dave's girlfriend."

"Oh." Cecile's face heated, burning crimson.

Charlotte didn't even glance in Cecile's direction when I spoke with her. I'd hoped that maybe she'd be able to see Cecile if I pointed her out, but she couldn't. She'd paid attention to Cecile when she'd gotten close to whatever was in this room that was important to Charlotte. Chances were good that something was the reason she'd stayed.

Oleana had been able to see Chrissie, but she'd haunted her directly. Besides Isaac, Oleana's spirit had been the only one that seemed to understand and want to pass along a parting word. I'd kind of hoped that maybe Charlotte would be similar. If she had been, I would have tried harder to get Dave up here. But Charlotte wouldn't recognize him either. It was a heartbreaking truth.

I may not be Dave's girlfriend, but I was his sister in every way but genetics. "Dave's my best friend, more like a brother, he's . . ." my breath caught, choking on words that could never do Dave justice. "Dave's important to me," I finally settled on. "I wouldn't hurt him for all the world, at least not intentionally. But, Charlotte," I moved in closer, "Dave is hurting. He knows you didn't pass on, and none of us know why. Dave wants you to be at peace."

Charlotte looked devastated, her bright blue eyes awash in a fresh haze of tears. Curling in on herself, she pulled the blanket tighter, cocooning her frail body within. Shaking her head, Charlotte stared at the floor. "That's not . . . it was never my intention . . . I just . . ." Her eyes flashed toward mine, cracked lips parted. "I couldn't go. I didn't have enough time."

"Leah," Cecile's worried voice broke through my screaming thoughts, "she's getting upset again. It's getting harder to keep her calm."

In other words, we needed to get a move on. "Charlotte, what do you mean, 'you didn't have enough time'?" The answer seemed obvious. Charlotte had died young, but if she'd stayed because she didn't want to leave Dave, then it made more sense she'd haunt him, not this room.

Charlotte's eyes flashed toward the row of binders before they snapped back to me. "He can't know. I have to protect Dave." Fear laced Charlotte's words, but so far, Cecile was doing a great job tempering it, keeping Charlotte's spirit sane enough to continue speaking with.

"Charlotte, Dave's an adult now. He can take care of himself. He doesn't need you to do that for him anymore." I tried to keep my tone gentle. As a mother, it was probably difficult for Charlotte to hear that her son didn't need her anymore.

Spirit snapping back, Charlotte floated a little deeper into the room. Her bare toes just skimmed the surface of the wooden floor. "Oh." The word was so softly spoken I had to strain to hear it. "He doesn't live here anymore? With Dean?"

"No, he—" I started to say that Dave had moved out at sixteen but thought that might upset Charlotte. "No, he owns his own home. He bought it because it reminded him of something you might like."

Charlotte's smile was bright.

"He's not dependent on his dad at all. There's nothing Dean can do to hurt him, not anymore." I didn't think that was strictly true, but it was close enough for my purpose. The wash of relief that flowed across Charlotte's face told me I'd said the right thing. Deciding to go for broke, I said, "Whatever it is in this room you're protecting, you don't need to anymore. You've done all you can."

Again, Charlotte's gaze fell on the binders, only this time, it lingered. "I should have destroyed it sooner, before I got too sick. But I didn't want to erase the words." Head hanging, Charlotte's shoulders trembled. "I was selfish, and I put Dave at risk. If Dean had found out, he would have . . ." Charlotte's eyes were pleading pools of blue. "Dean has a temper."

I shoved down the shot of worried fear those words had sent into me. Dave had promised me Dean had never laid a physical hand on him. Words were weapons too—the kind that produced lasting, festering damage. Dave had shared a precious few of those words with me. He tended to generalize his relationship with his father, the specifics lacking.

Swallowing down my flood of emotions, I was suddenly glad Cecile couldn't hear Charlotte. Would she be able to keep up the positive emotional mood if she could? Doubtful. Cecile was emotionally healthier than me, but she was just as protective of Dave as I was, maybe more so. Hearing the worry in Charlotte's voice would definitely rattle Cecile's emotional cage. As it was, she'd probably gleaned enough from my side of the conversation to figure part of the story out. The harsh intakes of breath and wheezed gasps I caught every so often more than proved that.

"Dave's safe now. Dean can't hurt him anymore."

Another sharp intake of breath sounded from Cecile's direction.

Ignoring my cousin, I kept my focus on Charlotte. I hadn't thought we'd get this far, and I wanted to see if we could go the distance. "Charlotte, Dave wants you to rest. He wants you to find peace, and that's not something you'll find here, in this room. Tell me what it is you're guarding, and I'll keep it safe for you."

"I'm trying to let her know just how much we care about Dave." Cecile didn't whisper. She didn't need to.

Whatever mojo Cecile threw Charlotte's way worked.

Toes still barely skimming the floor below, Charlotte moved to the bank of binders. Shifting the spiritual blanket, Charlotte's arm raised, and a finger moved toward a yellow binder. The appendage passed through the binder and left her wrist and arm protruding.

"There," she said. "It's behind here."

I waited until she backed up before I pulled on the yellow binder she'd pointed to. Behind it, innocent in its lavender jacket cover, little white daisies splashed throughout, was a smaller book that looked like a journal.

Pulling the book down, its thin body was stuffed with envelopes, letters, and pictures—all peeking around the edges of the book. I started to open it but stopped. Staring up at Charlotte, I asked, "Do you want me to look?"

Her lips pursed. "You can. Dave should see it too. There's information in there that he . . ." Charlotte drew in a deep breath, something her spiritual body no longer needed. "I hope this doesn't change how he feels about me, but Dave should know." Charlotte gave a decisive nod, as if she'd finally convinced herself of this truth.

Clutching the book against my chest, I made sure to keep it tight enough that none of the loose pieces fell out. I didn't want to leave anything behind.

Finally breaking my attention from Charlotte, I stared at Cecile, her eyes wide and focused on the lavender-colored book in my arms. "I think we have what we came for," I told Cecile.

"Then . . ." Cecile's raised eyebrows looked expectant. Hopeful too.

"It's worth a try." Attention back on Charlotte, I said, "I'll give this to Dave. He loves you, and Dave's not the kind of person to abandon that love, no matter what these pages contain."

I didn't know if the hope I saw shimmering in Charlotte's

eyes was of her own making or a reflection of Cecile. Either way, it was a positive sign.

"It's time to rest, Charlotte. I've got it from here."

Andy's warmth was second nature to me now, something so familiar that I hardly registered its tantalizing beginnings. That warmth grew, spreading through my chest and warming my belly. The soft squeeze of unused hinges announced Andy's presence into the room. Turning slightly, I let the sight of Andy wash over me. My lips curved into a smile, whatever tension I'd been carrying melted away when our eyes connected, and I saw my feelings reflected back at me.

"Charlotte Masters," Andy's reaper voice slithered down my spine, sticking like warm honey. "Are you ready to pass on?"

Dave's larger frame filled the doorway before he pushed inside, those blue eyes so similar to the ones I'd been staring into for the last few minutes, a mixture of desperation and hope.

Charlotte didn't even glance in Dave's direction. Her attention was all for the reaper who'd come to claim her. And just like Sarah Nichols, Charlotte's gaze fell lower than it should have, staring down at something or someone I couldn't see. Her hushed, "David. Is that you?" Cracked my heart wide open and drew a gasped breath from my throat.

"It's time to rest," Andy cajoled.

"Leah?" Dave's long strides ate up the short distance between the doorway and Cecile and me. "What's going on? Is she—"

"She's passing now," I told Dave. I reached out and grasped hold of the hand Cecile wasn't clinging to.

"It's okay, Dave," Cecile's voice sounded far away. "She's happy." Cecile sniffled. "So very happy."

"Where? Where is she?"

"Just a foot or two in front of Andy. She's fading."

Charlotte's spirit looked like spun gold, shimmering and glistening—brighter toward its center. Her form faded, that beautiful gold color burning hotter and brighter until I could no longer watch. The intensity burned my eyes, and I slammed my lids closed.

The warmth of Andy's fingers wrapped around my wrists pulled my damp hands from my covered eyes. Blinking rapidly, emerald-green met my vision, little spots of gold dancing around their edges. The scar running through Andy's eyebrow pinched with his narrowed brows. "She's gone, Leah."

Andy's arms drew me in, encircling me in his warmth as Cecile did the same with Dave. Small gasps filtered through Dave's lips. I could count on one hand the number of times I'd seen Dave cry over the years, all of them connected to me somehow. Twisting my head against Andy's chest, my gaze fell on Dave's shaking shoulders, his body hunched and folded into Cecile's arms.

Quiet, muffled sobs met my ears. Cecile's murmured words were too soft for me to make out. Seconds passed into a minute, maybe two before Dave pulled away, rubbing his red, tear-stained eyes. Clearing his throat, Dave took a couple of seconds to let his eyes survey the room before he said, "We better get out of here." Taking a moment to clear his throat, Dave backed away from Cecile but still kept their fingers linked. "I, uh . . . I'm not sure how long the reaper whammy lasts, but Dad will probably come out of it soon."

"Dave's right," Andy agreed.

It was still weird to me how much better Dave and Andy got along. I waved them off. "It'll kick back in the moment Dean sees you again."

Andy shrugged while Cecile backed me up. "True, but I'd still like to get out of here. That is, if you're ready, Dave."

Dave glanced around again. "She's gone. Right?"

"Your mother has been reaped, Dave." Andy kept the words politely neutral.

Dave squeezed Cecile's fingers tighter. "Will she come back? Like Bobby?"

I stiffened. I hadn't considered that. I should have and felt like an idiot all over again.

"I don't know, Dave. I'm sorry." Andy sounded truly apologetic.

The small book in my arms dug into my skin as I tugged it even closer. "I can't be sure, but I don't think she'll wind up like Bobby. Guilt and regret," I reiterated. "Before she passed, I think Charlotte was relieved of those two things."

"I agree," Cecile thankfully chimed in. "I could feel her emotions, and all I felt was joy. Charlotte was happy when she passed. I'm not sure what she saw, but—"

"Dave," Andy and I answered at the same time. Looking down at me, Andy raised his eyebrows and nudged his head in Dave's direction. Taking that as my cue, I added, "She saw you, Dave. Only, I think what she saw was you as a child, not . . ." I waved a hand in Dave's direction, indicating his fully grown status. "And she called you David."

Choking on a gasped breath, Dave rubbed his forehead, the ghost of a smile hinting across his lips. "She used to call me that. Dad hated it. I have no idea why, but it pissed him off. She'd only call me that when we were alone."

"What the fuck is taking you so damn long?" Dean Masters's gruff, anger-filled voice drifted up the stairs, contaminating Charlotte's sanctuary.

"That didn't take long," Dave grumbled.

"And that's our cue to go." Holding up the stuffed lavender book, I looked to Dave and said, "Besides, we got what we came for."

17

We headed back to my house. It still felt weird thinking of it that way. I still called it Rose's house most of the time—mentally and verbally. Removing some of the wallpaper and moving in different furniture helped, but the vibe still felt like Rose. All in all, there were far worse vibes my home could carry, and it didn't upset me.

We left Marshall's stuffed bags and duffels in Dave's Jeep. I led the way to the front door, and Phoenix came running when I turned the key. Her small, fluffy white body slid across the hardwood floor, slamming into a wall. Completely unaffected, she scurried over to me, clawing up my leg.

"Hey. Ow." Bending over, I pried her claws out of my jeans, cradling her in my arms. She was so tiny that sometimes I was afraid I'd hurt her. But kittens were nothing short of resilient. Loud purrs filled the hallway.

"Damn, she's loud," Dave groused but scratched behind Phoenix's ears, ratcheting up her purrs another octave.

As far as I was concerned, Phoenix could purr all day long. I'd missed the sound. Ashes's purrs were always soothing. Those last few weeks of her life, her purr had diminished to an echo of its past glory.

"She's so cute." Cecile snatched Phoenix out of my hands, getting her fill of fluffy cuteness. "When's she coming into the clinic?"

"I'm not sure. I haven't made the appointment yet." I took off my coat and hung it on a nearby hook Chrissie had installed. What I didn't say, what I couldn't put into words, was that I just couldn't make the call.

Phoenix's purr ratcheted up yet another notch, leaning into Cecile's fingers as she continued scratching my kitten's face. I stood there, staring at the sugary sweet picture the two of them made, wishing it stirred my heart more. I wanted to love this kitten, wanted to care for her with the same depth I'd cherished Ashes, but something held me back. Some undefined emotion that felt similar to guilt and yet didn't one hundred percent deserve that moniker. It was confusing and made me feel even guiltier that I couldn't connect with her the way Phoenix deserved.

Unaware of my inner turmoil, Cecile beamed, her baby blues lighting up. "I can't wait for Dr. Anderson to meet her. She's been worried since . . ." Cecile didn't need to finish. We all knew what *since* she was talking about.

Charlotte's lavender book still in hand, I pushed down my internal turmoil and gave Cecile an understanding smile before I followed Dave farther into the house. I found him sitting on the couch, elbows on his knees and leaning forward heavily. Andy had been called away soon after we'd left Dave's childhood home. I didn't know when he'd be back. That was part and parcel of dating a reaper.

I left the seat beside Dave open for Cecile, opting for the floral chair we'd salvaged from my apartment. It didn't seem to mind my weight as much as it did Dave's. Lilly had taken to the chair as well. She liked the fact it swiveled and rocked. Her small body wasn't enough to tax it too much.

Dave sat there, silently staring at his feet while Cecile rubbed comforting circles on his shoulder. Sharing a worried look over the top of Dave's bent head, Cecile finally cleared her throat. "Are you all right? Is there anything I can do?"

Dave's garbled laugh frightened Phoenix, and she skittered out of Cecile's arms, dashing down the hall and into Lilly's bedroom.

"Dave—"

"She's gone. She's really gone." Dave ran the palms of his hands over his head, his short hairs bristling with the action. "Christ, I didn't think it would happen that fast."

Truth be told, I hadn't either, and I said as much. "I don't think it would have without Cecile."

Cecile's head shot up, eyes wide. "I didn't do much. I just—"

"She wouldn't let me finish a sentence before you hit her with your emotional Zen bomb, Cecile. It would have been like talking to Eliza Morgan all over again, and we didn't have that kind of time." It had taken more than a few rounds of *conversation* between Eliza and me, and weeding through her jealous anger had been excruciating and time-consuming.

"I . . ." Cecile sputtered, her cheeks pinking. "I think that's overstating things."

"It's not," I argued, "but that's beside the point. Thankfully, Charlotte told us what was so important, or at least pointed us in the right direction." Holding up the lavender book, I asked Dave, "Does this look familiar to you?"

Dave shook his head while holding out his hand. "No, but that's not saying much. Mom had a lot of books and binders, especially in that room. My memories are vague, but they aren't bad. Mom was happy there."

The book made an odd creaking sound as Dave opened the cover, large and small pieces of paper, envelopes, and pictures shifted, desperate to be free.

"I doubt anyone's opened it since your mom died," Cecile said as her nimble fingers rescued a photo that slid free. Face scrunched, Cecile looked at the photo in her hand, flipping it over. From my vantage, I could see the back was clear, not a name or date to label it. "Do you know who this is?" Cecile handed the photo to Dave.

With his mom's book open on his lap, Dave snatched the photo from Cecile's hand, its edges slightly yellowed. Dave's eyes narrowed, lips twisting. "Not a clue. No one in my family has ever been in the military, at least not as far as I know." Dave flipped the photo over, much like Cecile had, its blank back no more illuminating this time.

Dave handed the photo to me. I had no more clue than he did, but looking at the face in the photo, there was no denying this guy had to be some kind of relative. He looked too much like Dave not to be.

"Are you sure your mom didn't have a brother, or maybe a cousin in the military?" I asked as I handed the photo back to Cecile.

"No, not one hundred percent positive, but if so, I've never heard of them." Dave shuffled through some more loose items tucked inside the book, handing them to Cecile to start going through while he skimmed the bound pages.

"Shit." I'd never heard that curse word sound so mournful. "It's her writing." Dave's fingers lightly traced the neat scroll on the page. "It's been a long time, but I'd recognize her style anywhere." A drop of liquid fell on the open page, and Dave quickly brushed the tear away.

Cecile wrapped her arm around Dave's shoulders, tucking him in a little closer. Quietly we sat there, allowing Dave time to absorb and process the flood of memories assaulting his senses. Sucking in a deep breath, Dave's chest expanded before collapsing back down, shoulders slumped. "Whatever's in here, it's important, or was important to my mom."

Reaching across the small living room space, Cecile handed me the loose papers she'd been holding onto so she could focus more on Dave, reading over his shoulder. I got to work sorting through the mismatched items. As I was sorting, a narrow strip of photos slid free. It was one of those strips the photo booth spat out at you. I held it up, twisting it in the light, swallowing hard. Unless Charlotte had been into incest, that man in the photo wasn't Dave's uncle or cousin.

"Um . . . Dave . . ."

"What is it?" Dave's head snapped up, the whites of his eyes bloodshot and lids rimmed in red.

I opened my mouth, words nowhere near at the ready. Pursing my lips, I handed the photo strip over. Cecile's gaze connected with mine, her baby blues full of legitimate concern.

"What the hell?" Dave's eyes quickly skimmed the strip, seeing the same thing I'd seen—Dave's mom locking lips with the guy from the earlier photo. "Who the hell is this?"

Mind tumbling, a nagging tingling pulled at the back of my brain. It was uncomfortable but persistent, demanding attention and refusing to be pushed aside.

Scrambling through the stack of loose papers and envelopes in my lap, I scanned for names and addresses. I found both. "Christopher Monahan. Does that name ring any bells?"

"Not a damn one." Dave sounded perplexed.

"How about Chris?" Cecile asked while pointing to something I couldn't see written within Charlotte's notebook. "I've seen that name a couple of times now. It's probably the same guy."

Dave looked from Cecile to me, confusion clearly written across his watery eyes. My world tilted, wobbling on its already shaky axis. Dave wasn't supposed to look like that. Dave was the strong one, the one person in my life that didn't waver, that never faltered. Dave wasn't having a breakdown, but he was off-kilter. I knew the feeling and hated that his foundation had been shaken.

"I have no idea." Dave's voice was as shaky as the rest of him. Looking back down at the stream of pictures pinched between his fingers, Dave's voice was whisper-soft when he said, "Mom's young here. Her hair's about the same style and length as in my baby pictures. She's so . . . happy." Dave's eyes went distant. "I sort of remember her this happy, or maybe it's just pictures of when I was a baby that I remember, not the actual experience itself. Mostly though, I remember her like she was right before . . . that fucking cancer stole more than her life." Dave growled at the end.

Dave snatched the larger photo out of Cecile's hands, the one with this mystery man dressed in military garb. I didn't know my military uniforms well enough to know which branch he belonged to. Thumb running over the guy's face, Dave said, "He does kind of look like me, doesn't he?"

Cecile and I shared a look, both our eyebrows arched high. This guy more than *kind of* looked like Dave.

"Let's read some of these letters," I offered, trying to break the growing tension. "I'll dig into these while you two start reading Charlotte's . . ." I wasn't really sure what this book was.

"Journal. Or maybe diary." Cecile helpfully answered. "At least that's what I think it is. I haven't gotten the chance to get very far into it yet."

A journal or diary made the most sense. "Right. You two read that, and I'll sift through what I've got." I held up the thin stack of papers as if they hadn't already seen them.

Plan in place, quiet descended. Time slipped by with only the sound of shuffling pages and shifting paper to mark its passing. It didn't take me long to figure out what I held in my hands. Love letters. Their dates were brief, all of them containing an April date. There was one exception, the last letter, dated May 3. That's where they ended.

My cheeks flushed as I read through the letters—pieces of well-worn papers, fragile, their creases had been opened and closed numerous times. It was obvious Charlotte had read them. Repeatedly. What was also obvious was the deep love and affection this Christopher person had for Charlotte. There were several comments about the brevity of their interaction, the time they'd had together, and yet that time was seen as precious.

"Shit," Dave's whispered curse echoed into the silence, a wealth of feeling packed within that singular word. "Shit, shit, shit." Dave rarely strung the word together like that.

Cecile's added, "Oh my god," got me off my feet, rounding the couch so I could stare over their shoulders, reading what they'd found.

I skimmed Charlotte's words, re-reading them to verify what my gut had already suspected. My hands gripped Dave's shoulders, squeezing down tight. The words on the page were heartbreaking. I'd always thought my life was tragic. Charlotte's journal reminded me I didn't have the market cornered on family drama and trauma.

Charlotte's journal slipped from Dave's legs and hit the floor with a soft thud. Dave just sat there, staring at his knees, where the book should be. His breathing was labored —harsh and uneven.

"Dave?" Cecile's barely audible cadence drifted through the air, worry clearly lacing its edges. "Dave, talk to me."

Dave's answer was an incomprehensible grunt.

Quickly moving around the couch, I knelt down, grabbed

Charlotte's journal, and tossed it onto the nearby chair. Grabbing the coffee table, I pulled it over and plopped down in front of Dave. Cecile's scared eyes caught mine, her arms tightly wrapped around her boyfriend and hugging him as tightly as she could. Leaning forward, I grabbed Dave's hands and squeezed them within my own.

For the past six years, Dave had been the one holding me together. If mental duct tape was a thing, then Dave would have been wise to buy stock in it. He'd used enough on me to fund a Caribbean compound. Now it was my turn. I just hoped all my stuck-together pieces would hold long enough to be there when Dave needed me.

"Dave, I need you to look at me. Now."

Dave's head slowly came up, his blue eyes distant with hurt.

All those times I teetered on the edge of mental abyss. Was this what Dave had been forced to see with me? Was this the same kind of hell I'd pushed on him? If so, I owed Dave far more than I thought, and I was already in such a deep hole of indebtedness I'd never climb my way free.

Swallowing down my own pain, I sat up a little taller, forcing my body into a confidence I didn't feel. Breathing in deeply, I said, "This sucks. I know it does. But you need to process it, and to do that, you need to use words Cecile and I can understand. We can't help you if you don't speak with us."

Dave had told me that countless times. It felt weird throwing it back at him.

"It's okay, Dave," Cecile sounded surer than me.

I didn't exactly agree with Cecile. This wasn't okay, but it would be. We'd make it okay.

Dave's disbelieving grunt let me know he agreed with me more than Cecile. "How is this okay?" Reaching down, Dave grabbed his mother's journal, snapping it closed and tossing it at Cecile. "She lied. She lied to me and my fa—" Dave choked, body jerking back as if he'd been punched in the gut.

"She did," I agreed, settling back on the hard surface of the coffee table. It was kind of like sitting on the chairs in the Covetous Police Station. "But she had her reasons, and those reasons don't erase how much she loved you." I pointed at the book in Cecile's hands. "Your mother didn't follow her reaper. She chose to stay to protect that book so that she could protect you. Don't go twisting this into something ugly, something that changes the way you feel about your mom."

Dave blinked, eyes flaring wide with disbelief. "How can you sit there and say that? She lied. She—"

"And I'm not debating that. What I'm saying is that she had her reasons." I thought of Rose and Isaac, of all the choices Rose had had to make to secure a future for her and Melody. I'm sure those choices hadn't been easy, and there were probably more than a few she regretted. Inhaling, I allowed the air to fill my lungs, counting to five before releasing it. "We all read her words, the pain her decision carried. It's obvious she loved your father—your real father."

I let those words sink in, giving Dave time to ruminate on them.

After a few seconds, Dave stubbornly said, "But she was already involved with my . . . with Dean when she shacked up with Chris."

Cecile and I cringed at the caustic accusation. Cecile jumped in first to defend Charlotte. "But they weren't married yet. Charlotte didn't mean to cheat on your . . . on Dean." We were all struggling. Dean Masters wasn't Dave's biological father. But ten minutes of knowledge didn't negate twenty-four years of fatherhood. "She was on vacation with friends, and Christopher was on leave. They . . ."

Cecile looked to me for help, but I didn't know how to

give it. I knew what she was going for, what road her mind had taken. It was the same path mine had wandered down. The affair wasn't intentional, but it had happened, and if Chris hadn't . . . my brain cut off. Some days, there was only so much tragedy your thoughts could contain.

"They fucked like bunnies," Dave crassly picked up the threads of conversation. "And *viola*—" Dave leaned back, running his hands up and down his torso—"here I am."

I loved Dave, but his attitude was starting to piss me off. "Yes, here you are, and I'm damn grateful for that fact. I don't give a damn who your father is, Dave. All I care about is the man sitting before me. The man that pulled me out of the gutter more times than I had a right to expect. The man who has my back no matter what. The man who's loyal to a fault. The man who doesn't give a shit if his brother is gay, bi, or whatever else. The man who loves my cousin and treats her like the capable woman she is. The man who is my best friend. And if that," I pointed at the picture in Cecile's lap, "is the genetic donor that made all that possible, then I'm going to find his grave, fall down on my knees, and thank every star I can find that he hooked up with your mother, if only for a few, short, precious days."

Dave's shocked look would have been priceless if it hadn't been so haunting. Leaning back into the couch cushions, Cecile's arms no longer wrapped around him but gripping his hands within her own, Dave's blank eyes stared back at me. His next words filled me in on the real source of his grief. "He's dead. He died before I was born, before Mom even knew she was pregnant."

And that was the true tragedy of this whole, fucked-up situation. A little over a month into his deployment in the Middle East, Dave's biological father had been killed in the line of duty. There weren't a lot of specifics in Charlotte's notes. Only that final piece of mail, the one dated in May that wasn't from Christopher Monahan, but a friend he was serving with—a friend who'd taken the time to notify Charlotte.

Dave's biological father was dead. He was a man, a haunting figure from Dave's unknown past. He'd been in Charlotte's life a brief time, but it had been long enough.

Eyes fixed on the aged lavender cover of Charlotte's journal, Dave's fingers ghosted over it. "I'm the reason she married that asshole." Dave sounded one part furious, two parts guilty.

Cecile took up the conversation reigns. "I suppose, in a way, that's true. But that was Charlotte's decision, Dave, not yours. Don't blame yourself. Not for that."

"She's right, and you know it. You'd tell either one of us the same thing. I can't say if Charlotte was in love with Chris when you were conceived or if love came later. From what I can tell on Chris's end, it was certainly love he felt for Charlotte. You might have been a surprise child, but you weren't an unwanted one, Dave. Your mom loved you. If there had been any doubt regarding the depths of her affection, they were erased the moment I learned why she hadn't followed her reaper."

Thinking of that, I reached for Charlotte's journal, stuffing the papers and pictures back inside. "She couldn't bear to lose this, to destroy it, but it was also a risk, keeping it." I set the book beside me on the coffee table. "Dean doesn't know. Charlotte didn't want him to know, especially after she'd passed."

Slapping his hands on his thighs, Dave abruptly stood, pacing the room with agitation. "Of course she didn't." Dave threw a hand out in Cecile and my direction. "Can you imagine what he would have done if he knew?" Dave grunted, placing his fisted hands on his hips before pacing again.

I wasn't sure I did know what Dean Masters would have done and asked just that.

Dave stopped pacing, his head tilted and eyes staring out the back door. "Honestly, I'm not sure. I think if he could have, he would have kicked me out a helluva a lot sooner than I willingly left. If not that, he would have made my life even more hellacious than it was." Shoulders slumping, Dave ran his hand over his bristly hair. "Da—" Dave sighed, long and mournful. "I don't remember things as clearly as I'd like. I was only five when Mom died. Mostly it's images and feelings instead of exact memories. One of the most prevalent feelings is how possessive Dean was with Mom. I remember raised voices a lot, and that Mom wanted to go out, to do other things, but Da—Dean—wouldn't let her. Dean worshipped my mom, and it killed him when she died. I don't know if you'd call that love or not. In Dean's own way, I suppose that's the way he felt."

Cecile stood, closing the short distance between her and Dave. Rubbing a hand up and down his arm, she leaned in, resting her cheek against his chest. "It would have killed Dean to know you weren't his."

Dave wrapped his arms around Cecile, pulling her in tight, his chin sitting atop the crown of her head. "It would have killed his pride. And if there's one thing a man like Dean Masters has in abundance, it's misplaced pride. You don't tread on that lightly."

No, you certainly didn't. We needed to look no farther than how Dean had reacted to Cindy leaving him. The victim of that reaction was his own son—Marshall.

My gut crashed with the realization of exactly what Charlotte had saved Dave from. Dave's life in that house hadn't been sunshine and roses, but it could have been worse. Much worse. And Dave wouldn't have had an older sibling to step in and take him in. Dave would have been all alone in a house with a man with an emotional ax to grind.

Charlotte had turned from her reaper, and in the process, she'd allowed Dave to grow up as protected as possible. She'd allowed Dave to grow into the man he'd become. She'd not only saved Dave's life but mine too. And by default, Cecile's.

As far as I was concerned, Charlotte Masters was a fucking hero.

18

"We have to keep this a secret." Dave leaned back, heavily resting within the cushions of the couch. Cecile was snuggled in beside him. At some point, I'd found my way back to the floral chair.

"I got no plans on telling," I answered. "But just out of curiosity, why are you so adamant that he can't know? It's not like you live under Dean's roof anymore."

"No, I don't. But he's still Marshall's dad. So far, Dean doesn't act like he wants custody of Marshall even if he was granted it. Cindy seems content to wash her hands of him too, but that shit could change, and I don't want to take that risk. I'm trying to officially adopt Marshall, and I've got a lot better chance if we're biologically related."

Suddenly that innocuous lavender cover looked a lot more sinister. "Shit, I didn't even think of that. Like I said, I've got no plans to tell."

"Me neither," Cecile agreed before drawing her bottom lip into her mouth, chewing on it. "But—"

"But what?" Dave asked.

"*But*, I, for one, would like to know more about your biological father." Twisting in Dave's arms, Cecile tilted her head and gave Dave pleading eyes. "You could have uncles or aunts out there that you don't even know about. Grandparents too."

Dave blew out a troubled breath. "I haven't had time to think about that."

"I know." Cecile ran a finger down Dave's scruffy jaw. "And you don't have to think about it yet. Marshall's the priority. We'll get that situation locked down, but in the meantime, I can do a little digging around, see what I can find out about Christopher Monahan. I'm happy to do that, but only if you're okay with it."

Dave's gaze tracked to his lap before finding me. "What do you think, small fry?"

I shrugged. "I think it's up to you, but for what it's worth, looking into things further would be a good idea. Maybe you're not ready yet, but eventually, you will be." I knew Dave well enough to feel certain of that.

"Yeah. Okay." Dave didn't sound as sure as I'd have liked, but he gave his permission anyway. "You know, I was glad it was Andy who came for my mom." The deep blue of Dave's eyes hit me hard. "I don't know what I would have done if it had been Bobby or worse, Elijah."

It was my turn to snort. "If Ellen Dykstra was good enough to avoid Elijah as her reaper, your mom was a shoe-in for Andy."

The corner of Dave's mouth flirted with a smile. "Yeah, but you never know, do you?"

"No, I suppose not." Everyone had secrets. I guessed it just depended on how deep and dark those secrets ran and maybe the damage they'd done.

"But still, I'm glad it wasn't Bobby." Dave's hinted smile

vanished. "I don't think I could take it, watching him reap someone. I know I wouldn't be able to see the whole reaping business, but I don't want to think about him doing it."

"Or hear his voice." Cecile shivered beside Dave.

Having witnessed it firsthand, I could completely understand.

"Yeah, that too," Dave readily agreed. "But I would like to see him." Fingering the charm hanging around his neck, Dave's head tilted down so that his chin almost rested on his chest. "Now that I've got this, I could actually see Bobby. The real Bobby. We could even talk. I could tell him . . . I'm not sure what I want to tell him. I just know I want to see him again." Dropping the crystal back against his skin, Dave asked, "Do you think that would be possible?"

I wasn't sure. "I can ask Andy." It was the only thing I could think of. Long ago, I'd asked Isaac to contact Andy for me, but Isaac was gone, and I didn't have another capable spirit stashed in my back pocket anymore.

Dave's face scrunched into something unpleasant, his lips pursed with the distaste of that idea. Dave and Andy got along better, but there was still some odd, lingering animosity. I was saved from hearing whatever Dave had to say when the front door opened.

Chrissie's feet pounded through the hall and into the living room.

I raised my head, ready to offer a greeting but the fiery glow of Chrissie's green eyes stopped me cold.

"Do you know what that fucker did?" Chrissie's voice held a strange quality, a sinister edge that raised the little hairs running along my arms and down my spine. The air in the living room crackled with something I couldn't name. It smelled like ozone, like the sky was getting ready to unleash Mother Nature's fury.

Chrissie threw an envelope into my lap. It was stuffed

with papers, thick and heavy. I didn't know if I was supposed to open it or not. Shifting the envelope in my hand, I glanced over at Dave and Cecile. They'd both scooted to the edge of the couch, eyes wide and mouths slightly parted.

"Chrissie, you mind taking it down a notch or two," Dave bravely suggested.

Chrissie's hiss of anger made Dave flinch back. "No, Dave, I will not *take it down a notch or two*." Aggressively pointing to the evidently toxic letter sitting in my lap, Chrissie spat, "That bastard is after my daughter." Stabbing a finger at her chest, Chrissie emphasized, "*My* daughter. The daughter I've been raising. The daughter he abandoned before she was a year old."

Blowing through the living room, Chrissie slammed through the swinging door leading to the kitchen, the door flailing back and forth, unable to settle completely before she stormed through it again, a bottle of water in her hand.

Staring down at the manilla envelope, I asked, "I assume this is about Mark?"

"Of course this is about that asshole. It's not like Lilly has two sperm donors out there."

Dave snickered, and Cecile slapped his arm while she threw him a warning glance.

Anger fading to fear, Chrissie paced to the nearby fireplace, setting her half-empty bottle of water on the mantel. "He's really doing this." Chrissie sounded lost, the green fire of her eyes fading to their usual hazel beauty. "What in the hell is Mark thinking? I always knew he had more looks than brains, but this . . ." She tossed her head back and forth causing her long blond ponytail to dance across the black of her Crossroads t-shirt. "He came by work with his lawyer and his fucking private investigator." Chrissie turned, eyes narrowed and arms crossed over her chest. "And would you like to know who my *wonderful* ex has hired to investigate me?"

My mind tumbled into a black abyss. "It can't be." I stupidly tried to hold off the inevitable.

"Oh, it can. And it is. Levi Small Dick."

"Christ." Dave shot up from the couch, filling the room with his pacing. "Tell me you're not serious."

"I'm as fucking serious as I've ever been." Chrissie cursed almost as much as Dave and me, but even for her, this was a lot. She was really pissed, and I couldn't even begin to blame her. "He's suing for custody—full custody. I don't know who's funding him. Mark's family isn't wealthy, and this has to cost a small fortune. Not to mention the fancy car Mark drove off in today when Doug basically threw him out of Crossroads. I'm not joking or even being mean when I say Mark isn't smart. He's not especially lucky either. Someone with deep pockets is funding this disastrous endeavor of his. Someone's after my daughter."

Chrissie's crossed arms wrapped around her middle, pulling tight.

"What in the hell am I going to do? I can't afford to—"

"Shh." Dave pulled Chrissie into his arms, temporarily protecting her from all the shit being thrown her way. "Take a breath. Let it all out now, before Lilly gets home from school. When she walks through that front door, you'll be the badass mother and witch we all know and care about."

Chrissie let out a choked sob that turned into a garbled laugh. Guiding her to the couch, Dave settled Chrissie between him and Cecile. Five minutes of deep breathing and more than a few mantras of, "I've got this," and Chrissie settled.

"Good," Dave praised. "Now, tell us what happened, from the beginning. You're not alone. We've got this."

Chrissie deflated as her mouth opened, spewing the ugly

details. As she talked, we focused on our latest crisis, ignoring the fact that Dave's dad wasn't really his dad, that his real father had died half a world away without knowing Dave had been conceived.

"I need to get home." Dave looked as exhausted as the rest of us. "Marshall will be home soon from school, and I want to be there."

I checked my watch, noting that it was now early afternoon, and that meant Lilly would be home soon too. Phoenix had yet to come out of Lilly's room, as if she knew there was still too much turmoil to risk it. Cats were smart that way.

Cecile got up and followed Dave. Along the way, her gaze tracked down the hall, toward Chrissie's closed door. Worrying her bottom lip, Cecile asked, "You think Chrissie will be okay?"

I took a minute to consider it before I nodded. "She has to be."

Lilly's future depended on Chrissie getting her collective shit together. We needed a plan. We had the start of one, and that was talking to the same lawyer currently helping Dave. Cecile also planned on grilling her dad about Chrissie's chances and what might be coming. Being prepared was over half the battle.

Dave made his way toward the door. Shoulders rounded and looking beat down, I didn't like the heavy weight Dave carried. "Are you going to be okay?" I parroted Cecile's earlier question, this time aimed Dave's way.

Silent for half a beat, Dave finally gave a slow nod. "Yeah. Honestly, it's a relief, knowing I'm not biologically related to the man who raised me. It also stings. It's hard to come to terms with those two mixed feelings. I think I'll be working through that for a while."

"That's understandable."

"And very mature," Cecile added in a teasing tone.

"Thanks, honey bunny." Dave leaned down, pressing his lips to Cecile's and drinking her in. Dave's body relaxed into the kiss. Pulling away, he gave her a lighter peck. I averted my eyes, finding something on the wall far more fascinating than what it truly was.

Clearing my throat, I asked what was really on my mind. "Are you going to say anything to Marshall?"

"You mean about what Dean said? That Marshall's gay?" Dave didn't use any of the derogatory words we'd all had the misfortune of hearing Dean spew. "Not right now. Maybe not ever. Dean could be full of shit. You know I don't care either way, but I won't push Marshall to tell me something he's not ready to. The kid barely knows me, and that's as much my fault as it is Dean's and Cindy's."

I started to protest, but Dave stopped me. "I should have kept trying, Leah. I shouldn't have given up. Biologically related or not, they're my brothers."

Nothing I could say would ever convince Dave he'd been a victim too, that Dean and Cindy's actions had hurt him as much as his brothers. Knowing that, I offered up an understanding smile.

"Eventually," Dave continued, "Marshall will understand that I don't care who he's attracted to. Once he feels safe with me and that I'm not gonna kick him out over something that stupid, he'll trust me enough to open up. Or, at least, I hope that's what will happen. It's hard enough to know what an adult is going to do, let alone a teenager."

"We were all there at one time or another, and technically, Cecile's still there." At nineteen, my cousin was on the cusp of twenty but technically still in her teens.

Cecile's baby blues drifted from me to Dave. "I don't think any of us ever qualified as typical teens."

Dave and my silence were agreement enough. The past was a funny thing. It carved you up and pieced you back together, spitting you out into the future in different shapes. All three of us wore our scars—some visible, some you had to dig for.

19

I had the afternoon-slash-evening shift the following day. Lenny did too, something I'd become accustomed to being grateful for. Unfortunately for both of us, Ricky did too. Lizzie had the day off, which almost evened the scales regarding working with Ricky. Almost.

We were barely an hour into our shift when I heard raised voices an aisle or two over. I was in the process of restocking the leaf debris bags when I recognized one of the raised voices was Lenny's.

I didn't stop to think. Abandoning my work, I quick-stepped toward Lenny's increasingly loud voice. Lenny being loud wasn't necessarily unusual. But the angered tenor that accompanied that booming voice was. Perpetually happy, Lenny rarely raised his voice in anger, and I hated to contemplate what could be the root of it now.

Coming around the aisle, my toe scuffed the floor, rolling up the packaging tape affixed to the sole. "Fucking hell," whispered through my lips, heat rising in my cheeks and heart starting up a painful rhythm.

"Levi." His name was more growl than word when it exited my lips.

"Stay away from her!" Lenny stepped in, pushing his body toward Levi. "Chrissie's a nice person, and she's a great mother. Lilly's a happy kid."

Levi didn't look all that impressed by Lenny's anger or the fact Lenny had gotten up in his face. Levi probably had a couple of inches on Lenny and about twenty pounds of muscle too. Hands clasped behind his back, Levi stood there, shoulders square but far from tense. A single blond eyebrow tilted up, and an obnoxious smirk pulled at his lips. His hair was longer than it had been when he'd worn police-issued blue. Levi tilted his head, the soft waves of his dirty blond hair shifting ever so slightly.

"I didn't say she was a bad person," Levi defended whatever he'd said before. "I'm just trying to get the facts. Lilly isn't the Messiah. She didn't spring from Chrissie alone. Lilly has a father and—"

"Lilly has a sperm donor," Lenny spat in Levi's face. "That's all Mark ever was. He willingly walked out on his daughter and the mother of his child. He gave up whatever fatherly rights he had a long time ago."

Internally, I beamed. I was so damn proud of Lenny. Moving to back up my friend, I said, "I couldn't agree more."

Lenny stumbled back a couple of steps, and his face relaxed with obvious relief when I came into view.

Levi didn't look relieved. He looked feral, like a predator who'd just spotted a wounded gazelle on the Serengeti.

"Leah," Levi's voice sounded thick and sugary sweet. Reaper voices sounded similar, but Levi's tone distinctly lacked anything remotely tempting. "It's been a while since I've seen you."

"A lifetime of not seeing you wouldn't be enough," I shot

back before offering Lenny a supporting hand. "You okay?" I shot a look Levi's way as I asked.

Lenny blew out a breath that ruffled his lips, making a sputtering noise. "This guy's trying to dig up dirt on Chrissie." Lenny threw a thumb in the direction of Levi. "I don't know how many times I told him to go away, that I didn't have anything to say. But he just kept on pushing."

I knew the feeling all too well. "Yeah, Levi's kind of like a nasty rash you just can't seem to shake." It was the politest disease I could think of to compare Levi with. "He can hear just fine. It's the listening bit he has some trouble with." I enjoyed that I no longer had to call Levi "Officer Dickerson." He'd willingly given up that title a few months ago. Even without it, Levi was still a pain in the ass. Maybe even a bigger pain than he'd been with it.

"That's a little crass, don't you think?" Levi didn't sound very upset. In fact, he seemed amused.

"Not hardly crass enough."

We were starting to draw a group of people who acted like they weren't paying attention but hung on to every word. Making a spectacle of myself had lost appeal when Justin Turlington used my brother's body to murder my parents. I'd had more than my fifteen minutes of fame.

"What in the hell is going on here?"

I rolled my eyes, visions of overhead ductwork swimming through my gaze as Ricky's annoying cadence joined in on the party. Where the hell were Berta or Daryl when you needed them? Hell, I'd even take Lizzie popping up unexpectedly if it would get me out of this clusterfuck.

"Richard Levitson," Levi sang, rocking back on his heels, a twisted but pleased smile lighting up his face. "Two birds, one uncomfortable visit. How are you doing this afternoon? How's Shelly?"

Ricky barely spared Lenny and me a glance. Ricky's

emotional struggle played out across his face. For the barest of moments, the old and true Ricky broke through. His rough, irritated declaration a couple of minutes ago warred with this new, weirder polite version. I watched, completely fascinated, waiting to see which personality would win.

I was infinitely disappointed when Ricky's posture relaxed, limbs going lax, fingers dangling at his sides. Ricky answered with a slow grin, "Shelly and I are great. She's been so busy at home recently, what with her online coursework. It's been keeping her days so full that she hardly has time to speak on the phone, let alone leave the house and visit anyone."

This time, both of Levi's eyebrows shot up. "*Online coursework*? What's she studying?"

"Medical transcription," Ricky answered without so much as a second of hesitation. A wide, wicked smile lit up his face, contrasting sharply with the wide-eyed innocence he aimed for.

It was still difficult for me to stomach, thinking Levi and I agreed on anything. For a split second, our eyes connected, and, in the silence, I heard the word *bullshit* echo through my head. I wasn't sure if it was my inner voice or Levi's.

"Really," Levi drew the word out. "Huh, I'll have to ask her brother, Brandon, if he was aware Shelly had that kind of interest."

Ricky didn't act the least bit concerned. "I think it's a relatively new thing, but you can feel free to question Brandon all you like." Taking a step closer to Levi, Ricky tilted his head down. The fluorescent lights above glinted off the crown of his brown hair. Unlike when Lenny had gotten up in his face, Levi was more alert this time. Eyes narrowed and muscles pulled taught, Levi was wary.

"Now, Mr. Dickerson"—it looked like I wasn't the only one taking pleasure in no longer having to place "officer" in front of Levi's last name—"this is a place of business, and Lenny is currently on the clock. If you'd like to speak with him further, perhaps a phone call or scheduling something when he's not at work would be best."

"He can call me all he wants. I'm not talking to him. I've said all I'm going to," Lenny shot off before he turned and stomped away, leaving me alone with two vipers and a handful of gawking spectators.

"Hmm, surprisingly, I agree with Lenny." With a final twisted smile, Ricky followed Lenny's retreat. I should have beelined it out of there too. Either my reflexes or sense of self-preservation weren't what they should be. History told me it was probably the latter.

"Everyone always thinks they can hide from the truth," Levi muttered, more to himself than me.

"That's rich, coming from the man who spouted lies for over six years about me," I challenged.

"I've already apologized for that." Levi sounded exasperated, like he just couldn't believe I was still upset about something so trivial as being constantly accused of murdering the people I loved.

I wanted to rail, wanted to scream and shout at the rafters. But the rafters wouldn't listen any more than Levi Dickerson would. Both of them were incapable of giving me what I wanted. It was a waste of energy I couldn't afford to spare.

Finally getting my collective shit together, I turned, more than ready to get away from all that was Levi Dickerson. I was never that lucky. Human, reaper, or management, everyone wanted to get in the last word.

"I understand Christine and Lilly Hollybrook are living with you now. Is that correct?"

Cold chills danced their way down my spine, lifting the hairs on my arms. "They are."

"Interesting friends you have, Leah." Levi's voice sounded closer. Having turned from him as I began walking away, I quickly faced Levi. I didn't like him at my back. I didn't like him at my front, either.

"Oh, and why's that?" I shouldn't have asked, but I was curious. Mark knew about Chrissie, or at least he knew something about her. I'd never gotten a clear answer from Chrissie what Mark did and didn't know. The question was —what had Mark told Levi? And what did Levi believe? I was starting to think Levi Dickerson was far more open-minded than I was comfortable with.

Levi gave me another one of those irritating half smiles, the one where it looked like he was placating a small child with an intellectual disability. "I think you know, Leah. I think there's a reason you brought Christine Hollybrook to our earlier meeting."

My pulse quickened again. "I suppose you'd think that, wouldn't you? Friendship would never be a good enough reason. There's always got to be something else underlying, something more sinister. Newsflash, Levi, sometimes friendship *is* enough. Sometimes there is no ulterior motive. Sometimes, people simply do things for each other—support each other, because they care."

Levi acted stuck for half a second, as if what I said made a hint of headway through his thick skull. Whatever inroads my words made came to a halt when Levi threw up his mental roadblocks. "That's a nice but very naïve thought, Leah."

Just like before, it wouldn't do me a damn bit of good trying to argue with him.

"I'll be by to speak with Chrissie sometime soon. Please let her know that."

"You can come by. It's up to Chrissie if she wants to speak

with you or not. Personally, I wouldn't even open the door to slam it in your face."

I didn't wait to see if my words would have any effect. Finally hightailing it out of there, I took off for the break room. I didn't know if Lenny would be there or not, but I thought it was probably a fair bet. I was used to dealing with Levi Dickerson's bullshit. Lenny wasn't.

"I can't believe Mark," Lenny fumed. I'd been right. He was in the break room, pacing back and forth, weaving between chairs and around the lockers. Fingers repeatedly flexing, Lenny's body vibrated with anger. "What the hell is he thinking? And why now? Why is he coming after Lilly after all these years?"

I didn't have the answers to those questions, only speculation that I wasn't ready to share. "I'm not sure. I gave up on trying to figure out asshole's motives a long time ago."

Lenny's feet stuttered to a stop, almost tripping. Hand catching a chair for balance, Lenny stared at me, his lips parted before sweeping up into a smile. With a soft chuckle, Lenny pulled out the chair he clasped and sat heavily upon the seat.

"He is an asshole, isn't he?" Lenny didn't sound as sure as his words.

I pulled out a chair and sat opposite Lenny. The break room door cracked open, and Janelle started to step inside. I'm not sure exactly what the look on my face conveyed, but her eyes widened before she offered a quick nod. Backing up, Janelle let the door ease closed behind her, leaving Lenny and me alone.

Focusing on Lenny again, I answered, "I didn't know him

well in high school, but everything I've learned about him since doesn't point in another direction."

"Trust me, he was an asshole back then too." Lenny fidgeted with the corner of his Handy Helpers vest. "I didn't like to say anything . . . you know, when I was younger. Mark was a bully. He was mean to everyone, and I always wondered what a girl like Chrissie saw in him. Of course, Mark was good-looking, but that seemed to be all he had going for him."

"It took her a bit, but I'm pretty sure Chrissie figured that out too." I felt confident Chrissie wished she'd realized it sooner than she had. But if that had been the case, Lilly wouldn't be here. I was also confident Chrissie considered it a decent trade-off, no matter how rocky it was being young and pregnant. Being a single mother was brutal, but Chrissie wouldn't give Lilly up for all the world.

Head hanging low, Lenny stared down at his lap. I wasn't sure what was going through his head. "At least Chrissie's taste in men is a lot better than it used to be."

Lenny's eyes drifted up, staring at me from beneath his lashes. "Why do you say that?"

I didn't mind stroking Lenny's ego. "Because she likes you. Don't act like that's a surprise."

Lenny blushed and looked off to the side.

"We both know it's true, and I'm damn happy for the both of you. Chrissie's a lucky lady."

Lenny gave a disbelieving snort. "I think you've got that turned around."

"I'm sure you think so, but no, I don't. What I just witnessed out there, in aisle eleven, proved that. I'm so glad Chrissie and Lilly have you in their corner. You're loyal, and you'll be there when they need you. I've got absolutely no doubt about that."

Posture finally relaxing, Lenny scooted down in his chair,

slumping forward as his shoulders rolled inward. "You're a nice person, Leah."

I didn't think I was all that nice, at least not all the time, but answered, "I'm glad you think so, but kindness isn't why I just said all that. I said it because it's true." Getting more serious, I added, "What's also true is that Levi Dickerson isn't someone to mess around with. And to be truthful, I kind of feel like Mark isn't either."

I'd never seen that serious of a look on Lenny's face. Eyes narrowed, their deep brown color glinted with alertness. The wheels of his brain turned. "Mark? Or someone Mark's associated with?"

The question brought a surprised gasp from my throat. "What do you know?"

"Not much. Nothing, really. But that doesn't mean I don't notice things. Chrissie and Lilly . . . they're different. I know they're special, and not just because I care about them. Something more is going on there." Lenny's eyes turned downcast, his shoulders even more rounded. "I know that sounds nuts. You probably think I've been playing too many video games, that I'm just seeing stupid shit that isn't there."

Sitting there, all I could do was stare, wondering how on earth I'd underestimated Leonard Filliman this badly for all these years. Maybe Elijah was right. Maybe I really was an idiot. "You do play a lot of video games—"

"See, I knew it."

"I wasn't finished," I scolded. "But you're also perceptive, Lenny. I can't talk to you about this. That's Chrissie's decision. All I can say is that I think, with time and patience, she'll fill you in. Chrissie's been hurt before."

"By Mark," Lenny guessed correctly.

"And a few others. She's understandably cautious. Just keep doing what you're doing, Lenny. I think Chrissie will come around."

Offering a soft smile, Lenny said, "Thanks, Leah."

"You're welcome. But my earlier warning still stands. I'm not sure who Mark's gotten mixed up with or why, but knowing the lawyer he's hired, plus employing Levi, whoever it is has deep pockets and is in this to win it. I don't want you to get hurt in the crossfire, and I know Chrissie doesn't either."

"I don't care," Lenny argued back. "I'll do whatever I can to help."

The sentiment was appreciated, especially since Lenny obviously understood what was going on here was more than a simple child custody case. He may not know everything, none of us did, but what he'd figured out shocked me.

Lenny continued surprising me when he asked, "What did Levi mean when he told Ricky that thing about the two birds?" I opened my mouth, ready to ask if Lenny had really never heard that expression before when he stopped me with a roll of his eyes. "Yeah, I know that. What I don't know is why Levi wanted to see Ricky. And then he asked about Shelly. Is she okay?"

None of us knew Shelly well, but we all knew Ricky and, by default, had an immediate concern for Shelly. Blowing out a deep breath, I answered, "I'm not sure, but I don't think so. I don't think Shelly's okay at all."

20

Chrissie was still up when I got home later that night, sitting in the dark with a glass of red wine perched on the arm of the couch.

"Drinking alone?" I asked while plopping down in the floral chair.

"Not if you'd like some too. There's still a half a bottle open in the kitchen." Chrissie didn't look drunk. She didn't sound drunk either. She sounded a little tipsy and maybe more than a little depressed.

"Thanks, but no thanks. I don't drink." Sometimes I wondered if I could now. I wasn't on meds, and I was older. Glancing down at my covered wrists, I knew I couldn't afford to take the risk.

Blinking, Chrissie stared at me as if she'd never seen me before. "I'm sorry. I should have asked before I brought it into the house." She started to get up. "I'll go dump it. I—"

"Sit. Drink," I ordered. "I don't mind. I just can't risk drinking it. Don't worry, it's not a big temptation or anything." From what I was beginning to understand, the same couldn't be said for the man we'd all thought had been Dave's father.

"Are you sure?"

"Positive."

"Okay." Chrissie took a big gulp of the dark red liquid. "Grams always said this was the devil's brew." Chrissie swirled the glass, watching the wine tilt back and forth. "She always made the worst decisions when she drank." The edge of her lips quirked up, and Chrissie glanced my way. "Do you think she was drunk when she decided to hex my mom?"

Yup, definitely a few sheets to the wind. "I don't know. Possibly." For a split second, I almost wished we hadn't reaped Oleana's spirit. Chances were good she'd be giving Chrissie the business right about now, not that Chrissie would have been able to hear it.

Head tilted back, Chrissie rested on the edge of the couch. "I can't lose her."

"I know." I didn't tell Chrissie that she wouldn't lose Lilly. I didn't have the power of clairvoyance, which made me wonder if anyone really did. Maybe there was a witch in that little black book of Chrissie's that could see the future. Knowing what had happened in my life, I thought that was more a curse than a gift.

"I called my dad tonight," Chrissie offered after a beat of silence. "I asked him if he had anything to do with Mark coming after Lilly." Chrissie snorted. "You know what that bastard said?"

The cold snaking down my skin gave me a hint. I remained silent.

"He said, 'not directly.' When I asked him what the hell that meant, my oh-so-loving father told me that after what happened with my mom, after he learned what Grams did, what I could do to reverse it, he got worried about Lilly." Chrissie sat up, sloshing her wine. "Can you believe the gall of that man? He hasn't wanted a fucking thing to do with me since he dropped me off on Grams's doorstep, and as for Lilly . . . he didn't even come to the hospital to see her when I gave birth. As far as I know, he's never even seen Lilly, let alone met her. And now he's, what? Concerned?"

I let Chrissie vent, spewing words laced with venom and fear into the room. Given the time, Lilly was in bed and hopefully fast asleep. Chrissie was too responsible to start drinking before Lilly was tucked in. Shifting on the couch revealed Phoenix's small, furry body tucked in between Chrissie's hip and the arm of the couch. Peeking her head up, I caught a glance of sleepy eyes before the kitten ducked back down, snuggling into the warmth. Chrissie set the glass down on a side table, petting Phoenix as she filled the living room with purrs that twisted my heart.

I had no idea what to say, no clue how to soothe my friend's worried heart. All I could offer was an ear, a soft place for Chrissie's venting to land.

"I should have just let her die." Chrissie sounded wrecked. "I never should have gone to the hospital. I never should have saved Mom. If I'd left it alone, let the hex destroy her, Dad would have kept on ignoring me, and Lilly would be safe."

Unable to let that go, I said, "And your grams would be stuck on the plane of the living."

"She would have deserved it." I knew Chrissie didn't mean those harsh words, not deep down. "Fuck, this is messed up."

It was. The million-dollar question was how we got it un-fucked-up. "Did your dad say anything else? Did he hint at who might be behind this if it's not him?" From what I understood, Fergus Hollybrook had been the spark, but he wasn't the gasoline.

Chrissie reached for her glass of wine, draining the last of it. After a couple of beats, she said, "Maybe."

When nothing else appeared to be forthcoming, I prompted, "Maybe? Is that a strong or half-ass maybe?"

"I'm not sure yet." Turning to fully face me, Chrissie very solemnly added, "I hope I'm wrong. The minute one of them comes into contact with the wards I put around the house, I'll know for certain."

"We have to wait for this person to get that close?" I didn't like the sound of that.

"Yeah. And FYI, saying *person* is using the term loosely. And it could be several *persons*, not just one. They hunt in packs."

Wait? "What?" It was late, and I was tired, but I was fully awake now. "What are you talking about?"

"I told you a long time ago, Leah, there are a lot of things out there, a lot going on that you don't have a clue about. Some of them are harmless. Lots of them just want to be left alone, to live their lives. And then there are others. Power is a temptation, no matter what the species."

Picking Phoenix up, Chrissie settled the sleeping kitten in her lap. A fresh, brief episode of purrs rattled through Phoenix's chest before she settled into slumber again. "I don't want to say more, not until I'm positive." Rolling her head along the back of the couch, Chrissie's eyes glimmered, not with the witch fire within her but with pain and grief. "We'll move out if that's what you want. You didn't sign up for this, and—"

"You're not going anywhere and that's final." I wasn't about to abandon them. My aunt and uncle had taken me in when Bobby was on the loose, when no one knew if he planned to come back for me or not. They risked their lives to protect me. Dave had done the same thing when he'd taken me in once we'd known Bobby was back, Justin's spirit riding him hard and gunning for me. It was time to pay it forward.

"But we—"

"You need to tell Lenny something," I cut Chrissie off, ready to be done with that end of the conversation.

Chrissie's large, hazel eyes blinked, the haze of alcohol heavy within them. "Lenny? What does he have to do with this?"

I gave Chrissie a pass on this one, considering how tipsy she was. "Levi was in the store today, asking Lenny questions."

"What the fuck?" Chrissie sat up fast, dislodging Phoenix and earning a mew of protest.

"It makes sense. You're dating Lenny, and Levi's been hired to dig up dirt on you to try to help Mark's case. Lenny's involved, and he's not going anywhere. You can offer him the same out you just offered me, but I guarantee he'll tell you to stuff it. Lenny's all in—committed. He loves Lilly, and it's not a stretch to say he loves you too. And he's . . . Lenny's not as oblivious as you might think." I repeated my earlier conversation. By the end, Chrissie looked like I'd punched her in the gut.

"Oh my god." Chrissie frantically looked around the room, as if there was an escape route hidden somewhere in Rose's living room.

"Stop," I ordered, keeping my voice soft. I was painfully familiar with the roads Chrissie's mind raced down. "Stop thinking worst-case scenarios. We've talked about this before. Lenny's not like Mark. He's not like your mom and dad either. Lenny's the real deal, and he won't abandon you or Lilly. He'll accept you, Chrissie. Just like Dave, Cecile, and I do. Trust him."

"I—" Chrissie's voice trailed off, unable to form the words, or maybe she didn't know what the words were.

Warmth seeped deep into my soul, pushing into my skin and deep into my pores. Andy was nearby. I'd felt him earlier, lingering somewhere. For whatever reason, he kept some distance, hovering outside.

Chrissie stared at her empty glass, its clear edges streaked in red. "You're right," she finally admitted, voice small and hesitant. "I know you're right. I don't know why I've waited so long."

I did. "Fear is a powerful thing."

"It is," Chrissie agreed. "And I've been letting mine get the better of me."

"Sometimes fear can be a good thing. Fear can save your ass."

"It can, but not in this case." Standing, Chrissie stretched and took a step, her body wobbling. "Whoa, got up a little too fast."

I stood too, steadying Chrissie as we made our way down the hall to her bedroom. I didn't even ask if that's where she wanted to go. Regardless, Chrissie didn't fight me. She let herself be led. I helped her get undressed and settled under her covers. Before I could leave, Chrissie snatched my wrist. She didn't even flinch when the pads of her fingers brushed against my raised scars.

"I don't think I've had enough to drink to affect my memory, but just in case I do forget, remind me in the morning that I need to talk to Lenny. Okay?"

"No problem. Go to sleep. I'll clean up in the living room and kitchen."

Chrissie's eyes softly stared up at me. "Thanks, Leah. You're a godsend."

I didn't think I was even close, but it was never a good idea to argue with someone who'd been drinking. "Night," I answered before I walked through the door, closing it softly behind me. Before heading back to the living room and the couch I'd most likely spend the night on, I ducked my head inside Lilly's room. She was a small lump huddled underneath the covers, her blond hair a halo of gold laid out across her pillow.

"She sleeps very peacefully," Andy whispered over my shoulder, his breath warm against my skin.

"She does."

"Most people assume children are oblivious, but I've found that to rarely be the case." I'd heard that tone before from Andy. It was the one that spoke of experience—too much experience.

"I don't have much experience with kids," I admitted, leaning back into Andy's warmth. It still amazed me when he didn't pull away. "Maybe it's just that kids see things differently. Or maybe process differently." I wasn't a psychiatrist and should probably leave the psychoanalysis to Dr. Cross.

"Hmm . . . maybe." Andy's arms wrapped around me, pulling me away from Lilly's door and toward the living room.

Andy settled on the couch, and I squeezed in tight beside him, snuggling in. The cushion was still warm from where Chrissie had sat earlier. Her empty wine glass was in easy reach.

"It appears as if Chrissie had a bad day." Andy twisted the wine glass stem within his fingers before setting it back on the table. I'd never seen Andy the least bit interested in alcohol. Sweets were his vice. The contents of my cabinets made it seem like I was perpetually ready for Halloween.

"Is that why you stayed outside?" I asked on a yawn.

"It looked like you and Chrissie were having an important conversation." Andy's fingers carded through my hair, his nails gently rasping against my scalp. "I could feel your worry—your concern. I thought it best to stay away and give the two of you some privacy. Chrissie is very tolerant of my presence, but I know she's still uncomfortable around me. I didn't want to upset her further."

"That's very sweet of you." I kept my voice light and teasing, covering the fact that I really did think it was sweet.

Andy just hummed again. His fingers continued their soothing path through my hair. Every once in a while, he'd tug at one of my longer strands, but it was always gentle. My eyelids drooped further. Andy's presence relaxed me in ways I hadn't thought possible since violence decimated my family.

The conversation I'd had with Chrissie played through my head as I lay against Andy's side. Worry niggled my core. That worry must have been stronger than I'd thought because Andy couldn't ignore it. "I hate to agree with Dave, but whatever you're thinking about shouldn't stay locked up in your head. What's wrong?"

I sucked in a deep breath, expanding my chest, holding that precious air before releasing it with a heavy sigh. "It's something Chrissie said."

"About Mark trying to take Lilly away?"

"Yes, but no." Twisting, I wiggled into a position where my head was cradled within Andy's lap. I could easily look up into his green eyes. I loved those gold-flecked eyes. I loved them more now that they reflected my own emotions and didn't burn with condescension. "Yes, I'm worried about the legal aspects of Mark's claim. But more than that, I'm worried about something else Chrissie said. You know we've suspected someone, or maybe a group of someone's, are bankrolling Mark's bid for Lilly."

"I remember." Andy stared down at me, his fingers finding my scalp again and continuing their soothing pattern.

"I asked Chrissie tonight if she knew who it might be. She said she had an idea but isn't sure." I twisted my sweatshirt within my fingers, wadding it up and pulling tight. "It didn't sound good. Chrissie wouldn't elaborate beyond telling me that if they try to get in the house—pass through her wards—she'll know for sure. And then she said . . ." I hesitated, swallowing hard. "She said they *hunt in packs.*"

Andy's fingers stopped, his body frozen and eyes glinting with something I couldn't name.

"Andy, do you know who she's talking about?" Maybe asking *what* would have been better.

Ever so slowly, Andy's muscles loosened, but he remained tense, like a spring ready to jump into action. Emotions flitted across his face. Minuscule changes that my eyes barely caught, my mind barely processed, before being replaced by another.

Seconds ticked into minutes before Andy's lips parted on a barely audible, "Perhaps."

I took a minute to process that before asking, "*Perhaps?* Care to elaborate, or is this one of those reaper laws that you can't comment on?"

Andy's jaw worked, grinding his teeth. "No, this does not fall under reaper purview. If it's one of the possibilities I'm thinking of, it doesn't fall under management either. And before you ask, I'm not sure whose authority they might be under. Maybe they don't have an authority. That kind of thing is way above my paygrade."

I'd figured out over the last few months that Andy wasn't lying when he said reapers were little more than peons in the whole afterlife scheme of things.

"I don't know much, only what I've seen, and much of that has been from far away. Reapers linger on the sidelines. We don't engage the living, whether that be living humans or . . . something else."

Chrissie had more than implied what we might be dealing with wasn't human. I didn't like hearing it the second time any more than the first. Ignoring that part, I said, "Except you and me."

Andy gave me a soft smile. "Except when it comes to you and me." He leaned down, his lips a barely there touch against my forehead.

I wanted to lay there and bask in Andy's affection. Unfortunately, reality demanded otherwise. "This *something else . . .* can you tell me anything more about them?"

Leaning back into the couch, Andy's eyes strayed to the ceiling, giving me an excellent view of his chin. Andy's facial hair never changed. There was always just a hint of stubble. I wasn't positive reapers' true appearances mirrored what they'd looked like at the time of death or not. Bobby's spirit had been that of his teenage self, before Justin had hooked his claws deep into his soul and taken over his body. Bobby as a reaper looked like he had in that hospital bed, muscles wasting away, skin pale and paper-thin, hair barely grown out after I'd shaved the bleach blond out of it.

If reapers really did hold the appearance of their final living days, then Andy had needed to shave.

I waited as patiently as I could. When I asked Andy questions, I never knew if I would get an answer or not. I got more answers now than I used to, but it wasn't a sure bet. I could tell Andy would answer this time. He was just taking his time to formulate his response.

I was almost asleep when he finally said, "There are a few possibilities, but only two that make the most sense when I think of the situation as a whole. Chrissie said they hunt in packs. Most things that are . . . *other* seem to be solitary creatures. In my limited experience, that is the case more often than not. The only pack hunters that I can think of that would care about getting a witch into their fold would be shades or wolves."

Given how far into slumber my mind had wandered, it took me a couple of seconds for that to sink in. It took a couple more for it to process and even longer to utter a completely useless, "Huh?"

Andy's chest rumbled with suppressed laughter. I wasn't offended. "Oddly enough, that simple word sums things up well. Or at least it sums up the way I felt when I first found out about them. Like I said, I don't know much and have only experienced shades once. Wolves I've seen more often, but considering the decades I've been a reaper, those times are very low too. Neither is pleasant, but for wholly different reasons. By far, Chrissie would know more than me. Witches are a very knowledgeable group. I suppose Chrissie could be talking about a rival coven who might be after her daughter, but I doubt it. Children are precious to witches, and taking the child of another witch would damn the caster."

"Just like hexing Chrissie's mother damned Oleana?"

"Something very similar." Andy's face tilted down, his eyes fixing on me again. "Though, I'm far from an expert. As I said before, Chrissie would know more."

"Yeah. I get that feeling. She just doesn't seem to be in a sharing mood. At least not yet."

Andy's fingers continued to dance across my scalp, his body relaxed once more. "Chrissie cares about you. She's fiercely loyal to her friends and family. Most witches are. She wants to protect you. When she has a better handle on what's coming, she'll let you know."

"But wouldn't being prepared be better?" My thoughts faded, drifting out to sea, floating on Andy's calming breeze.

"Shh." The sound of Andy's voice was far away. "Sleep, Leah. Those are worries for another day."

And just like all the other times when Andy was close to me, I did sleep. It seemed like my body remembered how, even if my brain argued otherwise.

21

"You're coming over for Thanksgiving, aren't you, Leah?"

I'd shared Thanksgiving with Uncle Jack, Aunt Joyce, and Cecile on and off for the past few years. I'd never looked forward to it as much as I did this year. Aunt Joyce and I got along better than I'd ever dared hope. She'd never be my mom, and I'd never think of her that way, just like I didn't see Uncle Jack as my dad. That didn't mean it wasn't nice to have their surrogate support.

"Handy Helpers is open until one that day. I can come over after if that's okay. I don't want to make you guys wait to eat, so if—"

"We'll plan to eat at two." Aunt Joyce shut down any question about me being there. "I've got the day off, which means I'll most likely be scheduled on Christmas." Aunt Joyce was busy going through bills, clicking different websites and paying them online. Like most mothers, she was a pro at multitasking.

I'd dropped by to pick up Cecile. We were headed to Dave's. We needed to do more than a little recon on Thomas

Birkingham. I also planned on picking their brains about what Andy had said to me last night about shades and wolves. I'd wanted to ask Chrissie when she got up this morning, but one look at her mussed hair, pinched eyes, and sour face, and I'd swallowed my words. Grilling people when they were hungover wasn't any better use of my time than arguing with them when they were three sheets to the wind.

"That sucks," I offered, wondering if Tyson would have to work the holidays considering he had lower seniority.

Aunt Joyce gave a little shrug. "It is what it is. Someone has to work. The ER doesn't close down, even if the rest of the country does. People can't help when they get sick."

No, I guessed they couldn't. I turned my head when I heard Cecile's soft footsteps coming down the stairs. Hair in a high ponytail, Cecile wore a heavy, long-sleeved navy shirt. Her dark jeans were almost the same color. The shirt hid the charms nestled against Cecile's chest. The color made her milky skin gleam.

"Hey, Leah. Sorry." Cecile blushed, and I knew she was up in her room, primping a little heavier than usual. This thing between her and Dave was still relatively new. Slipping on her sneakers, Cecile hurried into the kitchen and gave her mom a half hug. "Hey, Mom. Leah and I are gonna take off. I'm not sure when I'll be home."

Aunt Joyce partly turned, her eyes glued to something on her computer screen. Leaning in, she hissed something gently under her breath. I thought I caught a comment about something Uncle Jack had purchased, but Aunt Joyce only appeared slightly irritated, so it must not have been anything important.

"Have a good time, sweetie." Aunt Joyce planted a quick kiss on Cecile's cheek before she got back to the ugly business of paying bills.

As Cecile and I walked out the door, it hit me just how

normal that scene had been. There were no agonized looks of disapproval thrown my way, no list of where we could and couldn't go, no pointed stares or demands for an itinerary and ETA. Chrissie's charm had freed Cecile and her mom. I got the feeling Chrissie had no idea just how significant an impact she'd made on all our lives. If I hadn't been certain before about doing everything I could to help Chrissie and Lilly, I was then.

Marshall was in the living room when we got to Dave's. It was weird seeing him out in the open and not tucked away in his room. Marshall and Dave were eating sandwiches, a bag of chips laid out on the coffee table in front of them. A college football game was playing on the TV. I had no idea who the teams were. Sports weren't my thing, especially football. My dad had been more of a college basketball man. I'd try to catch some of the NCAA tournament each year, but that was about it.

"What the hell?" Dave yelled at the screen, coming off the couch, landing back on its edge. "Did you see that?" He turned to Marshall, so far mostly ignoring Cecile and me.

"Yeah." Marshall didn't sound as upset as Dave. Maybe more disgusted. "Dumbass move. Dev would scream at the screen too." I rarely heard Marshall mention his brother's name, but he often called Devlin *Dev* when I did. I had no idea if Devlin called Marshall *Marsh*. I didn't even know if Devlin and Marshall had spoken since Dave had taken the younger sibling in. It didn't exactly sound like the two of them were close.

Cecile wisely walked around the back of the couch, not breaking Dave's line of sight to the TV. Sitting beside him, Cecile leaned in and gave Dave a kiss on his cheek. Dave's face lit up, a soft smile pulling at his lips. "Hey, sweetie." The nickname carried a totally different weight when Dave said it compared to Cecile's mom.

"Game's almost over," Dave offhandedly offered, even though neither Cecile nor I asked.

"*Almost?*" Marshall grunted. "There's no almost about it. OSU just ended the game with that last move." Marshall reached into the bag, grabbed a handful of chips, and stuffed them into his mouth. I was happy to see his bruises had faded to nothing. Marshall's split lip had healed too. Good thing considering all the salt in those chips.

"Yeah, you're probably right." Dave stood, ignoring the *duh* look Marshall threw his way. "You ladies want anything to eat?" Dave asked while heading to the kitchen.

"I don't. Cecile and I stopped by a drive-thru on the way."

"Maybe some Oreos. If you've got them." Cecile had become as addicted to them as Dave and me. Andy was always down for them too, though I wasn't sure if it was the Oreo or just the fact it was sweet.

"Pfft . . . Do I have Oreos? What kind of a question is that?" Dave came back in, carrying a box that was about two-thirds full. "There are a couple more boxes in there if we get really desperate."

"You guys are nuts," Marshall announced with the surety all teenagers seem to have. "This game's over. I'm gonna head to my room."

"Homework before gaming, Marshall." Dave twisted on the couch, leaning over it so much that if Cecile's weight hadn't been sitting there too, the whole thing might have toppled over.

I caught Marshall's eyes roll before he headed for the stairs, walking right through where Eliza Morgan had spent the better part of her first seven years in the afterlife.

"I mean it!" Dave hollered after him.

"I heard you the first time," Marshall fired back.

Dave craned his neck, watching Marshall's ascent until he could no longer see him. Twisting back around, Dave slumped into the cushions.

"Problems?" I asked, working my way over to the couch and claiming Marshall's vacated spot.

"Probably not." Dave shrugged before a grin twisted his lips. "I think we're getting to the 'normal,'"—Dave made little hand quotes—"part of teenage rearing."

"Joy," I deadpanned.

"It kind of is," Dave answered. "I'd rather deal with this than the silent treatment. He's finally started to come out of his room. He even eats with me and watches some TV. It's good. Better than I thought it might be."

I was glad to hear it. "I take it his counseling sessions are going well."

Marshall had a different psychiatrist than I had. So far, Marshall had seen his counselor a couple of times.

"As far as I know. He doesn't talk about it with me. So far, he hasn't said anything his counselor thinks I need to know —nothing life-threatening or anything like that. He's keeping Marshall's privacy, and I'm good with that. I think it helps build the trust."

"That's great, Dave." I was beyond relieved, even if that meant we'd all be subject to some of Marshall's less than pleasant personality traits in the future. Teenagers were a breed all their own, or at least most of them were. I had no idea where I'd fit into that click when I'd been one. My circumstances molded me into something a little . . . different.

OSU scored another touchdown, and Dave grabbed the remote, turning off the TV. "Marshall's right. The game's over." Sliding his laptop around, Dave pulled the coffee table closer to the couch. "Okay, ladies. Let's see what we can find out about ol' Thomas and Dr. Benjamin Davidson."

"My guess is not much." Cecile's thoughts echoed my own. "All that happened before the days of social media and instant, flooded news stories."

Despite our dubious hopes, Cecile and I leaned farther in, staring at the screen as Dave typed in different search words. But no matter what he plugged in, we didn't learn anything new. It was the same information we'd found before. Even having Beth's full name didn't help.

"Damn," Dave muttered. "This is frustrating. What in the hell did people do before everything about everyone was set free into the digital world?"

"Had a private life." I was more than a little bitter over society's voracious desire for salacious news. It sucked being on the entertainment side of it.

Dave rubbed my shoulder in silent support. "There just isn't a lot of info. You'd think there would be if Thomas was as rich as Dr. Meyer said. But that was a long time ago, and even in a smaller town like Covetous, people have short memories of things like that. It looks like Elizabeth was Thomas's only heir. His estate was sold off and probably given to charity or gobbled up by distant relatives. There's not much left of his legacy."

"Not much of Dr. Davidson either," Cecile's saddened voice joined in as she leaned forward, clicking on the one link we'd found to the man. "It looks like his son was his only child. And then he . . . Well, he didn't live long enough after to father any other children."

"Beth's actions destroyed a lot of lives," Dave said with disgust. "Just like my fath—" Dave sucked in a deep breath. "Just like Dean's drinking is doing to him and almost did to Marshall."

"It's a disease." I tried to remind Dave. "Just like my

mental health issues. It's hidden," I tapped my temple, "up here, out of sight. It's easy to forget that."

Dave's shoulders slumped. "Yeah, I know."

"And not everyone has a Dave and Cecile in their lives to pull them out of the darkness," I added, just in case the two of them hadn't realized by now how important they were to me.

"Ashes too." Cecile reached across Dave's lap, briefly squeezing my wrist.

"Ashes too." I softly agreed.

We silently sat there. I couldn't say what Dave and Cecile were thinking. My own thoughts were morbid. It was amazing how one bad decision—one thoughtless act—could cause so much destruction. A few seconds of violence could lead to a lifetime of pain and grief. Time was weird like that.

Desperate to get off my morbid thoughts, I mentally flipped to a different, although equally, disturbing mental topic. "Do me a favor, Dave, and look up shades."

"Why?" Dave asked, his fingers already typing.

"Something Chrissie mentioned."

"Shit, that could be anything," Dave grouched.

"It could be," Cecile agreed, "but I doubt it has anything to do with paint colors."

I stared at the screen and what had come up. Cecile was right. All the links had something to do with color. "Maybe try shade creature. Or maybe being . . . We're looking for something living."

Dave snorted. "Of course we are. Couldn't just be thinking about doing some remodeling, sprucing the joint up a bit." After a couple more corrections, Dave muttered, "Christ, what in the hell is going on?"

Cecile and I leaned forward again, reading through the list. Dave clicked on a couple of easy, quick links, waiting for the two of us to read through the minutia. On the surface, shades sounded like something right up Chrissie's witch alley. Somehow though, it just didn't fit.

"This says it's an evil warlock, or maybe someone possessed with the spirit of one, or . . ." Cecile faded off until she finally admitted, "I'm kind of confused."

"I think Google is too, honey," Dave agreed with Cecile.

"None of that sounds right," I finally offered.

"Why don't you give us a little more info?" Dave said the words, but Cecile's curious gaze more than said she wanted to know too. I spent the next few minutes telling them what I knew. Dave ran a hand over his stubbled jaw by the end. As for Cecile . . . she just kind of sat there, mouth hanging open. Without looking her way, Dave reached over and gently pushed on Cecile's lower jaw, closing her mouth.

All of us sat there, staring at one another. Finally, Cecile broke the silence. "That's . . . I don't know what that is."

"Neither do I. That's why I thought we could look it up. I think I know what *wolves* probably are. Unless that's a code word for some group that's not actually werewolves." My lips twisted on the word, shocked I said it with any seriousness.

"You mean, like a biker gang or something?" Cecile asked.

Dave's eyebrows drew tight, scrunching his face. "I doubt it would be something like that, but in general, yeah, I guess a group of people using the word as their title. But Chrissie said they weren't *people* or that using that term wasn't accurate. Andy also said they weren't under his purview or management's. All that sounds like these guys aren't straight-up human."

"Agreed." I stared back at the internet search we'd done. "But they also don't sound like that." I pointed at the screen. "Andy said he doubted a witch was involved. I'm not sure where warlocks fit into things, but they sound pretty solitary and not like something that hunts in packs. That was the one thing Chrissie seemed sure about." It was also the only bit of extra information she'd parted with.

Silence filtered in again. The pinging of Dave's baseboard heat crackled and popped into the room as the boiler kicked in again. "I don't know what this is," Dave started, "but I don't like it."

"Nothing like stating the obvious," I offered, earning me a glare.

Cecile ignored Dave and my staring contest and asked, "Do you think the wards Chrissie placed around the house will be enough to protect you? I don't like the idea of you being there. What if one of these . . . things . . . gets through? What if—"

"I won't abandon Chrissie or Lilly."

"I wasn't suggesting that," Cecile hastily corrected. "I was only asking if there was something more that could be done to help keep you all safe. The legal system is one thing. Fighting a battle in court is completely different from what we're talking about here."

"Yeah, I get that." And I truly did. "I'm not a lawyer. I can't help Chrissie on that aspect of things. I don't even know how to help with this, but I figure I've got a better shot at being useful on the home front." Besides, it was Rose's home—the one she'd unknowingly shared with Isaac. I'd be damned if I'd abandon it or let something out there harm it. As far as I was concerned, I was living on hallowed ground.

Blowing out a deep breath, I scooted down and flopped into the corner of the couch, sliding a bent knee up and staring at Dave and Cecile. "I don't think there's a ward in the world strong enough to keep Levi from our door."

"Levi?" Dave sat up straighter, shoulders tense and body immediately on the defensive. "Why is Levi Small Dick showing up at your door?"

I quickly ran down my latest encounter with Levi at

Handy Helpers. I didn't skimp on the details about how Lenny had defended Chrissie and Lilly. It was also a good time to bring up my hope that Chrissie would fill in Lenny on her witch secret soon. It was a huge show of trust on Chrissie's part. I didn't have to worry that Lenny would let her down.

Dave fumed by the time I was done. Cecile looked more worried than angry. Growling low in his throat, Dave looked furious. "That guy just won't go the fuck away. He—"

"Has no one really seen Shelly?" Cecile interrupted Dave's growing rant, something I was grateful for, even if I didn't like the direction the conversation veered.

Ignoring Dave, I tilted my head so I could better see Cecile. "I don't know. She hasn't been by Handy Helpers in a few weeks. The last time I saw her was at Rose's funeral services. Ricky was his normal assholish self to her."

Cecile drew her bottom lip in and chewed the hell out of it. "Do you really think something's happened to her?"

"I have no idea. And the shitty thing is that there's no way for me to find out. I gave her my cell phone information, but I don't have hers. Besides, from the snippet of conversation I heard at Rose's services between Levi and Ricky, it sounds like her brother, Brandon, can't get a hold of her either. If she's not answering for him, even if I did have her number, I doubt Shelly would pick up for me."

My brain was a wicked beast, its timer always set to obsessiveness. I had trouble letting things go. They'd nag at me until exhaustion set in, and then they'd nag some more. You'd think there'd be enough for my brain to latch on to—with everything going on with Chrissie and Lilly. It looked like my noggin always had room for another worry to obsess over. They say everyone has something they're good at. I just wish my *something* was a tad more productive and a hell of a lot less self-destructive.

"What's Ricky say?" I don't think Dave had let go of his angered frustration regarding Levi, but he'd gotten it under control enough to join in on the current conversation.

I snorted a laugh. "What? Other than that bogus story about Shelly being too busy with medical transcription courses to talk to anyone?"

"Yeah, besides that bullshit."

"Nothing more than his creepy, smiling façade." A shiver worked its way down my back. "I've never seen anything like it." And I hoped with everything in me that I never did again. "I'd be impressed if I weren't too busy being disturbed and wigged out."

"It's a bad situation," Cecile accurately summed up. "I'm about to say something I never dreamed I'd say, but I hope Levi keeps digging until he gets to the bottom of things."

"What's that I hear?" Dave leaned toward me, hand cupped to his ear. "Did I just hear Satan ask for a winter coat? Seems like Hell just got chillier."

Cecile smacked Dave's shoulder and huffed. Wrapping her up in his arms, Dave squeezed Cecile tight, peals of laughter ringing through the room.

"Hey," Marshall shouted from the top of the stairs. "You guys want to keep it down out there? I can't hear you when I'm gaming, but I'm *supposed* to be doing homework."

"Sorry," the three of us yelled up in unison. None of us looked the least bit serious about our apology.

"At least he's studying," I told Dave.

"I'm not complaining," Dave threw back. "Yet. I'm sure the attitude will get old eventually."

Oh, it would get old, but I understood. Sometimes normal was better than anything in the world. I didn't think I'd ever fit into that lofty ambition, but I was closer now than I'd been in the past six years.

"Do we have any type of plan? About Thomas," Cecile

clarified when Dave and I stared at her like the idiots we probably were.

"You mean, besides cornering him in a closet and having an unhealthy heart-to-heart?" I'd already tried that method, and it hadn't gone smoothly. The bruise on my arm was long gone. The memory wasn't.

Cecile squirmed. "You know, it might not be that bad this time."

"No?" I didn't sound any more convinced than I looked. "Why not?"

"Because," Cecile's shoulders confidently went back, thrusting out her chest, "this time, you've got me."

22

Reprieves come in bursts. I just wished my bursts would turn into months' long vacations instead of weekend getaways. Three days of relative peace—shifts without Ricky (only one with Lizzie), no Levi sightings, and two out of three nights spent cuddled up in Andy's arms. I'd gotten so much sleep in the past seventy-two hours that my body hardly knew what to do with it.

True to her word, Chrissie had spoken with Lenny. Our following shift had been . . . interesting. Lenny had been dying to talk to me, finally cornering me in the Wasteland. We stood there, in the blowing wind and cold. In the end, I'd been glad for the space. Lenny had gesticulated wildly, his voice starting out hushed but building to a crescendo. I hadn't been certain if Lenny's cheeks were flushed by the cold or his excitement. I figured it was one part Mother Nature and two parts Chrissie's witchcraft revelation.

Lenny's response wasn't surprising in the least. But it was gratifying. He was thrilled, more because Chrissie had trusted him with her secret than the secret itself. I was righter than I'd thought, something far too rare.

It was evening when our peaceful normalcy inevitably came to an end. We all knew it was a matter of time. Just enough days had passed to ease the tension from our bodies. Phoenix was sitting on my lap, something she'd started doing more often. Cats were funny that way. They always seemed to know who wasn't as interested and were either determined to change that person's mind or wanted to take advantage of a warm lap at zero cost.

It wasn't that I didn't want her with me. I just couldn't shake the guilt that ate at my soul. Or the disappointment that Phoenix would never be Ashes. Adding to my guilt was the feeling that I was letting Francis down, that he'd trusted me with a precious gift, and I was squandering it. I wanted to love Phoenix. I wanted to bond with her just like I had with Ashes. That proved more elusive than I'd thought it would be.

"Have you made an appointment with the vet yet?" Chrissie asked while she scraped the last of her mac and cheese off her plate. Lilly had already eaten and was in her room, doing her homework. I couldn't remember having homework at six years old, but maybe I had. A lot of things from my past weren't exactly clear.

"I called today. They have an opening next week. Cecile's working that day, so she'll be there too." I set my plate on a side table before I downed the rest of my lemonade. Chrissie and I hardly ever used the table in the kitchen. Sometimes we sat at the barstools, mostly when Lilly ate too.

"Good. I know you've been dragging your feet." Chrissie gave a pointed look at the white lump in my lap.

I stared too, while my fingers worked their way into Phoenix's long fur. When she first arrived, I wasn't sure if she had long or short fur. It was obvious now that she'd have a long mane of white. Soft purrs filled the living room.

Clearing my throat, I admitted, "It's been harder than I thought."

Chrissie cocked her head to the side, her long ponytail drifting over her shoulder. She was still wearing her Crossroads work t-shirt and a pair of jeans. A long-sleeved white shirt was underneath the black t-shirt since the weather had turned colder. "I get it. Don't beat yourself up."

Sometimes living with Chrissie was like living with a sterner, more abbreviated version of Dave. Thinking of Dave . . . "I called Dave today too."

"Yeah?" Chrissie gave that pronouncement the attention it deserved. Me calling Dave was a daily occurrence. Sometimes more than daily.

"I decided to add some more ink."

That got Chrissie's attention. Head snapping up, she asked, "What and where?"

My eyes strayed to the wooden box holding Ashes's ashes. It was tucked away on a shelf; the picture of Rose and Isaac Melody left behind sat beside it. Leaning against the wall behind the box was an ink print of Ashes's paw. Nodding in the general direction of her ashes, I said, "He's going to copy her paw print and add her name. I'm not sure about the location yet. Most likely on my arm."

"Cool." Chrissie gave an approving smile. "I think that's a great idea."

I did too. I wasn't sure if she'd think my next one was as sound. "That's not all."

Chrissie's eyebrows shot up. "No? What else?"

I rubbed the area on my chest where the other one would go, right above my heart, tucked away and kept secret from the rest of the judgmental world. Clearing my throat, I said, "Bobby." I tapped the area in question, watching Chrissie's eyes track the movement.

Surprise widened Chrissie's eyes before they softened. "I get it. Are you going to tell Bobby?"

I hadn't considered it. "I'm not sure." I didn't see a reason to shout it and couldn't imagine a conversation where it would come up. Hidden beneath my clothes, Bobby would never see it. The tattoo was meant to comfort me, not Bobby.

Getting Ashes's name tattooed on my body was an easy decision. Bobby's wasn't. Technically, Bobby was dead. Funny how the word "technically" could have so many different meanings and connotations. Regardless, the Bobby I knew and loved died a long time ago. The Bobby who became a reaper was a different person than the one I was about to ink over my heart.

"Does Dave know you want to get Bobby's name too?"

"Yeah, I told him. Dave was quiet for a second or two but recovered quickly. I think on some level, he'd been expecting the call." Dave had been the one to suggest the tattoos on my wrists. It hadn't taken a lot to convince me. I hated the raised red and pink scars littering them. The scars were still there, but they were hidden. I could see them when I turned my wrists in the light, and I felt them every time I touched that part of my skin. My actions weren't forgotten, but they were forgiven—as much as they could be.

Chrissie started to rise off the couch, ready to take her plate and glass into the kitchen. Halfway through the motion, she stopped. A hissed breath escaped her lips, and her eyes flashed brilliant green.

"What is it?" I scooted toward the edge of my chair, disrupting Phoenix. Her tiny head bobbed up, ears perked. Her whiskers twitched, nose pointed up. The slightest hiss erupted from her open mouth, exposing tiny, pointed, sharp baby teeth. Puffed up, Phoenix let out a low growl before she jumped off my lap and slinked off toward Lilly's room. I'd never seen her act like that.

Fully standing, Chrissie rounded the couch on her way to the door. Tension sang through every molecule of her being. The air felt charged, like the cusp of a violent thunderstorm.

"Chrissie, what—"

"Wolves. Watch Lilly. Don't let her out of her room," Chrissie ordered.

I took off down the hall and peeked into Lilly's room. She was at her desk, her too-short legs swinging from her seated position. She was practicing her writing. I didn't see Phoenix anywhere and figured she was tucked away, hiding.

Trying to keep as calm as possible, I said, "Lilly, I'm going to close the door. Your mom wants you to stay inside. Don't come out until one of us gets you. You remember how we taught you to lock the door?"

Lilly jumped up. She hurried toward the door with a worried expression and grabbed the handle. I ran a hand over her head, offering up a confident smile I didn't feel. "We'll come get you soon. It'll be okay."

Chrissie had spoken with Lilly. I wasn't present during their conversation, but Chrissie had given me the run-down on the basics. Lilly was prepped for moments like this.

"Be careful, Aunt Leah." Lilly had started calling me her aunt when they moved in. Considering Bobby would never father any children, it was the closest I'd ever get, and I had no plans to deny the title.

"I will." I managed a brighter smile. "I've got your mom, and we both know she's badass."

Lilly grinned before she closed the door with a quiet snick. The squeal of the hinges wasn't nearly so silent, and I made a mental Post-it Note to buy a bottle of WD-40 at work. My dad had sworn by the stuff.

I waited to hear the turn of the lock before heading back to the living room with a pounding heart. I had no idea what kind of help I could possibly be, but if nothing else, I'd be there for moral support. Cold sweat beaded down my back. Raised voices met my ears as I rounded the corner of the hall leading to the door. Chrissie's back blocked my view.

"I told you I'd be back," Mark's smug voice filtered into the house over Chrissie's shoulder.

"And I told you that you're not welcome. You abandoned your daughter five years ago. Why in the hell would I willingly let you back into her life now?" Chrissie's cold voice sent shivers down my spine. "You are nothing to her, and you never will be."

"Now, now, Miss Hollybrook"—I didn't recognize the voice, but the tone was simperingly condescending—"in the eyes of the law, Mr. McKinney has a legal right to see his daughter. Mark never signed over complete custody to you, and you never sued him for those rights. You have no ground to deny—"

"Get the fuck off my porch." Chrissie wasn't any more impressed than I was.

"You can't keep me from my—"

"The hell I can't." Chrissie took a step outside, allowing me to move closer. I got a view of who our *guests* were. I'd known about Mark and what I figured was his lawyer. I hadn't expected Levi along with another brutish man. Levi stood there, arms crossed over his chest, tugging at the heavy coat protecting him from the cold November wind. Levi was dwarfed by the figure looming behind the guy I pegged as the lawyer. That guy made Dave look small. Tall and beefy, this guy had a t-shirt on, the sleeves pulled tight and ready to rip at a moment's notice. I halfway expected the whole shirt to split in two with the slightest movement. With a heavy brow and shaggy and unkempt chestnut hair, he looked like the antithesis of Mark and his lawyer—both of whom looked coiffed and styled within an inch of their lives.

Levi's deep blue eyes connected with mine. I'd expected a

smirk or something equally bratty. Instead, Levi looked . . . cautious. His eyes darted to the side, warily looking not only at the giant at the lawyer's back but also the lawyer himself. It didn't escape my notice that Levi had positioned himself farther off to the side, a spot that afforded him a decent sightline to Chrissie *and* the people he'd come with.

Mark took a step forward, emboldened by the company he'd brought. Nose held high, Mark taunted, "You can't keep me out this time." Throwing a thumb over his shoulder, Mark crowed, "I've got help, and they're not scared of what you are."

Levi's eyes narrowed, and his lips pursed into a near-invisible line. My skin crawled. I hated that he stood there, listening to Mark's loose tongue and even looser words. Levi didn't need encouragement when it came to this kind of shit.

"No?" Chrissie's hands fisted. I caught movement out of the corner of my eye, but it wasn't of the human variety. Rose's rosebushes shuddered, their green leaves long gone but their thorns forever present. Twisting and turning, they reached forward, stretching toward our invaders.

The men stepped back. Mark's eyes were large orbs of fear. Levi was too curious for my liking. As for the two strangers, they looked . . . impressed.

The rosebushes stopped moving just shy of touching. Throwing out an arm, Chrissie pointed toward the strangers, her attention zeroed in on Mark. "You're such an idiot, Mark. You stand there and think I'm the one you need to be afraid of." Chrissie laughed, low and dark. "You have no idea who, or more importantly, *what* you've hopped into bed with. You've made a deal with the devil, Mark, and trust me, you're going to get burned. When this is all over, you're the one that will pay the most."

Mark mustered up courage from somewhere. Or maybe it was desperation. "Are you threatening me?"

I caught the edge of Chrissie's smirk. I'd never seen her like that—so very vicious. "Oh, I don't have to threaten you, Mark. Like I said, it's not me you need to be afraid of. I'll only hurt you to protect Lilly, and you'll live to bitch about it. You won't get that kind of offer from the *things* you think are guarding your back."

It was easy to see the confusion coloring Mark's fear. Chrissie had planted a seed that wouldn't easily be rooted out. Shaking his head violently, Mark tugged on his coat, taking a step closer, wary of the rosebushes but pushing through that anxiety. "I want to see my daughter. Move out of the way or bring Lilly to the door. She has a right to know her father."

Words, angry and lit with dynamite, flew through the air. The cold suffusing my body thawed as warmth clawed its way through my soul and pushed the frigid fear to the side. *Andy.*

"Leah," Andy's honey-warm voice dripped through the misty cold. It was his reaper voice, the one that would have broken through Dave's bandanna of truth. "Is everything all right?"

It was more than obvious it wasn't. But it would be soon. All eyes turned toward Andy, and one by one, their expressions softened—drifting and peaceful. All but one. The man I pegged as the lawyer stood there and shook his head like a dog with an ear infection. A low, guttural, inhuman growl echoed from deep within his throat. Lips pulled back, the large, sharp canines they exposed weren't even close to human.

"Reaper."

The word was so guttural that I barely understood it.

"Wolf," Andy returned. "And a charmed one too. I don't think your witch is as talented as mine." Andy cocked his head in Chrissie's direction. "Your charm helps, but it's painful and has left you more exposed than your master would desire. No wonder he's after a new witch." Andy's head lowered; his green eyes stared up through dark fringed lashes. "But to go after a child." Andy tsked. "That seems like a new low."

A deeper, meaner growl erupted. The well-groomed lawyer was long gone, replaced by something that still looked human overall but had too feral a quality to it to easily pass. Mark, Levi, and big-and-brawny all looked wonderstruck. I had no idea what each of them saw when they looked at Andy, but it was pleasing, or at the very least, calming.

Andy easily moved through the crowd, coming to stand beside me. I leaned in closer, barely touching but needing the contact. The lawyer sneezed as he continued to shake his head. His hair now haphazardly spread around his face as drool and snot flowed down his chin. His fingernails pressed against his chest were no longer well-manicured, blunt tips. Thick, heavy, yellowed claws clutched at his suit jacket. His claws were nothing like the slender, razor-like talons Lizzie had.

Continuing his thick-as-molasses reaper voice, Andy said, "I think you should reevaluate your position. Or do you want to push your luck by yourself? Your muscle," Andy pointed to the brawny man at the lawyer's back, "is a little out of it right now. I suppose you could go it alone." Andy shrugged as if it didn't matter to him. "But I doubt you'd get very far."

On cue, the rosebushes started rustling again. One of their branches shot out, tangling with the lawyer's pants, clinging tight as he struggled to free himself.

"Think about this, Chrissie. You don't want to make an enemy of us." The lawyer's words were clearer but still sounded like they'd come through a garbled filter.

Chrissie stepped forward. "I think you've got that the

wrong way around. And I'm not the one trying to make enemies. You want my daughter. What in the hell did you think I'd do?"

The lawyer pressed the hidden charm against his skin as hard as he could. He seemed uncertain, and Andy helped him with his decision. "I think it's time all of you left. Thank you for visiting. Goodbye."

The three affected by Andy looked bereft for a half minute before they turned and walked away, leaving the lawyer stuttering on our stoop.

Bravado all used up, our final unwelcome visitor growled, "This isn't over," before he turned and bounded off the porch, his gait as unnatural as his teeth and claws.

"Shit," Chrissie whispered before she slumped against the side of the house. When I glanced over, her body was shaking.

"Are you okay?" It was a stupid question. Four men had been a few feet away from her daughter, their intentions less than stellar. Of course Chrissie wasn't okay.

"Yes. No." Chrissie gave a hysterical laugh. "I have no idea. I could use some sugar."

"Sugar is always a good idea," Andy readily agreed as he followed us into the house.

I sat Chrissie down on the couch before I ran into the kitchen. I poured her a glass of OJ and grabbed a bag of left-over Halloween candy. I thrust the OJ into her hand so force-fully that some spilled over the side. Chrissie didn't seem to mind.

She drank about half the glass before setting it on the table beside her, popping a piece of hard candy into her mouth and sucking on it hard. Andy rummaged around in the bag and took a few things too.

Chrissie's trembling eased into gentle spurts of soft quivers. Lifting the juice back to her lips, she drank the remainder. Breathing deeply, Chrissie's chest expanded before deflating with her exhale. "Grams would never believe this, but thank you, Andy. That was about to escalate into . . . something." Chrissie's lips twisted. "I guess we know who's bankrolling Mark now."

"Hmm, indeed," Andy answered while crunching SweeTARTS.

"Wolves?" I asked and then clarified, "Werewolves?"

"Nasty fuckers." Chrissie's mouth screwed up. "But not as nasty as shades."

I still wasn't clear on what shades were, at least when Chrissie spoke of them, but I thought I knew about werewolves. Well, not *knew* knew but had some general concept.

Deciding maybe I could use some clarity, and all too aware that I was really about to ask this question, I asked, "Are these traditional werewolves, as in, the things I've read about in books?"

Chrissie shrugged. "Pretty much. I'm sure there are differences here and there, but the concept is accurate enough. They're a pack. The biggest difference between what you've read and the real deal is that they've got one grand master. There are smaller groupings that have individual leaders, but they all answer to one man." Chrissie's shimmering green eyes bore into mine. "Samuel Hartman."

The name didn't mean anything to me. I hadn't expected it to.

"I've heard the name before." Evidently, I was the only one totally in the dark. "But I've never met the man, or perhaps, wolf."

"Neither have I." Chrissie let loose a soul-deep sigh. "God, I wish Grams were here. She'd know what to do." Scrubbing her hands over her face, Chrissie pushed off the couch. "I need to go get Lilly to tell her everything's fine." Chrissie choked on a laugh. "For now."

A faint knock on Lilly's door preceded the squeak of the hinges. Chrissie's soft, reassuring voice drifted down the hall and into the living room.

"You really do have a death wish, don't you?" Andy moved closer, and I leaned back into his chest.

"In my defense, I don't think this one is my fault."

"No. I suppose not." Andy's arms wrapped around my middle, his body bent over to accommodate the movement. "Regardless, I don't like this new danger. What I did today won't always work. By all accounts, Samuel Hartman is very intelligent. One of his wolves will remember what happened today, and soon, all of them will wear a charm, even if they are a poor imitation of what Chrissie can do. It will work well enough."

"I guess that makes you a one-trick pony," I teased.

"I suppose it does." Andy's breath blew across the top of my head, teasing my hair.

"Will you get in trouble? For what you just did?"

Andy had told me time and time again that there were rules.

"Doubtful. Management isn't keen to upset you or lose you. I have more leeway where your safety is concerned. And two of those affected aren't under management's concern. They couldn't care less about what I did to the wolves."

"Hmm." I wasn't sure what to say but was grateful Andy didn't expect any blowback. I had enough crisis to manage without adding to that shitty list.

"This won't be the end, Leah. If anything, it is only the beginning. They will be back and better prepared. You were the one anomaly they hadn't accounted for."

"I doubt they know anything about me," I argued despite the cold vying to beat back Andy's warmth.

"That may be, but they know about me and that I'm connected to you and, by default, their primary target. And that makes you a target too. I don't know how to protect you from that kind of threat."

Andy tightened his arms around me and pulled me in closer. I didn't know how to protect us either. That didn't mean I wouldn't do everything I could to keep Lilly and Chrissie safe.

23

Quiet descended again into our little world, but it was a charged silence. All of us were waiting for a repeat performance, wondering where the next attack would come from. It seemed like Mark was content to leave it in the hands of the lawyers and courts. Chrissie didn't seem surprised. She said that creating a charm like the one she'd made for Dave and Cecile took time. It wasn't something that could be accomplished overnight. It would be a few days, or maybe weeks, before the wolves would try again.

Chrissie drove herself into the ground. She warded the house and communicated with other witches who offered help. We had a few visitors here and there that did things around the house I didn't understand. Overall, I didn't ask a lot of questions. This wasn't in my wheelhouse.

Phoenix's appointment time rolled around, and I bundled her up in the new carrier Dave and Cecile had gotten for her. She meowed the entire way there. Rose's house was about the same distance from Dr. Anderson's clinic as my apartment had been, just in the opposite direction.

Everyone in the clinic came in to see her, their faces beaming with smiles. I returned those smiles, even if mine were only skin deep. Phoenix was a good kitty. I could only hope that one day I didn't look at her and wish she were a cat she wasn't.

Phoenix didn't appreciate her blood draw, but her viral testing came back negative. A wave of relief settled over me. I wasn't as attached to her as I'd been to Ashes, but I was happy she had a clean bill of health.

A round of vaccinations and a follow-up appointment made for boosters later, and we were out the door. Cecile's mom could pick her up later today. I had the day off and would have offered, but I had plans involving Dave and a spot in his chair. Cecile made me promise to take some photos of my new ink and text them to her later.

I dropped Phoenix off at home. Thankfully Chrissie was off work today and could keep an eye on her to make sure she didn't have any reactions to her vaccines. Dr. Anderson told me that most likely Phoenix would sleep the rest of the day away. I didn't see how that was a lot different than her normal activity.

With my kitten safely deposited back at home, I drove to Ink No Evil. It was weird. For a time, I'd called the space home, but I hadn't been back since I'd moved into Rose's old house.

Evening was approaching. The sky darkened earlier than during the summer months. Our earlier sunshine had been obliterated by low-hanging clouds, and I longed for summer's warmth.

Tugging my coat tighter, I scurried up to the door. This time, I used the store one instead of the apartment door. The metal bells above announced my arrival. Hampton ducked her head out from deep within the hall leading to Dave's room. "I'll be with you in a minute." Hampton's voice had a lilting quality that always reminded me of a song.

"It's okay, Hampton. It's just me."

"Well, *just me*, I'm glad to see you." Hampton's long, lean, jean-clad legs sauntered down the hall and into the lobby. As per usual, she pulled me into a tight, air-crushing hug. Hampton's well-endowed chest cushioned my cheek. "I feel like it's been an age since I've seen you. How are you doin'?"

Pulling away, Hampton held me at arm's length. A hint of a smile lifted her lips. She looked pleased. "You're lettin' your hair grow out." Hampton's fingers slid through my longer length while her crimson-painted nails gently scratched my neck. "I like it. And please don't take this the wrong way, but you've plumped up a little. You've got a little meat on your bones. It's a good look."

Easing behind the counter, Hampton clicked a couple of things on the keyboard. "Dave told me you were comin' in today to get some fresh ink. I'm glad to hear it. You ever decide you want a little jewelry here and there, you let me know. I'll fix you up right."

"If I ever want a piercing or two, I wouldn't dream of asking anyone else," I assured Hampton.

Her smile was wide. Hampton's white teeth shimmered against her dark, sepia skin. "Good answer. I'll let Dave know you're here."

I quietly waited for Hampton to go down the hall. She would have told me to head on down myself if Dave had been alone. That meant he was still with another customer. The sky continued to darken outside, and I sat down to wait. Another customer came in, this one had an appointment with Hampton, and she took them to a back room I'd seen maybe once or twice but never had a reason to peek into often.

I'd seen Tonn Tonn's Camaro in the parking lot. Chama's

truck was absent. I hadn't seen a lot of him recently. Dave said Chama had taken his mother's passing pretty rough and was considering moving back to New Mexico to be closer to family. Dave was crushed by the idea but understood it.

I was fiddling with the strap of my purse when the chimes above the door sounded their metal medley. Their tinkling automatically brought my head up. My open, gaped mouth was all my doing. *Holy shit.*

"This is an interesting establishment." The man was tall, lean, and covered from head to toe in a dark black coat that swished around his ankles. His bare hands hung at his sides. Reddish-brown skin peeked around all the black encasing his body. Even his hair was jet black, just this side of blue. His facial features were sharp angles, his eyes covered by a pair of dark, impenetrable sunglasses. I took a second glance outside and noticed night had encroached even farther.

"I said you could wait in the car." The woman was dressed similarly, only her hands were covered by a pair of the smoothest leather I'd ever seen. A wide-brimmed, scarlet hat sat atop her head. She had skin paler than mine. Her sleek, dark brown hair tumbled over her matching scarlet coat. I didn't know if she wore lipstick or if her lips were naturally that plump and deep red. She also had large, oversized sunglasses covering her eyes.

"I'm more than capable of entering a building by myself, John. My nephew is hardly a threat." She sounded irritated, a huffing quality that implied she wasn't used to being told what to do or when to do it.

Her head twisted, and her hair shifted along her coat, the long strands stuck here and there. When her gaze landed on me, she asked, "Do you work here?"

I sat there, dumbfounded and staring. I'd seen a lot of beautiful people in my day—mostly on television or airbrushed in a magazine. I'd never seen anyone like this, though.

I was silent too long, and her lips pressed into an irritated line. "Are you dim? Or perhaps hard of hearing. I asked if you worked here."

"Oh, um . . . No. I—"

"Aunt Gussie, is that you out there harassing Leah?" Tonn Tonn sounded far away, his words muffled by the long hall separating us.

"I wouldn't know." The woman I suspected was Tonn Tonn's *Aunt Gussie* crossed her arms over her chest, head tilted, and mouth set in obvious irritation. "She's barely spoken, let alone offered up a name or her position here."

Tonn Tonn chuckled, low and warm. The sound grew in volume as he drew closer. "Leah doesn't work here, though she used to spend enough time hanging around you'd think she did. Leah's a friend, and from what Dave said, a customer tonight too."

Smiling so hard it looked like his cheeks should hurt, Tonn Tonn took three long strides and pulled his aunt into his arms, squeezing the life out of her. She was stiff at first but melted into the contact, lifting her arms and hugging Tonn Tonn back.

"How many times have I told you not to call me that ridiculous name?" she asked as Tonn Tonn released his firm hold.

"About as many times as I've called you Aunt Gussie. Doesn't matter. The rest of the world can call you Augusta. Mom and I get away with Gussie."

Augusta gave a grunt of irritation, but her lips tipped up at the edges, and a dusting of pink colored her cheeks. "Yes, well . . . I suppose it's no worse than the ridiculous nickname you insist upon being called. You'll always be Antony to me."

Stepping back, Augusta set her coat to rights, tugging down the places that had been displaced with their hug.

Tonn Tonn's laughter cut off jarringly. His sharp eyes widened, and that odd amber glow I sometimes caught shimmered between darkened eyelashes. Taking a step back, Tonn Tonn's gaze traveled between his aunt and the stranger behind her. Swallowing hard, Tonn Tonn's Adam's apple bobbed. Briefly, that gaze flashed toward me. I couldn't read the emotions simmering behind it.

"Aunt Gussie, you've brought an interesting . . . *friend* with you."

Augusta waved a crimson gloved hand behind her, dismissing the looming figure standing there. "Don't mind John. Currently, he's allowing his paranoia to override good sense."

Tonn Tonn looked like the last thing on his mind was *not minding* John.

Ink No Evil's waiting room was probably larger than a lot of tattoo shops. Having transformed a previous car dealership into the store, Dave and Chama had turned the old service reception area into the lobby. Normally there was more than enough space. John filled that space to the brim, overflowing into every nook and cranny.

Moving around Augusta, John's sleek, tall form glided more than walked. Hands clasped low on his back, John didn't offer to shake Tonn Tonn's hand. Instead, he eased forward enough to offer the barest hint of a bow. "Youngling," John addressed Tonn Tonn, his voice low and raspy. The scent of charred smoke filtered into my nose, and I wondered if someone had started a bonfire nearby.

I was so distracted by the sound and new scents that it took me longer than it should have to realize what John had just called Tonn Tonn. *"Youngling?"* Tonn Tonn was *young*. I wasn't exactly sure of his age. My best guess was mid-to-late twenties. Regardless, it was an odd way to greet someone.

Tonn Tonn's head didn't move—just the barest hint of his eyes shifted in my direction. John didn't acknowledge me, his attention all on Tonn Tonn. Only Augusta seemed to care that I'd spoken. "He's not that much younger than me," Augusta huffed with an eye roll of irritation. "Honestly, you say the oddest things sometimes." Augusta ended with a breath of irritation and an equally dismissive wave of her leather-covered hand.

John's head dipped ever so slightly while taking a step back. "Forgive me, youngling."

Hands fisted on her hips, Augusta gave John a withering look I would have been frightened to mimic. Huffing seemed to be her way of ignoring John.

Tonn Tonn didn't exactly relax, but he did ease down some. "I'm sorry, Aunt Gussie. I should have turned the lights down." Without waiting for a response, Tonn Tonn walked behind the counter and hit the overhead lights, turning off the fluorescent shine from above. Once those lights were off, Augusta removed her glasses and pulled off her hat. I didn't think I'd ever seen someone with as pale blue eyes as this woman. Set against her dark lashes, eyebrows, and hair, they were stunning.

"It's fine. I'm used to it and came prepared." Augusta held up her hat and sunglasses.

John, I noticed, didn't remove his dark lenses.

"I know, but it was rude." Turning, Tonn Tonn addressed me for the first time. I'd started to think maybe they'd forgotten I was in the room. "Aunt Gussie has a medical condition. She's sensitive to light."

"Really?" I jerked back, realizing how rude that had probably sounded. "Um, sorry, I didn't—"

"Not that I'm not happy to see you, but what are you

doing here?" Tonn Tonn asked, interrupting what was sure to be a weak-ass apology on my part.

Augusta's smile turned brittle. "Mom and Dad. They're holding a fundraising gala this year."

Tonn Tonn's eyes rolled, their color still amazing but no longer glimmering. "They hold a fundraising gala every other month."

I sat there, mind silently whirling. Dave had made hints, little comments here and there over the years that Tonn Tonn didn't have financial worries, but he'd never indicated what I was beginning to guess. Average American families didn't hold fundraising galas, let alone one every other month. Just who was Tonn Tonn? Or, more importantly, who was Tonn Tonn related to?

Augusta tugged at the fingers of her gloves and pulled them off with a little more force than was strictly necessary. "Your mom hasn't told you yet, has she?"

Tonn Tonn leaned against the desk, his casual stance betrayed by the tick in his jaw. "She told me you were thinking about moving back from Virginia."

"Yes, well . . . you can remove the thinking aspect from that sentence. Looks like I will once again call the Hoosier state home." Augusta didn't sound all that pleased, more resigned than anything.

"Mom will be thrilled," Tonn Tonn said hesitantly. "But you don't sound too excited."

Augusta shot a quick look behind her. John's looming presence was a constant heaviness. "Circumstances have . . . changed." Augusta's plump lips pinched when she turned her attention back on her nephew. "Sometimes needs outweigh desires. Besides, the situation with my work in Virginia has become untenable. It's time for a change."

"And how does that change relate to one of Nana and Papaw's galas?"

Blowing out an exasperated breath, Augusta slapped her gloves against a pale hand. Her manicured nails were white against the crimson leather. "The veterinary clinic in Clementine is abysmal. Your nana has decided that if I'm going to spend any time in that facility, there needs to be a few upgrades. I'll also continue my research on my own terms and without the backing of an established institution. All of that requires money, and no one is better at getting the wealthy to part with their beloved cash than your nana."

"True." Tonn Tonn gave an affectionate smile before his eyes hardened, their gaze no longer on Augusta but the man standing behind her. "And John," Tonn Tonn's head jerked in John's direction. "He decided to come along because . . ."

"That's a longer story than we have time for." Eyes traveling around the lobby, Augusta didn't look like she missed a thing. "So, this is where you work? Do I get a tour? Covetous isn't exactly on the way to Indianapolis from Clementine."

"Yeah, of course." Stepping away from the counter, Tonn Tonn offered, "John, would you like to come or—"

"I will wait in the car." John's covered eyes swept the room again. "This facility appears harmless. Augusta, call if I am required. Youngling, it was an honor to meet you." John tipped his head in what sort of looked like a bow but wasn't. The tinkling sound of the overhead bells chimed as John stepped out the door and back into the night.

By the time I looked back, Augusta's crimson coat had disappeared down the hall, her faded complaint, "I told him to just stay in the car," drifted lowly into the lobby I sat in dumbfoundedly.

Blinking, my dry eyes complained about that earlier lack of action. *What in the hell had that been?* I'd seen a lot of *strange* in the past few months, but that . . . I didn't even know how to define it. Isaac had implied long ago that there were *other* things out in the world. Knowing Chrissie had solidified that fact.

By the time Dave's customer left, checking out with Hampton, I was convinced what I'd just experienced fit into Chrissie's world a hell of a lot more than mine. Right before Dave came to get me, I managed a brief and all too underwhelming, "Weird."

Dave put the finishing touch on Bobby's name scrolled across my heart in beautiful cursive. My mom's name had daisies around it. My dad's had little nails. Bobby's name was kept clean. Dave had already finished Ashes's tattoo, her paw print inked below her name, both on the inside of my right forearm. No leather wrist straps would cover it. But Ashes's tattoo wasn't like my parents'. Hers didn't cover raised scars of self-harm. I had no intention of covering Ashes name.

Bobby's would stay forever tucked away, safe from prying eyes and judgmental thoughts. I'd keep him safe in his afterlife, even if I hadn't been able to do the same while he'd been alive.

Dave quietly worked while my jaw and hands clenched. My body was used to mental pain more than physical. Regardless, pain was pain, and I cordoned this off similarly. At least this pain would eventually end. It was more than tolerable.

"Wolves."

Dave had repeated that singular word more times than I cared to hear it. There hadn't been a doubt in my mind about telling Dave what had happened last night. Before, when we'd sort of been researching shades, we'd known that werewolves were a possibility. Theoretical and right in your face were two different things.

"That one's hard to swallow. What's next? Vampires?"

I sucked in a breath—a piercing pain stronger than before rocketed up from Dave's tattoo gun. When the pain was manageable again, I filled Dave in on a conversation I'd had with Chrissie this morning. "Chrissie says no, or at least not like we traditionally think of them. There's no corpse-like thing out to suck your blood. But there are other kinds of things—humans that have the ability to suck energy off people. Chrissie said some of the humans who do this don't even know they're doing it. Most of the time, it's harmless."

Dave's motions stopped. Sitting back, he stared at me with wide eyes. "Well, that's . . . I don't know what that is."

Neither did I. "I also asked about shades."

Dave leaned over, the whine of the tattoo gun picking up again.

"I'm sure that's something *pleasant* too."

"I doubt that's the right word." Honestly, I wasn't sure what the right word was for what I'd found out. Maybe creepy would fit. "Chrissie said shades can mean different things, but the type of shades she's most worried about are those that come after infant witches."

Dave stopped again, and his head jerked up. "They go after babies? Christ, what kind of monster are we talking about?"

I considered my words, trying to remember how Chrissie had phrased it. "It's not as bad as you think, or maybe not as malicious. According to Chrissie, shades are the remnants of leftover human emotions—emotions that are so strong they form an entity all their own. These entities tend to gather, forming groups that become bound together. Alone, they're mindless and driven by that singular emotion. Together, they begin to form a being, yet they can never be whole and alive. Not without the help of a host body."

"A host body? Jesus, are we talking Justin Turlington level shit again?"

"I don't think so."

Dave wiped away some more blood. The scent of it was by far worse than the physical pain of the needle. Dave lit a cinnamon-scented candle, trying to distract me from the nauseating copper tinge. I didn't have the heart to tell him that it made things worse, that it just made me think of cinnamon-flavored blood.

"Then what are we talking about?"

"Chrissie says it's like a permanent bonding but has to happen with an infant or young child. Chrissie says the instances of it happening are extremely rare. Some witches think it's just a fable. Oleana didn't think so, and the first charm that was ever laid against Lilly's skin was one to protect her against shades. She still wears it. That's one of the reasons Chrissie thought it was probably the wolves and not shades that were out to get Lilly."

Dave wiped more blood away, staring at his work. "Is it in her bracelet?"

Lilly always wore a bracelet with little charms worked into the hemp. They didn't dangle like a lot of bracelets did. They were all tucked firmly against her skin.

"Yeah, though I'm not sure which one."

"You can sit up now. I'll get the mirror." The wheels of Dave's rollie chair sounded against the concrete floor as he scooted across the room. Dave grabbed a handheld mirror and handed it over. I stared at my brother's reflected name, tears gathering in the corners of my eyes. "That's . . ."

"I kept it simple, just like what you wanted. If you ever change your mind and want a little more detail or flourish, I can add to it."

"No, at least not right now." I managed a smile for Dave. "It's beautiful." And right where it should be. "I asked Andy about talking to Bobby and seeing if he could stop by sometime, that you wanted to see him." I wanted to see Bobby too, just about as equally as I longed not to see him. I was so damn confused when it came to my brother that I didn't know what to wish for. Given how infrequently wishes came true, that was probably for the best.

"What did he say?" Dave snapped off his gloves and tossed them in a nearby biohazard box. Dave busied himself, cleaning up his station. I wasn't sure if he was avoiding my gaze or not.

"He said he'd talk to him, but ultimately, it's up to Bobby. Unless management has different ideas," I amended.

"Management sounds like a bunch of dicks to me," Dave grunted.

I didn't argue.

"Samuel Hartman sounds like an even bigger dick."

I didn't argue that either.

"Hartman?" Tonn Tonn pushed Dave's curtain aside, leaning against the frame. With his fingers clenching the fabric, Tonn Tonn looked like he was aiming for relaxed but missed the emotion by a mile.

"Yeah," Dave answered, smearing a cream over my newest tattoo and covering it. "Don't take that off for about three days. Got it?" Dave instructed me before turning his attention back to Tonn Tonn. "Do you know him?"

Tonn Tonn shrugged. Again, the action more casual than the tension that filled his body. "Not specifically. The name just sounded familiar." His gaze focused in on me

I pulled my shirt up, covering my fresh ink and preserving what little dignity I might have left.

"Is he someone who's bothering you?"

I sat up a little straighter, righting the rest of my shirt.

"Not me in particular, but a friend of mine who became my roommate."

"Hmm . . ." Tonn Tonn's eyes looked distant, as if he were seeing something other than the pictures on Dave's desk. Shaking himself free of whatever thoughts circulated through his head, Tonn Tonn's face morphed into an easygoing smile, the image a familiar and much more welcome one. "Sorry to interrupt. I was just curious to see how your new ink turned out."

I happily showed Tonn Tonn the latest additions to my skin. His fingers were warm against my wrist as he twisted my arm, allowing better light onto it. "Looks good."

"Of course it looks good," Dave gruffed. "I did it."

Tonn Tonn chuckled, releasing my arm and holding his hands up in a defensive manner. "So sorry. Didn't mean to offend."

Dave threw up the middle finger, and they seemed to be good after that.

Sliding around so I could stand up, I asked, "Is your aunt gone?"

Tensing ever so slightly, Tonn Tonn's shoulders slowly relaxed. "She is. I'm sorry if she was a little gruff with you. Aunt Gussie can be . . ." Head tilted to the side, Tonn Tonn's smile was fond. "Sometimes she can be kind of abrasive. She's wicked smart though," he tapped his temple, "and doesn't always have a lot of patience for those that can't follow along. She's also been through a lot and has to still put up with a lot, what with her medical condition and all."

It was an odd condition, one I hadn't really heard of before. "She's really that sensitive to light?"

"Light and temperature fluctuations," Tonn Tonn answered offhandedly, effectively dismissing the conversation and whatever questions I had brewing. "I also wanted to stop in and let you know I'm heading out for the night, Dave.

Hampton left about fifty minutes ago, so you've got the place to yourself."

"I'll lock up. Thanks."

"No worries." Tonn Tonn turned, releasing the fabric drape. The curtain was almost completely closed when he caught it again and ducked his head back in the room. "Listen, Leah. If that Hartman guy keeps giving you shit, you let me know. Okay?"

My mouth opened, shutting again on words I couldn't find. Eventually, I settled on, "Okay?" which came out more question than answer.

"Catch you later." Tonn Tonn gave me a wink before he released the curtain again, this time allowing it to close.

For the second time that evening, the only word I could come up with was a wholly inadequate, "Weird."

Dave didn't disagree.

24

The house was unusually calm for the next couple of weeks. It was a quiet sense of foreboding—constant waiting for the other proverbial shoe to drop. Thanksgiving rolled around, and Aunt Joyce and Uncle Jack's table was fuller than in years past. The tension Chrissie and I'd carried around momentarily eased as we all sat down to a spectacularly carbolicious Midwestern meal. Noodles, mashed potatoes, rolls, corn, green beans . . . and of course, turkey, littered the table. Deserts were laid out along the nearby counter.

Dave, Chrissie, and Lilly all found a place at the table. Chrissie and Lilly planned to head over to Lenny's place after eating a late lunch with us. Aunt Joyce had several containers full of food at the ready to take over. Lenny didn't cook and had told Chrissie that they usually didn't do anything fancy for Thanksgiving. Aunt Joyce was determined to change that. Next year we'd probably have to add another seat for Lenny and one for his mom too. I wasn't sure what restrictions Lenny's mom had or if she could get out of the house and come over at all. I planned to find out before Christmas.

After Chrissie and Lilly left, the rest of us had another brainstorming session about Thomas. We didn't have much more information than before, and the plan mostly came down to cornering Thomas's spirit and hoping that Cecile could tame his anger. I didn't like our so-called *plan* much. If Dave's continued huffs and drawn eyebrows were anything to go by, he didn't either. Dave took every opportunity to remind us that Thomas could move things—throw objects at us that could do some serious damage. Silently, I wondered if we could get by with taking shields in with us. I was sure that wouldn't look weird at all.

Sitting around, discussing deceased, lingering spirits made me long for Andy. I had no idea if he had a spirit to reap today or not. Andy couldn't be around Aunt Joyce and Uncle Jack without affecting them. We could have asked them to cover their eyes the entire time, but that didn't seem very kind.

I needed to ask Chrissie if she could make them charms too, but given everything she currently had on her plate, I didn't want to push it. I'd never seen Chrissie so exhausted. Chrissie had pulled Lilly out of school, deeming it too dangerous. On top of everything else, Chrissie was trying to homeschool Lilly. She'd cut her hours back at Crossroads but hadn't given work up completely. Chrissie was determined to finish this semester of college classes. Next semester was anyone's guess.

I'd told Chrissie she didn't have to work, that I could cover us for a while. Chrissie refused, or at least she refused to take my *charity*. She said she'd work enough to at least cover the cost of her and Lilly's food and to help out as much as possible with the utilities. There was also the hefty cost of the lawyer Chrissie had hired. Custody battles weren't cheap —monetarily or emotionally. Chrissie didn't have a lot saved. Everything she did have had gone into a single payment.

Future bills were sure to come, and Chrissie had no idea how she would pay them.

Dave's frustrated tone caught my attention, pulling me away from thoughts of Chrissie. "I think you should wait until after the holidays."

"Why?" Cecile sounded genuinely curious.

Instead of answering Cecile, Dave asked, "Joyce, correct me if I'm wrong, but I'm gonna take a wild stab and say the hospital decorates for Christmas."

With a bite of pumpkin pie halfway to her lips, Aunt Joyce set her fork on her plate, tilting her head before saying, "Some. It's the ER, so not a ton, but there are decorations."

Dave twirled his fingers in the air. "Lights, trees with ornaments, things like that?"

"Yeah." Aunt Joyce nodded, her eyes flicking toward Uncle Jack. When he shrugged his confusion, they turned on me.

"I've got nothing," I answered before she could ask me what in the hell Dave was going on about.

Huffing, Dave crossed his arms over his chest. "Thomas can throw shit. I don't see how going in and getting him all riled up and angry while he's got more ammunition around is a good idea. And some of those ornaments are probably fragile and will shatter on impact. You two are going in to help cleanse the hospital, not become patients."

"That's . . . surprisingly practical thinking, Dave." Uncle Jack appeared to be fishing for compliments or something to say.

Cecile got up, plopped down on Dave's lap, and wrapped her arms around his shoulders. She succeeded in flushing Dave's cheeks rosy-pink with a quick peck. "That's so sweet of you to think of something like that."

I groaned. I just couldn't help it. "Yeah, real sweet of you, Dave."

Dave ignored me. Wrapping his arms around Cecile, he pulled my cousin in closer. Uncle Jack just kept eating his pie while Aunt Joyce looked like she might melt into a puddle of pumpkin goo.

I leaned back against the couch, wishing it would swallow me whole.

My phone distantly sounded from inside my purse. "Thank god," slipped through my lips before I could even attempt to pull it back.

Dave threw me the one-finger salute behind Cecile's back. Uncle Jack chuckled around his bite of pie. Aunt Joyce acted like she didn't see a thing. I was too late getting to my purse, and the call had ended. Checking the number, I didn't recognize it and chalked it up to spam. I waited a minute to see if there was a voicemail, but nothing showed up. Stuffing my phone back into my purse, I headed back into the living room and the sugary sweetness that had nothing to do with desserts.

<hr>

Christmas was out and in full swing the day after Thanksgiving. Black Friday hit us fast and hard. Gary typically tried to accommodate those who wanted the day off, which left us shorthanded on a day where we should have had more, not less employees. To help out, Gary and Judy were both in the store, working their fingers to the bone. Lizzie was on as manager. Berta had the day off to be with her kids, and Daryl was scheduled to come in during the afternoon-slash-evening shift to relieve Lizzie, not that she looked like she needed relieved. If there was one thing Lizzie Johnson appeared to thrive upon, it was chaos.

"Can you believe this?" Lenny asked as we snuck off to the break room to at least get some water and a candy bar.

Lenny shoved some Doritos into his mouth too. "It's weird to think this many people have the day after Thanksgiving off."

I'd never given it much thought either way. This was the first year Thanksgiving hadn't been an awkward verbal dance since my parents died. Years past, I'd been anxious to get back to work, back to something I knew I could do well. This was the first time in a long time I thought it may be nice to have the day off.

"Your aunt's a great cook," Lenny went on, thankfully swallowing the handful of chips he'd stuffed in his mouth before praising Aunt Joyce. "And it was super nice of her to send all that food over. Mom loved it and having Chrissie and Lilly there too . . ." Lenny's face flushed, and his fingers scratched the back of his neck with his embarrassment. "It was nice, you know?"

I did indeed know, just in a different way than Lenny spoke of. The employee break room door swung open. For the briefest moment, before he realized he wasn't alone, Ricky's true colors showed through his pissed-off eyes and snarled lips. Even when his eyes landed on me, that look remained for a split second longer than it should have.

"Leah. Lenny." Ricky recovered, moving into the room and allowing the closing door to mute the cacophony of sound brewing outside. "Busy day, isn't it?" Ricky beamed, his fake smile strained.

"Really busy," Lenny offered, voice quieter than usual. Shifting from foot to foot, Lenny thumbed toward the door. "Better get back out there. You coming?" Lenny's gaze flicked toward Ricky's back as he dug inside the refrigerator for a drink.

"Yeah, I've just gotta check my messages first." Chrissie had taken to checking in with me when I was at work, just to let me know if things were okay or not. It felt weird, being on the other end of the stalking line.

Lenny gave me a dubious look, eyes skittering in Ricky's direction again. Silently, I mouthed, "I'll be fine." I didn't plan on staying long.

Lenny still looked doubtful but nodded before he left.

I quickly got into my locker and pulled my phone out. Chrissie had texted a brief, "We're okay." I texted back a relieved emoji and hit send. It was then I realized I had a missed call. The number looked kind of familiar but not something I recognized right away, and there was no name attached, so it wasn't a number in my contacts. There was no voicemail.

Tucking my phone back into my purse, I turned to leave. At some point, Ricky had moved close—too close. Jumping back, my heart thumped loud and heavy in my chest. "Jesus, Ricky. What the hell?"

Ricky grinned, slow and malicious. "Sorry, Leah. I didn't mean to frighten you."

Like hell he hadn't. Slamming my locker door, I thought about telling Ricky all the reasons I'd nominate him for asshole of the year, but those words didn't come. Instead, I pointed at the sleeve of his typically meticulously white shirt. A fresh stain of red seeped around the cuff. "What's that? Are you okay?" I probably couldn't smell the blood soaking into Ricky's bleached white shirtsleeve. Most likely, it was imagined—a memory that would never leave.

Ricky's bravado faded into a look of brief shock. Quickly tucking his arm behind his back, Ricky took three large steps away. "It's nothing. Just an accident."

Blood did funny things to me. One of those funny things was that it made me concerned about Ricky Levitson. "Do you need me to get you a Band-Aid?" From the length of red, it looked like it might take more than one.

"No. I said I'm fine."

Ricky had *not* previously said that. I chose not to point

that out. Knowing how put out Ricky had been about the motor oil stain, I couldn't imagine what he'd feel like going back out on the floor with blood on his shirt. "Do you want me to call Shelly? I don't have her number, but maybe she could bring you—"

"I do not need your help, Leah," Ricky spat.

There was so much vitriol, so much venom and anger in his voice that I took two healthy steps toward the door.

"This," Ricky held up his arm, "is nothing. An accident that I'm more than capable of handling on my own. Besides," Ricky turned to his locker, opening it and pulling out a fresh, clean white shirt, "I learned from my last mistake." Ricky smiled again, the malice of earlier fading to little more than a whisper of what it had been. "This time, I'm prepared."

Fresh shirt in hand, Ricky headed out of the break room to change. I stood there, mouth parted and brain uselessly tumbling. Ricky was such an ass. I had no idea why, but I'd been concerned. I hadn't been flippant in my questions and sincerely wanted to know if he was injured and if there was anything I could do to help him. Obviously, my concern was wasted. Why Ricky's rejection of my help stung was beyond me. Dr. Cross would probably tell me my response was naturally human, that many of us were hardwired to worry about others, even when we didn't like them.

If that were the case, my body was in serious need of a fresh rewire. It was a stupid thought, but only because that was a fact I hadn't needed Ricky Levitson to expose.

The door had just swung closed when I heard the ping of a new text message sound from my phone. Keeping a wary eye on the break room door, I headed back to my locker and quickly located my phone. My eyebrows shot up when I read Dave's message. "Lawyer just called. Cindy wants to sign custody of Marshall over to me. Dean already signed papers.

Appt on Monday." The message was followed by a row of grinning emojis.

I texted back an equally ecstatic-looking smiley face before placing my phone back into my locker, closing the metal door with a quick snick. It was probably stupid, but I still hadn't placed a padlock on the door. No one else had either. With Justin's spirit reaped, I hadn't seen the need. Staring over at Ricky's locker gave me second thoughts.

With no desire to see Ricky again, I headed for the door and back out into the chaos that was Black Friday. No matter what was going on out there, it had to be better than being alone with Ricky Levitson.

Cyber Monday was a lot calmer of a workday. Almost everyone else was back at their jobs, scrounging the internet for the best sale while on the clock. I guess I could have done something similar with my phone during break. I didn't.

Lenny and I worked the morning shift together and headed out to our cars the same way. The sky was overcast, with low-hanging, heavy clouds that spoke of rain. The forecast didn't call for any, but it was depressing all the same. I hated this time of year.

We'd reached a fork in our common passage. Lenny was parked off to the right while I was left. Stopping, Lenny asked, "You headed home?"

"No." I shoved my hands into the pockets of my heavy coat. The wind was particularly biting today, and I bounced on my toes, trying to keep warm. "I'm headed over to Dave's. He signed the paperwork today, making him Marshall's legal guardian. We're not having a party, just a small get-together to celebrate."

"Is Marshall okay with that?" Lenny looked more concerned than dubious.

"He is. Marshall's the one who asked for it. Dave said his little brother's relieved." I'd be relieved too, knowing I didn't have to go back and live with Dean Masters. I still wasn't sure about Cindy. Despite Dave, Bobby, and I growing up together, I barely knew the woman.

Lenny beamed. "That's great. Hopefully we'll all celebrate something like that soon with Lilly and Chrissie."

"Yeah. Hopefully." I managed a smile. Lenny wasn't the idiot I used to think he was. He knew it was an uphill battle. There'd be no small amount of bloodshed left on that hill. Lilly's situation was wholly different from Marshall's. Lilly was a prize, and the stakes were high. As for Marshall . . . neither of his biological parents wanted him. It would have been sadder if Marshall wasn't better off without them.

No more convinced than me that Lilly's situation would resolve as easily as Marshall's, Lenny offered up a small wave of goodbye. Head down and unusually subdued, Lenny faced the wind and hustled toward his car.

The cold, north wind left no time to linger. Just like always, my little blue Toyota started up on the first try. Heat blasting, I headed for Dave's.

***

There weren't a lot of cars parked on the street near Dave's house. It was still early enough in the afternoon that many residents were at work. That would change in the next hour or two. Cecile was scheduled to work until six. Uncle Jack and Aunt Joyce planned to pick her up and meet us for a nice, quiet dinner. I'd picked up the cake at the grocery. It wasn't very big, but it was full of chocolatey goodness. Scrolled in blue icing were the words WELCOME HOME.

Cake in hand, I got out of my car and headed for the front door. I gave a cursory knock before I let myself in. The front door wasn't locked, and even if it had been, I had a key.

Cindy's loud, mocking voice smacked into my ears the moment the door cracked open. "I never wanted Marshall, not even while I carried him."

I nearly dropped the cake, stumbling over my feet as those words hit me in the chest. Facing away from me, Cindy's fisted hands rested on her hips, pushing out the long, dark brown coat she'd failed to remove. Given what she'd just said, I doubted Cindy planned on staying long. Technically, Dave faced me, but his furious eyes were all for his stepmother. Neither realized I'd walked through the door.

"Then you're an idiot," Dave shot back. "And a shitty-ass mother."

The small heel of Cindy's shoe clacked against the hardwood of Dave's refinished floors as she stepped back. "I'm not a shitty mother," Cindy defended herself. "If I were, I would have abandoned Marshall a long time ago. I stayed there, raised him the best I could. He's fourteen, more than old enough to take care of himself now."

Dave's eyebrows shot up so high I thought they might hit the ceiling. "*Old enough?* By what standards? The 1800s? Marshall's a teenager, and you left him alone in a home with a verbally and physically abusive father. An alcoholic, no less. Forgive me, Cindy, but that certainly doesn't nominate you for mother of the year."

Back bristling, Cindy's nose pointed toward the sky. "I had Devlin to think about. It was his first year in college. His—"

"Exactly." Dave took a step closer, getting up into Cindy's face. "College. Devlin's eighteen, nineteen in another month. Why do you think your fourteen-year-old son is old enough to fend for himself but not his older brother? That makes no sense."

Silently, I agreed with Dave.

Cindy just scoffed. "You make it sound like I left him on the corner with no roof over his head."

"I'm not sure that would have been worse." Dave backed up, pacing in front of the opening leading to the kitchen. "What the hell, Cindy? Marshall's a good kid. He's smart and has a good head on his shoulders. Anyone would be happy to have a son like Marshall, so what the hell's your problem?"

Cindy's arms dropped, her hands still fisted. "That's none of your concern."

"None of my concern? Like hell it isn't. I'm responsible for Marshall now. Knowing neither of his parents want him has to mess up his head. I'm going to be dealing with that, with the mess you and Dean have left behind. This is my business." Dave stopped pacing, and his eyes locked on Cindy.

Turning, Cindy walked to the fireplace and gripped the mantle, her knuckles white against the aged wood. Her reluctant words gritted through her teeth, their sound like broken glass. "Marshall is *his* child."

Dave's gaze landed on me for the first time, startling him. Just like I'd thought, he hadn't realized I'd walked in. I offered up a half-ass smile, something that was meant to be supportive but probably fell short.

He gave me an abbreviated nod of acknowledgment before he headed toward Cindy, careful to keep a few feet of distance between them so as not to crowd her. "What do you mean by that? Marshall's Dean's kid, right?"

Cindy laughed, a startling sound that sliced more than soothed. "Oh, Marshall's Dean's child all right. One drunken night . . . That's all it took for Dean to plant his seed in me."

My breath caught. Dave's hiss of shock sounded the same. "Did he—"

"No. It was mutual consent, albeit inebriated," Cindy clarified. "I wasn't so drunk that I didn't know what I was doing, just tipsy enough to make it sound like a good idea."

Dave and I shared a look, neither sure where that murky line of consent fell. Clearing his throat, Dave said, "I still don't understand. Marshall and Devlin are both Dean's kids, so why is Marshall different? Why . . ." Dave's words stuttered to a stop. Head turned from me, I couldn't see Cindy's face, but Dave could. Whatever he saw there made him hesitate, made his words dry up.

Licking his lips, Dave stared, realization dawning and throwing his eyes wide. "Devlin's not Dean's, is he?"

Cindy looked down toward the crackling, roaring fire.

I figured she had to be sweltering still in her winter coat.

"Dean never knew, still doesn't. I had an affair with a married man. He wouldn't leave his wife, not even when he found out I was pregnant. I was still sleeping with Dean off and on at the time, and he just assumed Devlin was his. It never occurred to him that I'd strayed." Cindy's quiet voice turned mocking. "Your father has always been so cock sure of himself. Even when he wasn't . . . Well, that doesn't matter now." Pulling away from the fireplace, Cindy tugged her coat a little tighter. "Dean's always been so proud of Devlin. That boy is everything Dean imagined his son would be—athletic, popular, good with the ladies . . . Sometimes I want to tell him, throw it in his face that his real son is a fag. That's what Dean Masters's genetic contribution was."

The barest hint of a gasp drew my eyes up toward the top of the stairs. Marshall sat there at the top landing. Knees drawn up and arms wrapped around his legs, Marshall's shadowed face held the hint of a terrified teenager. I wanted to run up those stairs, wrap my arms around him, and tell him that Cindy's hateful words wouldn't mean shit to Dave. As usual, I didn't need to defend my best friend.

"Like I give a flying fuck who Marshall's attracted to." Dave got up in Cindy's face, looming over her. Taller than me, Cindy wasn't as intimidated as I would have been. "I also don't give a shit who his dad is or isn't. As far as I'm concerned, Marshall's my brother, and that's all I need to know." Backing up, Dave's grin turned feral. "Thank you, Cindy, for signing custody of Marshall over to me. That might be the most *motherly* action you've ever committed where he's concerned. I'll let Marshall decide if he wants to pursue a relationship with you in the future. Marshall's upstairs if you want to say goodbye, but I'm warning you, if you say any of this stupid ass shit to him, you'll—"

"It's okay, Dave." Marshall walked down the stair treads, his pace slow but deliberate. Hands fisting the banister, Marshall stared at his mother. Cindy's parted lips slammed closed, thinning and blanching. "I think Mom said enough. It sounds like she's ready to go." Marshall shot Dave a look, his tight features relaxed into the hint of a smile before his eyes hardened, gaze traveling back to his mother. "Tell Dev I said hi and that he can call if he wants. I won't call you, and I don't want to hear from you either."

"Marshall, I—"

"No, Mom. I think you better leave."

Cindy took a step toward Marshall. There was a brief moment of longing, something that spoke more affection than Cindy had. Whether she'd wanted him or not, Cindy had carried and raised Marshall for many years. The softness disappeared, and Cindy turned on her heel. Her eyebrows shot high when she saw me standing by the door, cake still in hand. I wasn't sure she recognized me, and then she said, "Excuse me, Leah."

Stepping to the side, I watched Cindy Masters walk out

the front door and hoped I'd never witness her step back through.

Quiet descended, the crackle of the fire the soundtrack to what was left of Marshall's childhood.

Blowing out a deep breath, Dave ran his hands over the top of his head, scrubbing vigorously. Marshall turned, starting to go back upstairs. Dave wasn't having it. Footsteps heavy on the wooden floor, Dave cleared the living room in less than five strides.

"Marshall," Dave hollered.

Marshall stopped, almost to the top of the stairs. Head down, he turned it ever so slightly. Hair longer and hanging low, I couldn't make out his face.

Voice barely above a whisper, Marshall asked, "You want me to leave?"

Dave jerked back like he'd been slapped. "Why would I want you to leave?"

Marshall turned a little more, his hair parting enough for me to see a singular, shimmering whiskey-colored eye. "You heard her. I'm a fag. I like di—"

"Is that all?" Dave's shoulders relaxed. Rolling his neck, Dave cranked his head, staring up the stairway and toward Marshall. "I wasn't aware you were deaf, Marshall. We'll need to get you into a specialist, see just how bad the hearing loss is and if—"

"I'm not fucking deaf," Marshall whirled, shouting at Dave. Stomping down the stairs, Marshall came around the landing, a finger pointed at Dave and pressed into his chest. "I'm a fucking homosexual. I'm just like Mom said. Don't make this into a joke."

Dave sobered. "Sorry. I was just trying to lighten the mood."

"Well, it was a shitty attempt." Marshall wrapped his arms around his chest, squeezing tight. Marshall probably had twenty-five pounds at least on me, and yet at that moment, he looked small and fragile. Young too.

I wanted to support Dave. I'd thought his comment was funny, and it was classic Dave. But I didn't say a word. I just stood there, the cake in my hands getting heavier by the minute.

"Come here." Dave didn't give Marshall time to escape. Wrapping Marshall up in one of his bear hugs, Dave squeezed tight. Voice low, Dave rocked Marshall in his arms, holding on until he stopped struggling for release. "I want you to listen to me and listen well. Hear what I'm saying, and never doubt me. I don't care that you're gay. As long as you stay safe and happy, that's all I care about. I meant what I said. You're my brother, and that is the only thing that matters. Do you understand?"

Marshall's stiff body relaxed into the hold. Burying his face into Dave's neck, Marshall squeezed back just as hard. A faint "Got it" barely met my ears.

"Good." Finally pulling back, Dave placed Marshall at arm's length. Flashing me a wicked, teasing grin, Dave patted Marshall's arm. "Besides, you've got nothing on all the baggage Leah's carrying around, and if I can put up with her, then I—*oof.*"

I threw a pillow at Dave's head. "Ass," I hissed, finally setting the cake on the coffee table. I heard it slide within the package. I'd probably just screwed up the icing.

Dave laughed, low and deep.

Marshall stared at him like he was crazy. Sputtering, Marshall's lips twitched until he finally gave in and joined Dave in his lunacy. "I can't believe you just said that."

"Believe it." I picked the cake back up, heading for the kitchen. "Your brother is something else."

"Yeah, he is." Marshall agreed, his voice soft and far away as I moved deeper into the kitchen. Distantly, I heard

Marshall say something about needing to finish up some homework before dinner.

This time, Dave let him go.

"Sorry, short fry." Dave's heavy hand pawed at my head, messing up my hair. "The moment screamed for some levity."

"At my expense." I peeked in on the cake, glad to see it hadn't been messed up too badly. "That's okay, though." I wasn't really that upset about it. Besides, it wasn't like Dave had said anything that wasn't true. "Are you making dinner, or are we ordering out?"

Dave walked to the fridge and pulled out a pan of lasagna. "I made it last night. All I have to do is put it in to cook." Dave set the oven to preheat.

My mouth watered when I noticed a couple loaves of garlic bread nearby. I loved Dave's lasagna.

Hovering over the cold pan of soon-to-be-cooked deliciousness, Dave's hands rested on the counter beside me. "Ironic, isn't it?"

"What's that," I hummed, visions of lasagna goodness swimming through my senses and clouding my brain.

"Dean. He thinks he has three sons, but biologically, he only has one, and he's turned his back on that child more than Devlin or me." Dave's gaze swept toward the empty living room, a deep frown marring his face.

"Do you plan on telling Marshall the truth?"

Dave's deep blue eyes slanted toward me. "That Dean's not my biological dad either?"

"Yeah."

Dave shrugged, leaning heavily on the countertop. "Maybe someday, but not right now. I meant what I said. As far as I'm concerned, Marshall's my brother. Devlin too. Genetics don't have shit to do with it."

I leaned into Dave. "You plan on contacting Devlin soon?"

He gave a slow nod. "I do. I should have kept in contact

with them this whole time. I should have tried harder, pushed more. When Marshall talks about Devlin, it's with this odd sort of hero worship. It's hard to tell what the truth is behind their relationship, but I do know that Devlin's called him a few times. I think there might be hope there. I think it's time I got to know all my siblings."

I thought about bringing up the side of Dave's family that he had no clue about—his biological father's side. Dave could have uncles, aunts, cousins, grandparents, and even possible siblings out there somewhere for all we knew. But that was a discussion for another time. Right now, Dave had his hands full with a lost fourteen-year-old. I didn't envy my friend's task, but if anyone could paddle through those murky waters, it was Dave.

26

Stuffed on Dave's lasagna, garlic bread, and the cake I'd picked up at the grocery store, my stomach was only slightly heavier than my eyes when I pulled onto the darkened road leading to Rose's old house. Spotty outdoor lights from my neighbors' yards lit up the dark patches here and there. The cold mist hanging in the air made interesting halos in their light.

I was almost to my driveway when movement caught my eye. The headlights of my little blue Toyota illuminated a figure I didn't recognize. Breaking hard, my car rolled to a slow halt. My once heavy eyes widened with a mixture of confusion and concern. When a second figure walked into the light, my concern quickly shoved my confusion aside. Heart pounding, I pulled out my phone and pulled up Chrissie's number. I punched the send button.

"Hello, Le—"

"There are two strangers in front of the house," I quickly interrupted Chrissie's greeting. As far as I was concerned, we didn't have time for pleasantries.

Chrissie didn't sound as concerned as me when she asked, "What are they doing?"

"What are they . . ." Hitting my wiper blades again, the mist covering my window dissipated, leaving a clearer view. Phone hanging lower than my mouth, I mumbled incoherent words as I took a few seconds to watch the strangers. "I . . . uh . . ." I couldn't really figure out what they were doing. That's why I'd been confused when I first pulled up. "I'm not sure. They keep turning around, walking toward the house, but when they get to the edge of the road, they just stand there, moving from side to side before turning around and heading in the opposite direction. They take a few steps and then do it again." One of them fisted their hands, throwing their arms up in the air as they turned to their colleague. I couldn't hear what either said, but by the wild gesticulations, they weren't happy.

"They look pissed off."

I pulled the phone away from my ear as Chrissie's gleeful cackle assaulted my poor ears. "Good. Do me a favor, Leah, and record some of it for me."

"I . . . What? You want me to record this?"

"You bet," Chrissie happily answered.

I took a few seconds to absorb that before asking, "What's going on?"

"Oh, just a little confusion casting. Mina came up with that little gem. I can feel when they get close to the barrier I placed around the house, but there's a layered casting over my own that confuses anyone with ill will. When they trigger my original casting, the secondary layer automatically kicks in. From what I understand, they can see and sense the house a certain distance out, but as they move closer and hit my barrier, everything disappears. Mina described it as a dense fog they can't see, hear, or smell through. They get confused and turned around."

Chrissie's giggle was anything but childlike. "As an added bonus, if they get too far in, all of a sudden the house seems to be behind them. They turn around and head that direction only for it to change again."

"Huh." I didn't sound very elegant, but that summed up what I saw sufficiently. Now that I knew what was going on, their actions suddenly made sense. "I'll bet that's frustrating."

"Oh, I certainly hope so." Chrissie's voice dropped an octave. "You don't come after my daughter. Period."

I swallowed hard. I'd never been afraid of Chrissie. I wouldn't call what I felt right now fear either. What I did feel was a sense of wariness. Chrissie and her *friends* could pack more of a wallop than the charms Cecile and Dave wore around their necks. Lizzie had recoiled when she'd seen those charms, hissing the word *witch*. I'd thought she was overreacting at the time. Maybe I'd been wrong.

Pushing those thoughts aside, I stared at my driveway, wondering how on earth I was supposed to get inside the house. I didn't have any ill intentions toward Chrissie or Lilly, but I wasn't sure how to get past the two goons lumbering around in front. And if they saw me pull into the drive, would that allow them to follow? I didn't want to take a chance on Lilly's safety.

Foot still firmly planted on the brake pedal, I asked just that. "Is it safe for me to pull into the drive? Can they follow my car?"

"They'll probably try, but the same thing will happen. Once you're inside the barrier, you'll be safe."

"You sure?"

Chrissie sounded confident, but I wasn't.

"I could always go stay with Dave, or—"

"I promise, Leah. You'll be safe. Lilly and I will be too. I wouldn't do anything to keep you from your home."

I didn't for a minute think Chrissie would do something

like that intentionally, though that might have been naïve on my part. Regardless, I trusted Chrissie.

With that thought in mind, I told Chrissie I'd see her in a few minutes. Hitting the end button, I switched to the video app and recorded the odd scene playing out in front of our house. Thankfully the evening was dreary, and none of my neighbors seemed the wiser. If one of them did happen to look out and see this, they'd probably call the cops because these guys were obviously up to no good.

Done obtaining Chrissie the entertainment she wanted, I waited until both men were once more headed back across the road and out of my way. They didn't even turn their heads as I crept by. I pulled into the driveway, got out, and turned around, staring in disbelief as they headed my way again. Heart pounding, I watched the same scene play out. They got to the edge of the grass and stopped. Now out of my car, I heard the low growls of bitter frustration roll through the night. One of them even took a swipe at the air in front of him. Even in the dim light, their movements looked unnatural. Or at least inhuman.

"You coming in?" Chrissie asked from the cracked door. I hadn't even heard it open.

"How long have they been at it?" I asked, amazed as they both turned and headed back across the road.

"Fifteen, maybe twenty minutes." Chrissie sounded far from upset. "Stop soaking up the mist and come on in."

I shut my car door and took one last glance behind me before heading inside. Chrissie was right. My hair was damp. A chill ran through me as I removed my coat, setting it on a nearby rack Chrissie had installed. It was weird seeing other coats hanging around it. Lilly's small pink one was the bright standout.

"I've got a fire going." Chrissie waved me inside. She had a glass of wine in her hand, but she was far from drunk.

I plunked down in the floral chair. Chrissie took the couch. It had become our standard seating arrangement.

Glancing back toward the door, I asked, "How long do you think they'll keep trying?"

Chrissie shrugged, sipping her wine. "No idea."

"Will the barrier hold up?" I scooted forward in my chair, drawing Chrissie's attention. "I mean, does this thing you and Mina set up have a time limit, or maybe a point of stress where it falls apart?" I had no idea how Chrissie did what she did. The rules and regulations of witchcraft were lost on me.

Staring into the fire, an odd smile tilted the edge of Chrissie's lips. "It'll last as long as I can maintain it. My power is the fuel. Mina's secondary casting feeds off me."

That didn't relieve me in the least. "Is that safe? Will that hurt you?" I remembered Chrissie's concerns about Oleana's castings. She'd been wrong regarding what hastened her grams's death, but from what I understood, her concern hadn't been misplaced.

Chrissie shrugged. "It is what it is. Lilly's all that matters, and I'll do what's necessary to keep her safe. So far, it's not too much of a drain. Winter might be knocking on nature's door, but there's still enough life in the ground to pull from." Smile widening, Chrissie tipped her glass of wine in the direction of Rose and Isaac's picture. "Thanks to Rose's love of plants, I've got a lot to work with."

I relaxed, slumping into the softness of the old chair cushions. As if Phoenix had just realized I'd gotten home, she scurried down the hall. She'd probably been in Lilly's room. She was small enough that climbing seemed more economical than jumping. Thankfully my heavy jeans took the brunt of her tiny but sharp claws. Within seconds, her head peeked over my knee, and the rest of her fluffy white body followed suit.

"Did she do okay today?" I asked while pulling Phoenix

into my lap. Her loud purr would have been enough to wake the dead. "She seemed sore after her vaccinations."

"She slept most of the day." Pointing her wine glass in my direction, Chrissie added, "That's the most activity I've seen out of her."

Enjoying her scritches, Phoenix leaned into my touch. "I guess she's feeling better and not holding a grudge about getting poked the other today."

Chrissie chuckled. "Give her time. She's still young. Grudges generally wait until their teens."

I figured Chrissie was a better judge of that, considering she had a six-year-old daughter and I couldn't remember ever being that young.

With Phoenix settled, I stared at Rose and Isaac's picture, finally absorbing Chrissie's earlier words. "I think Rose would like that, knowing the house and surrounding land are helping to protect you and Lilly."

Chrissie didn't turn her head, just the hint of her hazel eyes shifting in my direction as she asked, "Are you sure? She didn't even know me."

"Hmm . . . true, but I stand by my statement. Rose would be happy. I'm sure of it." And I was. I didn't know Rose's full history, but I felt safe saying she would have done anything and everything she could to protect Melody. Good mothers always did.

27

"I'm glad to hear you have a new kitten." Dr. Cross looked pleased as she stared at me over her clasped hands. Her reading glasses were perched low on her nose, and her deep brown eyes peeked over their rims. She had a small Christmas tree sitting on the corner of her desk, tiny white lights barely visible in the bright overhead lights. As far as holiday decorations went, it was sparse.

I twisted in my seat. I'd cut my visits with Dr. Cross back. The frequency was no longer needed. I didn't feel ready to cut the cord completely. Not that I'd truly ever do that. I learned that lesson earlier this year when I restarted my sessions with her.

"Yeah." I cleared my throat. "It's good." I nodded for extra emphasis. I wasn't sure if I was trying to convince Dr. Cross or me of my sincerity.

"That didn't sound particularly convincing, Leah." Dr. Cross didn't sound so much disappointed as concerned. "Are there problems?"

"No." I twisted my purse strap, wrapping it around my fingers, cutting off their circulation and turning their tips reddish-purple. Some days it seemed like I just couldn't stop hurting myself. "Phoenix got a clean bill of health from the vet. She seems well."

"Hmm, that's good to hear but not exactly what I meant, and I think you know that." I'd heard that mild rebuff in Dr. Cross's voice before. It was just shy of scolding.

Looking off to the side, I stared at the floral-curtained window. It was sunnier today. I'd had the morning into afternoon shift at Handy Helpers and gone straight from work to my appointment. The sun was nice. It wasn't necessarily warm, but it did brighten my mood. Or at least it had been brightened before I'd sat down across from the woman in front of me.

"Leah?" Dr. Cross prompted. "I can't help if I don't know what's going on inside your head. Talk to me. Please."

I released my purse strap. The tips of my numb fingers tingled as blood flowed back in. My prickling fingertips traced over the covered tattoo of Ashes name and paw print.

Taking a deep breath, I released my worry, throwing it into Dr. Cross's lap. "I feel guilty."

Dr. Cross silently sat there, tapping her fingers. Finally, she repeated, "Guilty. About what?"

Shrugging, I knew my nonverbal response was terribly unhelpful. But the truth of the matter was that I didn't know. Or at least it wasn't clear.

Not content with my silence, Dr. Cross started asking me leading questions. "Do you think Ashes would be hurt by the fact you have another cat in your life?"

When the words were put out there like that, it sounded stupid. Ashes hadn't been human. I had no idea if cats felt jealousy or not. She hadn't liked other cats in her territory, but I didn't think that automatically equated to jealousy.

Looking down at my lap, I finally answered, "No. I mean, she didn't really like other cats, and if she were still alive, she'd be pissed if I'd brought Phoenix into her home." I didn't tell Dr. Cross that Phoenix's entry into my life hadn't gone down like that. Francis had carried her into my home, not me. Getting into the topic of Francis wouldn't do Dr. Cross or me any favors.

"Okay. Not guilty for that reason then." Dr. Cross sat back, letting that settle, waiting to see if I'd fill in the pieces or if she'd need to prompt me again.

I could have sat there longer, but I was here for a reason. Keeping my mouth shut was a waste of my money, time, and energy. "I just can't connect with her. Not like I did Ashes." I sounded as exasperated as I felt. "I want to. Really, I do. I just . . . can't."

"I see."

My head snapped up, eyes wide and eager. "You do?"

Dr. Cross gave me a soft, understanding smile. "I do. Now we just have to get you to see." I was afraid she'd stop at that. Sometimes Dr. Cross did that. Most of the time, she wanted me to figure things out on my own. "Tell me, Leah, why do you think you should connect with Phoenix on the same level you did with Ashes?"

"I . . . because . . . she's a cat. I like cats. I loved Ashes. She was everything to me." I couldn't figure out why Phoenix should be any different.

"All those things are true. But things aren't the same with you now as they were with Ashes. You were a child when Ashes came into your life. Your perceptions and bonding would have been different then. And then there's what happened with your parents and your brother. Ashes was a kindred spirit. She was a survivor, just like you. And let's not forget, you and Ashes were together for nineteen years. She had a terminal condition which you valiantly warred against. You've had this new kitten, what . . . a couple of weeks?" Dr. Cross leaned back into her chair, hands resting somewhere I couldn't see. "I think your expectations are maybe a little too high."

My mouth dropped, lips parting in a hollow "O."

"Don't be too hard on yourself, Leah. Enjoy Phoenix for the new and exciting things she brings to your life. It's early yet, and even if you don't bond with her on the same level as you did with Ashes, that's okay. Phoenix will still feel loved, she'll still be cared for, and she'll still have a wonderful life with you. At the end of the day, that's enough. Let it be enough for you too."

I was still in a weird fog when I walked through the door of Rose's old house. Dr. Cross's words stuck with me the way a heavy meal did. I'd be digesting her thoughts for a long time to come. Phoenix, just like all animals, couldn't have cared less about my mental fugue. The door opened, and she came running, sliding around the corner and slamming into the hall wall. Not even a little phased, she scurried toward me. I reached down and lifted her into my arms before she had a chance to climb my pants leg.

Lilly's giggle caught my ear, piercing through the mad purrs rumbling through Phoenix's tiny chest. As I moved down the hall, Lilly's musical laughter played along to a classic Christmas station Chrissie had playing. I caught Lenny's voice in there too and vaguely remembered he'd told me he planned on coming over to help put up the Christmas tree. It never occurred to me that he meant that would happen in my home.

I still had my coat on when I rounded the corner, staring open-mouthed at the domestic bliss unraveling within my living room.

The Christmas tree had to have come from Chrissie. I

hadn't put one up since my parents' murders. Just like every-thing else from my childhood home, I had no idea what had become of our ornaments or the tree itself. I could guess that the tree was long gone. I didn't think Uncle Jack or Aunt Joyce would have thrown out the ornaments.

Holding Lilly around the waist, Lenny lifted her into the air and allowed her to hang an ornament higher in the tree. They'd already put the colored lights on, and the tree shim-mered in the evening light. Standing there, holding Phoenix in my arms, her purrs thrumming in the back-ground to Nat King Cole, the sting of tears pricked the backs of my eyes.

"Aunt Leah!" Lilly shouted from her perched position. "We're decorating the tree!"

Lenny lowered Lilly to the ground. Her shorter legs ran around the couch, and her body slammed into mine. Head tilted, she had the biggest, goofiest grin on her face. "Mom said we could put it up today. Are you going to help?"

"I . . ." My wide eyes looked from Chrissie to Lenny and back again.

Chrissie had two ornaments dangling from her fingers. Her raised eyebrows and drooped lips looked confused before worry took over. "I'm sorry, Leah. I probably should have asked first. I just assumed . . ." She stared at the tree. "I figured it would be okay, but maybe I shouldn't have."

"No," I hurried to reassure her, shifting Phoenix from my arms to Lilly's. The distraction worked, and Lilly took off back to the tree. I didn't even want to think about the mischief Phoenix was bound to get into with a tree decked out in ornaments in the house. "It's fine," I finally added while removing my coat.

"Are you sure? We can—"

"We're good." Even if putting up a tree hadn't been okay with me, seeing the joy in Lilly's face, there was no way I was going to tell them to take it down. "I just haven't . . . It's been a while, that's all."

Lenny scrounged around in one of the boxes. I thought about warning Chrissie that Lenny had a knack for breaking things—that he was banned from restocking fragile items at Handy Helpers. I kept my mouth shut. Chrissie knew Lenny. She was well aware of his positive and negative traits. They were her ornaments on the line, not mine.

"We're making sugar cookies after." Lilly looked disappointed when Phoenix jumped out of her arms but quickly got over it at the thought of cookies.

"Oh?" I asked after hanging up my coat. "Have you made those before?" I had vague memories of baking them with my mom and dad, but that was about it.

"No need." Chrissie waved me off. "The premade dough is great. We just roll it out and cut out the designs."

"I picked up icing, sprinkles, and other things to decorate them with," Lenny chimed in, his face flushed. "I probably got too much."

"No such thing," I assured while walking farther into the room. I stayed away from the tree, almost like it might suddenly reach out and bite me. But this was a fake tree, not something I figured Chrissie could control.

"Do you have ornaments to add too?" Lilly asked innocently.

Chrissie and Lenny pulled up short while both of their gazes shot in my direction.

Swallowing, I sat down on my chair and patted my leg. Lilly immediately came and plunked herself on my lap. Wrapping my arms around her middle, I pulled Lilly into my body as I leaned back, rocking us both. Finally, I answered her the best I could. "Not this year. Maybe next year. We'll have to see."

"Okay," Lilly readily agreed.

Chrissie looked relieved and gave me a grateful smile. Something I returned easily.

Lilly stayed with me for a few more minutes until the draw of the tree was too much and she wiggled off my lap. No one asked me to help decorate, something I was eternally grateful for. I could wrap my head around having a Christmas tree again. I didn't think I was ready to participate in its grooming.

Leaning my head back, I bathed in the normalcy of holiday decorating. A fire was crackling, warming the room. Somewhere along the line, Lenny snuck away and made all of us hot chocolate. Miniature white marshmallows bobbed up and down on the frothy top. Everything was going blissfully well.

And then the doorbell rang.

2 8

Chrissie's body stilled. I should have caught that before the ring of the doorbell pulled me from my hot chocolate bliss. We stared at each other. The edge of my mug sat at my lips, the heat of hot cocoa warming my rapidly chilling body. Chrissie had an idea who was at our doorstep with the warding around the house, and her tense shoulders told me it wasn't Dave or Cecile.

The bell sounded again. I set my cup on the side table, a quiet "I'll get it" passing my lips as I made my way to the door. I took a minute to peak through the hole. My head jerked back when I recognized who was on the other side. I slid the lock open without a second thought.

"Jenny?" I looked behind Detective Riggins to the officer at her back. I knew this woman too. "Officer Supinsky? What's going on?" My mind whirled as my stomach fell into the pit of my belly. My thoughts spiraled out of control. There were only a handful of reasons I could think of for the police to show up at my doorstep, and none of them were good.

Latching onto the doorframe, I barely kept my wobbling

knees from collapsing. "What happened? Is it Dave? Cecile? Aunt Joyce or Uncle Jack?" I fired off names nearly as quickly as I could think of them. "Did something happen to one of them? Are they—"

"They're all okay." Jenny held up a halting hand. Her fingertips barely touched my quaking shoulder. "Calm down, Leah. They aren't the reason we're here."

"Thank god." It was all I could do to keep my body upright. Generally speaking, life had been pretty good to me recently, and my body wasn't as used to fight or flight mode.

"Leah, who's at the door?" Chrissie's wary voice grew louder as she walked up behind me. Standing in the narrow hall, she filled the space up even more.

"Christine Hollybrook?" Jenny's shoulders drew back, straightening her spine and making her look stern.

"Yes, that's me." Chrissie sounded as confused as I felt. "Who are you?"

I answered for Jenny. "This is Detective Riggins. She worked Bobby's case. The woman behind her is Officer Supinsky. She . . . She helped me out once with Levi."

"Oh." Chrissie didn't sound any less confused, but her voice was softer. "Why are you here now? The situation with Leah's brother has been resolved. Right?" Chrissie knew it had, better than Jenny did.

"We're not here about Bobby," Jenny answered before asking, "Can we come inside?"

I felt like an idiot, or maybe just a really bad hostess. "Yeah. I'm sorry. I should have offered that sooner." As winter closed in, it would get a hell of a lot colder outside, but that didn't mean it was warm out there currently.

Both women shuffled in, and I took their coats, hanging them over the ones already on the rack, nearly blocking the hall with coat debris.

We made our way into the living room. Jenny's eyes

widened before they softened when she saw the tree standing there. Lenny and Lilly temporarily halted in their decorating efforts. "Is that your daughter?" Jenny asked while looking at Chrissie.

Immediately Chrissie's hackles went up. "She is." Without asking another question, Chrissie turned to Lilly and Lenny. "Can you take Lilly and stay with her in her room for a little while?"

Lenny barely shot the police a second look. Crouching, he took Lilly by the hand and led her down the hall. Lilly didn't say a word. She scooped Phoenix up with one hand, the other firmly latched on to Lenny. A brief backward look was the only concern she showed.

We silently waited until the snick of Lilly's door sounded. With Lilly and Lenny gone, Jenny took a moment to look around the house. "This is a nice place, Leah. I heard Rose VanDillard left it to you in her will."

I didn't catch any censure in Jenny's voice, only simple curiosity.

"She did. It shocked the hell out of me."

Jenny aimed another one of those soft smiles in my direction. "I'm sure it did. I didn't know Rose personally, but some people at the station did, and they always spoke highly of her. I was happy to hear the news." Turning her attention toward Chrissie, Jenny's smile faded into thinly pinched lips. "I was glad to hear you'd taken on a roommate too."

Her tone made me think Jenny wasn't so certain now.

Chrissie's body tensed further. Officer Supinsky's did the same in response. I still wasn't sure what was going on, but whatever it was didn't need to escalate in my living room. Stepping slightly in front of Chrissie, I asked, "Jenny, what's this about?"

Inhaling deeply, Jenny let her breath out slowly. "We're investigating two missing persons reports. Interestingly enough, one of them involves Miss Hollybrook, and the other involves you, Leah."

"Huh?" Chrissie and I said in unison.

"Who's missing?" I got out before Chrissie could.

Officer Supinsky stepped up beside Jenny, flipping open a spiral-bound notebook and a pen. "Mark McKinney was reported missing this afternoon by a Mr. Fergus Hollybrook, Christine Hollybrook's father."

Chrissie sucked in a whistling breath before shouting, "What?" Her eyes danced between Jenny and me. I thought I caught a glow, but it was low enough Jenny would probably think it was an effect of the Christmas tree lights behind us. "What do you mean Mark's missing? And why in the hell would my father be the one to call that in?"

"That's what we'd like to know," Jenny stated calmly. "It's our understanding that Mark is Lilly Hollybrook's biological father and that he recently came back into your lives and is currently suing for custody of his daughter. Is this true?"

Chrissie threw up her hands while she paced toward the fireplace. A hushed "Unbelievable" fell from her lips.

Walking toward my friend, I placed a hand on Chrissie's shoulder. Her muscles vibrated beneath my fingertips. Head tilted down, she turned her eyes toward me, their glow unmistakable. Under my breath, I whispered, "Calm down."

It took a few deep inhales and probably more counting than I had the patience for, but Chrissie eventually regained enough control to turn around. Inhaling one final time, she nodded. "That's true. Mark walked out on Lilly and me before she turned a year old. He popped back up a few weeks ago, demanding custody. Naturally, I didn't just hand my daughter over to him."

"*Naturally,*" Jenny inclined her head toward Chrissie. "And just as naturally, I'm guessing the two of you shared a few words regarding the situation."

"Of course," Chrissie agreed.

"Heated words?"

Chrissie darkly chuckled. "Heated or ice-cold, take your pick. I'm not going to lie here, there was no love lost between Lilly's sperm donor and me. Mark walked out on us. I haven't seen or heard from him in the past five years, and that includes any type of financial assistance where his daughter is concerned. Call me what you want, think of me what you will, but I wasn't about to cave to his most recent whim."

Jenny nodded like she understood. Officer Supinsky scribbled letters and words across the paper she cradled in her hand.

"When was the last time you saw Mark?" Jenny asked.

Chrissie looked at me. "It's been a while. Before Thanksgiving. All our communication is supposed to go through our lawyers."

Legally, that was true. The wolves recently outside our door told a different story.

"Are you certain?" Jenny followed up.

Chrissie scoffed. "I'd think I'd know if Mark showed up."

Jenny didn't know just how true that was. With the warding around the house, Chrissie would know even if she weren't at home.

Officer Supinsky was the one who asked, "Any reason it would be your father who reported Mark missing?"

"No idea. I haven't spoken with my father in weeks."

"Do you mind if we check your phone records to confirm that?" Officer Supinsky asked.

"Check away. I haven't called my father or Mark."

Jenny nodded before she turned and confirmed something I couldn't hear with Officer Supinsky. Attention back on us, Jenny said, "That's all the questions we have for now.

Unless Mark McKinney shows up soon, chances are we'll have follow-up questions."

Chrissie didn't look happy, but she did look resigned.

It looked like it was my unfortunate turn. "Leah, what can you tell me about your relationship with Shelly Christiansen?"

My blood rushed through my body, hammering within my skull. Hazy fuzz filled my head, blocking out words and all other sounds. "Sh-Shelly?" I only knew one Shelly. I had no idea what Ricky's fiancée's last name was, though. "Are you talking about Ricky Levitson's fiancée?"

"Yes," Officer Supinsky answered. "Her brother, Brandon, has been concerned about her for some time. He's had Levi Dickerson," Officer Supinsky almost faltered over Levi's name, "investigating the matter. Brandon Christiansen asked the police to do a wellness check on his sister. When we went by Richard Levitson's residence, the place Brandon said Shelly is currently living, Mr. Levitson said his fiancée packed her bags a couple of days ago and walked out. He says he has no idea where she went."

"Shit." I backed up, running into Chrissie.

"Leah, what do you know?" Jenny stepped closer. The crow's feet around her eyes deepened with her interest. "We obtained Shelly's phone records, and it looks like she called you twice in the past few days. Once on Thanksgiving and again a few days later. The record indicates the calls were brief."

I stumbled to my floral chair. Chrissie had a hold of my arm, easing me into the cushioned seat. Furiously shaking my head, I finally settled my forehead in my hands.

Jenny crouched in front of me. "Leah. This is serious. If you know something, you—"

"But I don't. Not really. I don't know Shelly that well. I was afraid that her fiancé, Ricky, was abusing her. I asked Dr.

Cross about it, and she gave me a list of shelters and support groups Shelly could call. I wrote that down on a piece of paper, along with my phone number, and told her she could call me anytime. I've had a couple of phone calls that went to voicemail, but the person didn't leave a message. That could have been Shelly, but I don't know her phone number, so I can't be sure. You're welcome to my phone if that'll help."

Jenny sat back on her heels. "Do you think she went to one of those shelters? Maybe she called one of the hotlines and got some help?"

"I don't know. I hope so, but last I knew, Shelly was still pretty deep in denial. She didn't want to hear anything bad about Ricky, but . . . I was scared for her. I don't know what happened, but I can tell you that I saw bruises on her body, and I'm not the only one." I glanced down the hall toward Lilly's room. I didn't want to draw Lenny into this cluster-fuck, but he'd seen Shelly at the grocery, sporting a black eye she'd tried to cover with makeup. I decided not to bring Lenny's name up unless I had to.

I thought of the BBQ this summer. "You should ask Gary about it. There was an incident at a cookout at Handy Helpers this past summer. Ricky grabbed Shelly pretty rough, and a lot of employees saw it. Gary had more than one complaint, and I think he spoke with Ricky. I don't know what they talked about." I wanted to add that my car had been keyed that afternoon, after Ricky left. I kept that little gem to myself too.

Jenny stood, placing her hands on her hips. She didn't look happy. Jenny looked pissed. "Thank you, Leah. Shelly still might have wised up and taken off. But from what you've told me, combined with the information I've gotten from her family and . . . Levi, I'm inclined to believe this warrants further investigation."

"Okay." My voice was barely audible, so quiet I wasn't

sure I'd spoken at all. "I hope she's all right. The last time I saw her, Shelly looked like she'd lost a lot of weight, and she and Ricky were arguing in Handy Helpers' parking lot."

"Damn," Officer Supinsky cursed before tucking her notepad into one of the pockets on her belt.

Jenny sighed, long and put-upon. Pinching the bridge of her nose, she looked to the ceiling. "Why are you always in the thick of things, Leah?"

Hands tucked between my knees, I shook my head. "I have no idea, but I'd happily jump out of the thicket if possible."

"I know." Jenny offered me an understanding smile. "That's why we're doing this here and not at the station." Standing, Jenny tugged on the belt wrapped around her hips. Funny, when Jenny was here, I hardly noticed her gun. When Levi had been in uniform, it was the first thing my eyes zeroed in on.

"We'll let you ladies get back to your holiday decorations. As I said earlier, we'll probably have more questions as these cases develop." It wasn't a threat, per se, more a warning that Chrissie and I needed to be available at the drop of a hat. "Needless to say, if either of you hear from Mark or Shelly, notify me immediately. Hopefully we're jumping the gun and they're okay."

Jenny took a step toward the door, then stopped. Officer Supinsky pulled up short alongside. Jenny turned slightly, her narrowed eyes settling on Chrissie and then me. "Any chance the two of them know each other? That they could have taken off together?"

Chrissie looked just as taken aback by the question as me. Our eyes connected before I answered for the two of us. "Not that I know of. Admittedly, I don't know either of them well."

"Same," Chrissie added. "I only saw Shelly the one time, at

the barbecue Leah spoke about. I hadn't seen Mark in over five years. I have no idea where he's been or who he's been spending his time with." Chrissie's tone made it clear that she didn't give a damn, either.

"Okay. So far nothing points to the two cases being related. I just thought I'd pick your brains too. If anything further comes to mind, Leah knows where to find me. And for the record, I hope this—" Jenny's hand motioned toward the half-decorated Christmas tree—"works out. You look better, Leah. Better than I've seen you in a long time." Jenny offered a rare, soft smile. That softness radiated out from her eyes.

Chrissie showed Jenny and Officer Supinsky to the door. I heard the typical shuffling of coats. Cold air floated down the hall as our guests left. Chrissie followed that cold gust, flopping down on the couch. I wasn't sure if the wheezing sound came from the furniture or Chrissie.

"Thoughts?" I questioned when Chrissie remained silent.

Chrissie remained quiet for a few more seconds before she finally answered. "I think Lilly will never meet her biological father." Chrissie stared at the fire, the flames reflected in her shimmering hazel eyes. I couldn't tell if tears lurked there or not. Chrissie hated Mark, but at one time, she'd cared for him. Maybe even loved him.

"Do you really think he's dead?"

With a shrug, Chrissie blinked away whatever moisture might have been lurking. "If he's not dead yet, he soon will be. It's quicker than I thought it would be, but not unexpected." Inhaling deeply, Chrissie's focus turned back to the fire. "The question I need to focus on, the one that's important to me, is how this fits into Samuel's game plan. If Mark isn't around to sue for custody, then what's his next move?"

My mind tumbled over the possibilities. "Your mom and dad?"

Chrissie grunted her agreement. "Possibly." Her eyes narrowed, face hard, and fingers clenched. "There's another possibility, one that's worse."

It was hard for me to figure out what might be worse than your family conspiring to take away your child.

"Mark's missing," Chrissie stated the obvious. "There's a good chance he's already dead, and if he's not, then he will be soon. We already know what door the police came knocking on. If they find him dead, who do you think will be at the top of their suspected murderer list?"

My heart pounded deep and hard. I'd been on that less than illustrious list once upon a time. In the court of public opinion, I was still on it. Being on that list sucked.

"You don't think—"

"What I think is that I wouldn't put anything past Samuel Hartman. What I think is that Samuel's done playing nice. If the charms his goons were wearing the other day are any indication, the witch he's got on his payroll isn't all that talented, and Samuel knows it. I don't know why or how, but he's got his sights set on my daughter. So far, going through me hasn't worked. Going around me hasn't worked either. Getting rid of me is his best option. Killing me would be difficult, and if he'd kept Mark in play, then Lilly's sperm donor would have been the prime suspect. Now he's turned the tables."

My breath came in rapid pants as worry consumed me. It was weird, worrying about someone else instead of myself. Oddly enough, the emotional hit was worse. "We have to do something."

Chrissie barked a laugh. "What? There's nothing we can do, not until we know more. Like I said before, I'm not surprised by the move. The only thing I'm surprised about is that Samuel didn't give this time to play out in the courts. Lilly's young. Her abilities are promising but nowhere near where she'll be as she gets older. For some reason, Samuel doesn't want to wait. Maybe he wants more time to groom her while her mind's still malleable. I don't know and wish I didn't have to think about it. But wishing it away won't make it disappear."

"No," I agreed. "That has never worked out very well for me either."

Chrissie shot me a wry, understanding grin. It didn't last long, the grim reality of Mark's disappearance settling in. "I wonder what he did that pissed Samuel off." Chrissie hung her head. "He was always such an idiot." Her words were spoken with an odd kind of fondness. "If there was one thing Mark never seemed to lack, it was confidence. That confidence was often misplaced, but it was there nonetheless."

I stared at the Christmas tree. Its shimmering lights were ignorant of the trauma circling my life. Inanimate objects were lucky that way. "Are you going to say anything to Lilly?"

"Not yet. I'll wait until we know more. Too much has been thrown at her already. I'm going to give myself a couple more minutes, then I'm going to march down that hallway with a smile on my face. We're going to finish decorating the tree, and then we're going to bake the best damn sugar cookies premade dough has ever seen. We're going make the tackiest, overdecorated cookies in the world." Chrissie looked at me and asked, "You in?"

I pulled my lips back in a horrible excuse for a smile.

"Well, not like that. Lilly will go running and screaming back to her room," Chrissie teased.

My face relaxed into something close to normal.

"I'll help bake and decorate. I'll also do my best not to think about Mark and Shelly."

"Shit. I was so concentrated on Mark, I forgot all about Shelly." Scooting forward on the couch, Chrissie rubbed her hands up and down her jeans. "Any chance she's safe at a shelter somewhere?"

I rubbed my temples, a headache beginning to pound. "That's my hope, but hope hasn't been kind to me over the years. I'm afraid of what the truth is." Chewing on one of my nails, I thought back on what Jenny had said. "You know what bothers me the most?"

Chrissie softly laughed. "Gee, Leah, there's so much to choose from. I don't know where to start."

"Yeah, stupid question," I agreed. "What bothers me the most is what Ricky told Jenny. He said Shelly packed her things and left. Up until now, he's been giving Shelly's brother some bullshit story about Shelly being too busy to call—that she's been tied up with online classes. Now all of a sudden, she's taken off? *And* more importantly, Ricky admitted that Shelly left him?" I violently shook my head. "Ricky's too pompous to admit to something like that. If she was really gone and okay, he'd tell everyone he kicked her out. Not the other way around. Ricky's ego wouldn't allow Shelly to leave him."

"Damn."

"I wish I'd known it was her number on my caller ID. I would have called her back. I would have . . ." I wasn't entirely sure what I would have done.

"I wonder why she didn't leave a message."

"Me too." I had a sinking feeling it was a mystery Shelly had taken to her grave.

Pushing off the couch, Chrissie ran a hand over her tightly pulled hair, smoothing away the little wisps that had come loose from her ponytail. It was amazing, watching her morph from worried mother to holiday cheer. I'd never thought myself a very good actress, and seeing Chrissie now, I knew I was right.

"Okay," Chrissie said with a genuine-looking smile. She

repeated, "Okay," with more emphasis. "Time to release Lilly and Lenny. Let's turn up the music, decorate the hell out of this tree, and then stuff our faces with sugar cookies. Maybe we'll even leave some for Andy."

My laughter joined Chrissie's as we headed down the hall toward Lilly's bedroom door.

Fake it till you make it. I'd tried to fulfill that statement off and on for years. Looked like tonight I was going to give it another try.

"Oh my god, Leah. Did you hear?" Lenny whispered in my ear the next morning at work. "Oh, of course you heard. You were there, with Chrissie, weren't you?" At least Lenny answered his own question before I had a chance to say something uncharitable. "Do you think Shelly's okay?"

Lenny had waited for me in the parking lot. The sun was barely a hazy gray tint on the horizon. The air was cold, and frost was on the ground. Whatever summer plants that had been clinging to life would be all but gone in a couple of hours. It was one of the saddest times of the year. The only thing that made it a little more bearable was the Christmas lights pilfering the suburban landscape.

We made our way through the gloomy gray parking lot. Handy Helpers was lit up inside like a shining, welcoming beacon. The doors slid open, and warmth slammed me in the face. I hadn't answered Lenny yet.

Safe within Handy Helpers' brightly lit halls, I finally said, "I don't know. I hope she's okay, but I'm not sure." I didn't tell Lenny that I put the odds of Shelly being okay around twenty-eighty, leaning heavily toward the twenty or less part of that percentile.

"God, this sucks."

Chrissie and I'd thought something similar last night.

"I hope she really did leave him and is safely tucked away somewhere." Lenny grabbed his timecard, stamping it a little harder than usual. "And Mark's missing too. What's going on?"

Too much was going on. I was ready for some peace and smooth sailing in my life. The poor little life raft my sanity clung to was tired of getting beaten up and tossed about in the waves of life. I wanted to find a nice little wading pool instead of floating in the middle of the Atlantic during hurricane season.

A couple more bleary-eyed employees lumbered into the break room. Lenny and I returned their half-coherent attempts at morning greetings before we headed out on the floor too. Lizzie was on as manager this morning, and she seemed unusually . . . chipper.

After sort of, kind of winning my battle with management regarding Andy, Lizzie had been polite, and her too-wide smiles had fallen into something closer to natural. This morning, it was as if time had been rolled back. Lizzie bounced about, her grin near maniacal. Those bright white teeth shimmered under Handy Helpers' fluorescent lights. I'd thought about asking Chrissie to make me a charm too, so I could see Lizzie for what she was. Today was one of those days I didn't want the reminder. Those smiles were disturbing enough without the addition of pointed teeth.

Despite Lizzie's weirdness, the morning flew by into the early afternoon. By two thirty, I was ready to clock out. A couple of months ago, I would have puttered about, trying to find something else to do. Anything to keep my mind attached to something productive. Usually, that meant engaging my body too.

Things were different now. I was ready to go home. Ashes's purrs wouldn't greet me when I walked through the door, but Phoenix would. I was trying to follow Dr. Cross's advice and not be too hard on myself where the newest member of my family was concerned. She was right. The bond would come, or it wouldn't. Regardless, I still enjoyed Phoenix's company. Her antics made me laugh, and running my hands through her fur was soothing. She wasn't Ashes, just like Aunt Joyce wasn't my mom and Uncle Jack wasn't my dad. Loss happened. The voids they left were individually shaped, and finding something or someone to fill them exactly was close to impossible. Trying to shove living creatures into an existing mold was futile. It was also self-destructive.

Surprisingly, I was trying to be a little less hard on my mind and body these days.

Lenny was helping a customer when I headed for the break room. He gave me a minuscule nod, acknowledging that he'd be late clocking out. That was the policy. You didn't up and leave a customer you were helping just because your shift was over.

Grabbing my purse and coat from my locker, I glanced at the pictures taped there. There was a newer one—one that hadn't been present a few months ago. Dave had gotten a copy of the photo he had of the three of us when we were kids—our faces gooey with melting popsicle juice. It was obvious in that photo that we hadn't had a care in the world.

I ran my finger over Bobby's face. The smile that raised his cheeks was at once foreign and yet as familiar as the tattoos and scars stretched across my wrists. I hadn't seen Bobby since he reaped Oleana's spirit. Dave hadn't seen him at all. Andy said he passed along Dave's message. So far, silence was our only reply.

Heart heavy, I closed my locker with a barely audible snick. Shoving my arms through my coat, I zipped up the front and swung my purse over my shoulder. Lenny was still helping the same customer when I passed him in the aisle. I offered a wave of goodbye, happy to see that it looked like he was wrapping things up and would be able to get out of there soon. Chrissie was scheduled to work tonight, and I figured Lenny would pop in to say hi to her. I'd volunteered to keep an eye on Lilly. I'd never been one for kids and still didn't want one of my own. Lilly was different. I couldn't explain it, but I didn't mind being around her.

Janelle was at the help desk, just settling in for her afternoon-slash-evening shift. She was still in school, so she usually came in later. I offered a smile and wave to her too, one that was genuinely returned.

As my eyes drifted away from the help desk, I caught Lizzie standing at the end of an aisle. Her smile was wider than ever, with a sinister glee that sent shivers racing up and down my spine. As I stared, her eyes shifted toward me—her posture never moved an inch. If possible, that smile grew. She looked delighted, like Christmas had come early and she was sure what she'd asked for was wrapped up under the tree.

My feet caught on the cement as the packaging tape wrapped around one of my soles rolled and stuck to the floor. Cursing under my breath, I shifted my purse. It was time to get the hell out of there. Lizzie was seriously starting to freak me out.

Pulling my attention from Lizzie, I started for the main doors again. Only this time, it wasn't just my foot that caught, but my whole body. My chest seized, the air pushed out as if someone had punched me. The blood slid from my face, the rush of its movement a cacophony of deafening sound. My fingers trembled, every hair on my body standing on end as I watched Ricky Levitson saunter into the store.

Ricky wore a dark brown leather coat—a deep blue scarf wrapped around his neck. The wind outside had ruffled his hair, and he ran his fingers through its length, taming the strands and making sure every follicle was neatly in place. Ricky's dark khaki pants were pressed. His polished patent leather shoes shimmered against Handy Helpers' concrete floors.

Everything about Ricky Levitson was immaculate. When he walked by, his woodsy cologne would fill my senses. Yes, Ricky Levitson was handsome, well-put-together, fashionable, and falsely affable. What Ricky Levitson also was, was a murderer.

The spirit trailing after him proved that.

Shelly's depressed spirit hovered nearby, keeping a small distance, as if she were still frightened of Ricky even in death. Cheek's hollow, Shelly's spirit was gaunt. Arms wrapped around her, she hugged her body tight. Her thin arms were a shadow of the beautiful woman she'd once been. Shelly and Ricky were polar opposites. Ricky walked into the store as if he hadn't a care in the world. For the first time in months, the pleasured ease Ricky portrayed didn't carry a hint of falseness. Comparably, Shelly looked devastated and horribly small.

My heart hammered away, painfully beating a drum inside my chest. I grabbed the fabric of my coat, clenching it over my runaway heart. Ricky shifted, turning slightly as he headed toward me and the break room to clock in. Shelly turned with him, and I stopped breathing. From this angle, it was easy to see.

Shelly had been pregnant. Ricky hadn't murdered just

one person when he took Shelly's life. He'd killed his child too.

"Oh, he's definitely one of mine."

I jumped a mile. Thankfully the store was loud enough most of the customers missed my panicked squeak. Lizzie was too close. Her bobbed hair swung back and forth as her gaze shifted from me to Ricky.

"Elijah will be so pleased," Lizzie went on as if my world hadn't imploded once again. "He'll enjoy dragging Ricky's spirit into the afterlife." Lizzie stepped away, the smile on her face no less gleeful than it had been all day. "Imagine Ricky's surprise when he finds out I'll be his manager for eternity."

Heart thudding and skin ice cold, I watched Lizzie walk away. Her laughter pushed out the cacophony of noise bouncing through Handy Helpers' open rafters. By the time I turned around, Ricky was gone, tucked away in the break room, Shelly's spirit gone with him.

I ran.

Lenny's voice trailed me, fading into the background. I dodged shopping carts and the humans attached to them. I ran through the doors, out into the cold, and to my old blue Toyota. I don't remember shoving the key in the door or turning on the car. I don't remember the trip home or how I got inside.

The next thing I knew, I was in Andy's arms as his warmth struggled to push away the cold. Naively, I'd thought everything would be all right if I had Andy. I should have known better. Andy helped, but he couldn't erase what I knew, what I'd seen. I knew my mind well enough to know that Shelly's ghost would haunt me far worse than her murderer.

"Thank you for meeting me, John." Tonn Tonn walked into the open field behind Ink No Evil. Darkness had long ago settled in for the night, and the stars struggled to shine through the floodlights illuminating the parking lot behind them.

"Soul Eater." John inclined his head, keeping to the darkened shadows.

Tonn Tonn eased back, shoving his hands into the back pocket of his jeans. The metal chain attached to his belt loop sang into the night. "That's my father's title. I haven't decided when I'll take up the family profession."

"Understandable." John's answer was brief, not a hint of judgment. "Does your mother know?"

"About what Dad is? What I am?" Tonn Tonn raised an eyebrow, staring off into the distant field. "No. She believes Dad is aging naturally, following her mortal path to an inevitable grave. I think it's a kindness, keeping the truth from her."

"Undoubtedly so," John agreed. "A soul eater's loved one is

precious. It does not surprise me that your father has her best interests at heart."

"Hmm. And what of you, John? What interest do you have in my aunt?" Tonn Tonn reached for the true reason he'd asked for this meeting.

John moved, and despite himself, Tonn Tonn took a step back. It was unlikely he had anything to fear from John, but sometimes battling instinct was impossible. John's new position placed him more in the faint light coming from the parking lot. Dark glasses still covered John's eyes. Earlier, when he'd walked into Ink No Evil's waiting room, John had looked almost human. Now, out here in the open, John didn't waste as much energy to keep up the façade.

Tonn Tonn heard the click of John's talons as his fingers twitched. The sway of John's body was more laborious yet no less graceful. There was greater bulk there, and as John turned, Tonn Tonn caught the movement of a massive tail.

Swallowing thickly, Tonn Tonn asked again. "Aunt Gussie, what—"

"Augusta Mayfield has nothing to fear from me. I have given my word, to the last of the line I've sworn my life to."

Tonn Tonn sucked in a hissing breath. "Ariana Preston? She's still alive?"

John chuckled, the sound low and menacing. Embers ghosted into the night, carried on the wings of John's breath. "She is, despite Samuel's efforts to the contrary. It is her I serve. She asked me to watch over Augusta, to protect her. I will fulfill my oath."

Tonn Tonn's skin prickled, the palms of his hands sweaty. "What does Aunt Gussie have to do with Ariana?"

"Apparently, they were college friends. When Ariana's situation became . . . untenable, she requested Augusta's assistance."

"*Assistance?* With what?" Tonn Tonn racked his brain, trying to make the connection.

John shifted again, his talons clacking louder. "It seems Samuel was busy while I was . . . indisposed," John hedged. "He is not content with the wolves he holds dominion over. He wishes to turn humans into something they are not. Ariana's town, her home, and the people she cares for have been infected with something of Samuel's making. Ariana believes your aunt can assist them."

"Shit." Tonn Tonn kicked a cold clump of earth. "And Ariana can't help because . . ."

"It is impossible," John answered, the discussion closed.

Grabbing his hair, Tonn Tonn tugged the edges. "I don't like this. Aunt Gussie doesn't know about . . . about any of this shit. She'll be an easy target. Samuel will—"

"I wonder, young Soul Eater, if you truly know your aunt. Augusta Mayfield is one of the most capable humans I have met. She is not as ignorant as you may think."

Tonn Tonn stilled. There was something in John's voice, something in his tone. John was one of the oldest creatures living on the planet. He was there long before Tonn Tonn was born, and he would be there long after Tonn Tonn was gone. He'd heard stories about John, mostly frightened tales spun over darkened nights and barely lit campfires. When he and his father were alone. Affection had never been hinted at as one of John's qualities.

Taking John's word regarding his aunt, Tonn Tonn said, "Samuel is becoming increasingly dangerous. He's threatening friends of mine. He's after one of their daughters—a young but very promising witch."

John hissed, more embers flying into the night. "Samuel has embraced the human quality of greed."

"He needs to be removed." Tonn Tonn took a risk. From what his father had said, all wolves were descended from

John. Although distantly removed, Samuel was one of his offspring. "And you are the only—"

"Samuel cannot be removed. There is no other to lead, and the wolves would be worse without him."

Tonn Tonn wasn't deterred. "He has a son: Jason. From what I've heard, Jason isn't as—"

John roared, low and deep. Strips of fire lit the night, followed by the scent of burning smoke. "Jason Hartman is as deceptive as his father. Regardless, he is no longer an option. Samuel murdered him."

Tonn Tonn's feet stumbled back. "His father killed him?" The very thought was inconceivable. Family was the most precious thing, the only thing. They were loved and protected above all others. Should someone kill his mother, or somehow kill him, Tonn Tonn's father would wreak the kind of vengeance none would risk. Soul eaters were feared for good reason. Soul eaters consumed everything you were.

The anger fueling John's fire dimmed, and his body slumped. The tail dragging behind him rustled fallen leaves as he began to move on. "Jason did the unforgivable. He fell in love with Ariana."

Tonn Tonn stared, eyes wide and heart thudding as John walked deeper into the night, back into the darkened shadows that hid what he truly was. From a great distance, Tonn Tonn heard John's whispered words, "I will protect Augusta. You are all that is needed to protect the witch child."

Heavy flaps of wings broke the still of the night, and their wind blew up dead leaves and debris. Shielding his eyes with his hands, Tonn Tonn caught a glimpse of something massive move through the sky, blotting out the stars struggling for attention.

Standing in the cold, Tonn Tonn tucked his hands deeper into the pockets of his pants while mumbling, "Oh, Aunt Gussie. What have you gotten yourself into?"

Available and Coming Works by MJ May
The Reaping Covetous Series:
Sow What You Reap: Reaping Covetous I
Dead Women Tell Tales: Reaping Covetous II
Dying to Reap You: Reaping Covetous III
Brother's Keeper, Brother's Reaper: Reaping Covetous IV
Ashes to Ashes: Reaping Covetous V
Pushing Up Roses: Reaping Covetous VI
Coming Soon—The final book in the Reaping Covetous
series, Reaping Consequences: Reaping Covetous VII

M/M Fantasy Romance
Coming this fall: Imperfectly Perfect Pixie

ACKNOWLEDGMENTS

As with most writers, there are a few people I'd like to take the time to thank because, without you, this book might have happened, but it would have been a pale imitation of the outcome.

My friend Kathy has been supportive through this whole process. She encourages me when I feel discouraged. Kathy is my biggest cheerleader and thinks everyone should read my books. If she could, she'd place a copy in every single household. That level of support can be hard to find and is precious when you do.

My sister, Julie, is an incredible nurse. She's been an RN for years and has always loved her chosen profession. These past couple of years have tried her resilience, much as it has most of our health care professionals. Thank you to everyone working hard to keep the human race on the living side of life.

I've written for several years but only revealed this fact to my parents one to two years ago. Since learning, they have been very supportive. My mom enjoys reading. My dad . . . not so much. I'm not lying when I say that my dad had never read a book before I published my first one. He wanted to read it. And when the second one came out, my dad read that one too. By his own admission, they are the only books he's ever read.

Michelle Rascon has been exceedingly helpful to this newbie, and I can't thank her enough. Michelle offers constructive criticism along with praise. She continues to open my eyes to glaring mistakes. Rogena Mitchell-Jones proofreads and polishes my writing into something infinitely more enjoyable to read.

The book cover for *Pushing Up Roses* was done by cheriefox. She was patient, asked many questions, and brought Leah and Phoenix to life. Cheriefox was open to small changes, and I enjoyed swapping ideas with her.

I'd also like to give a shout-out to my work family. The ladies I trudge through the day with have suffered through long diatribes regarding characters, storylines, and the hurdles of publishing. Thank you so much for listening and for your encouragement.

Last, but never, ever least—my pets. It is no small thing to say that my two cats and my dog are the pillars in my life. I'm lucky enough to be able to take my dog to work with me. Fennik is a source of solace and comfort when my paying job goes to hell in more than a few handbaskets. My cats, Newton and Copernicus, are there when I get home with soul-soothing purrs. I can't imagine living without pets in my life. In many ways, they are my chosen family—the furry kiddos I can't wait to get home to, even when they sit in front of the computer screen demanding attention, their plump, furry butts sitting on my arm and preventing me from typing. I wouldn't trade those moments of irritation for all the world.

Author Bio

MJ May lives in the Midwest with her two cats and one dog. She is passionate about her furry children, the wild birds eating her out of house and home, and her garden. MJ May is a firm believer that changing the sheets on your bed with housecats involved should be an Olympic event. Scores should be based on speed, accuracy, creative cursing, and how many times you have to toss a cat off the bed.

Connect with MJ May at her website: https://blogawaywithmjmay.com.

In the United States, the national suicide hotline number is 1-800-273-8255.